Midwinter of the Spirit

PHIL RICKMAN was born in Lancashire and lives on the Welsh border. He is the author of the Merrily Watkins series, and *The Bones of Avalon*. He has won awards for his TV and radio journalism and writes and presents the book programme *Phil the Shelf* for BBC Radio Wales.

PHIL RICKMAN

Midwinter of the Spirit

CORVUS

First published in Great Britain in 1999 by Macmillan.

This paperback edition first published in Great Britain in 2011
by Corvus, an imprint of Atlantic Books Ltd.

1 3 5 7 9 10 8 6 4 2

A CIP catalogue record for this book is available from the British Library.

ISBN: 978-0-85789-010-8

Printed in Great Britain by CPI Bookmarque, Croydon

Corvus
An imprint of Atlantic Books Ltd
Ormond House
26-27 Boswell Street
London WC1N 3JZ

www.corvus-books.co.uk

Midwinter of the Spirit

PART ONE
IMPRINT

1

It

This is where it walks...

Washing her hands, Merrily looked up and became very still, convinced in this grey, lingering moment that she was seeing the *imprint*.

What she saw, in the cracked and liver-spotted mirror, was a smudgy outline hovering beyond her left shoulder in the women's lavatory with its stone walls and flagged floor. Through the bubble-glass in the door, a bleary ochre glow seeped from the oil lamp in the passageway where, for some reason, there was no electricity.

This was where it walked, Huw had explained in his soft, mat-flat Yorkshire voice – David Hockney on downers.

It.

Rumoured, apparently, to be the shade of a preacher named Griffith who heaped sermons like hot coals on hapless hill-farming folk towards the end of the nineteenth century. But also known as the Grey Monk because this was what it most resembled, and this was where it walked.

Where it walked.

Merrily focused on her own drained face in the mirror.

Was this where madness began?

'Are they often caught short, then?' the ex-Army chaplain, Charlie Headland, had asked a few minutes earlier, while

Merrily was thinking: *Why do they always walk? Why don't they run like hell, in desperation, looking for a way out of this dismal routine?*

The course tutor, Huw Owen, had blinked, a crumpled old hippy in a discoloured dog-collar.

'No, I'm serious,' Charlie insisted. 'Do any of them still feel a need to pee, or do they leave all that behind?'

'Charles…' Huw being patient, not rising to it. 'There hasn't always been a lavatory at the end of that passage.'

Not smiling, either.

Huw would laugh, sometimes wildly, in the pub at night, but in the stone-walled lecture room he never lost his focus. It was about setting an example. Outside of all this, Huw said, you should always strive to live a full, free life but in 'Deliverance' remain watchful and analytical, and careful not to overreact to something as innocuous as an imprint.

This whole Grey Monk thing had arisen because of Huw needing an example of what he meant by '*imprints*'.

As distinct from '*visitors*', who usually were parents or close friends appearing at your bedside or in a favourite chair on the night of their deaths, often a once-only apparition to say: Everything is OK. Or '*volatiles*' – loose-cannon energy forms dislodging plates and table lamps, and commonly but some-times inaccurately called poltergeists.

When this place was a Nonconformist chapel, Huw had told them, the present women's toilet had been some kind of vestry. Which was where Griffith the preacher – apparently helpless with lust for a married woman in Sennybridge – had been drinking hard into the night, was subsequently seen striding white and naked on the hill at dawn, and then had been found dead back here, his head cracked on a flagstone, the room stinking of brandy.

Sure – these things happened in lonely parishes. Merrily pulled down a paper towel and began to dry her hands, not hurrying – resisting the urge to whirl suddenly around and catch Griffith, crazed and naked, forming out of the dampness in the wall.

She would *not* be bloody-well scared. She would observe with detachment. *Imprints* were invariably harmless. They appeared, vanished, occasionally messed with the atmosphere, but they never accosted you. They were, in fact, unaware of you, having no feelings, no consciousness. Their actions rarely varied. They appeared like a wooden cuckoo from a clock, only silently. And, no, they did not appear to feel the need to pee.

If an *imprint* responded to you, then it was likely to be something else – a *visitor* or, worse, an *insomniac* – and you had to review your options.

'And how, basically, do we know which is which?' big, bald Charlie Headland had demanded then. Charlie was simple and belligerent – Onward, Christian Soldiers – and needed confrontation.

'We have tests,' Huw explained. 'After a while, you might start feeling maybe you no longer have to apply them. You'll feel you know what's required – been here before, already done that. You'll feel you've attained a sensitivity. Now you've got to watch that temptation, because—'

'Meaning psychic powers, Huw?' Clive Wells interrupted. Clive was old-money and High Church, and naturally suspicious of Huw with his ancient blue canvas jacket, his shaggy grey hair, his permanent stubble. 'Psychic powers – that's what you mean by sensitivity?'

'No-oo.' Huw stared down at the holes in his trainers. 'It's not necessarily the same thing. In fact I'm inclined to distrust people who go on about their powers. They start to rely on what they think of as their own ability, and they – and anybody else who relies on what they say – can be deceived. I was about to say I've found it dangerous to rely too heavily on your perceived sensitivity. That feeling of heightened awareness, that can be an illusion too. We still need, all the time, to stay close to an established procedure. We need that discipline, Clive; it's one of the Church's strengths.'

Charlie the chaplain nodded briskly, being all for discipline and procedure.

'Make sure you put reason above intuition,' Huw said. 'Beware of inspiration.'

'That include divine inspiration?' Clive demanded.

Huw directed a bleak blue gaze at him. 'How do you know when it's divine?'

Clive stiffened. 'Because I'm a priest. Because I have faith.'

'Listen, beware of being too simplistic, man,' said Huw coldly.

They'd all gone quiet at this. Dusk clogging the grimy, diamond-paned window behind Huw, melding with mountains and low cloud. Late October, long nights looming. Merrily wishing she was home in front of the vicarage fire.

'I mean, don't get me wrong...' Huw was hunched up on a corner of his desk by the bare-stone inglenook. 'All I'm saying is' – he looked suddenly starved – 'that we must strive to know the *true* God. Evil *lies* to you. Evil is plausible. Evil butters you up, tells you what you want to hear. We need to beware of what you might call disinformation.'

'Hell's bells.' Charlie chuckled, trying to diffuse the atmosphere. 'Times like this you begin to wonder if you haven't walked into the wrong course. More like MI5 – *imprints* and *visitors*, *weepers*, *breathers*, *hitchhikers*, indeed.'

'Important to keep them in their place, lad. If we over-dramatize, if we wave our arms and rail against the Powers of Darkness and all this heavy-metal crap, if we inflate it... then we glorify it. We bloat what might simply be a nasty little virus.'

'When all it requires is a mild antibiotic, I suppose,' said Barry Ambrose, a worried-looking vicar from Wiltshire.

'If you like. Take a break, shall we?' Huw slid from the desk.

Cue for Merrily to stand up and announce that she was going to brave the ladies' loo.

Deliverance?

It meant exorcism.

When, back in 1987, the Christian Exorcism Study Group had voted to change its name to the Christian Deliverance Study Group, it was presumably an attempt to desensationalize the job. 'Deliverance' sounded less medieval, less sinister. Less plain weird.

But it changed nothing. Your job was to protect people from the invasion of their lives by entities which even half the professed Christians in this country didn't believe in. You had the option these days to consider them psychological forces, but after a couple of days here you tended not to. The journey each morning, just before first light, from the hotel in Brecon to this stark chapel in the wild and lonely uplands, was itself coming to represent the idea of entering another dimension.

Merrily would be glad to leave.

Yesterday, they'd been addressed by their second psychiatrist, on the problem of confusing demonic possession with forms of schizophrenia. They'd have to work closely with psychiatrists – part of the local support-mechanism they would each need to assemble.

Best to choose your shrink with care, Huw had said after the doctor had gone, because you'd almost certainly, at some time, need to consult him or her on a personal level.

And then, noticing Clive Wells failing to smother his scorn, he'd spent just over an hour relating case histories of ministers who had gone mad or become alcoholic or disappeared for long periods, or battered their wives or mutilated themselves. When a Deliverance priest in Middlesbrough was eventually taken into hospital, they'd found forty-seven crosses razored into his arms.

An extreme case, mind. Mostly the Deliverance ministry was consultative: local clergy with problems of a psychic nature on their patch would phone you for advice on how best to handle it. Only in severe or persistent cases were you obliged to go in personally. Also, genuine demonic possession was very rare. And although most of the work would involve hauntings, real ghosts – unquiet spirits or *insomniacs* – were also relatively infrequent. Ninety per cent were basic *volatiles* or *imprints*.

Like the monk.

Ah, yes… monks. What you needed to understand about these ubiquitous spectral clerics, Huw said, was that they were a very convenient shape. Robed and cowled and faceless, a monk lacked definition. In fact, anyone's aura – the electro-magnetic haze around a lifeform – might look vaguely like a monk's cowl. So could an *imprint*, a residue. So that was why there were so many ghostly monks around, see?

'Oh, just bugger… *off!*' Merrily crumpled the paper towel, tossed it at the wall where the smudge had been and went over to investigate.

The smudge turned out to be not something in the air but in the wall itself: an imprint of an old doorway. The *ghost* of a doorway.

Three days of this and you were seeing them everywhere.

Merrily sighed, retrieved the towel, binned it. Picked up her cigarette from the edge of the washbasin. There you go… it was probably the combination of poor light and the smoke in the mirror which had made the outline appear to move.

It was rare, apparently, for Deliverance ministers or counsellors actually to experience the phenomena they were trying to *divert*. And anyway, as Huw had just pointed out, a perceived experience should not be trusted.

Trust nothing, least of all your own senses.

Merrily took a last look at herself in the mirror: a small dark-haired person in a sloppy sweater. The only woman among nine ministers on this course.

Little dolly of a clergyperson... nice legs, dinky titties.

Dermot, her church organist, had said that the day he exposed to her his own organ. She shuddered. Dermot had worn a monkish robe that morning, and no underpants. So naturally she no longer trusted monks. Or, for that matter, priests like Charlie Headland who looked as if they wouldn't mind spanking you. But she *was* inclined to trust the Reverend Huw Owen, faded and weary on the outside but tough and flexible as old leather. Something of the monk about Huw, also – the Celtic hermit-monk in his lonely cell.

She dropped her cigarette down the loo.

Oh well, back into the twilight zone.

The passage still had lockers and iron hooks on the wall, from when the chapel had been an Outward Bound centre owned by some Midland education authority. It had changed hands discreetly a couple of years ago, was now jointly owned by the Church of England and the Church in Wales, although it seemed few people, even inside the Church, knew it was currently used as a training centre for exorcists.

The door to the big stone room was open; she heard muted discussion from inside, a shrill, affected laugh. Charlie Headland was wedged against the jamb, crunching crisps. He shook the packet at Merrily.

'Prawn mayonnaise flavour.'

Merrily helped herself to a crisp. Charlie looked down at her with affection.

'You've got a lot of bottle, Mrs Watkins.'

'What? Just for going for a wee in a haunted loo?'

Charlie chuckled. On occasion, he would fling an arm around Merrily and squeeze her. Twice he'd patted her bottom.

'You wouldn't be laughing,' Merrily said, 'if that thing was in the Gents' instead.'

Charlie grimaced and nodded, munched meditatively for a while, then patted her arm lightly. 'Got a little girl, I hear.'

9

'Not any more. A woman, she tells me. She's sixteen – just.'

'Oh, blimey. Where'd you leave her? Suitably caged, one hopes.'

'She's staying with friends in the village. Not this village – back home.'

Charlie balled his crisp packet, tossed it in the air and caught it. 'I reckon he made that up, you know.'

'Who?'

'Huw. That story about the hellfire preacher-man who died in the ladies' bogs. It's too pat.'

Merrily pulled the door to, cutting off the voices from the stone room. 'Why would he do that?'

'Giving us all little tests, isn't he? You particularly. You're the only woman amongst us, so there's one place you need to visit *alone*. If you'd suddenly started crossing your legs and holding it till you got back to the hotel, he'd know you were a little timid. Or if you came back rubbing your hands and saying you'd detected a cold patch, you'd be revealing how impressionable you were.'

'Be difficult to *spot* a cold patch in this place.'

'You're not wrong,' said Charlie. 'Talk about Spartan. Not what most of them were expecting. Neither's Huw. Awfully downmarket, isn't he? Clive's quite insulted – expected someone solemn and erudite like his old classics master at Eton.'

'What about you?'

'After fifteen years with the military? No problem at all for me. Funny chap, though, old Huw. Been through the mill, you can tell that. Wears the scar tissue like a badge.' Charlie dug his hands into his jacket pockets. 'I think Huw's here to show us where we stand as of now.'

'Which is?'

He nodded at the closed door. 'Out in the cold – lunatic fringe. Half the clergy quite openly don't believe in God as we know Him any more, and here we all are, spooking each other with talk of *breathers* and *hitchhikers* and *insomniacs*.'

10

Not for the first time since her arrival, Merrily shivered. 'What exactly *is* a *hitchhiker*, Charlie?'

'What's it sound like to you?'

'Something that wants a free ride?'

'All the way to hell, presumably,' said Charlie.

'Mustn't overdramatize,' Merrily reminded him as the door opened and Huw stood there, unkempt, his dog-collar yellowing at the rim.

'Putting the telly on now,' Huw said hesitantly. 'If that's all right?'

Merrily said cheerfully, 'I didn't notice anything at all in the lavatory, Huw.'

Huw nodded.

There was a clear dent in the woman's forehead. Also a half-knitted V-shaped scab over her left eye, the bruised one.

Merrily had seen several women in this condition before, although not recently. And not under these circumstances, obviously. Mostly in the hostel in Liverpool, when she was a curate.

'This was what done it.' The woman was holding out a green pottery ashtray. An old-fashioned pub ashtray like a dog bowl. 'See? Chipped all down the side. Not from when it hit me, like. When it fell on the floor afterwards.'

'I see.' The man's voice was calm and gentle and unsurprised. Not Huw – too deep, too posh. 'So it came flying—'

'I should've saved the other pieces, shouldn't I? I didn't think.'

'That's quite all right, Mrs... *bleep*... We're not the police. Now, the ashtray was where?'

'On the sideboard. Always kept on the sideboard.'

You could see the sideboard behind her. Looked like early sixties. Teak, with big gilt knobs on the drawers. On the once-white wall above it was a half-scrubbed stain. As though she'd started to wipe it off and then thought: *What's the bloody point?*

11

'So you actually *saw* it rising up?'

'Yeah, I... It come... It just come through the air, straight at me. Like whizzing, you know?'

This was a very unhappy woman. Early thirties and losing it all fast. Eyes downcast, except once when she'd glanced up in desperation – *You've got to believe me!* – and Merrily could see a corona of blood around the pupil of the damaged eye.

'Couldn't you get out of the way? Couldn't you duck?'

'No, I never...' The woman backing off, as though the thing was flying straight at her again. 'Like, it was too quick. I couldn't move. I mean, you don't expect... you can't believe what's happening, can you?'

'Did you experience anything else?'

'What?'

'Was there any kind of change in the atmosphere of this room? The temperature, was it warmer... or colder?'

'It's always cold in here. Can't afford the gas, can I?' Her eyes filling up.

'No,' he said. 'I'm sorry. Tell me, where was your husband when this was happening?'

'What?'

'Your husband, did *he* see anything?'

'Nah, he... he wasn't here, was he?' Plucking at the sleeve of her purple blouse.

Merrily wrote down *husband* on her pad.

'He was out,' the woman said.

'Has he had any experiences himself? In this house?'

'He ain't seen nothing. Nothing come flying at *him*. I reckon he's heard, like, banging noises and stuff, though.'

'Stuff?'

'You better ask him.'

'Have you discussed it much between yourselves?'

Minimal shake of the head.

'Why not?'

'*I* dunno, do I?' A flicker of exasperation, then her body went slack again. 'What you supposed to say about it? It's the kids, innit? I don't want nothing to happen to the ki—'

The woman's face froze, one eye closed.

'All right.' Huw walked back to his desk pocketing the remote control, turning to face the students. 'We'll hold it there. Any thoughts?'

Merrily found she'd underlined *husband* twice.

They looked at one another, nobody wanting to speak first. Someone yawned: Nick Cowan, the former social worker from Coventry.

Huw said, 'Nick, not impressed?'

Nick Cowan slid down in his canvas-backed chair. 'Council house, is this, Huw? I don't think you told us.'

'Would that make a difference?'

'It's an old trick, that's all. It's a cliché. They want rehousing.'

'So she's faking it, is she?'

'Well, obviously I can't... I mean you asked for initial impressions, and that's mine, based on twenty-five years' experience and about a thousand reports from local authorities after that rubbishy film came out... *Amityville* whatever. It's an old scam, but they keep on trying it because they know you can't prove it one way or the other. And if you don't rehouse them they'll go to the press, and then the house'll get a reputation, and so...'

Nick felt for his dog-collar, as if to make sure it was still there. He was the only one of the group who wore his to these sessions every day. He seemed grateful for the dog-collar: it represented some kind of immunity. Perhaps he thought he no longer had to justify his opinions, submit reports, get his decisions rubber-stamped and ratified by the elected representatives; just the one big boss now.

'All right, then.' Huw went to sit on his desk, next to the TV, and leaned forward, hands clasped. 'Merrily?'

He was bound to ask her, the only female in the group. On the TV screen the woman with one closed eye looked blurred and stupid.

'Well,' Merrily said, 'she isn't faking that injury, is she?'

'How do you think she got the injury, Merrily?'

'Do we get to see the husband?'

'You think he beat her up?'

'I'd like to know what he has to say.'

Huw said nothing, looked down at his clasped hands.

'And see what kind of guy he is.'

Huw still didn't look at her. There was quiet in the stone room.

There'd been a lot of that. Quite often the course had the feeling of a retreat: prayer and contemplation. Merrily was starting to see the point: it was about being receptive. While you had to be pragmatic, these weren't decisions which in the end you could make alone.

Beyond the diamond panes, the horn of the moon rose over a foothill of Pen-y-fan.

'OK.'

Huw stepped down. His face was deeply, tightly lined, as though the lines had been burned in with hot wire, but his body was still supple and he moved with a wary grace, like an urban tomcat.

'We'll take another break.' He switched off the TV, ejected the tape. 'I'd like you to work out between you how you your-selves would proceed with this case. Who you'd involve. How much you'd keep confidential. Whether you'd move quickly, or give the situation a chance to resolve itself. Main question, is she lying? Is she deluded? Merrily, you look like you could do with another ciggy. Come for a walk.'

2

Fluctuation

THE MOUNTAINS HUNCHED around the chapel, in its hollow, like some dark sisterhood over a cauldron. You had to go to the end of the drive before you could make out the meagre lights of the village.

It was awesomely lonely up here, but it was home to Huw, who sniffed appreciatively at Merrily's smoke, relaxing into his accent.

'I were born a bastard in a little *bwddyn* t'other side of that brow. Gone now, but you can find the foundations in the grass if you have a bit of a kick around.'

'I wondered about that: a Yorkshireman called Huw Owen. You're actually Welsh, then?'

'Me mam were waitressing up in Sheffield by the time I turned two, so I've no memories of it. She never wanted to come back; just me, forty-odd years on. Back to the land of my father, whoever the bugger was. Got five big, rugged parishes to run now, two of them strong Welsh-speaking. I'm learning, slowly – getting there.'

'Can't be easy.'

Huw waved a dismissive arm. 'Listen, it's a holiday, luv. Learning Welsh concentrates the mind. Cold, though, in't it?'

'Certainly colder than Hereford.' Merrily pulled her cheap waxed coat together. 'For all it's only forty-odd miles away.'

'Settled in there now, are you?'

'More or less.'

They followed a stony track in the last of the light. Walkers were advised to stick to the paths, even in the daytime, or they might get lost and wind up dying of hypothermia – or gunshot wounds. The regular soldiers from Brecon and the shadowy SAS from Hereford did most of their training up here in the Beacons.

No camouflaged soldiers around this evening, though. No helicopters, no flares. Even the buzzards had gone to roost. But to Merrily the silence was swollen. After they'd tramped a couple of hundred yards she said, 'Can we get this over with?'

Huw laughed.

'I'm not daft, Huw.'

'No, you're not that.'

He stopped. From the top of the rise, they could see the white eyes of headlights on the main road crossing the Beacons.

'All right.' Huw sat down on the bottom tier of what appeared to be a half-demolished cairn. 'I'll be frank. Have to say I were a bit surprised when I heard he'd offered the job to a young lass.'

Merrily stayed on her feet. 'Not *that* young.'

'You look frighteningly young to me. You must look like a little child after Canon T.H.B. Dobbs.' Huw pronounced the name in deliberate block capitals.

'Mr Dobbs,' Merrily said, 'yes. You know him, then?'

'Not well. Nobody knows the old bugger well.'

'I've never actually met him – with him being in and out of hospital for over a year.'

'There's a treat to look forward to,' Huw said.

'I've heard he's a… traditionalist.'

'Oh aye, he's that, all right. No bad thing, mind.'

'I can understand that.' Merrily finally sat down next to him.

'Aye,' Huw said. 'But does your new bishop?'

It was coming, the point of their expedition. The pale moon was limp above a black flank of Pen-y-fan.

'Bit of a new broom, Michael Henry Hunter,' Huw said, as a rabbit crossed the track, 'so I'm told. Bit of a trendy. Bit flash.'

'So he appoints a female diocesan exorcist,' Merrily said, 'because that's a cool, new-broom thing to do.'

'You said it.'

'Only, he hasn't appointed me. Not yet. Canon Dobbs is still officially in harness. I haven't been appointed to anything.'

'Oh, really?' Huw tossed a pebble into the darkness.

'So are you going to tell him?'

'Tell him?'

'That he shouldn't.'

'Not my job to tell a bishop what he can and can't do.'

'I suppose you want *me* to tell him: that I can't take it on.'

'Aye.' Huw gazed down at the road. 'I'd be happy with that.'

Shit, Merrily thought.

She'd met the Bishop just once before he'd become the Bishop. It was, fatefully, at a conference at her old college in Birmingham, to review the progress of women priests in the Midlands. He was young, not much older than Merrily, and she'd assumed he was chatting her up.

This was after her unplanned, controversial speech to the assembly, on the subject of women and ghosts.

'Shot my mouth off,' she told Huw, sitting now on the other side of the smashed cairn. 'I'd had a… all right, a psychic experience. One lasting several weeks. Not the kind I could avoid, because it was right there in the vicarage. Possibly a former incumbent, possibly just… a *volatile*. Plenty of sensations, sounds, possibly hallucinatory – I only ever actually *saw* it once. Anyway, it was just screwing me up. I didn't know how to deal with it, and Jane saying: "Didn't they teach you anything at theological college, Mum?" And I'm thinking, yeah, the kid's right. Here we are, licensed priests, and the one thing they haven't taught us is how to handle the supernatural. I didn't know about Mr Dobbs then. I didn't even know that every diocese needed to have one, or what exactly they did. I just wanted to know how many other women felt like me – or if I was being naive.'

'Touched a nerve?'

'Probably. It certainly didn't lead to a discussion, and nobody asked me anything about it afterwards. Except for Michael Hunter. He came over later in the restaurant, bought me lunch. I thought, he was just… Anyway, that was how it happened. Obviously, I'd no idea then that he was going to be my new bishop.'

'But he remembered you. Once he'd got his feet under the table and realized, as a radical sort of lad, that he could already have a bit of a problem on his hands: namely Canon T.H.B. Dobbs, his reactionary old diocesan exorcist. *Not* "Deliverance minister". *Decidedly* not.'

'I'm afraid "Deliverance consultant" is the Bishop's term.'

'Aye.' She felt his smile. 'You know why Dobbs doesn't like the word Deliverance? Because the first two syllables are an anagram of *devil*. That's what they say. Must've been relieved, Mick Hunter, when the old bugger got his little cardiac prod towards retirement.'

'But he hasn't gone yet, and I'm only here because the Bishop wants me to get some idea of how—'

'No, luv.' Huw looked up sharply. 'This *isn't* a course for people who just want to learn the basics of meta-physical trench warfare, as Hunter well knows. He wants you, badly.'

It's a sensitive job. It's very political. It throws up a few hot pota-toes like the satanic child-abuse panic – God, what was all that about, really? Well, I don't want any of this bell-book-and-candle, incense-burning, medieval rubbish. I want somebody bright and smart and on their toes. But also sympathetic and flexible and non-dogmatic and upfront. Does that describe you, Merrily?

Mick Hunter in his study overlooking the River Wye. Thirty-nine years old and lean and fit, pulsing with energy and ambition. The heavy brown hair shading unruly blue eyes.

'So,' Huw Owen said now, mock-pathetic, slumped under the rising moon. 'Would you come over all feminist on me if I begged you not to do it?'

Merrily said nothing. She'd been expecting this, but that didn't mean she knew how to handle it. Quite a shock being offered the job, obviously. She'd still known very little about Deliverance ministry. But did the Bishop himself know much more? Huw appeared to think not.

'I do like women, you know,' he said ruefully. 'I've been *very* fond of women in me time.'

'You want to protect us, right?'

'I want to protect everybody. I'll be sixty next time but one, and I'm starting to feel a sense of responsibility. I don't want stuff letting in. A lot of bad energy's crowding the portals. I want to keep all the doors locked and the chains up.'

'Suddenly the big, strong, male chain's acquired all these weak links?'

'I've always been a supporter of women priests.'

'Sounds like it.'

'Just that it should've all been done years ago, that's the trouble. Give the women time to build up a weight of tradition, some ballast, before the Millennial surge.'

'And how long does it take to build up a weight of tradition? How long, in your estimation, before we'll be ready to take on the *weepers* and the *volatiles* and the *hitchhikers*?'

'Couple of centuries.'

'Terrific.'

'Look…' Silver-rimmed night clouds were moving behind Huw. 'You're not a fundamentalist, not a charismatic or a happy-clappy. You've no visible axe to grind and I can see why he was drawn to you. You're in many ways almost exactly the kind of person we need in the trenches.'

'And I would keep a *very* low profile.'

'With Mick Hunter wearing the pointy hat?' Huw hacked off a laugh. 'He'll have you right on the front page of the *Hereford Times* brandishing a big cross. All right – joke. But you'll inevitably draw attention. You're very pretty, am I allowed to say that? And *they'll* be right on to you, if they aren't already. Little rat-eyes in the dark.'

Merrily instantly thought about Dermot Child, the organist in the monk's robe. 'I don't know what you mean.'

'I think you do, Merrily.'

'Satanists?'

'Among other species of pond life.'

'Isn't all that a bit simplistic?'

'Let's pretend you never said that.'

A string of headlights floated down the valley a long way away. She thought of Jane back home in Ledwardine and felt isolated, cut off. How many of the other priests on the course would agree with Huw? All of them, probably. A night-breeze razored down from crags she could no longer see.

'Listen,' Huw said, 'the ordination of women is indisputably the most titillating development in the Church since the Reformation. They'll follow you home, they'll breathe into your phone at night, break into your vestry and tamper with your gear. Crouch in the back pews and masturbate through your sermons.'

'Yes.'

'But that's the tip of the iceberg.'

'Rather than just a phase?'

'Jesus,' Huw said, 'you know what I heard a woman say the other week? "We can handle it," she said. "It's no more hassle than nurses get, and women teachers." A priest, this was, totally failing to take account of the... the overwhelming glamour the priesthood itself confers. It's now a fact that ordained women are the prime target for every psychotic grinder of the dark satanic mills that ever sacrificed a chicken. And there are a lot of those buggers about.'

'I've read the figures.'

'Exaggerated – two million in Britain alone, that sort of level. I don't think so. I'd guess no more than a thousand hard-liners and another five or six thousand misfit hangers-on. But, by God, that's enough, in't it? It's a modern religion, see, masquerading as something ancient. I've not said much about it down there yet.' Jerking a thumb towards the chapel. 'I like to save it for the end of the course, on account of some priests find it harder to take seriously than spooks.'

A blur of white: an early barn owl sailing over on cue.

Merrily said, 'What do you mean by a modern religion?'

'Well, not in principle, though it got a hell of a boost in the eighties. All that worship of money and sex and wordly success – Lucifer as patron saint of greedy, self-serving bastards, the Lord of this World. Goes back to some of the old Gnostic teachings: God's in His Heaven, while the other feller runs things down here.'

'You can't imagine people actually believing that.'

'Why not? If you want to get on in the world, you have to join the winning team. That's not evil, it's pragmatic. It's being level-headed, recognizing the set-up. A jungle, every man for himself, that's the manifesto. That's the spin. Got this amazing charge in the eighties. Took off faster than mobile phones.'

'Which was when you—?'

He lifted a hand. 'I only talk about me when I'm drunk, and I don't like to get drunk any more.'

She stood up and walked, with determination, around to his side of the stones. 'Why are you here, really, Huw? I mean out here in the sticks. Are you in hiding?'

'Eh?'

'I just don't go for all that Land of my Fathers bullshit. Something happened to you in Sheffield and you felt you couldn't—'

'Cut it any more?'

'I'm sorry. It's none of my business.'

21

She *was* sorry. She wished she could see his eyes, but his face was in deep shadow.

'Aye, well, it wasn't Sheffield,' Huw said.

'You don't have to—'

'I won't. I'm just saying it wasn't Sheffield. I just... Look, don't try and turn this round, Merrily. You should consider your situation. You're on your own, your daughter won't be around much longer—'

'And I can't possibly hold myself together without a man.'

Huw stood up, the rising moon blooming on his left shoulder. 'This is not just wankers in the back pews, you know.'

She looked at him. 'I've encountered evil.'

'Face to face? Hearing it call your name? And your mother's name, and your daughter's name? Feeling it all over you like some viscous, stinking—'

He turned away, shaking his head, shambled back on to the track towards the chapel.

'Look, those blokes down there – solid, stoical, middle-aged priests: I can tell you four of them won't go through with it. Out of the rest, there'll be one broken marriage and a nervous breakdown. Are you listening, Merrily?'

'Yes!'

She stumbled after him, and he shouted back over his shoulder, 'Woman exorcist? Female guardian of the portals? You might as well just paint a great big bullseye between your tits.'

When they got back, the chapel was in near-darkness, only an unsteady line of light under the door of the stone room.

Inside, the oil lamp which normally hung in the passage now stood on Huw's desk, next to the TV.

'Power's gone,' someone said. They were all standing around in the lamplight looking guilty like small boys. There was a smell of burning.

'Ah, Huw, ah...' The Rev. Charles Headland flicked at the letter-box mouth of the VCR. 'Some of us wanted to have another look at that lady. Couldn't make up our minds. Dodgy items, poltergeists.'

'It was mainly me,' said Barry Ambrose, the worried vicar from Wiltshire. 'I half-believed her, but I think I'd have wanted to go back and talk to her again.'

'Yes.' Huw closed the door of the room. 'That was what they did. It was a rector in Northampton. He felt bad about them recording the first interview on tape for the likes of us, and just giving her a token prayer, so he went back to talk to her in private.'

Merrily felt a tension in the room.

'Sorry, Huw.' Charlie held up his hands, something ribboning and rustling there, and glistening in the lamplight. 'Don't know what happened here.'

Holding up the video cassette. About four yards of tape had become unravelled.

'Screen went blank. Ejected the tape, and the damn thing was on fire. Had to rip it out and stamp on it. Extraordinary thing. Wasn't your only copy, was it?'

'Doesn't matter.' Huw accepted the remains of the video. 'Coming to the end of its shelf-life anyway, that particular case-history.'

'Need a new player, too, I'd guess.'

Merrily leaned in and saw that the lips of the machine were scorched and warped. She'd never known this happen to a VCR before.

'That's the fourth one in two years,' Huw said. 'It's a right difficult place, this.'

'Jesus.' Merrily's legs felt weak; she clutched at a chair. 'You're not saying…?'

'No, luv. I don't say anything, me.'

Silence in the stone room. One of those moments when spiderwebs of cracks appeared in the walls of reality, and Merrily thought: *Do I really want to be doing this? Should anyone be doing it?*

23

Huw looked over the lamplit assembly of bemused vicars and rectors and priests-in-charge. *God's elite commando unit*, Merrily thought, and wanted to give in to hysterical laughter, except one or two of them might then think she was possessed.

'So, lads,' Huw said, 'which of you would like to practise his cleansing routine?'

Charlie Headland's mouth tightened. Merrily guessed he was wondering if Huw had rigged this. And she even wondered that, too. *Tests – little tests. Lies. Disinformation.*

'And should we bless and cleanse the entire premises? Or perhaps each other?'

Merrily thought, horrified: *It's getting completely out of hand. How quickly we all rush to the edge.*

'This is insane,' Nick Cowan, the ex-social worker, said. 'It's nonsense. There was obviously some sort of electrical fluctuation. A power surge, that's all.'

Huw beamed at him. 'Good thought, Nicholas. You do get problems like that in the mountains. That's a very good thought. There you are...' He spread his hands. 'Lesson for us all. Always consider the rational nuts-and-bolts explanation before you get carried away. Why don't you go and check the fuse-box, Charles? In the cupboard over the front door. There's a torch in there.'

When Charlie had gone, Merrily sat down. She felt tired and heavy. To break the uncomfortable silence, she said, 'Was that a genuine case – the woman on the video?'

'Ah,' said Huw. In the wavery light, he looked much younger. Merrily could imagine him in some rock band in the sixties.

'You said they went back to talk to her again.'

'Well.' He began to wrap the unravelled videotape in a coil around his hands until it was binding them together. 'Our man in Northampton knocks on the door and gets no answer, but he can hear a radio playing loudly inside the house, and the door's unlocked, so he goes in and calls out, like you do. And the radio just goes on playing, and our man's beginning to get a funny feeling.'

'Oh, dear God, no,' said Clive Wells. 'Don't say that.'

'Afraid so, Clive.' Huw held out his hands, pressed together as though in prayer but bound tight, somehow blasphemously, with black videotape. 'There she is on the settee with a bottle of whisky, nearly empty, and a bottle of pills, *very* empty, and Radio Two playing comforting sixties hits.'

Merrily closed her eyes. Huw wouldn't be lying about this. He wouldn't be that cruel.

'And we still don't know if she was genuine or not,' Huw said sadly. 'The bottom line is that our man in Northampton should not have left before administering a proper blessing to leave her in a state of calm, feeling protected. Psychological benefits, if nothing else. The worst that could've happened then was he'd have looked a pillock if it came out she'd made the story up. But, then, looking like a pillock's part of the clergyperson's job, in't it, Merrily? Get used to it, don't we?'

Merrily was still staring into the scorched and grinning maw of the VCR when the lights came on again.

'First law of Deliverance,' Huw said. 'Always carry plenty of fuse wire.'

PART TWO
VIRUS

3

Storm-trooper

THEY WENT TO look at Hereford Cathedral – because it was raining, and because Jane had decided she liked churches.

As distinct, of course, from the Church, which was still the last refuge of tossers, no-hopers and sad gits who liked dressing up.

Jane wandered around in her vintage Radiohead sweatshirt, arms hanging loose, hands opened out. Despite the presence of all these vacuous, dog-collared losers, you could still sometimes pick up an essence of real spirituality in these old sacred buildings, the kid reckoned. This was because of where they'd been built, on ancient sacred sites. Plus the resonance of gothic architecture.

Merrily followed her discreetly, hands in pockets, head down, and didn't argue; a row was looming, but this was not the place and not the time. And anyway she had her own thoughts, her own decision to make. She wondered about consulting St Thomas, and was pleased to see Jane heading for the North Transept, where the old guy lay. Kind of.

They passed the central altar, with its suspended corona like a giant gold and silver cake-ruff. On Saturdays, even in October, there were usually parties of tourists around the Cathedral and its precincts, checking out the usual exhibits: the Mappa Mundi, the Chained Library, the John Piper tapestries, the medieval shrine of…

'Oh.'

In the North Transept, Merrily came up against a barrier of new wooden partitioning, with chains and padlocks. It was screening off the end wall and the foot of the huge stained-glass window full of Christs and angels and reds and blues.

Jane said, 'So, like, what's wrong, Reverend Mum?' She put an eye to the crack in the padlocked partition door. 'Looks like a building site. They turning it into public lavatories or something?'

'I forgot. They're dismantling the shrine.'

'What for?' Jane looked interested.

'Renovation. Big job. Expensive. Twenty grand plus. Got to look after your saint.'

'Saint?' Jane said. 'Do me a favour. Guy was just a heavy-duty politician.'

'Well, he was, but—'

'Thomas Cantilupe, 1218 to 1282,' Jane recited. 'Former Chancellor of England. Came from a family of wealthy Norman barons. He really didn't have to try very hard, did he?'

Well, yes, he did, Merrily wanted to say. When he became Bishop of Hereford, he tried to put all that behind him. Wore a hair shirt. And, as a lover of rich food, once had a great pie made with his favourite lampreys from the Severn, took a single succulent bite, and gave the rest away.

'Must have had something going for him, flower. About three hundred miracles were credited to this shrine.'

'Look.' Jane pushed her dark brown hair behind her ears. 'It's the power of *place*. If you'd erected a burger-bar here, people would still have been cured. It's all about the confluence of energies. Nothing to do with the fancy tomb of some overprivileged, corrupt…'

She stopped. A willowy young guy in a Cathedral sweatshirt was strolling over.

'It's Mrs Watkins, right?'

'Hello,' Merrily said uncertainly. Was she supposed to recognize him? She was discovering that what you needed more than anything in this job was a massive database memory.

'Er, you don't know me, Mrs Watkins. I saw you with the archdeacon once. Neil Cooper – I'm kind of helping with the project. It's just... I've got a key if you want to have a look.'

While Merrily hesitated, Jane looked Neil Cooper over, from his blond hair to his dusty, tight jeans.

'Right,' Jane said. 'Cool. Let's do it.'

Under the window, a fourteenth-century bishop slept on, his marble mitre like a nightcap. But the tomb of his saintly predecessor, Thomas Cantilupe, was in pieces – stone sections laid out, Merrily thought, like a display of postmodern garden ornaments.

There were over thirty pieces, Neil told them, all carefully numbered by the stonemasons. Neil was an archaeology student who came in most weekends. It was, he said, a unique opportunity to examine a famous and fascinating medieval tomb.

Jane stood amongst the rubble and the workbenches, peering around and lifting dustcloths.

'So, like, where are the bones?'

An elderly woman glanced in through the door, then backed quickly away as if dust from the freshly exposed tomb might carry some ancient disease.

Jane was prepared to risk it. She knelt and stroked one of the oblong side-slabs, closing her eyes as though emanations were coming through to her, the faint echo of Gregorian chant. Jane liked to feel she was in touch with other spheres of existence. Nothing religious, you understand.

'Sorry,' said Neil. 'There aren't any.'

'No bones?'

Hands still moving sensuously over the stone, Jane opened her eyes and gazed up at Neil. He looked about twenty. An

31

older man; Jane thought older men were cool, and *only* older men. It was beginning to perturb Merrily that the kid hadn't found any kind of steady boyfriend her own age, since they'd arrived in Herefordshire.

Neil glanced at Jane only briefly. 'What happened, Mrs Watkins, is some of the bones were probably taken away for safekeeping at the time of the Reformation. And some were apparently carried around the city during the plague in the hope they might bring some relief, and I expect a few of those didn't come back. So he's widely scattered, although part of the skull's supposed to be back in Hereford, with the monks over at Belmont Abbey.'

Jane stood up. 'So it was like completely empty when you opened it, yeah?'

'Lot of dust,' said Neil.

The side-slab was divided into six sections; on each a knight in armour had been carved, their swords and shields and helmets and even chain-mail fingers crisply discernible, but all the faces gone – flattened, pulped. It didn't look as if time was entirely responsible.

'So, in fact,' Jane said, 'this great historic, holy artefact is like an empty shell.'

'It's a shrine,' Merrily said.

'Of course, that's one of the continuing problems with the Anglican Church.' Jane smiled slyly, before sliding out the punchline. 'So *much* of it's just a hollow shell.'

Merrily was careful not to react. 'We're delaying you,' she said to Neil Cooper. 'It was good of you to let us in.'

'No problem, Mrs Watkins. Drop in any time.' He smiled at Merrily, ignoring Jane.

Jane scowled.

'I expect you'll be around quite often,' Neil said. 'I gather they're giving you an office in the cloisters.'

'Nothing's fixed yet,' Merrily said, too sharply. 'And, anyway, I'd only be here one-and-a-half days a week. I have a parish to run as well.' *God*, she thought, *does everybody know about this?* So much for low-profile, so much for discretion.

'Look in anytime,' Neil repeated. 'Always nice to see you.'

'The trouble with older men,' said Jane, as they left the Cathedral, 'is that the cretins seem to fancy even *older* women.'

As they walked into Broad Street, the rain dying off but the sky threatening more, Merrily noticed that Jane seemed taller. A little taller than Merrily in fact, which was not saying much but was momentarily alarming. As though this significant spurt had occurred during the few days they'd been apart: Merrily experiencing weirdness in Wales, Jane staying with trusty villagers Gomer and Minnie, but returning to the vicarage twice a day to feed Ethel the cat.

Merrily felt disoriented. So much had altered in the ten days since she'd last been to the Cathedral. Ten days which – because the past week had been such a strange period – seemed so much longer, even part of a different time-frame.

She felt a quiver of insecurity, glanced back at the ancient edifice of myriad browns and pinks. It seemed to have shrunk. From most parts of the city centre, the spires of All Saints and St Peter's were more dominant. The Cathedral had long since lost its own spire, and sat almost modestly in a secluded corner between the River Wye and the Castle Green and a nest of quiet streets with no shops in them.

'Tea?' Merrily said desperately.

'Whatever.'

The late-afternoon sky was a smoky kind of orange. Merrily peered around for cafés, snackbars. She felt like a stranger, needing to ground herself.

'The Green Dragon? They must do afternoon tea.'

Jane shrugged. They crossed towards Hereford's biggest hotel, nineteenth-century and the longest façade on Broad Street.

'So you've learned about Thomas Cantilupe at school?'

'Only in passing. He didn't figure much nationally. Nothing that happened in Hereford seems to have made much of a difference to anything in the big world.'

Useless arguing with Jane in this mood. The kid had consented to come shopping, a big sacrifice on a Saturday; it was now Merrily's task to tease out of her what was wrong, and Jane wasn't going to assist. Tiresome, time-honoured ritual.

They found a window table in the Green Dragon, looking back out on to Broad Street, the Saturday crowds thinning now as the day closed down. Sometimes November could bring a last golden surge, but this one had seemed colourless and tensed for winter. Merrily was aware of a drab sense of transience and futility – nothing profound. Maybe just wishing she was Jane's age again.

'Cakes,' she said brightly.

'Just tea, thanks. Black.'

Merrily ordered two teas and a scone. 'Worried about our weight, are we, flower?'

'No.'

'What *are* we worried about then?'

'Did *we* say we were worried?'

The bored, half-closed eyes, the sardonic tuck at the corner of the mouth. It was pure Sean – as when Merrily was trying to quiz him about some dubious client. You don't see your daughter for a week, and in the interim she's readmitted her father's soiled spirit.

Merrily tried again. 'I, er... I missed you, flower.'

'Really?' Jane tilted her soft, pale face into a supportive hand, elbow on the table. 'I'd have thought you had far too much to think about, poncing about in your robes and practising your *Out, Demons, Out* routine with the soul police.'

'Ah.'

'What?'

'That's what this is about – the soul police? You think I'm...'

34

What? An anachronism? A joke? Though Jane was basically spiritual, she just didn't believe the Church of England was. Bad enough to have your own mother walking around in a dog-collar, never mind the holy water and the black bag now. Was that it?

That was probably too simple. Nothing about Jane was ever really simple.

A man striding up the street towards All Saints glanced through the window, blinked, paused, strode on. *Oh God, not him, not now.* Merrily turned away from the window, stared across the table at Jane.

The kid pushed back her tumbling hair. 'OK, look...'

Yes? Merrily leaned forward. A crack, an opening? *Yes...*

Jane said, 'I'm uncomfortable about what you're doing, Merrily.'

'I see.'

Jesus. *Merrily?* A major development. Now we are sixteen, time to dump this Mum nonsense. We are two grown women, equals.

This needed some thinking about.

'I don't think you do see,' Jane said.

'So tell me.'

'They're dragging you in, aren't they?'

'Who?'

'The Church. It's all political.'

'Of course it is.'

'All those fat, smug C-of-E gits, they're worried about losing their power and their influence, so they're appointing cool bishops: smooth, glossy people like Michael Hunter... *Mick* Hunter, for God's sake.'

'Bishops are still appointed by Downing Street.'

'Yeah, well, exactly. Old mate of Tony Blair's. I can just see them swapping chords for ancient Led Zeppelin riffs. Like, Mick's superficially cool and different, but he's really Establishment underneath.'

'Phew,' said Merrily theatrically. 'Thank God, my daughter has finally become a revolutionary. I thought it was never going to happen.'

Jane glared at her.

'You really don't understand, do you?'

'Sure. You think I'm a glossy, superficial bimbo who's—'

'More like a trainee storm-trooper, actually.'

'What?'

'Look...' Jane's eyes flashed. 'It seemed really interesting at first when you said you were going to do this Deliverance training. I'm thinking, yeah, this is what it's all about: the Church actually investigating the supernatural nitty-gritty instead of just spouting all this Bible crap. And this course and everything, it all seemed really mysterious. So, like... Wednesday night, I go back to the vicarage to feed Ethel. I think maybe I should check the answering machine, see if there's anything urgent. So I go into your office and I find... hang on...'

From a pocket of her jeans, Jane dragged a compacted square of printed paper which she opened out on the tabletop.

'And suddenly I saw what it was all really about.'

Merrily pulled towards her a Deliverance Study Group pamphlet heralding a forthcoming seminar entitled:

NEW AGE... OLD ENEMY.

She'd forgotten about it. It had come in a package from the DSG the morning she left for the Brecon Beacons.

'I haven't read it, flower.'

'I bet.'

'But, sure, I can guess what it's about.'

She picked up the leaflet.

Meditation-groups, sweat-lodges, healing-circles... it may all seem innocuous, but so-called New Age pursuits are often the

marijuana which leads to the heroin of hard-core Satanism.
Introducing the discussion, Canon Stephen Rigbey will
examine the allure of alternative spirituality and suggest ways
of discouraging harmful experimentation.

Merrily said steadily, 'You happen to notice the key word in this?'

'Don't try and talk all around it.'

'It's "discussion" – meaning debate.'

'It's bloody spiritual fascism,' said Jane.

'Oh, Jane, listen—'

'*You* listen, for once. The New Age is about… it's about millions of people saying: I want to know more… I want an inner life… I want to commune with nature and the cosmos and things, find out about what we're really doing here and who's running the show, and like what part I can play in the Great Scheme of Things. Right?'

'Pretty much like Christianity, in fact.' Merrily lit a cigarette.

'No, that's bollocks.' Jane shook her head furiously. 'The Church is like: Oh, you don't have to *know* anything; you just come along every Sunday and sing some crappy Victorian hymns and stuff and you'll go to heaven.'

'Jane, we've had this argument before. You just want to reduce it to—'

'And anybody steps out of line, it's: Oh, you're evil, you're a heretic, you're an occultist and we're gonna like burn you or something! Which was how you got the old witch-hunts, because the Church has always been on this kind of paternalistic power trip and doesn't *want* people to search for the truth. Like it used to be science and Darwinism and stuff they were worried about, now it's the New Age because that's like *real practical spirituality*. And it's come at a time when the Church is really feeble and pathetic, and the bishops and everybody are shit scared of it all going down the pan, so now we get this big

Deliverance initiative, which is really just about... about *suppression*.' Jane sat back in her chair with a bump.

'Wow,' Merrily said.

'Don't.'

'What?'

'You're gonna say something patronizing. *Don't*.' Jane snatched back the leaflet and folded it up again. Evidence obviously. 'I bet you were mega-flattered when *Mick* offered you the job, weren't you? I bet it never entered your head that they want people like you because you're quite young and attractive and everything, and like—'

'It did, actually.'

'Like you're not going to come over as some crucifix-waving loony, what?'

'It *did* occur to me.' Merrily cupped both hands around her cigarette; she wasn't sure if they allowed smoking in here. 'Of course it did. It's *still* occurring to me. Not your let's-stamp-out-the-New-Age stuff, because I can't quite believe that. But, yeah, I think he does want me for reasons other than that I'm obviously interested in... phenomena, whatever. Which is one reason I haven't yet said yes to the job.'

Jane blinked once and they sat and stared at one another. Merrily thought about all the other questions that were occurring to her. And what Huw Owen had said to them all as they gathered outside the chapel in the last minutes of the course.

Maybe you should analyse your motives. Are you doing this out of a desire to help people cope with psychic distress? Or is it in a spirit of, shall we say, personal enquiry? Think how much deeper your faith would be if you had evidence of life after death. How much stronger your commitment to the calling if you had proof of the existence of supernatural evil. If that's the way you're thinking, you need to consider very carefully after you leave here. And then, for Christ's sake, forget this. Do something else.

Merrily dragged raggedly on her cigarette.

'You really want it, though, don't you?' Jane said. 'You really, really want it.'

'I don't know,' Merrily lied.

Jane smiled.

'I have a lot of thinking to do,' Merrily said.

'You going to tell *Mick* you're in two minds?'

'I think I shall be avoiding the Bishop for a while.'

'Ha.' Jane was looking over her mother's left shoulder.

Merrily said wearily, 'He just came in, didn't he?'

'I think I'll leave you to it. I'll go and have a mooch around Waterstone's and Andy's. See you back at the car at six?'

The waitress arrived with the tea.

'The Bishop can have mine if he likes,' Jane said.

4

Moon

IT WAS WHAT happened with the crow, after the rain on Dinedor Hill. This was when Lol Robinson actually began to be spooked by Moon.

As distinct from sorry for Moon. Puzzled by Moon. Fascinated by Moon.

And attracted to her, of course. But anything down that road was not an option. It was not supposed to be that kind of relationship.

Most people having their possessions carried into a new home would need to supervise the operation, make sure nothing got broken. Moon had shrugged, left them to get on with it, and melted away into the rain and her beloved hill.

There really wasn't very much stuff to move in. Moon didn't even have a proper bed. When the removal men had gone, Lol went up to the Iron Age ramparts to find her.

He walked up through the woods, not a steep slope because the barn was quite close to the flattened summit where the ancient camp had been, the Iron Age village of circular thatched huts. Nothing remained of it except dips and hollows, guarded now by huge old trees, and by the earthen ramparts at the highest point.

And this was where he found Moon, where the enormous trees parted to reveal the city of Hereford laid out at your feet like an offering.

Lol was aware that some people called the hill a *holy* hill, though he wasn't sure why. He should ask Moon. The ancient mysteries of Dinedor swam in her soul.

She was standing with her back to him, next to a huge beech tree which still wore most of its leaves. Her hair hung almost to the waist of the long medieval sort of dress she wore under a woollen shawl.

Making Lol think of drawings of fairies by Arthur Rackham and the centrefolds of those quasi-mystical albums from the early seventies – the ones which had first inspired him to write songs. The kind of songs which were already going out of fashion when Lol's band, Hazey Jane, won their first recording contract.

Moon would still have been at primary school then. She seemed to have skipped a whole generation, if not two. Hippy *nouvelle*. Down in the city, she sometimes looked pale and nervy, distanced from everything. Up here she was connected.

Dick Lyden, the psychotherapist, had noticed this and given his professional blessing to Moon's plan, despite the fears of her brother Denny, who was jittery as hell about it. *'She can't do this. You got to stop her. SHE CANNOT LIVE THERE! OUT OF THE FUCKING QUESTION!'*

But she was a grown woman. What were they supposed to do, short of getting her committed to a psychiatric hospital? Lol, who'd been through that particular horror himself, was now of the opinion that it should never happen to anyone who was not dangerously insane.

When he first saw Moon on the ramparts, even though her face was turned away, he thought she'd never seemed more serene.

She glanced over her shoulder and smiled at him.

'Hi.'

'OK?'

'Yes.' She turned back to the view over the city. 'Wonderful, isn't it? Look. Look at the Cathedral and All Saints. Isn't that amazing?'

From here, even though they were actually several hundred yards apart, the church steeple and the Cathedral tower overlapped. The sky around them was a strange, burned-out orange.

Moon said, 'Many of the ley-lines through other towns, you can't see them any more because of new high-rise buildings, but of course there aren't any of those in Hereford. The skyline remains substantially the same.'

Lol realized he'd seen an old photograph of this view, taken in the 1920s by Alfred Watkins, the Hereford gentleman who'd first noticed that prehistoric stones and mounds and the medieval churches on their sites often seemed to occur on imaginary straight lines running across the landscape. Most archaeologists thought this was a rubbish theory, but Katherine Moon was not like most archaeologists. *It's at least spiritually valid,* she'd said once. He wasn't sure what she meant.

'Moon,' he said now, 'why do some people call it a holy hill?'

She didn't have to think about it. 'The line goes through four ancient places of worship, OK? Ending at a very old church in the country. But it starts here, and this is the highest point. So all these churches, including the Cathedral, remain in its shadow.'

'In the poetic sense.'

'In the spiritual sense. This hill is the mother of the city. The camp here was the earliest proper settlement, long before there was a town down there. Over a thousand Celtic people lived up here.' She paused. 'My ancestors.'

There was a touching tremor of pride in her voice.

'So it's kind of…' Lol hesitated, '… holy in the pagan sense.'

'It's just holy.' Moon still had her back to him. 'This was before the time of Christ. Over a thousand people keeping sheep and storing grain, doing their spinning and weaving and dyeing. It would've been idyllic – for a time.'

'What happened to them? The Dinedor People.'

'Some of them never went away. And the spirit remains.'

Moon gazed down over the spread of the city towards the distant Black Mountains and Welsh border. Slowly she turned towards him.

'And some... some of us have returned.'

He saw tears shining in her eyes.

And then he saw the black thing clasped to her stomach.

Katherine Moon...

Dick Lyden, the therapist, had briefed Lol as best he could about three months ago.

Twenty-six. Bright girl, quite a good degree in archaeology, but an unfortunate history of instability. Runs in the family, evidently. Her brother Denny, he's the sanest of them; might look like a New Age traveller, but Denny's a businessman, has his head screwed on.

After university, Dick said, Katherine had spent a couple of years freelancing on various archaeological digs across Britain. This was how she became obsessed with dead Celtic civilizations. Began wearing primitive clothing and strange jewellery, smoking too much dope, tripping out on magic-mushroom tea. When she arrived back in Hereford, the Katherine bit had gone; she was just Moon, and more than a little weird.

The reason she'd come back to Hereford was the lure of the big Cathedral Close dig. Also, perhaps, the impending death of her mother – as if Moon had sensed this coming. Her mother had died after several years in and out of expensive psychiatric residential homes – one of the reasons Denny had kept working so hard. Now it looked like he had another one to provide for.

But Denny's wife, Maggie, had decreed that Katherine wasn't living with them, no way – this stemming from the Christmas before last, when Moon had come to stay and Maggie had found her stash under the baby's cot. What a dramatic Christmas *that* had been. Now it was: Let her take her inheritance, smoke it, snort it, inject it into her arm... Just keep the mad bitch well out of our lives.

No wonder Maggie was paranoid. Denny's mother seemed to have picked up psychiatric problems simply by marrying into the Moon family, like their instability was infectious.

Meanwhile, Katherine had flipped again. Bought some speed from a dealer in Hereford, disappeared into pubs and clubs for three days, and been pulled in by the police after nicking two skirts from Next. Denny had taken her to Dick Lyden, as part of the deal for a conditional discharge by Hereford magistrates.

He'd refurbished the flat over one of his shops for her, suggesting she ran the store for a while. Knowing this wasn't entirely satisfactory – right in the city centre, too convenient for pubs and clubs and dealers, it was not really where he'd wanted her. But where *did* he want her? Well, somewhere safe. Somewhere he wouldn't have to visit her too often and risk domestic strife.

But certainly not Dinedor Hill. Not in a million years. As for fucking Dyn Farm…

We got to stop her, man! Denny with his head in his hands, beating it on the shop counter when he heard about the barn. *She can't DO this!*

But Moon had the money from her mother's bequest. She'd already signed the lease with the latest people to own the farmhouse and its Grade Two listed outbuildings.

Think about it this way, Denny, Dick Lyden had suggested. *The hill might have terrible memories for you, but she was just a child at the time. She has no memories of it at all. To Moon it's simply the birthright of which she was robbed. So going back to the hill – to part of the actual family farm – could be a healing thing. Who knows? Might even be the making of her. If I were you, Denny, and I couldn't disguise my feelings, I'd keep my distance. Now she's done it, it would not be good for her to be exposed to any negativity.*

And then Dick had said, *Tell you what, why don't we get Lol here to keep an eye on her? Most inoffensive chap I know, this.*

Patting Lol on the arm. *No threat, you see? She mustn't feel pressured in any way – that's the important thing.*

So Lol Robinson, ex rock-star (almost), sometime songwriter, former mental patient, had become Moon's minder. Possibly because no one else really wanted to take that responsibility.

But that was OK. Lol needed some responsibility. It was fine.

Until this.

The rain had begun again. It misted Lol's glasses and made a glossy slick of Moon's waist-length hair, falling black and limp down her back.

As black and limp as the dead crow she held.

She was leaning back against the tree now, her right hand cupped under the bird.

'Moon?' Lol took a step backwards, stumbled to his knees in the mud, looking up at her. She was beautiful. Her big eyes were penetrating, like an owl's.

'Look,' she said.

There was a spreading patch of blood, already the size of a dinner plate, on her dress from the stomach to the groin.

'It fell dead at my feet,' Moon said, 'out of the sky. Isn't that incredible?'

'Is it?' Lol said faintly. Appalled to see that her left hand, bloodied to the wrist, was actually moving *inside* the body of the crow. Loose feathers were sticking to the blood on her dress.

'To the ancient Celts the crow or raven was a sacred and prophetic bird.' Moon spoke as though she was addressing not one person but a group of students in a lecture room. 'The hero Bran was possibly a personification of a raven god. There were also several crow or raven goddesses: Macha, Nemain, Badb and the Morrigan.'

Lol stood up but moved no closer to her.

'It fell dead at my feet,' she said again. 'It was a gift – from the ancestors. A greeting on this the day of my homecoming.'

'Like a housewarming present,' Lol said before he could think.

He expected her to flare up, but she smiled and her eyes glowed.

'Yes!' She looked at Lol for the first time, and began to cry. 'Oh, Lol, I can't tell you. I can't express…'

Her hand came out of the crow then, full of organs and intestines and bloody gunge.

Lol felt sick. 'Moon, if it's a gift—'

'The gift,' Moon said happily, 'is *prophecy*! And inner vision. The point is that the crow was endowed with supernatural powers. It was honoured and feared and revered, OK? When this one fell to the earth, it was still warm and there was a small wound in the abdomen and I put my little finger into the wound and it just…'

'Why did you do that?'

'Because it was *meant*, of course! By bathing my hands in its blood, I'm acquiring its powers. There's a legend of Cuchulainn, where he does that. I…' She held out the bird to Lol. 'I don't know what to do next.'

'Bury it, I think,' Lol said hopefully.

And Moon nodded, smiling through her tears.

Lol let her put the mutilated bird into his hands, trying not to look at it, fixing his gaze out over the city, where the Cathedral tower still merged with the steeple of All Saints under an orange-brown cloudbank.

Down below the ramparts, in the bowl of the ancient camp, they covered the crow with damp, fallen leaves. Lol wondered if maybe he should say some kind of prayer, but couldn't think of one.

'You'll fly again,' he said lamely to the leafy mound. 'You will.'

He felt dazed and inadequate.

Poor crow. Poor bloody Moon.

She stood up, her long grey dress hemmed with mud. As he followed her out of the hollow, Lol thought of Merrily Watkins, whom he hadn't seen since leaving Ledwardine. Would a priest conduct a funeral service for a carrion crow? He thought Merrily would.

Moon gathered her dark woollen shawl around her. Numbed, he followed her along the slippery path. Ahead of them was a now-familiar oak tree with the single dead branch pointing out of the top like a finger from a fist. This was where another steep, secret path dropped towards Moon's new home in its dripping dell.

When the path curved to the left, and the barn's metal flue poked out of the trees, Moon's mood changed. Her face was a tremulous dawn.

'I still can't believe it.' She stopped where the path became a series of long, shallow earthen steps held up by stones and rotting boards. 'I'm back. I'm really back. And they *want* me back. They've given me their sign. Isn't that just...?' Moon shook her head, blown away.

Leaving Lol in a quandary – his hands sticky with crow bits and blood. Should he tell Denny about this? Or just Dick? Or not mention it at all?

'I'd like to sleep now, Lol,' Moon said.

'Good idea,' he said gratefully.

'I can't tell you how wonderful I feel.'

'Good,' Lol said. 'That's, er... good.'

Driving the old Astra back through the semi-industrial sprawl of Rotherwas and into the city, he couldn't even think about it. He thought instead about stupid things, like maybe buying a bike, too, and getting fit like Moon who insisted she'd be pedalling to the shop in Capuchin Lane six days a week all through the coming winter.

He parked in a private yard behind the shop, in a spot which would have been Moon's if she possessed a car, and he walked through an alley and into Capuchin Lane. It was also known these days as Church Street, but he and Moon both preferred its old name.

This was a wonderful street to live in: narrow, ancient, cobbled and closed to traffic, full of little shops and pubs, and ending at the Cathedral – presenting, in fact, the most medieval view of it, especially at dawn and in the evening when all the shops were closed and the hanging signs became black, romantic silhouettes.

The flat over the shop called John Barleycorn – one of Moon's brother's shops – had been semi-derelict when Moon had first lived here. This was when she was helping with the archaeological excavation in the Cathedral Close, before the digging site was released for a new building to house the Mappa Mundi and the Chained Library. More than a thousand skeletons had been unearthed, and Moon had spent her days among the dead and her nights on a camp bed in this same flat. Walking out each morning to the Cathedral – the dream developing.

She kept a photograph of herself holding two medieval skulls from the massive charnel pit they'd found – all three of them wearing damaged grins. When the excavation ended and the bones were removed, Moon wanted to stay on there and Denny wanted her to leave, so there was tension, and soon afterwards Moon stole the skirts from Next, and the police found her stoned on the Castle Green. And that was when Dick had finally agreed to renovate the flat over the shop as a proper home for her.

Moon had seemed fairly content here in Capuchin Lane. Only Dinedor Hill, in fact, could have lured her away – and it did.

Lol, in need of somewhere to live, had then himself taken over the flat. Denny was glad about that, as it meant Lol could keep an eye on Moon during her working hours, and watch out for any hovering dope-dealers.

He had his key to the side door, but went in through the shop to report to Denny.

Moon's much older, and very much bulkier, brother sat on a stool behind the counter, trying to tune a balalaika. Although there was only one customer in the store, a girl flicking through the CDs, it seemed quite full; for in a street of small shops this was the very smallest. And it was full of the busy sound of Gomez from big speakers – and Denny was here, a one-man crowd in himself.

'It go all right then, my old mate?'

'Fine.'

'Shit.'

As well as this shop, Denny ran a specialist hi-fi business, and his own recording studio in the cellar of his house up towards Breinton. Lol had produced a couple of albums for him there: local bands, limited editions. Denny was keen to get him back on to the studio floor, but Lol wasn't ready yet; the songs weren't quite there – something still missing.

Denny said, 'No fights, breakages, tears?'

'Would you count tears of joy?'

'Shit.'

Lol decided to keep quiet about the crow.

Denny twanged the balalaika and winced. 'Don't get yourself too comfy in that flat, mate. She changes like the wind, my little sister.' He shook his bald head, and his gold-plated novelty earring swung like a tiny censer.

'You hope.' Lol couldn't remember feeling exactly comfy anywhere.

'Yeah,' Denny said. 'Don't go back, that's my philosophy. *Never* in life do you fucking well go back.'

Lol shrugged, helpless. 'Whatever that place does to you, it has the opposite effect on her. You can't get around it: she's happy. She walks into the woods, up to the camp—'

'Yeah… and all the time passing the place where her fucking father topped himself! What does that say to you?'

Denny sniffed hard and plucked twice at the balalaika's strings, then laid it on the counter in disgust. 'What use is a three-string shoebox on a stick? Kathy bought it from this poor, homeless busker, probably got the BMW parked round the corner.'

'Soft-hearted,' Lol said.

'Soft in the head! I'll tell you one thing: first sign of unusual behaviour, any hint of dope up there – she's *out*. Kicking and screaming or…' The CD ended and Denny lowered his voice. 'Or however. Right?'

Lol nodded.

'Long as we agree on that, mate,' Denny said, as the girl customer turned around from the CD racks clutching a copy of Beth Orton's *Trailer Park*, a slow delighted smile pushing her tongue into a corner of her mouth.

'Hey,' she said. 'Lol Robinson, wow.'

'Oh,' Lol said. It seemed like ages since he'd seen her. He smiled, realizing how much he'd missed her even though sometimes, like Moon, she could be trouble. Well, not *quite* like Moon.

'Hey, cool,' the girl said. 'And that same old Roswell sweatshirt. *Is* that the same one, or did you buy a set?'

'Hello, Jane,' Lol said. He wondered how much she'd overheard.

'So, like who's Kathy?' Jane Watkins said. Dark mocking eyes under dark hair. A lot like her mother.

5

The Last Exorcist

THE BISHOP SMILED hard, talked fast, and wore purple as bishops do.

'The Church, OK?' His voice was public-school with the edges sanded off. 'The Church is… hierarchical, conservative, full of rivalry, feuding, back-stabbing. And inherently incapable of ever getting anything bloody well *done*.'

The Bishop wore purple all over: a tracksuit and jogging gear. The Bishop jogged all over the city and its outskirts, usually in the early mornings and the evenings, covering, according to the *Hereford Times*, a minimum of thirty miles a week.

'Now you'd think, wouldn't you, that organizing an office in the Cathedral cloisters would be the *easiest* thing? Scores of cells and crannies and cubicles, but… all of them the Dean's. And if the Dean says there isn't an office to spare, I'm not even permitted to argue. Within the precincts of the Cathedral, even God bows to the Dean. So we shall have to look elsewhere. I'm so sorry, Merrily.'

'It's probably meant, Bishop.'

'Mick,' corrected the Bishop. 'Meant? Oh it was meant, for sure. The bastard means to frustrate me. Who, after all, is the oldest member of his Chapter? Dobbs.' The Bishop tossed the name out like junk-mail. 'The old man's ubiquitous, hovering silently like some dark, malign spectre. I'd like to… I want to *exorcize* Dobbs.'

'Well, I feel very awkward about the whole thing.' Merrily poured tea for them both.

'Oh, why?' The Bishop quizzically tilted his head, as though he really didn't understand. He sugared his tea. 'You know the very worst thing about Dobbs? He actually *frightens* people – imagine. You have what you are convinced is an unwelcome presence in your house, your nerves are shot to hell, you finally gather the courage – or the sheer desperation – to go to the Church for help. And what should arrive at your door but this weird, shambling creature dressed like an undertaker and mumbling at you like Poe's doleful raven. Well, you'd rather hang on to the bloody ghost, wouldn't you?'

The Bishop, Merrily had noticed, said 'bloody' rather a lot, but nothing stronger, always conscious of the parameters of his image as a cool Christian. She was determined to be neither overawed nor underawed by Mick Hunter this afternoon, neither bulldozed nor seduced. She wished he was more like Huw Owen, but men like Huw never ever got to be bishops.

'Listen... Merrily...' His voice dropping an octave – late-night DJ. 'I realize how you must feel. If you were the kind of person who was utterly confident about it, I wouldn't want you in this job.'

... not a fundamentalist, not a charismatic or a happy-clappy, you've no visible axe to grind and I can see why he was drawn to you. You're in many ways almost exactly the kind of person we need in the trenches.

'Do you know Huw Owen?' she asked.

'Only by reputation. Quite a vocal campaigner for the ordination of women long before it became fa... feasible.'

Fashionable, he'd been about to say. Until it became *fashionable*, Mick Hunter would have kept very quiet on the issue. Merrily was trying to see him as Jane saw him, but it wasn't easy; Mick's blue eyes were clear and blazing with a wild integrity. He had a – somehow unepiscopal – blue jaw. He smelled very lightly of clean, honest, jogger's sweat and of something smokily indistinct which made her think, rather shockingly, of what a very long time it had been since she'd last had sex.

'Your late husband was a lawyer, wasn't he?' he said, startling her upright, tea spilling.

'Yes.' She was blushing. 'I... me too. I mean, I was going to be one too. Until Jane came into the picture, and a few other things changed.'

'Shame,' the Bishop said. 'Road accident, wasn't it?'

'On the M5. He... he hit a bridge.'

They hit a bridge. Sean and Karen Adair, his clerk and girl-friend and accomplice in a number of delicate arrangements with iffy businessmen. Dying flung together in a ball of fire, at the time when Merrily was balancing an inevitable divorce against her chances of ordination, and Jane was just starting secondary school. How much of this did the Bishop know? All of it, probably.

'Look,' she had to say this, 'the thing is, Huw's position on the ordination of women doesn't extend to Deliverance ministry – did you know that? He doesn't think we're ready for all that yet.'

His eyes widening. She realized he'd probably sent her on this particular course precisely *because* he knew Huw was sympathetic to women priests.

'Not ready for all that?' The eyes narrowing again. 'All what?'

'He doesn't feel that we have the necessary weight of tradition behind us to take on... whatever's out there.'

'Which is a little bit preposterous' – Mick Hunter leaned back – 'don't you think?'

'It's not what *I* think that matters.'

'No, quite. At the end of the day, it's what *I* think. The Deliverance consultant's responsible to the Bishop, and only to the Bishop. And *I* think – without any positive discrimination – that, if anything, this is a job a woman can do better than a man. It demands delicacy, compassion... qualities not exactly manifested by Dobbs.'

'I've... I've been trying, you know, to work out exactly how you do see the job.'

Mick Hunter stirred his tea thoughtfully. Two tables away, a couple of well-dressed, not-quite-elderly women were openly watching him. Beefcake bishop – a new phenomenon.

'OK, right,' he said. 'While you were in Wales, we had some basic research carried out. Quick phone-call to all the parish clergy: a few facts and figures. Did you know for instance that in the past six months, in this diocese alone, there have been between twenty and thirty appeals to the Church for assistance with perceived psychic disturbance?'

'Really? My God.'

'And rising.' Mick smiled. 'If the Church was a business, we'd be calling this a major growth area.'

The Bishop then talked about apparent psychic blackspots revealed by the survey – the north of the diocese was worst – and Merrily thought about how fate pushed you around, all the unplanned directions your life took. Whether she would ever actually have become a lawyer had she not become pregnant while still at university. If she would ever have become a priest had Sean not died when he did and if she hadn't discovered he was a crook. If she would ever have been drawn into the strange shadow-world of Deliverance, had her own vicarage in Ledwardine not been tenanted by an essence of something which no one else had experienced.

She felt targeted, exposed. She wanted to leap up from the table and run to the car and smoke several cigarettes.

Instead she said, 'What exactly are we talking about here?'

The Bishop shrugged. 'Mostly, I suspect, about paranoia, psychiatric problems, loneliness, isolation, stress. Modern society, Merrily. Post-millennial angst. We're certainly *not* talking about the medieval world of Canon Dobbs. Nor, I think, should we be sending the local vicar along just to have a cup of coffee and intone a few prayers, which is what happens in most cases now.'

She began to understand about the office. He would want one that actually said DELIVERANCE CONSULTANT on its door. He wanted to bring the job out of the closet.

'I'm glad the awful word Exorcism's been ditched,' he said, 'though I'm not entirely happy with Deliverance either. A less portentous term would be "*rescue*", don't you think?'

Rescue Consultant? Spiritual Rescue Service? SRS? She raised her cup to mask a smile. He didn't notice.

'It would still be part of the parish priest's role to deal, in the initial stages, with people who think they're being haunted or little Darren's got the Devil in him or whatever. But the public also need to know there's an efficient machinery inside the Church for dealing with such problems, and that there's a particular person to whom they can turn. And I don't want that person to look like Dobbs. We need to be seen as sympathetic, non-judgemental, user-friendly. You've read Perry's book on Deliverance?'

'The set text, isn't it?'

'It's a start. I find Michael Perry rather too credulous, but I like his insistence on not overreacting. The job's about counselling. It's about being a spiritual Samaritan – about listening. You notice that Perry seldom seems to advocate exorcizing a place?'

'He suggests a Major Exorcism should primarily be focused on a demonically possessed person, and then only when a number of other procedures have proved ineffective.'

Mick Hunter put down his cup. 'I *never* want to hear of a so-called Major Exorcism. It's crude, primitive and almost certainly ineffective.'

Merrily blinked. 'You don't think that in the presence of extreme evil…?'

'Evil's a disease,' the Bishop said. 'In fact it's many diseases. If we're going to deal with it, we have to study the symptoms, consider the nature of the particular malady, and then apply the correct treatment with sensitivity, precision and care. The

Major Exorcism, quite frankly, is the kind of medieval bludgeon which in my opinion the post-millennial Church can do without. Are you with me here?'

I don't know, Merrily thought wildly. *I don't know...*

'It's hard...' She took a breath to calm herself. Mick Hunter's enthusiasm picked you up and carried you along and then put you down suddenly, and you didn't know where you were. 'It's hard to express an opinion about something you've really had no experience of. I don't think anyone can possibly—'

'Merrily...' He put his hand over hers on the white tablecloth. 'One of my faults is expecting too much of people too soon, I realize that. But I know from my predecessor that you've proved yourself to be a resourceful, resilient person. The appalling Ledwardine business – I know you don't like your part in all that to be talked about...'

'No.'

'But you've shown you have nerve and wisdom and you can think on your feet. OK, I'm aware that we're breaking new ground here, but it's the direction I believe every diocese will be going in within five years.' He paused. 'I've had a word with Gareth, by the way.'

'The Archdeacon?'

'Under the reorganization, you were due to be awarded two extra parishes before the end of the year. I pointed out to Gareth that, under the circumstances, that would be far too much of a burden.'

'You mean it's either the Deliverance role or two more parishes to run?'

'The two parishes would be a lot easier, Merrily – a quieter life.'

'Yes.'

'If it's a quiet life you want?'

What she wanted was a cigarette, but she knew the Bishop hated them. What she wanted was for Huw Owen to have been proved wrong, but everything Huw had forecast had been dead right. She *would* wind up with her picture in the *Hereford Times*, although probably without the crucifix.

'I'm going to have to play this slowly and diplomatically,' Mick Hunter said. 'Dobbs won't go until he's too shaky to hold a cup of holy water, and as long as he's here he has the support of the Dean's cabal. Well, all right, he can still be an exorcist if he wants. That doesn't prevent me appointing a consultant to, say, prepare a detailed report on the demand for Deliverance services.'

Merrily said, 'I don't like this.'

'Merely politics. I'm afraid I'm quite good at politics.'

She sighed. 'You've given me a lot to think about, Bishop.'

'Mick.'

'Could I have some time?'

'To pray for guidance?'

'Yes,' Merrily said, 'I suppose that's what I'll do.'

'Call my office if you'd like another meeting.' Mick stood up, zipped his purple tracksuit top.

'Er... if you can't get an office in the cloisters, that means I'd be working from home then?'

At least she wouldn't have to see the rather scary Dobbs.

'Oh no.' Mick grinned. 'The Dean doesn't screw me so easily. I told you I'm quite good at this. I'm going to put you in the Palace.'

In the car going home, Merrily put on Tori Amos's *From the Choirgirl Hotel* because it was doomy and gothic and would keep Jane quiet. The kid would want to know what the Bishop had been so keen to talk about, but first Merrily needed to work it out for herself.

It certainly wasn't what Jane had imagined, a clandestine return to witch-hunting, sneaky rearguard action by a defensive Church. There was no sign of *New Age, Old Enemy* paranoia in Mick Hunter. He was simply enfolding the Deliverance ministry into his campaign to project the diocese further into the new millennium as a vibrant, caring, essential institution. Was that so wrong? But what did he see as the enemy?

… paranoia, psychiatric problems, loneliness, isolation, stress, post-millennial angst…

Clearly, the Bishop's liberalism did not extend to the supernatural. Merrily suspected he didn't believe in ghosts, and that for him the borderline between demonic possession and schizophrenia would not exist – which was worrying. To what extent was healthy scepticism compatible with Christian faith? And what did he mean: *Put you in the Palace*?

'… little record shop in Church Street?'

'Huh? Sorry, flower.'

Jane reached out and turned down the stereo. Merrily glanced across at her. Jane turning down music – this had never happened before.

'I said, who do you think I ran into in that poky little record shop in Church Street?'

It was almost dark, and they were leaving the city via the King's Acre roundabout, with a fourteenth-century cross on its island.

'Close. Lol Robinson.' Jane said. 'You do remember… ?'

'Oh,' Merrily said casually. There was a time when she could have become too fond of Lol Robinson. 'Right. How is he?'

Jane told her how Lol had just started renting this brilliant flat over the shop, with a view over the cobbles and two pubs about twenty yards away.

'Belongs to the guy who owns the shop. His sister used to live there but she's moved out. Her name's Katherine Moon, but she's just known as Moon, and I think she and Lol… Anyway, he looks exactly the same. Hasn't grown, same little round glasses, still wearing that black sweat-shirt with the alien face on the front – possibly symbolic of the way he feels he relates to society and feels that certain people relate to him.'

'So, apart from the sartorial sameness, did he seem OK?'

'No, he was like waving his arms around and drooling at the

mouth. Of course he seemed OK. We went for a coffee in the All Saints café. I've never been in there before. It's quite cool.'

'It's in a church.'

'Yeah, I noticed. Nice to see one fulfilling a useful service. Anyway, I got out of Lol what he's doing now. He didn't want to tell me, but I can be fairly persistent.'

'You nailed his guitar hand to the prayerbook shelf?'

'Look, do you want to know what he's doing or not?'

'All right.'

'You ready for this? He's training to be a shrink.'

'What? But he was—'

'Well, not a shrink exactly. He hates psychiatrists because they just give you drugs to keep you quiet. More a kind of psychotherapist. He was consulting one in Hereford, and the guy realized that, after years in and out of mental hospitals, Lol knew more -ologies and -isms than he himself did, so now he's employing him a couple of days a week for sort of on-the-job training, and Lol's doing these night classes. Isn't that so cool?'

'It...' Merrily thought about this. 'I suppose it is, really. Lol would be pretty good. He doesn't judge people. Yeah, that's cool.'

'Also, he's playing again. He's made some tapes, although he won't let anybody hear them.'

'Even you?'

'I'm working on it. I may go back there – I like that shop. Lots of stuff by indy folk bands. And I'm really glad I saw him. *I* didn't want to lose touch just because he moved out of Ledwardine.'

Merrily said cautiously, 'Lol needed time to get himself together.'

'Oh,' Jane said airily, 'I think he needed more than that, don't you?'

'Don't start.'

'Like maybe somebody who wasn't terrified of getting into a relationship because of what the parish might think.'

'Stop there,' Merrily said lightly, 'all right?'

'Fine.' Jane prodded the music up to disco level and turned to look out of the side window at the last of the grim amber sinking on to the shelf of the Black Mountains. A desultory rain filmed the windscreen.

'Still,' Merrily thought she heard the kid mumble, 'it's probably considered socially OK to fuck a bishop.'

That night, praying under her bedroom window in the vicarage, Merrily realized the Deliverance issue wasn't really a problem she needed to hang on God at this stage. Her usual advice to parishioners facing a decision was to gather all the information they could get from available sources on both sides of the argument, and only then apply for a solution.

Fair enough. She would seek independent advice within the Church.

She went to sit on the edge of the bed, looking out at the lights of Ledwardine speckling the trees. They made her think of what Huw Owen had said about the targeting of women priests.

Little rat-eyes in the dark.

She hadn't even raised that point with Mick Hunter. He would have taken it seriously, but not in the way it was meant by Huw.

Merrily shivered lightly and slid into bed, cuddling the hot water bottle, aware of Ethel the black cat curling on the duvet against her ankles, remembering the night Ethel had first appeared at the vicarage in the arms of Lol Robinson after she'd received a kicking from a drunk. She hoped Lol Robinson would be happy with his girlfriend. Lol and Merrily – that would never have worked.

Later, on the edge of sleep, she heard Huw Owen's flat, nasal voice as if it were actually in the room.

Little rat-eyes in the dark.

And jerked awake.

OK. She'd absorbed Huw's warning, listened to the Bishop's plans.

It was clear that what she had to do now, not least for the sake of her conscience, was go back to Hereford and talk to Canon Dobbs.

The Last Exorcist.

Merrily lay down again and slept.

6

Sweat and Mothballs

'OH YES,' MOON said, 'he was outside the window, peering in – his face right up to the glass. His eyes were full of this awful, blank confusion. I don't think he knew who I was. That was the worst thing: he didn't *know* me.'

'He was in the… garden?' *How do I handle this?* Lol thought. *She's getting worse.*

'I ran out,' Moon said. 'Then I saw him again at the bottom of the steps leading up to the camp. And then he wasn't there any more.'

She was sitting on a cardboard box full of books. There were about two dozen boxes dumped all over the living area. Lol hadn't been into the kitchen or the bathroom but, except for the futon in the open loft, it looked exactly the way it had been the last time he was here. She'd refused offers of help from Denny and Lol, and from Dick Lyden's wife Ruth. You had to arrange your possessions yourself, she'd insisted, otherwise you'd never know where anything was.

But nothing at all seemed to have been put away, nothing even unpacked. It was as though she'd gone straight to bed when he left her on Saturday and had just got up again, four days later.

Sleeping Beauty situation, fairytale again.

The point about Moon was that she was utterly single-minded. Most of the time she had no small talk, and no interest in other people, although she could be very generous when some problem was put under her nose – like buying the busker's balalaika.

But now she'd found her father, and nothing else mattered.

'Oh,' she said, 'and he was wearing a flat cap which I recognized.'

Moon was wearing an ankle-length, white satin nightdress which had collected a lot of dust, a thick silver torc around her neck. She'd had on nothing over the nightdress when she'd opened the door to Lol. She didn't seem cold. It was wildly erotic. Lol wondered how doctors coped with this.

'It was this grey checked one with all the lining hanging out. Mummy always kept it – I mean for years, anyway. She talked about all the times she used to try and get him to throw it away. Denny threw it away in the end, I suppose. Now my father has it back.'

Delusional, Lol thought. *Because she doesn't seem scared. It has to be wishful thinking.* But what did it mean, that she'd wished up a father who didn't seem to recognize her?

The long nightdress rustled like leaves as Moon stood up, glided to the window.

'When I was little, I used to wonder if that was the cap he'd worn when he shot himself, so that was why it was all torn. Of course, the gun would have made much more of a mess than that, but you don't know these things when you're little, do you?'

It occurred to him that this was the first time she'd spoken about her father.

Her father had killed himself when she was about two years old. Denny said she had no memories of him, but there was probably some resentment because his folly was the reason they'd had to sell up and leave the hill.

This fucking insane investment. Some mate of the old man's had developed this sweet sparkling cider he reckoned was going to snatch at least half the Babycham market. Dad threw everything at it – sold off about fifty acres, left the farm non-viable.

They'd lost the farm. Which was said to have been in the family since at least the Middle Ages. Or much longer, if you listened to Moon.

Denny had said, *The day we left, the old man took his shotgun for a last, short walk. It's a thing farmers do when they feel they've let their ancestors down.*

'How, um…?' Lol's mouth was dry. He sat down on another box of books. 'How do you feel about your dad now?'

Moon turned to Lol, her eyes shining. 'I have to reach out to him. The ancestors have enabled me to do that, OK?'

The crow. *By bathing my hands in its blood, I'm acquiring its powers.*

'They sent him back. He doesn't know why, but he will. He has to know who I am – that's the first stage. I have to let him know I'm all right about him.'

'You're not… just a bit scared?'

'He's my *father*. And I'm his only hope of finding peace. He knows he's got a lot of making up to do. To Mummy as well, but that's out of our hands now.'

She went silent, the fervour in her eyes slipping away.

'Your mum… do you feel *she's* at peace?' Lol didn't know why he'd asked that, except to get her talking again.

'I don't know. She was never the same afterwards. I mean, all my life she had problems with her nerves. It was lucky Denny was practically grown-up by then, and so he took charge. It was Denny who was always pushing me to do well at school, determined I should go to university because he hadn't. Taking the father's role, you know? He owes Denny too, I suppose.'

'How can he make it up to you?' Lol said softly. 'How can your father help?'

She blinked at him, as if that was obvious. 'With my book, of course – my book about the Dinedor People. He can help me

67

with the book. He can make them talk to me. They sent him to me, so I must be able to reach them through him.'

'Who?'

'The ancestors.'

The barn was quite small: just four rooms. It had been converted initially as extra holiday accommodation by the present owners of the farmhouse, some people called Purefoy, who apparently ran a bed-and-breakfast business. But this had not been a very good summer for weather or tourism, and they'd presumably realized they could make more money with a long-term let. Not much ground, of course. No room for a garage, quite difficult access, but a beautiful rural situation.

Moon had come up here on the mountain-bike Denny had bought her in the aftermath of the shoplifting case. It was a hot day and she was pushing the bike up towards the camp when she suddenly, as she put it, felt her ancestors calling out to her.

It was the most incredible experience. Like the one Alfred Watkins must have had, when he first saw those lines in the landscape. Except I was aware of just one line, leading from me to the hill and back through the centuries. The hill was vibrating under me. I was shaking. I realized this was what I'd been training for, during all those years of digging people up. But that was only bones. I want to unearth real *people. I want to communicate with them. I knew I had to discover the story of the hill and the Dinedor People. It was just an amazing moment. I felt as light as a butterfly.*

Moon had been up here until the dusk came. She'd found herself almost frantically knocking on the doors of farmhouses and cottages all around the hill to find out who was living here and who had lived here for the most generations. Discovering, as she'd suspected she might, that the oldest Dinedor family was her own. Moon maintained that her family had come out of the original settlement on Dinedor Hill, all those years before the time of Christ.

But none lived here any more. Her father had snapped the line.

Close to sunset, Moon had arrived at Dyn Farm, at the old, mellowed farmhouse near to the camp, to find the Purefoys – Londoners, early-retired – in the garden.

Usually, as you know, I'm so shy, unless I've taken something. But I was glowing. They didn't seem very friendly at first, a bit reserved like a lot of new people, but when I told them who I was, they became quite excited and invited me in. Of course, they were asking me all sorts of questions about the house that I couldn't really answer. I was just a toddler when we left.

Then they showed me the barn. And I felt that my whole life had been leading up to that moment.

Moon came over and stood in front of Lol, close enough for him to see her nipples through the nightdress. Oh God! He kept looking at her face.

'I wanted to tell him – my father – that it was OK, it was me, I was back. I was here. I wanted to tell him it was all right, that I'd help him to find peace.'

'You tried to talk to him?'

'No, not last night. I couldn't get close enough to him. This was the first night… last Saturday. Yeah, I had a sleep and then I went for a walk in the woods, where he shot himself. I went there when it was dark.'

'You saw him then?' *This is eerie. This is not good.*

'I didn't *see* him then. That was when I started to call out for him.'

'Literally?'

'Maybe. I remember standing in the woods and screaming, "Daddy!" It was funny… It was like I was a small child again.'

Lol said tentatively, 'You, um… you think that was safe, on your own?'

'Oh, nothing will ever happen to me on the hill. I intend to walk and walk, day and night, until I know every tree and bush of those woods, every fold of every field. I've got to make up for all those years away, you know? I have to absolutely immerse myself in the hill – until it goes everywhere with me. Until it fills my dreams.'

'So when you… when you saw him, *that* was a kind of dream, was it?'

She looked down at him. Her nightdress smelled of sweat and mothballs. Her hair hung down over each shoulder, like a stole.

She said, 'Are *you* supposed to be my therapist now, Lol?'

'I don't think so, not officially. I just help Dick.'

'Dick's hopeless, isn't he? Dick's a dead loss. He doesn't believe in anything outside of textbook psychology.'

'He's a nice bloke,' Lol said awkwardly. 'He wants to do his best for you.'

'He's an idiot. If you told Dick I'd seen my father, he'd come up with a beautiful theory involving hallucinations or drugs. But you see I don't *have* any drugs. I don't need anything up here; it's a constant, natural high. And it would be kind of an insult anyway. *And* I have never had hallucinations, ever.'

Her hair swung close to his face. It was the kind of hair medieval maidens dangled from high windows so that knights could climb up and rescue them.

'So it's not official,' she said. 'I mean us: we're not counsellor and patient or anything.'

Lol was confused. He felt himself blushing.

'We're a *bit* official,' he said.

'You have to report back to Dick?'

'I suppose so.'

'You'll tell him about this?'

'Not if…'

Moon turned away and dipped like a heron between two boxes, coming up with a dark green cardigan which she pulled on.

'Then it was a dream.' She bent and pouted at him, a petulant child. 'It was all a dream.'

70

7

Graveyard Angel

A MYSTERIOUS SUMMONS to the Bishop's Palace.

Wednesday afternoon: market day, and the city still crowded. Merrily found a parking space near The Black Lion in Bridge Street. She might have been allowed to drive into the Palace courtyard, but this could be considered presumptuous; she didn't want that – almost didn't want to be noticed sliding through the shoppers in her black woollen two-piece, a grey silk scarf over her dog-collar.

Looking out, while she was in the area, for Canon Dobbs, the exorcist.

What she needed was a confidential chat with the old guy, nobody else involved. To clear the air, maybe even iron things out. If she took on this task, she wanted no hard feelings, no trail of resentment.

Contacting Dobbs was not so easy. In Deliverance, according to Huw Owen, low-profile was essential, to avoid being troubled by cranks and nutters or worse. But his guy was *well* below the parapet – not even, as she discovered, in the phone book. As a residential canon at the Cathedral he had no parishioners to be accessible to, but ex-directory?

Evensong at Ledwardine Church had recently been suspended by popular demand, or rather the absence of it, so on Sunday night – with Jane out at a friend's – Merrily had found time to ring Alan Crombie, the Rector of Madley. But he wasn't much help.

'Never had to consult him, Merrily – but I remember Colin Strong. When he was at Vowchurch, there was a persistent problem at a farmhouse and he ended up getting Dobbs in. I think he simply did it through the Bishop's office. You leave a message and he gets in touch with you.'

Well, that was no use. It would get right back to Mick Hunter.

'So ordinary members of the public have no real access to Dobbs?'

'Not initially,' Alan Crombie said. 'It's strictly clergy-consultation. That's normal practice. If you have a problem you go to your local priest and he decides if he can cope with it or if he needs specialist advice.'

'What happened at Vowchurch? Did Dobbs deal with it?'

'Lord knows. One of his rules is total secrecy. Anything gets in the papers, I gather his wrath is awesome to behold. Do you have another little problem in that department yourself, Merrily?'

'No, I…' *Oh, what the hell!* 'Off the record, Alan, the Bishop's asked me to succeed Dobbs when he… retires.'

'Oh, I see.' Silence, then a nervous laugh. 'Well… rather you than me.'

'I realize I may have to buy a black bag and a big hat.'

'God, you don't want to go in for that kind of thing,' Alan had said with another nervous laugh. 'Have all kinds of perverts following you home.'

Merrily walked along King Street, the Cathedral up ahead filling her vision. She had no idea what Dobbs looked like and saw no men in big hats with black bags.

Although it didn't look much from the front, the Bishop's Palace was perhaps the most desirable dwelling in Hereford: next door to the Cathedral but closer to the River Wye, and dreamily visible from the public footpath on the opposite bank, with its big white windows on mellow red brick, tree-fringed lawns sloping to the water.

Inside, she'd never been further than the vastly refurbished twelfth-century Great Hall where receptions were held. Today she didn't even make it across the courtyard. Sophie Hill, the Bishop's elegant white-haired lay-secretary, met her at the entrance, steering her through a door under the gatehouse and up winding stone stairs, about twenty of them.

'It's not very big, but Michael thought you'd like it better that way.'

'I'm sorry?' Merrily pulled off her scarf.

'It could be quite charming' – Sophie reached beyond her to push open the door at the top of the steps – 'with a few pictures and things. To the left, please, Mrs Watkins.'

There were two offices in the gatehouse: a bigger one with a vista of Broad Street... and this.

Sloping ceiling, timbered and whitewashed walls, a desk with a phone. A scuffed repro captain's chair that swivelled, two filing cabinets, a small bookcase with a Bible and some local reference books, including Jane's one-time bible, *The Folklore of Herefordshire* by Ella Mary Leather.

Merrily walked uncertainly over to the window overlooking the courtyard and the former stables, a few parked cars and great stacks of split logs for the Bishop's fires.

'Welcome to Deliverance Tower,' said Sophie deadpan. 'The computer's on order.'

Walking dazed into the blustery sunshine on Broad Street, Merrily felt the hand of fate so heavily on her shoulder that she nearly threw up an arm to shake it off.

It had felt good up in the gatehouse, almost cosy. On top of the city and yet remote from it – a refuge, an eyrie. It had felt right.

Careful. Don't be seduced on the first date.

Sophie had said the Bishop had planned to see her himself, but Mrs Hunter had an important appointment and her own car was being serviced. This appeared to be true; through the window, Merrily had watched Mick, in clerical shirt under what was almost certainly an Armani jacket, accompany his wife to a dusty BMW in British racing green. She saw that Val Hunter was very tall, nearly as tall as the Bishop. Angular, heronlike, tawny hair thrown back, a beauty with breeding. They had two sons at boarding school; although Mick had confessed, in an interview with the *Observer*, to having very mixed feelings about private education. Merrily suspected his wife didn't share them.

'He's still rather feeling his way,' Sophie had confided, 'but he does want change, and I'm afraid he'll be terribly disappointed if you walk away from this, Mrs Watkins. He regards it as a very meaningful step for the female ministry.'

At the top of Broad Street now, Merrily stared at the rings in a jeweller's window, and saw her reflection and all the people passing behind her – one man with a briefcase looking over his shoulder at her legs while her back was turned.

She began to tremble. She needed a cigarette.

Actually, even stronger than that, came the realization that she needed to pray.

Like now.

Abruptly, as though obeying some hypnotic command, she turned back towards the Cathedral, rapidly crossing the green and once again guiltily winding the scarf about her throat to cover the collar. She wanted no one to see her, no one to approach.

Within yards of the north door, she thought of going around the back to the cloisters, asking the first person she didn't recognize where Canon Dobbs lived, but by now the compulsion to pray was too strong, a racing in the blood.

She breathed out. *Jesus!*

It happened only rarely like this. Like the day she drove into the country with a blinding headache, and ended up following a track to a cell-like church dedicated to some forgotten Celtic saint where – when she'd most needed it; when she was just finding out the sordid truth about Sean's business – there'd been this sudden blissful sense of blue and gold, and a lamplit path opening in front of her.

A group was entering the Cathedral; it looked like a Women's Institute party. 'Isn't there a café?' someone said grumpily.

Merrily felt like pushing past, but waited at the end of the line as the women moved singly through the porch. When she was inside, she saw them fanning into the aisles, heard echoes of footsteps and birdlike voices spiralling through sacred stone caverns.

And she was just standing there on her own and tingling with need.

'Welcome to Hereford Cathedral.' An amplified voice from the distant pulpit, the duty chaplain. 'If you'd all please be seated, we'll begin the tour with a short prayer. Thank you.'

Sweating now, almost panicking, Merrily stumbled through the first available doorway and slithered to her knees in the merciful gloom of the fifteenth-century chantry chapel of Bishop John Stanbury, with its gilded triptych and its luxuriously carved and moulded walls and ceilings merging almost organically, it seemed, in a rush of rippling honeyed stone.

When she put her hands together she could feel the tiny hairs on the backs of them standing electrically on end.

'God,' she was whispering. 'What is it? What *is* it?'

That sensation of incredible potential: all the answers to all the questions no more than an instant away, an atom of time, a membrane of space.

'There's this picture of her,' Jane said, 'that she once threw away, only I rescued it from the bin for purposes of future leverage and blackmail and stuff. I think she knows I've got it, but she never says anything.'

They walked past the school tennis courts, their nets removed for the winter, and across to the sixth-form car park where Rowenna's Fiesta stood, six years old and lime-green but otherwise brilliant.

'She's wearing this frock like a heavy-duty binliner, right? And her hair's kind of bunched up with these like plastic spikes sticking out. She's got on this luminous white lipstick. And her eyes are like under about three economy packs of cheap mascara.'

Rowenna shook her head sadly.

'Her favourite band,' Jane said, 'was Siouxsie and the Banshees.'

'Don't,' said Rowenna, pained.

'Well, actually they weren't bad.'

Rowenna unlocked the Fiesta. 'You could always sell the picture to the tabloids.'

'Yeah, but she'd have to do something controversial first, to get them interested. Just another woman priest who used to be a punk, that isn't enough, is it? I suppose I could take it to the *Hereford Times.*'

'Who'd pay you about enough to buy a couple of CDs.'

'Yeah, mid-price ones.' Jane climbed into the passenger seat. 'No, the point I was trying to make: you look at that picture and you can somehow see the future priest there. You know what I mean, all dark and ritualistic?'

'What, she's some kind of vestment fetishist?'

'No! It's just… oh shit.'

Dean Wall and Danny Gittoes, famous sad Ledwardine louts, were leaning over the car, Dean's big face up against the passenger window. Jane wound it down. Dean fumbled out his ingratiating leer.

'All right for a lift home, ladies?'

'Not today, OK?' Rowenna said.

'In fact, not *ever.*' Jane cranked up the window. 'Like, no offence, but we'd rather *not* wind up raped and the car burned out, if that's OK with you.'

Dean was saying, 'You f—' as Jane wound the window the last inch.

'Foot down, Ro.'

Rowenna drove off, smiling.

'Nicely handled, kitten. Thanks.'

Rowenna was new at the school, but nearly two years older than Jane. On account of her family moving around a lot and a long spell of illness, she'd got way behind, so she'd needed to re-start her A-level course. She was a cool person – in a way a kind of older sister, a role she seemed to like.

'You don't mean,' said Jane, astounded, 'that you *have* actually given those two hairballs a lift? Like, how did you get the slime off the upholstery?'

Rowenna laughed. 'I see now it was a grave mistake, and I won't do it again. What were you saying about your mother? I didn't quite grasp the nature of the problem.'

'Oh, it's just…' Jane cupped her hands over her nose and mouth and sighed into them, '… just she's worth more than this, that's all. Like, OK, maybe she was drawn into it by this spiritual need and the need to bring it out in other people, you know what I mean?'

'Maybe.' Rowenna drove with easy confidence. Within only a couple of hundred yards of the school, they were out into countryside with wooded hills and orchards.

'But I mean, the Church of England? Like, what can you really expect of an outfit that was only set up so Henry VIII could dump his wife? Spiritually they're just a bunch of no-hope tossers, and I can't see that the ordination of women will change a thing.'

'I suppose even the Catholics kind of look like they've got *something* together.' Rowenna's father was an Army officer, possibly SAS, and the family had spent some time in Northern Ireland.

'But you know what I mean?' Jane hunched forward, clasping her hands together. 'I imagine her in about forty years' time, sitting by the gas fire in some old clergyperson's home, full of arthritis from kneeling on cold stone floors, and thinking: What the hell was *that* all about?'

Rowenna laughed, a sound like ice in a cocktail glass. She looked innocent and kind of wispy, but she was pretty shrewd.

'And this Deliverance trip, right?' Jane knew she wasn't supposed to discuss this, but Rowenna's military background – high-security clearance, all that stuff – meant she could be trusted not to spread things around. 'It's obvious she thinks this is a kind of cutting-edge thing to do, and will maybe take her *closer*. You know what I mean?'

'To the spiritual world?'

'But it's actually quite the opposite. From what I can see, the job is actually to *stop* people getting close. She has to actively discourage all contact with the occult or anything mystical – anything *interesting*. I think that's kind of immoral, don't you?'

'It's kind of fascist,' Rowenna said.

'Let's face it, almost any kind of spiritual activity is more fun than going to church.'

'I wouldn't argue with that.'

And then, as usual, it was suddenly gone.

Sometimes you were left floating on a cushion of peace; occasionally there was an aching void. This time only silence coloured by the placid images of the Cathedral and the Wye Bridge in the small stained-glass window just above her head.

Merrily stood up shakily in the intimacy of Bishop Stanbury's exquisite chantry. She stood with her arms by her sides, breathing slowly. It was like sex: sublime at the time but what, if anything, had it altered? What progression was there?

Outside, in the main body of the Cathedral, the prayer was over and there was a communal rising and clattering. She stood quietly in the doorway of the chantry, her grey silk scarf dangling from her fingers.

'Go away. Go *away*.' A few yards away, a man's voice rose impatiently. 'I can't possibly discuss this here.'

'I don't understand…' A woman now, agitated. 'What have I been doing wrong?'

'Hush!'

A stuttering of footsteps. Merrily stepped out of the chantry, saw a woman, about sixty, who drew breath, stifled a cry, turned sharply and walked quickly away – across to the exit which led to the Cathedral giftshop. She wore a tweed coat and boots and a puffy velvet hat. She never looked back.

From the aisle to the left of the chantry, the man watched her go.

Merrily said, 'I'm so sorry, I didn't mean to—'

He wore a long overcoat. He glanced at her. 'I think your party is over in the Lady Chapel.'

Then he saw her collar and she saw his, and the skirt of the cassock below his overcoat. And although she'd never seen him before, as soon as she discerned cold recognition in the pale eyes in that stone face – the face of some ancient, eroded grave-yard archangel – she knew who he was.

And before she was aware of them the words were out. Possibly, under the circumstances, the stupidest words she could have uttered.

'Is there anything I can do, Canon Dobbs?'

He looked at her for a long time. She couldn't move.

Eventually, without any change of expression, he walked past her and left the Cathedral.

8

Beautiful Theory

FOR MANY YEARS, Dick Lyden had been something stressful in the City of London. Now he and his wife were private psychotherapists in Hereford. Dick was about thirty pounds heavier, pink-cheeked, income decidedly reduced, a much happier man.

'And Moon – in her spiritual home at last?' He beamed, feet on his desk. 'How is Moon?'

'Moon is…' Lol hesitated. 'Moon is what I wanted to see you about.'

Dick and Ruth lived and practised in half of a steep Edwardian terrace on the western side, not far from the old water-tower. Dick's attic office had a view across the city to Dinedor Hill, to which Lol's gaze was now inevitably being pulled. When Dick expansively opened up his hands, allowing him the floor, Lol turned his chair away from the window and told Dick about the crow which Moon claimed had mystically fallen dead at her feet.

Dick swivelled his feet from the desk, rubbed his forehead, pushing back slabs of battleship-grey hair. 'And do you think it really did?'

'I didn't see it happen.'

'So she may just have found it in the hedge and made the rest up.'

'It's possible,' Lol said.

'And the blood... she actually... That's extraordinary.' Dick rubbed his hands together, looking up at a plaster cornice above Lol's head. 'And yet, you know, while it might seem horrible to the likes of us, she's spent quite a few years scrabbling about in the earth, ferreting out old skulls with worms in their eyes.'

'This was a bit different, though.'

Yes, it was, Dick conceded. In fact, yes, what they were looking at here was really quite an elaborate fantasy structure, on the lines of one of those impossibly complicated computer games his son James used to play before he discovered rock music. Except this wasn't dragons and demons; this was built on layers of actual history.

'Let's examine it. Let's pull it apart.' Dick dragged a foolscap pad towards him, began to draw circles and link them with lines.

'What've we got? An extremely intelligent girl with a degree in archaeology, some years' experience in the field... and this absorbing, fanatical interest in the Iron Age civilization, which became an obsession – the Celtic jewellery, the strange woollens. She still wear that awful sheepskin waistcoat thing?'

'Not recently.'

'That's one good thing. Anyway... suddenly she's aware she can *explain* this obsession in the context of her own family history. She's been told the family roots in that particular spot go back to the Dark Ages and before – which is probably complete nonsense, but that's irrelevant. She forms the idea that this is what she was born to do, because of the *place* she was born – on the side of this Iron Age fort or whatever it is.'

Dick drew a crude hill with battlements.

'Perhaps believing... that there's some great *secret* here... that only she can recover. Some Holy Grail. But of course... what she *really* wants to find is a key... to her father's suicide.'

Dick smiled happily at Lol. He loved finding cross-references.

'Who knows, Laurence? Who knows what horrors lodged in the mind of a two-year-old child in circumstances like that? And Dinedor Hill never talked about, Denny going dark with anger if the subject of their father arises. So much *mystery*. Well, she doesn't want to believe her old man topped himself because he messed up his finances. It's got to be more profound than that.'

'It's profound enough,' Lol said. 'By losing the farm, he let down his family, and his ancestors. Scores of farmers have killed themselves in the past few years for similar reasons. And we're talking about a very historic family.'

'Absolutely. She's bunched all that together into an epic personal quest, with all the pseudo-mystical and supernatural overtones of James's trashy computer games.'

'Is that a good thing, though, Dick? Moon living at the centre of a fantasy?'

'I don't see that it's necessarily *bad*. And if it's all going to be providing material for her book... Do we know what kind of book she has in mind?'

'A history of Dinedor Hill seen through the eyes of the people who live there now—'

'Splendid,' Dick interrupted.

'—and the people who lived there over two thousand years ago.'

'Constructed from archaeological evidence and what she feels is her own instinctive knowledge of her ancestors? Well, that could be a very valid book, couldn't it? One can certainly imagine a publisher going for that. I could talk to some people myself.'

'I don't know.' Lol had been doubtful about this book from the start. A book wasn't like a song; you couldn't knock it out in a couple of hours when the inspiration was there. 'She doesn't seem organized enough for anything like that. For instance, Denny's managing the shop for a few days while she gets the barn sorted – supposedly. But this morning virtually nothing had changed: everything still in boxes. Which was what Denny said it'd be like: chaos – and Moon living inside herself.'

Dick shrugged. 'So after the excitement of the move, there's a period of emotional exhaustion. Then she dusts herself off, starts to pick up the pieces. Then the rehab begins. I'll give her a couple of days and then I'll go and have a chat myself. Or we can both go, yes?'

'OK.'

'You don't seem too sure. Is there something else?'

Dick's hopeless, isn't he? Dick's a dead loss. He doesn't believe in anything outside of textbook psychology.

Moon had predicted that Dick would come up with a beautiful theory, and he had – without Lol even mentioning her story about seeing her father at the window.

You have to report back to Dick? You'll tell him about this?

Dick tore off the top sheet of the pad and crumpled it up. 'I think you'd better spit it out, Lol.'

Yes, he had to. There was a professional arrangement here. Dick had insisted Lol should be paid a retainer to keep an eye on Moon and report back once a week. It was complicated: at first Lol had been paying Dick for analysis; now Dick was paying Lol.

In his kindly way, Dick was devious. Lol was still not sure whether observing Moon was not supposed to be part of his own therapy.

Women had been Lol's problem. Women and religion.

He'd wound up first consulting Dick Lyden during the summer, while still trying to sell his roses-round-the-door cottage on the edge of an orchard out at Ledwardine. To which he'd moved with a woman called Alison who he thought had rescued him from the past and the shadow of the psychiatric hospital. But Alison had her own reasons for coming to Ledwardine, and they didn't include Lol.

The people who actually *had* tried to rescue him had come from the village itself. They included a brusque old biddy called Lucy Devenish, now dead. And also the parish priest-in-charge.

At this stage in Lol's life, priests of any kind were to be avoided. His parents had been drawn into this awful evangelical-fundamentalist Christian church and had decided that Lol, with his strange songs and his dubious lifestyle, was no longer their son. At his mother's graveside, Lol's father had turned his back on him. Lol had henceforth been suspicious of everything in a dog-collar that was not a dog.

Until the Vicar of Ledwardine.

Who in the end had been the reason for him leaving the village. The Vicar was, after all, a very busy and respected person, and Lol was this pathetic little sometimes-songwriter living on hackwork and royalties from before the fall. He wasn't sure she realized how he felt. He *was* sure she didn't need this.

So he left her his black cat and moved to Hereford, putting his bits of furniture in store and lodging for a while in a pub just down the street from Dick Lyden. Dick's local, as it happened – also Denny Moon's. Which had led to several sessions in Denny's recording studio and a few consultation sessions with Dick, because Lol still couldn't rely on his own mental equilibrium.

Christ, Dick had said one afternoon, *you know more about this bloody trade than I do.* Fascinated by Lol's extensive knowledge of psychiatry – absorbed over hours, then weeks and months spent in the medical library at a lax and decaying loony-bin in Oxfordshire. *Apart from a general self-esteem deficit, this is probably your principal problem – you're a kind of mental hypochondriac. Perhaps you need to help diagnose other people for a while, to take your mind off it.*

Loonies taking over the practice. The idea had really appealed to Dick: the idea of Lol keeping an experienced eye on another of his clients – twenty-something, gorgeous, weird. Dick loved it when clients could help each other, his practice becoming a big family. It was still small, this city; he liked the way relationships and associations developed an organic life, spread like creeper on a wall, and therefore strengthened his own latent roots in Hereford.

Thus, Lol had been introduced to Katherine Moon – and perhaps also because Dick couldn't quite get a handle on Moon.

'Her father's ghost,' Dick said calmly.

'Twice.'

'Right.' Dick hunched intently forward. 'Now, think carefully about this, Lol. What effect did this alleged manifestation have on her? What kind of an experience was it? Soothing? Frightening? Cathartic?'

'Not frightening.'

'So, a man's face at the window at dead of night. A young woman all alone in a still-strange dwelling... and she's not frightened. What does that tell us?'

'She said she had the impression he was more scared than she was. Disturbed and confused. She thought he didn't recognize her. Didn't know who she was.'

'Interesting.'

'She said she wanted to tell him it was OK.'

Dick spread his hands. 'Moon as healer.'

'She wants him to find peace.'

'And when he does, she will too,' Dick said. 'I really don't see a problem there. Seems to be all bubbling away quite satisfactorily in Moon's subconscious. She finds a dead crow and inflicts upon the poor bird all of her not inconsiderable knowledge of Celtic crow-lore. The crow's been sent by the ancestors to give her *the sight*. So what's she going to see first?'

'That's very good, Dick.'

'It makes sense, my boy. It's about *belonging*, isn't it? Look at me. I do feel I've found my spiritual home here in this city – so tiny after London, and *knowable*. Ruth tells me I'm continually pulling this town to my bosom. But a hill… a hill's much more embraceable, isn't it?' Dick leaned over to the window to scan the horizon. 'You know, I'm not even sure I know which one it is.'

'The one with all the trees.'

In the afternoon sunshine, the woods were a golden crust on the long, shallow loaf.

'Hmm,' Dick turned away, 'not particularly imposing, is it? And this was where the first settled community was? This hill is what you might call the *mother* of Hereford, I suppose.'

'The holy hill.'

'Super,' Dick said with firm satisfaction. 'One must feel a weight of responsibility to one's ancestors if one was born on a holy hill. And her father's suicide… a ready-made open wound for her to heal?'

Lol felt unhappy. He didn't like the way Dick seemed to assume that once you'd made a neat psychological package out of something, that was it. Sorted. In Lol's experience, real life was endlessly messy.

Dick leaned back in his leather swivel-rocker, hands comfortably enfolded over his lightbulb gut. 'The way we create our destiny on an epic, computer-game scale – would that it was as simple for all of us. Do you know, I rather suspect there's a paper in this. Let's go and see her. What are you doing tomorrow morning?'

'So you think it was a dream?' Lol said.

'Hmm?'

'Her father – a dream? Or an invention?'

'Well, good God, man,' Dick threw up his arms, 'what the hell *else* could it have been?'

9

Clerical Chic

Driving home, Merrily hardly noticed the countryside: the shambling black and white farms and cottages, the emptied orchards. Over it all, as though bevelled in the windscreen glass, hovered the unchanging, weathered face of the archaic monument that was Canon T. H. B. Dobbs.

That silent confrontation in the Cathedral had erased time. She could no longer remember praying in Bishop Stanbury's beautiful chantry – only the stumbling in and the creeping out. The interim was like an alcoholic haze.

But she had her answer.

Didn't she just?

In the late afternoon the wind had died, leaving the sky lumpy and congealed like a cold, fried breakfast. Beneath it the historic village of Ledwardine looked sapped and brittle, the black and white buildings lifeless, as indeed several now were. Nothing remained, for instance, of Cassidy's Country Kitchen except a sign and some peeling apple-transfers on the dark glass; and five *For Sale* signs had sprouted between Church Street and Old Barn Lane.

The village looked like it needed care and love and a shot of something – an injection of spirit. Of God, perhaps? Introduced by a conscientious, caring priest without selfish ambitions she wasn't equipped to fulfil?

Confess: you were stimulated. You'd had a meaningful brush with the paranormal and you wanted to know more. In fact – admit it – it was you that Huw Owen was addressing when he said prospective Deliverance ministers should analyse their motives, consider if they needed evidence of life after death to sustain their faith, proof of the existence of supernatural evil to convince them of a power for good.

Huw had been full of foreboding. Jane had been dismissive. Only Mick Hunter was enthusiastic, and Mick Hunter was a politician.

And now God had arbitrated, signalling – in the silence of Canon T. H. B. Dobbs – His unequivocal negative.

Of course, that could have been pure coincidence – if we're being rational about this.

But the compulsion to rush into the Cathedral, the waiting chantry, Dobbs being right there when she emerged? She'd wanted a sign, she'd received a sign. End of story. Later this evening she would phone the Bishop and tell him what wasn't, after all, going to happen.

Mature trees seemed to push the old vicarage back from the village centre. Beneath them was parked a lurid luminous-green Fiesta.

Which had to be something to do with Jane. If it was a boy-friend, Merrily only hoped he was under twenty.

Because of the size of the house, Jane had taken over the entire top floor, formerly attics, as her private apartment, and had finally re-emulsioned her sitting-room/study as the Dutch painter Mondrian might have envisaged it – the squares and rectangles between the timbers in different primary colours. If the Inspector of Listed Buildings ever turned up, the kid was on her own.

She wasn't on her own up there now, though, was she? Merrily edged the Volvo around the little car and parked in the driveway. Although she talked a lot about 'totty', Jane's relations with boys had been curiously restrained. You waited with a certain trepidation for The Big One, because the kid didn't do things by halves, and the first stirring of real love would probably send her virginity spinning straight out of the window.

So Merrily was half-relieved when she opened the front door to find Jane in the hall with a girl in the same school uniform.

An older girl, though not as vividly sophisticated as Jane's last – ill-fated – friend, Colette Cassidy. This one was ethereal, with long, red, soft-spun hair which floated behind her as she gazed around.

'Oh, hi. I was just going to show Rowenna the apartment.' Jane gestured vaguely at Merrily. 'That's the Reverend Mum.'

The girl came over and actually shook hands.

Jane sat down on the stairs. 'Rowenna's dad's with the SAS.'

'With the Army,' Rowenna said discreetly. 'This is a really amazing house, Mrs Watkins. Wonderfully atmospheric. You can feel its memories kind of vibrating in the oak beams. I was just saying to Jane, if I lived here I think I'd just keep going round hugging beams and things. Our place is really new and boring, with fitted cupboards and wardrobes and things.'

'I bet it's a lot easier to heat and keep clean, though,' Merrily said ruefully. 'You live locally, Rowenna?'

'Well, you know, up towards Credenhill, where the base is.' Rowenna wrinkled her nose. 'I wish we *were* down here. It's on a completely different plane. The past is real here. You feel you could just slip into it.'

'Right,' Merrily said. 'If that's what you want.'

'Yes.' Rowenna didn't blink. 'Most of the time, yes.'

Merrily thought it was a sad indictment of society when young people wanted not so much to change the world as to change it *back* – to some golden age which almost certainly never was.

'Oh, hey, listen to this!' Jane sprang up. 'Rowenna's dad goes running – right? – with Mick Hunter.'

'Well, not exactly.' Rowenna looked a bit uncomfortable. 'The Bishop has this arrangement to go along with the guys on some of their routine cross-country runs. It's kind of irregular, apparently. I'm not really supposed to talk about it.'

God, thought Merrily, *he'd just have to go training with the SAS, wouldn't he?*

'Isn't that just so cool?' Jane drawled cynically.

Merrily smiled.

'She's not what I expected at all.' Rowenna went to sit on Jane's old sofa, staring up at the Mondrian walls. 'Most of the women priests you see around look kind of bedraggled. But with that suit and the black stockings and everything, she makes the dog-collar seem like... I don't know, a fashion accessory.'

'Clerical chic,' Jane said. 'Don't tell her, for God's sake. She only stopped wearing that awful ankle-length cassock because this guy was turned on by all those buttons to undo.'

'Which guy?'

'Her former organist, creepy little git.'

'No special person in her life?'

'Only the Big Guy with the long beard – and the Bishop.'

Rowenna shot her a look.

'Hey, just professionally,' said Jane, 'I *hope*. Sure, the first time I saw him, I thought, wow, yeah, this is the goods. But then I couldn't believe I'd been that shallow. Besides, he's got a wife and kids.'

'Whatever that counts for these days.'

'Yeah, he'd probably quite like to get his leg over Mum. If you can keep it inside the priesthood, it probably saves a lot of hassle. I just hope she's more sensible. You want a coffee?'

'No thanks, I have to be off in a minute.' Rowenna stood up and moved across to Jane's bookcase. 'You've got it all here, haven't you? Personal transformation, past-life regression, communicating with Nature spirits...'

'Yeah, I'm a sad New Age weirdo. Don't spread it around.'

'It's not weird to be interested in what's going to happen to us. Do you do anything like, you know, meditation or anything like that?'

'I've thought about it after... when I once had a couple of odd things happen to me.'

Rowenna sat down again. 'Go on.'

'It was probably just imagination. I mean, you can make something out of everything, can't you? Like, Mum, she reckons she sometimes gets these images of blue and gold when she's saying her prayers, and so she connects it with God because that's like the container she's in. But it could be anything, couldn't it?'

'So what happened to you?'

'I don't talk about it much. I reckon if you try to analyse this stuff it just evaporates.'

'Not around me, kitten.'

'OK, well, I just feel this intense connection to some places. Like you were talking about hugging beams, I feel I want to hug hills and fields and— Hey, this is really, really stupid. It's just hyper-imagination.'

'Oh, Jane! Don't stop *now*.'

'Sorry. OK, well, like time passes and you're not aware of it. It's like you're here but you're *not* here, and then you're here again – some kind of shift in reality. Maybe it happens to everybody but most people disregard it. There was an old woman in the village I used to be able to talk to about this stuff, but she's dead now.'

'I think there's another side to all of us we need to discover,' Rowenna said. 'Especially us... I mean our generation. We're growing up into this awesome millennial situation where all the old stuff's breaking down... like political divisions and organized religion. That's not knocking your mum or anything.'

'It's OK,' Jane said. 'She knows it's all coming to pieces. She got these quite sizeable congregations at first on account of being a woman, but the novelty's wearing off already. When the Church is just surviving on gimmicks you know it's the slippery slope. Go on.'

'All I was saying is that we shouldn't pass up on the opportunity to expand our consciousness wherever possible.'

'I'll go along with that. What sort of stuff have you done?'

'Oh, I've just kind of messed around the edges.' Rowenna flicked the pages of a paperback about interpreting dreams. 'Like, when we were in Salisbury I had this friend whose sister did tarot readings, and she showed me two layouts. I was doing it at school for a few weeks. It was really incredible how accurate it was. Then I did this reading for a girl who was getting to be quite a good friend, and it came out really horrible and she got meningitis soon afterwards and nearly died, and she never came back to school – which kind of spooked me.'

Jane shrugged. 'That doesn't mean it was the cards gave her meningitis. Can you still remember how? Would you be able to do a reading for me?'

'Mmm… don't think so. Rather not.'

'Wimp.'

'Maybe. Tell you what, though, I saw this poster down the health-food shop, right? There's a psychic fair on in Leominster next weekend.'

'Cool. What is it?'

'You've never been to one? There are loads about.'

'Rowenna, my mother's a vicar. I lead this dead sheltered life.'

Rowenna smiled. 'Well, actually I've just been to one and it was seriously tacky and full of freaky old dames in gypsy clobber, but good fun if you didn't take it too seriously. We could check it out.'

'OK,' Jane said. 'I suspect I'd better not tell Mum.'

'I suppose she wouldn't be cool about that stuff. Alternative spirituality – subversive.'

'Actually, she's pretty liberal. Well, to a point. Things could be just a tiny bit dicey at the moment, though. So I wouldn't want to, you know…'

Jane thought about the soul police. Then she looked at Rowenna and saw that this was someone intelligent and worldly and kind of unfettered. Someone she could actually share stuff with.

'I mean, I guess Mum feels that any kind of spirituality is better than none at all,' Jane grinned, 'which I suppose is how I feel about the Church of England.'

That night, Merrily and Jane made sandwiches and ate them in front of a repeat of an early episode of *King of the Hill*. And then Jane said she'd go to her apartment and have a read and an early night. So Merrily returned, as she usually did, to the kitchen.

She always felt more in control in the kitchen. It was a bit vast, but they'd had lots of cupboards put in, and installed a couple of squashy easychairs and some muted lighting. Recently, she'd converted the adjacent scullery into an office. She supposed this was *her* apartment.

Which meant that, with just the two of them, huge areas of the vicarage remained unused. Stupid and wasteful. No wonder the Church was selling off so many of its old properties, and installing vicars in modest estate-houses.

At least Merrily was no longer so intimidated by all those closed bedroom doors, which had played their own sinister role in the paranormal *fluctuations* that might – if she'd then heard of him – have sent her to consult Canon Dobbs. It had been quiet up there for several months now. A day or two ago she'd caught herself thinking she would almost welcome *its* return: a chance to study an *imprint* at close hand.

But, then, probably not. Not now.

It was ten fifteen. The Bishop had given her his private number, with instructions to call anytime, but she never had. This was probably too late.

Don't be a wimp.

Merrily went through to the scullery, switched on the desk lamp. The answering machine had an unblinking red light; for once, nobody had called. On the desk sat the Apple Mac she'd bought secondhand. God knows what was being installed in the Deliverance Office. If she didn't stop it now.

She pulled down the cordless phone and stabbed out the number very quickly. It rang only twice before Mick Hunter came on. The late-night DJ voice.

'Hi. Val and Mick are unavailable at the moment. Please leave a message after the tone. God bless.'

Merrily hesitated for a second before she cut the line. She'd do this properly tomorrow: call his office and make an appointment. She was aware that when you came face to face with Mick Hunter, your doubts and reservations tended to be tidal-waved by his personality, but that wasn't going to happen this time.

She thought of calling Huw Owen at his stark stone rectory in the Brecon Beacons. But to say what?

Realizing, then, that the only reason she would be calling Huw at this time of night was some tenuous hope that he'd changed his mind about the suitability of women priests for trench warfare.

Unhappy with herself, she switched out the lights, and went up to bed, Ethel the black cat padding softly behind her.

The bedside phone bleeped her awake.

'Reverend Watkins?'

'Yes.' Merrily struggled to sit up.

'Oh… I'm sorry to disturb you. It was your husband I wanted. Is he there?'

'I'm afraid he's dead.' Merrily squinted at the luminous clock, clawing for the light switch over the bed, but not finding it.

Nearly ten past two?

'I'm sorry,' the woman said. 'Have I got the right number? I'm trying to contact the Reverend Watkins.' Northern Irish accent.

'Yeah, that's me.'

'Oh. Well, I... This is Sister Cullen at Hereford General.'

'General? What... sorry?'

'The General Hospital.'

Jesus!

Merrily scrambled out of bed into a wedge of moonlight sandwiched between the curtains. 'Is somebody hurt? Has there been an accident?'

Jane!

She went cold. Jane had crept out again after Merrily had gone to bed? Jane and her friend in the car, clubbing in Hereford, too much to drink. *Oh no, please...*

'It's nothing like that,' the sister said, almost impatient. 'It was suggested we call you, that's all. We have a problem. One of our patients is asking for a priest, and the hospital chaplain's away for the night. We were given your number as somebody who should be the one to deal with this. There are some complications.'

'I don't understand. I'm ten miles away.' Scrabbling on the floor for her cigarettes. 'Who suggested...?'

'We were given your number. I'm sorry, they never told me you were a woman.'

'That make a difference?'

'I'm sorry, I didn't mean anything offensive. I don't know what to do now.'

'Look, give me half an hour, OK? I'll get dressed. What are the complications you mentioned?'

'I'm sorry, it's not the sort of thing we discuss over the phone.'

Give me strength!

'All right, the General, you said. It'll take me about twenty, twenty-five minutes, Sister...'

'Cullen. Ask for Watkins Ward.'

'What?'

It was starting to feel like a dream. The house had done this to her before.

'The Alfred Watkins Ward,' said Sister Cullen. 'Don't bother looking for your Bible. We've got one here.'

10

Denzil

REVERSING THE CLANKING Volvo out of the vicarage drive, she saw Dobbs's grim, stone face again, as though it was superimposed on the windscreen or the night itself. As if the old bastard had been in the car waiting for her. As if he was staying with her until she'd formally walked away from his job. As if—

This has got to bloody stop!

Merrily gripped the wheel, shaking it violently, but really shaking herself. She'd become oppressed by the dour image of Dobbs. When she'd had the chance to say a final *No, thank you* to Mick Hunter and to Deliverance, she was going to keep well away from the Cathedral precincts, because she – squeezing the wheel until her hands hurt – never... wanted... to... see... *him*... again.

OK – steadying her breathing – this was no state in which to minister to a dying man.

On the cobbles of the marketplace she thought she could see a glaze of frost. The wrought-iron mock-gaslamps had gone out, leaving only a small, wintry security light by the steps to the Black Swan.

She drove slowly across the square, not wanting to wake anyone. She'd left a conspicuous note for Jane on the kitchen table in case she didn't get home by morning; you never knew with hospital vigils.

Virtually alone on the country roads, too tense to be tired, she found the kid's all-time favourite album, the complex *OK Computer*, on the stereo and tried to concentrate on the words. But her perception of the songs, full of haunted darkness, only reminded her of Dobbs.

She stopped the music. She would go over this thing once more.

The truth was, after the shock of seeing Dobbs in the Cathedral, when she'd been all charged up and unstable, her mind inevitably had contrived this divinely scripted scene: *he* was there because *she* was.

But what about the unknown woman Dobbs had been with?

'What have I been doing wrong?' the woman had cried. What was all that about?

Well, it made no obvious sense, so forget it. The simple, rational explanation was that Merrily had walked, unexpected, into *Dobbs's* scene. Perhaps *he* was just as shocked when who should suddenly emerge from the chantry but the notorious female pretender.

All right. Stop it, there. Stop looking for a way out. You made your decision, you stick to it.

The General Hospital was an eighteenth-century brick building with the usual unsightly additions. Messy at the front but, like the Bishop's Palace, with a beautiful situation on the Wye, a few hundred yards downstream from the Cathedral. No parking problems at pushing three a.m.; Merrily left the Volvo near a public garden where a path led down to the suspension footbridge over the river, all dark down there now.

Been here many times to visit parishioners, of course, but never at this hour. And never to the Alfred Watkins Ward, named presumably after the Herefordian pioneer photographer, brewer, magistrate and discoverer of ley-lines. No relation of hers, as far as she knew, but then she didn't know the Herefordshire side of the family very well.

'Bottom of the corridor,' a passing paramedic advised. 'Turn left and immediately left again, through the plastic doors, up the stairs, left at the top and through the double doors.'

These old buildings were wonderful, Merrily thought, for almost everything except hospitals. A plaque on the wall near the main entrance discreetly declared that this used to be a lunatic asylum and, as you walked the unevenly lit, twisting passages, you could imagine the first ever patients wandering here, groping vaguely for their senses, the air dense with disease and desperation.

Despite the directions received, she lost herself in the dim labyrinth, and it was over five minutes before she found a sign to Alfred Watkins Ward. At its entrance, two nurses were talking quietly but with a lot of gesturing. When they saw Merrily, they separated.

She smiled. 'Sister Cullen?'

'On the ward,' the younger nurse said. 'Who shall I say?'

'Merrily Watkins.'

The younger nurse pushed through the double doors into the gloom of the ward itself. Merrily unzipped her waxed jacket, feeling better now she was here. The presence of the dying used to scare her, but recently she'd become more comfortable with them, even slightly in awe – aware of this composure they often developed very close to the end, a calm anticipation of the big voyage – assisted passage. And she would sometimes come away with a tentative glow. Over her past three years as a cleric, several nurses had told her shyly that they'd actually *seen* spirits leaving bodies, like a light within a mist.

'Oh hell!' The older nurse spotted the dog-collar, took a step back in dismay. '*You're* the priest?'

'At three a.m.,' Merrily said, 'you don't get an archbishop.'

'Oh, look…' The nurse was plump, mid-fifties, agitated. 'This isn't right. Eileen Cullen shouldn't have done this. She's an atheist, fair enough, but she should've had more sense. Isn't there a male priest you know?'

Merrily stared in disbelief at the woman's face, pale and blotched under the hanging lights. And fearful too.

'Don't look at me like that. I'm sorry, Miss... Reverend. It's just that what we don't need is another woman. Look, would you mind waiting there while I go and talk to Sister Cullen?'

'Fine,' Merrily said tightly. 'Don't worry about me. I don't have to go to work until Sunday.'

'Look, I'm sorry, all right? I'm sorry.'

'Sure.' Merrily sat down on a leather-covered bench, pulled out her cigarettes.

'And I'm afraid you can't smoke in here.'

Sister Cullen was about Merrily's age, but tall, short-haired, sombre-faced. *More like a priest than I'll ever look.*

Behind her, the ward diminished into darkness like a Victorian railway tunnel.

'I may have misled you on the phone,' Cullen said. 'I was confused.'

'*You're* confused.' Merrily stood up. 'Forgive me, but sometimes, especially at three in the morning and without a cigarette, even the clergy can get a trifle pissed off, you know?'

'Keep your voice down, please.'

'I'm sorry. I would just like to know what this is about.'

'All right.' Cullen gestured at the bench and they both sat down. 'It's Mr Denzil Joy... that's the patient. Mr Joy's dying. He's unlikely to see the morning.'

'I'm sorry.'

'With respect, Mrs Watkins, you'll be the only one.'

'Huh?'

'This is a difficult situation.'

'He's asked for a priest, hasn't he?'

'No, that... that's where I misled you. He hasn't.'

She jerked a thumb at the double doors. Behind the glass, Merrily saw the other two nurses peering out. They looked like they wanted to escape, or at least stand as close as possible to the lights outside.

'*They* did,' Sister Cullen said. '*They* asked me to call a priest.'

Following Cullen through the darkened ward, she was reminded of those war-drawings by Henry Moore of people sleeping in air-raid shelters, swaddled and anonymous. The soundtrack of restive breathing, ruptured snores, shifting bodies was inflated by muted hissings and rumblings in the building's own decaying metabolism. And also, Merrily felt, by slivers of tension in the sour sickness-smelling air.

'He's in a side ward here,' Cullen whispered. 'We've always had him in a side ward.'

'What's his... his condition?'

'Chronic emphysema: lungs full of fluid. Been coming on for years – he's been in four times. This time he knows he's not going out.'

'And he isn't... ready. Right?'

Cullen breathed scornfully down her nose. 'Earlier tonight he sent for his wife.'

Merrily looked for some significance in this. 'She's not here with him now?'

'No, we sent her home. Jesus!'

A metal-shaded lamp burned bleakly on a table at the entrance to the side ward, across which an extra plastic-covered screen had been erected.

'There's an evil in this man.' Sister Cullen began sliding the screen away. 'Brace yourself.'

Merrily said, 'I don't understand. What do you...?'

And then she did understand. It was Deliverance business.

Huw Owen had stressed: *Compose, prepare, protect yourself – ALWAYS.*

Directing them to the prayer known as *St Patrick's Breastplate*, very old, very British, part of our legacy from the

Celtic Church, Huw had said, and Merrily had seen the strength of the hermit in him, the hermit-priest in the cave on the island.

Christ be with me, Christ within me,
Christ behind me, Christ before me,
Christ beside me, Christ to win me,
Christ to comfort and restore me,
Christ beneath me, Christ above me,
Christ in quiet, Christ in danger...

Binding yourself with light Huw had said; this was what it was about. A sealing of the portals, old Christian magic, Huw had said. *Use it.*

But she hadn't even thought of that. She'd made no preparations at all, simply dashed out of the house like a junior doctor on call. Because that was all it was – a routine ministering to the dying, a stand-in job, no one else available. Nobody had mentioned...

We were given your number as somebody who should be the one to deal with this. There are some complications.

... it had simply never occurred to her that the hospital had been given her name as a trained Deliverance minister. It never occurred to her that this was what she now was. Who had directed them? The Bishop's office? The Bishop himself?

I've been set up, she thought, angry – and afraid that, whatever needed to be done, she wouldn't be up to it.

There were two iron beds in the side ward, one empty; in the other, Mr Denzil Joy.

His eyes were slits, unmoving under a sweat-sheened and sallow forehead. His hair was black, an unnatural black for a man in his sixties. A dying man dyeing, she thought absurdly.

Two pale green tubes came down his nostrils and looped away over his cheeks, like a cartoon smile.

'Oxygen,' Cullen explained in a whisper.

'Is he asleep?'

'In and out of it.'

'Can he speak?'

Trying to understand what she was doing here, looking hard at him, wondering what she was missing.

Like little horns or something? What do you expect to see?

'With difficulty,' Cullen said.

'Should I sit with him a while?'

'Fetch you a Bible, shall I?'

'Let's... let's just leave that a moment.' Knowing how ominous a black, leathered Bible could appear to the patient at such times, wishing she'd brought her blue and white paperback version. And still unclear about what they wanted from her here.

There was a vinyl-covered chair next to the bed, and she sat down. Denzil Joy wore a white surgical smock thing; one of his arms was out in view, fingers curved over the coverlet. She put her own hand over it, and almost recoiled. It was warm and damp, slimy somehow, reptilian. A small, nervous smile tweaked at Cullen's lips.

In the moment Merrily touched Denzil Joy, it seemed a certain scent arose. The kind of odour you could almost see curling through the air, so that it entered your nostrils as if directed there. At first sweet and faintly oily.

Then Merrily gasped and took in a sickening mouthful and, to her shame, had to get up and leave the room, a hand over her mouth.

The other hand, not the one which had touched Denzil Joy.

One of the patients on the ward was calling out, 'Nurse!' as loudly as a farmer summoning a sheepdog over a six-acre field.

At the door Merrily gulped in the stale hospital air as if it was ozone.

'Dr Taylor found a good description for it.' Eileen Cullen was standing beside the metal lamp, smiling grimly. 'Although *he*

105

never quite got the full benefit of it, being a man. He said it was like a mixture of gangrene and cat faeces. That seems pretty close, though I wouldn't know for sure. Never kept cats myself. Excuse me a minute.'

She padded down the ward towards the man calling out, one hand raised, forefinger of the other to her lips. As soon as she'd gone, the plump middle-aged nurse appeared from the shadows, put her mouth up to Merrily's ear.

'I'll tell you what that is, Reverend. It's the smell of evil.'

'Huh?'

'He can turn it on. Don't look at me like that. Maybe it's automatic, when his blood temperature rises. It comes to the same thing. Did you feel him enter you?'

'What?'

'We can't talk here.' She took Merrily's arm, pulled her away and into a small room lit by a strip light, with sinks and bags of waste. She shut the door. The disinfectant smell here, in comparison with that in the side ward, was like honeysuckle on a summer evening.

'I'm a strong woman,' the nurse said, 'thirty years in the job. Everything nasty a person can throw off, I've seen it and smelled it and touched it.'

'I can imagine.'

'No, you can't, my girl.' The nurse pushed up a sleeve. 'You have no idea. Look at that, now.' Livid bruising around the wrist, like she'd been handcuffed.

'What happened was: Mr Joy, he asked for a bottle – to urinate in, you know? And then he called me back and he said he was having… trouble getting it in. Well, some of them, they say that as a matter of course, and you have a laugh and you go away and come back brandishing the biggest pair of forceps you can find. But Denzil Joy was a very sick man and he seemed distressed, so I did try to help.' She pulled down her sleeve again. 'You see where that got me.'

'Oh.'

'Grip like a monkey-wrench, my dear. Thought I'd never get fooled again. You understand now why we wanted a male priest?'

Surely, what you wanted, Merrily thought, *was a male nurse.*
'Look, Nurse... I'm sorry?'

'Nurse Protheroe. Sandra.'

'Sandra, this is a dying man, OK? He knows he's dying. He's afraid. He's looking for... comfort, I suppose. That doesn't make him possessed by evil. I don't know what his background is. I mean...'

'Farm-labourer and slaughterman. Been in a few times before, he has. When he wasn't so bad – not so seriously ill, that is.'

'Farm-labourer? So his idea of comfort might be a bit... rough and ready?'

Sandra snorted. 'Oh, for heaven's sake, it's more than *that*, girl. You're not getting this, are you? I've dealt with that type more times than you've done weddings and funerals – rough as an old boar and ready for anything they can get. But Mr Joy, he's different. Mr Joy's an abuser, a destroyer – do you know what I mean? He likes causing pain and death to animals, and he likes doing it to women, too. Hurting them and humiliating them. Degrading them.'

'Yes. That might very well be true. But it doesn't—'

'That smell... that's not natural, not even in a hospital. That's *his* smell. That's the smell of all the things he's done and all the things he'd still like to do. We even put Nil-odour under his bed one night.'

'What's that?'

'Undertaker's fluid. They put it in coffins sometimes, so it's less offensive for the relatives.'

'You put undertaker's deodorant under a dying patient's bed?'

'It didn't work. You can't remove the smell of evil with chemicals. You spend a night in here with that man, you can't

sleep when you goes home. You keep waking up with that…'
Protheroe hugged herself. 'As for young Tessa – white, that girl
was. This was after his wife come in this afternoon.'

'Sandra, look…' Merrily moved to the door. This wasn't how
state-registered nurses were supposed to behave. She needed to
talk to the duty doctor. 'You say I don't get this. You're dead
right, I don't get this at all. All right, he might not be a very nice
man, he may not smell very good, but that's no excuse to make
his last hours a total misery. I mean, what does his wife say
about all this?'

'Mrs Joy don't talk,' said Sandra. 'Being as how you're a
priest, I'll tell you about Mrs Joy, shall I?'

'If you think it'll help.'

Sandra exhaled a sour laugh. 'About twenty years younger
than him, she is, but you wouldn't know it to look at her, state
she's in, the poor miserable cow. No, not a cow, a rabbit… a
poor frightened little wretch. We left them alone for about half
an hour, as you do at times like this. Then Dr Taylor comes on
his rounds and he has to see Mr Joy, obviously, and Tess goes
in to ask Mrs Joy will she come out for a couple of minutes,
and—'

Footsteps outside. Sandra stopped talking, looking at the
door. The footsteps passed. Sandra lowered her voice.

'The chair's pushed right up next to the bed, see? That chair
you were just sitting on?'

'Yes.' Merrily found her hands were clasped in front of her,
rubbing together. She wanted to wash them, but not in front of
Sandra Protheroe. 'Go on.'

'So Mrs Joy's standing on that chair, leaning over the bed.
She's holding her dress right up above her waist. She's got her
knickers round her ankles.'

Merrily closed her eyes for a moment.

'And Denzil's just lying there with his tubes up his nose and all
the spittle down his chin, wheezing and rattling with glee, and his
little eyes eating her up. But that's not the worst thing, see.'

She swallowed, backed up against a sink, looking down at her shoes and shaking her head.

'The worse thing is her face. What Tessa said was that woman's face was completely blank. No expression at all – like a zombie. She's just looking at the wall, and her face's absolutely blank. She knows Tessa's there, but she don't get down. Showing no embarrassment at all, though God knows she must have been as full up with shame and humiliation as it's possible to be. But she just stands there staring at the wall. Because *he* hadn't told her she could get down.'

Merrily's mouth was dry.

'This is a dying man,' Sandra said. 'And he knows it and she knows it, and she's still terrified of him. In his younger days, see, he thought he was God's gift. A woman who knows the family, she told me about all the women and girls he'd had, and the way he abused them but they kept coming back. He charmed them back, he did. Not by his looks, not by his manners, he just *charmed* them. And then he got older and he got sick and he got married, and he controls the wife by fear. And he's lying there delighting in Tessa seeing the poor little woman giving him an eyeful of what he owns. If that's not evil then I don't know what evil is.'

What is evil? Huw Owen had said. *It's the question you're never going to answer. But when you're in the same room with it, you'll know.*

Merrily said, 'I'm sorry. I don't know what I can do.'

'Protection. She wants protection.'

The door had opened. Sister Cullen was standing there, the darkness behind her.

'She's right, he's a bad man with a black charm. But he's just a man, and that's where it ends as far as I'm concerned. I'm from Derry, so I've seen what religion does to people, and I want none of it. But this is one patient where I'm more concerned about his nurses.'

'It's getting stronger the nearer he comes to death,' Sandra said. 'Tell her.'

'Sandra's convinced the smell's getting worse.'

'And if *you* don't do something, when he dies this ward's going to be polluted for ever. And I'm not coming back tomorrow. I'm out.'

'Let me get this right.' Merrily looked from one to the other, the believer and the atheist, but both essentially of the same mind. 'You've called me out in the middle of the night, not because you want comfort for a distressed terminal patient but because… you want protection from *him*?'

Cullen said with resignation, 'If there's anything you think you can do about it, feel free, but I'd strongly advise you not to touch the evil bastard again.'

'Sister…' The young nurse Tessa in the doorway. She was crying. 'Can you come, please?'

11

Scritch-scratch

MERRILY THOUGHT OF the almost-poetic abstraction of *imprints* and *visitors* and *weepers* and *breathers*.

She thought about the *hitchhiker* – the disembodied spirit which took over someone's body for a period, usually for some specific if illogical purpose, and then went away.

She considered probably the worst of them all – Huw had discussed this in detail over the last two days of the Deliverance course – the *squatter*.

And then thought about the pathetic, stinking, wheezing, nasal-cathetered reality of Denzil Joy, who fitted into none of the slick categories which Charlie Headland had said reminded him of the fictionalized world of espionage. What was Denzil Joy other than an unpleasant man coming to the end of his run? Was he, indeed, any of her business?

There were several tests you had to implement before a subject could reasonably be considered possessed by an external, demonic evil – most importantly, the psychiatric assessment. Now, how could anyone assess a man apparently in the last hours of his life, a person unable to speak? It was an impossible situation.

'I'm sorry, Sister,' Tessa said. 'It was just that his breathing sort of altered and I thought he was starting to… go.'

All four of them stood watching Denzil from outside the door.

'Gone, has he?' An old man warbling from the ward. 'What's happening over there?'

'Everything's fine, Francis,' Eileen Cullen hissed. 'Go to sleep now, will you.'

Merrily took a closer look at Denzil Joy, his face half-lit by the lamp on a table just outside the door. Black hair over shallow forehead, small, sucking mouth. His frame thin and wiry, with bony arms. *Grip like a monkey-wrench, my dear.*

'Does he never say anything? Never ask for anything? Doesn't he talk to you?'

'Doesn't like talking to women,' Cullen said. 'Prefers to communicate with us in other ways.'

Sandra instinctively massaged her bruised wrist. 'I reckon he didn't do this on his own. That's what I think now.'

Merrily turned to her. 'You're a Christian, Sandra?'

'I attend St Peter's,' Sandra declared piously. 'Well, not every week – sometimes shifts don't allow, obviously. But one week in every three – at least that.'

'And you don't believe, Eileen.'

'I'm aware of evil,' she snapped. 'Of course I am. I just think there's quite enough of it on this earth to be going on with.'

'Tessa?'

'I'm scared.' In her uniform, no make-up, Tessa looked about Jane's age, although she surely must be several years older. She had quite a posh accent. 'I thought he was Cheyne-Stoking. I didn't want to be alone with him when he died.'

Merrily glanced at Cullen, who beckoned her away from the door.

'She means the kind of sporadic breathing that tells you they're on their way out.'

Merrily nodded, remembering other bedsides.

'The smell's gone, Eileen. At least it's not what it was.'

'I don't know, he seems to be able to turn it on and off at will. That's what gets to Protheroe – him controlling his smell.

Particularly when a woman gets close. There's a psychological solution, if you ask me.'

'He's kind of drawing energy through sexual arousal?'

'I can't imagine there's any physical arousal, and I don't feel inclined to check. I've about had it with this one.' Cullen wiped her brow with the side of a fist. 'See, earlier on, Sandra was threatening to walk out. That's when I called you. She knows if I took any disciplinary action over this there'd be unfavourable publicity of the kind nobody wants. I'm going through the motions, so I am, and I'd be happy if you could just do the same.'

'Primarily, we need to consider what's best for him.'

'I just think he's an evil bastard, you know? I wish he'd just die, then we could get him portered the hell out of here.'

Merrily sighed. No putting this off any longer. 'I'll go in and say a few prayers for him.'

'That's it? I thought you were an exorcist of some kind?'

'Some kind,' Merrily said.

'I bind unto myself the Name,
'The strong Name of the Trinity.
'By invocation of the same,
'The Three in One and One in Three.'

She was back in the sluice-room, alone this time, murmuring *St Patrick's Breastplate* to the pale grey walls. A window was open; she heard a siren coming closer – police, or an ambulance bringing someone into Casualty. The normal world out there – and here she was in a former lunatic asylum, getting into Dark Age armour. Relying on her God to pull her out of this, if it should turn out to be misguided.

Don't ever fall into the trap of thinking it's you that's doing it, Huw had stressed. *You're never any more than the medium, the vessel. We don't want any of this Van Helsing crap, wielding the crucifix like it's a battle-axe. Always preferred a titchy little cross, meself. Lets you know where you stand in the great scheme of things.*

113

She wore her own cross under her jumper, and it too was pretty small.

What she could do was limited, anyway. She wasn't allowed to perform an exorcism – and quite right, too – without the permission of the Bishop. Knowing Mick Hunter, he'd call for a written report, spend at least two days considering the ethics of it and how he'd look if it leaked out.

Merrily stepped out on to the ward, where most of the patients slept noisily on, shuffling and muttering. Few people got a peaceful night in a hospital. The silent digital wall-clock said 4.25.

'I'd better come in with you,' the night sister said.

'Perhaps not, Eileen.'

Whenever possible, have other Christians with you as back-up – or witnesses in case there's any shit flying round afterwards in the media. Or, put it this way, if you're having people with you, make sure you know where they've been.

'Because I'm not a bloody Bible-basher? Jesus! All right… Nurse Protheroe, what about you? You started all this.'

Sandra shrank away. 'I can't.'

'Superstition,' Cullen said, with contempt. 'I can never accept that in a professional. Well, there has to be a staff nurse in there. This is a hospital, in case anybody's forgotten.'

'I'll do it,' Tessa said.

'Don't be stupid,' Sandra whispered harshly.

Merrily thought of Jane. She wouldn't want the kid within a mile of this. She thought: *My God, this is some kind of awful first. Four women gathering like a bunch of witches to plot against a dying man. This ever gets out, we'll look ridiculous or dangerously paranoid. Or cold conspirators – heartless, vindictive. Are we?*

'Look,' she said. 'I'll be all right on my own. I'm not going to be doing anything dramatic – no holy water. You can all watch through the window if you like.'

'No,' said Cullen.

'I teach Sunday school,' Tessa offered solemnly, and they all looked at her. 'I can handle it as long as I'm not alone in there.'

'All right, then.' Eileen Cullen shrugged, perhaps still wanting to shame Sandra Protheroe into it, but Sandra didn't react. 'Just as long as you realize it's not an instruction. And you make sure and stay well back from the Reverend, you hear? Any trouble, you come and get me. You know what I mean by trouble?'

'I think so.' Tessa nodded. She bit her upper lip, plucked a stray ash-blonde hair from her forehead.

Merrily put a hand on Tessa's shoulder, leaned in to look for her eyes. 'You sure about this?'

'It's best, isn't it?'

'All right. Do you want to come in here a minute.'

The sluice-room as temporary chapel. Merrily faced the girl over the rubbish sacks full of swabs and bandages soaked with bodily fluids and God-knows-what.

'Tessa, I... How old are you?'

'Nineteen.'

'OK, look... I just want to say I'm not too sure about any of this. Whatever Mr Joy's done in his time, it's not my job to judge him. We're just going in to pray with him and try to bring him some peace. To calm down whatever sick yearnings he's harbouring so that he can end his life in some kind of grace. I mean, probably none of this will be necessary, but when I've started, I've got rules to follow, so I'd like to... close our eyes a moment. *Our Father...*'

She said the Lord's Prayer softly, Tessa joining in, then placed her hands either side of the girl's bowed head.

'Jesus... surround her and hold her... safe from the forces of evil.'

It again entered her head that this was all a crazy, hysterical over-reaction; there were no forces of evil, no Je—

She kicked out mentally, sent the thought spinning away. She opened the door.

'Come on.'

* * *

Denzil Joy's terrible breathing was through the mouth: liquid, strangulated, the sound of an old-fashioned hot-water geyser filling up. In the side ward, with the door closed, it seemed all around them, underscored by that hum you couldn't seem to escape in hospital wards, and the throaty chortle of the overhead heating pipes.

The green oxygen tubes were clipped together behind his head, which was supported by three pillows. There were scabs of mucus where the tubes fitted into his nostrils.

'You want me to do anything?' Tessa asked.

'Just grab a chair from somewhere.'

'I'd rather stand. Is that OK?'

'However you feel comfortable.'

Merrily sat in the vinyl-covered chair on which the wretched Mrs Joy was said to have stood. Its seat was sunken in the middle.

OK. She pushed up a sleeve of her black jumper, reached over in the half-light and took Denzil's hand, instantly screwing up her eyes because it was undeniably vile, like picking up a cold turd.

Stop it!

Sliding her hand away from his fingers with their long yellow nails, and up to his bony wrist, holding it gently, calming her breathing.

'Denzil…' She cleared her throat. 'I don't know if you can hear me. My name's Merrily. I'm… er, the Vicar of Ledwardine. I'm just doing the rounds – as we vicars do.'

If he was even half awake, he wouldn't be aware of what time it was, how unlikely it was that a vicar would be doing the rounds. At all costs she mustn't alarm him.

'I wanted to say a few prayers with you, if that's OK.'

His breathing didn't alter. His eyes remained three-quarters closed. He seemed unaware of her. She looked down at his thin, furtive face, the spittle bubbling around his mouth. And she pleaded with God to send her some pity. Nobody should die an object of fear and hatred and revulsion.

'He's very, very weak,' Tessa murmured in her ear. 'I don't know how he's holding on.'

Merrily nodded. 'Almighty God, our Heavenly Father,' she said softly. 'We know, all of us, that we've done bad things and neglected to do good things we might've done.'

She felt Denzil's wrist turn under her hand: other than the breathing, the first sign of life. The wrist turned so that the palm was upwards, the position of supplication, as though he was responding, holding out his hand for forgiveness.

'For the sake of Jesus Christ, our Lord, Your Son, we beg You to forgive us, close the book on the past. Calm our souls.'

She squeezed the hand encouragingly. Outside, Nurse Sandra Protheroe passed the door without looking in.

'We know Your nature is to have mercy, to forgive. We beg You to free Denzil from whatever bonds are binding his spirit.'

One of Denzil's fingernails began to move slowly against her palm, like the claw of an injured bird. It felt, actually, quite unpleasant. Suggestive. She wished she'd never spoken to Sandra Protheroe.

Tessa was standing beside the door with her hands behind her back. She managed a rather wounded smile.

'We ask You this,' Merrily said, 'in the name of our saviour Jesus Christ.' She felt slightly sick and closed her eyes.

At once, the light scratching of Denzil's nail on her palm picked up momentum, acquired a rhythm. A small high-pitched wheeze was detectable under his rasping, snuffling breath, and the sweet sour stench was back – suddenly and rapidly unravelling from him like a soiled string, seeming to spiral through the thin, stale air directly into Merrily's nose and coil there.

Cat faeces and gangrene.

Oh God! She felt clammy and nauseous but also starved, like she had flu coming on.

I'll tell you what that is, Reverend. It's the smell of evil.

It's not evil. It's sickness. It's disgusting, but it's not evil.

Still, she tightened her lips against it, fighting the compulsion to snatch her hand away. She must *not*, she must let it lie there, mustn't react. *It's my job, it's my job, it's what I do, it's—*

She could almost hear it now. *Scritch-scratch* – the tiniest movement of a curling nail on the end of a yellow finger. Suspecting that in the mind of Denzil Joy this was not a mere finger.

He can enter you without moving an inch, that man.

Slide away, squirm away, get out of here.

Scritch-scratch, as though he was teasing away layers of skin in the centre of her palm to get his finger under the flesh. But that was imagination. His strength, his lifeforce, was so depleted this was the most he could manage: *scritch-scratch*. Poor guy – reach out to the humanity in him. *Poor guy, poor guy, poor guy, poor guy...*

She was aware of him taking in a long, long shuddering breath. Tessa moving towards the bed.

The breath was not released. There was an awesome cliff-edge of silence. The scratching stopped.

'This is it,' Tessa said quietly. So much composure in the kid. 'He's Cheyne-Stoking, no question this time.'

In the breathless silence, Merrily would swear she could feel the heat of him, slithering from his mind to her mind, while his finger lay still in her hand like a small cigar.

It seemed much darker and colder in here now – as though, in its hunger for life-energy, the shrivelled body in the bed was absorbing all the electricity, all the light, all the heat in the room.

'In fact I think he's gone,' Tessa said.

Darkness. Cold. Stillness. And the sinuous, putrid smell. Gently, Merrily attempted to slip her hand out of his.

And then it seized her.

Grip like a monkey-wrench.

Like a train from a tunnel, his breath came out and in the same moment his fingers pushed up between hers and tightened; a low, sniggering laugh seemed to singe the air between them.

And Merrily felt something slide between her legs.

Knowing in a second that she'd felt no such thing, that it was all imagination, conditioning. But it was too late: the cold wriggled fiercely into her groin, jetted into her stomach like an iced enema. She'd already torn her hand away, throwing herself back with so much force that she slipped from the chair to the shiny grey floor and slid back against the second bed, hearing herself squealing,

'*I bind unto myself the Name,*
'*The strong Name of the Trin—*'

And, hearing Tessa screaming shrilly, she cried out helplessly.

'Begone!'

Not knowing who or what she meant.

There was a wrenching, snapping sound; she saw the green tubes writhing in the air like electric snakes, torn from Denzil's nostrils as suddenly, in a single, violent ratchet movement, he sat up in his bed.

Tessa shrieking, 'Noooooooooooo!' and falling back against the door, stumbling out when it was flung open by Eileen Cullen – who just stood there with Denzil Joy's upright, stiffened, shadowed shape between her and Merrily.

12

Soiled

SHE DISCOVERED SHE was in the corridor outside. And that she was half sobbing and half laughing, but it wasn't *real* laughing. On the other side of a film of tears, a small flame was approaching.

'It's not allowed, is it?' Was that *her* voice, that mad cackle?

'The hell it isn't,' said Cullen, lighting Merrily's cigarette and then one for herself.

They sat on the bench outside the ward. It was no longer quiet in there.

'We told them Tessa had seen a mouse, but patients, especially old fellers – it's like spooking the horses in a stable, you know? We'll give them half an hour to get themselves back to sleep before we get somebody up here to take him out.'

'I'm sorry, Eileen.' Merrily blew her nose. 'This is ridiculous.'

'It's that, all right. How the devil he found the strength to sit up like that is beyond me. He was a husk, so he was. Nothing left. What the hell did you *do*?'

'Do?' She crushed the wet tissue into her palm – the palm of the *scritch-scratch*. 'God knows.'

'You reckon?'

'How would I know? I was completely out of my depth. No real idea what I was supposed to be doing. This is a bloody mug's game, Eileen. A charade, maybe. Play-acting?'

My bit was play-acting; his was real.

'Hey, I didn't hear that. This is your profession.' Cullen put a hand on her knee. 'We'll go into my office for a cuppa, soon as I get Protheroe to do the necessary.'

'The necessary?'

'Lay the poor bastard out. We're none of us scared of dead bodies, are we? Not even this one, although… you didn't see his face, did you?'

Merrily shook her head. 'I was on the floor by then. Could only see the back of his head and those tubes flying out of his nose when he… rose up.'

She shuddered. The snapping of the tubes; she could still hear it.

'That's lucky. You'll maybe get some sleep tonight.' Eileen Cullen dragged on her cigarette. 'Jesus, he was frightened. I thought at first it was me he was looking at. But he's staring over my shoulder, out of the door into thin air. Nobody there. Nobody *I* could see. And the look on his face: like somebody was coming for him, you know? Like the person he feared most in all the world was standing in that doorway, waiting to… Oh, Jesus, the things you see in this job, you could go out of your mind if you hadn't so much to bloody do.'

'Waiting to take him away,' Merrily said drably. 'Whatever it was was waiting to take him away.'

'It's the chemicals is all it is. The chemicals in the brain. Some people that close to the end, the chemicals ease the way, you know?'

'The angels on the threshold.' Merrily blew her nose again into the sodden tissue.

'Or the Devil. Whatever cocktail of volatile chemicals was sloshing round in that man's head, they must've shown him the Devil and all his works.'

'Which means I failed.'

'Natural justice, Merrily.'

'That's not the way it's supposed to work.' There was a question she needed to ask, a really obvious question. What was it? She couldn't think.

'Come and have that cuppa.'

'Thanks, but I need to get home. I've got my daughter.'

'You want someone to drive you? I think you're in shock, you know.'

'God no, I'll be fine. Maybe I should come back later and... cleanse the place?'

'What, with all the patients awake?' Cullen stood up. 'You in there flashing the big cross and doing the mumbo-jumbo? Forget it. Mop and bucket'll see it right. It's over.'

'Is it?'

'What do you want me to say? I'm a non-believer. Was all chemicals, Merrily, maybe a few of yours as well, don't you think? You go sleep it off. We'll tell the Bishop or who you like that you did a terrific job.'

The Bishop?

'I'd rather you said I'd never even been.'

'You don't mean that.'

'Tell them I didn't answer the phone when you rang.'

'Get yourself some rest. Call me at home sometime. I've written the number on your ciggy packet.' Sister Cullen squeezed her shoulder. 'Thank you, Merrily. You did OK, I reckon.'

'For a Bible-basher?'

The Bishop?

Had the Bishop set her up for it?

This was the question she'd meant to ask. She remembered that as she was leaving the building, pulling on her coat. Who exactly had told them to contact her? Who had advised them that Merrily Watkins was Deliverance-trained and available for work?

Had to be him. He was dangerous. Michael Hunter – Bishop Cool – was a dangerous man to have organizing your career.

There was light in the sky and a cold wind. What the hell time was it? Where had she left the car all those hours ago when all she'd had to think about was Dobbs? She hurried down the drive and into the deserted street full of fresh cold air from the hills.

It was the cold *inside* that scared her. She stood and shivered by the entrance to the shambling jumble of a hospital where the body of Denzil Joy lay cooling.

I was raped. Like icy letters in the sky. *He raped me.*

She felt greasy, slimy, soiled, used. He'd made his smell go into her, had scratched himself an entrance hole. And then he'd died, he'd gone away, but he'd left his filthy essence inside her. She needed a long shower, needed to pray. Needed to think. Because this would not, *could* not have happened to a male priest, a male exorcist.

I need exorcizing.

Violently she zipped up her fading waxed coat and strode away into the pre-dawn murk. She would find a church that was open or, failing that, would go to her own church in Ledwardine. She couldn't take the pitiful, disgusting dregs of Denzil home to Jane. She would have to go into a church and pray for his soul. Pray for it to be taken away somewhere and stripped and cleaned.

She saw that the old blue Volvo had been very badly parked, even for three in the morning: standing half on the grass near the little gardens where the footpath went up and then down to the Wye. Another six inches and she'd have backed into a sign saying: NO PARKING. KEEP ENTRANCE CLEAR. She fumbled out her keys.

'Excuse me, madam.'

He'd blundered out of the bushes, a big heavy guy in some kind of rally anorak, luminous stripe down one arm. 'Is this your car?'

'Who are you?'

'Police. How long has the car been here, please?'

All she needed.

'Look, I'm sorry, I was in a hurry and I thought it'd be OK.'

'When did you park it?'

'About three, I suppose.'

'To go to the hospital?'

'Yes.'

'Can I ask why?'

'Look,' Merrily said, exasperated, 'it could've been parked a whole lot better, I agree. I'm very sorry. Give me a ticket or whatever. I'm a bit knackered, OK?'

'It isn't about parking, miss. Would you mind telling me your name, please?'

'After I see your ID.' Merrily unlocked the Volvo. If he took any time producing his warrant card, she was out of here. You didn't trust big guys in the semi-dark – not these days.

'It's all right, Peter. It's her.' A woman in a long white rain-coat emerged from the river path. 'Ms Watkins, Person of the Cloth. I'll deal with this.'

The big man nodded, trudged back up the footpath.

Merrily sighed. 'DI Howe.'

'Acting DCI, actually.'

'The old fast track's moved up a gear, has it?' Weariness loosening Merrily's reserve. 'Let me guess, I've walked into some kind of stake-out. Colombian drugs barons are bringing a consignment up the Wye?'

Annie Howe didn't laugh. It occurred to Merrily that she had yet ever to hear Annie Howe laugh. Her short, ashen hair gleamed dully like a helmet in the early light.

'You priests work long hours. Sick parishioner?'

'Dead,' Merrily said. 'Just now.'

'Obviously a night for it, Ms Watkins.'

'For what?'

Annie Howe came to stand next to her, glancing into the Volvo. She was maybe five years younger than Merrily – a smooth, efficient, over-educated CID person, both feet on the escalator. During the police hunt in Ledwardine earlier this year, Jane had remarked that Howe reminded her of a Nazi dentist. You could tell where the kid was coming from.

'We've pulled a body out of the Wye, Ms Watkins. Just down there, not far from Victoria Bridge.'

'Oh God. Just?'

'Couple of hours ago.'

She remembered hearing the siren from the sluice-room window. 'What happened?'

'We're not sure yet. But it didn't appear to have been in the water an awfully long time, so we're rather keen to talk to anyone who might have seen something' – Howe smiled thinly – 'or heard a solitary splash, perhaps.'

'Not me.'

'You arrived about three, I hear that right?'

'Something like that.'

'Nobody about at all?'

'Not that I can recall.'

'You ever been down to the river this way?'

'Not really.'

'It's quite pretty,' Howe said. 'Come and see.'

Merrily sighed and followed her past some flowerless beds and a bench to a little parapet. Below them was a narrow suspension bridge, grey girders across the dark, misty river. A glimmering of pale plastic tape, and two policemen.

Howe said, 'It's just that if there's a particular parking place most convenient for the river, then your car's in it. We thought it might be the dead man's at first. Quite a disappointment really, when your name came up as the owner.'

'And when the body wasn't a woman about my age in a dog-collar.'

'Not quite what I meant. It just made it less easy to put a name to him. But we will.'

'How old was he?'

'Quite young. Thirties.'

'Suicide?'

126

'It's a possibility, given the time of day. So's accidental death.' Annie Howe looked at Merrily. 'So's murder.'

'He didn't drown?'

'We should know quite soon.'

'But he came off the bridge?'

Howe shrugged.

'If you knew it was my car, why didn't you come into the hospital and ask for me?'

'We did. Nobody seemed to know you were there.'

'The Alfred Watkins Ward, if you want to check. Ask for Sister Cullen. I've been with her for the last three hours or so.'

Howe nodded. 'So it's unlikely you would've seen anything. Ah, well, nothing's ever simple, is it, Ms Watkins? Thanks for your help. I don't suppose we'll be in touch, but if you remember anything that might be useful…' the wind whipped the skirt of Howe's raincoat against her calves, 'you know where to find me.'

Merrily looked down into the swirling mist and dark water. It looked somehow warmer than she felt – and almost inviting.

13

Show Barn

IT WAS RARE to see genial Dick Lyden in a bad mood.

When Lol arrived just after eight a.m., Dick was pacing the kitchen, slamming his right fist into his left palm.

'The little shit,' he fumed. 'The fucking little shit!'

'He's just trying it on,' Mrs Ruth Lyden, fellow therapist, said calmly. 'He knows you too well. He's got you psyched out. He knows your particular weak spot and he goes for it.'

There was plenty of room for Dick to pace; the Lydens' kitchen was as big as a restaurant kitchen, more than half as big as Lol's new flat over the shop. It was all white and metallic like a dairy.

'His psychological know-how goes out of the window when he's dealing with his own son,' Ruth told Lol. She was a large, placid, frizzy-haired woman who'd once been Dick's personal secretary in London.

'Well, you can't, can you?' Dick sat down at the banquet-sized table. 'You simply can't distance yourself sufficiently from your own family – be wrong even to try. I think we're probably even worse than ordinary people at dealing with our own problems.'

Lol didn't like to ask what the present personal problem was; Ruth told him anyway.

'James has been chosen as Boy Bishop.' She searched Lol's face, eyebrows raised. 'You know about that?'

'Sorry,' Lol said. 'I'm not that well up on the Church.'

'Medieval Christmas tradition. Used to happen all over the place, but it's almost unique to Hereford now. A boy is chosen from the Cathedral choristers, or the retired choristers, to replace the Bishop on his throne on St Nicholas's Day. Gets to wear the mitre and wield the staff and whatnot. Terribly solemn and everything, though quite fun as well.'

'It's actually a great honour,' Dick said. 'Especially for newcomers like us. Little shit!'

'And of course James now says he's going to refuse to do it.' Ruth poured coffee for Lol. 'When they offered it to him, he was very flattered in a cynical sort of way. But now he's announced it would be morally wrong of him to do it – having decided he's an atheist—'

'What the fuck difference does that make?' Dick snarled. 'At least twenty-five per cent of the bloody clergy are atheists!'

'—and that it isn't in line with his personal image or his musical direction. He's sixteen now, and at sixteen one's image is awfully well defined. How quickly they change! One year an angelic little choirboy, and then—'

'A bloody yob,' said Dick. 'Where's his guitar? I'm going to lock it in the shed.'

'He's taken it to school with him.' Ruth hid a smile behind her coffee cup. 'Told you he had you psyched.'

'Devious little bastard.' Dick drained his cup, coughed at the strength of the coffee. 'Right, I'll get my coat, Lol. Be good to go out and deal with something straightforward.'

'Moon is straightforward?'

'Well, you know what I mean. Straightforwardly convoluted.'

'Poor Dick,' Ruth said when he'd left the kitchen. 'It's an honour for *him* rather than James. A sign that he's really been accepted into the city. He needs that – needs to be at the hub of things. He's a terrible control-freak, really, in his oh-so-amiable way.'

Lol said, 'Do you guys psychoanalyse one another *all* the time?'

Ruth laughed.

Outside, it began to rain, a sudden cold splattering.

'Wow.' Jane was observing her mother from the stove. 'You really do look like shit.'

'Thank you. I think we've established that.'

Merrily had told her about being delayed by the police investigating a body in the Wye. But that evidently didn't explain why she looked like shit.

'You need a hot bath,' Jane said. 'And then off to bed.'

'The bath certainly.' No question about that. Merrily watched the rain on the window. It looked dirty. Everything looked dirty even after twenty minutes before the altar. *Scritch-scratch.*

'So.' Jane shovelled inch-thick toast on to a plate. 'You want to talk about the other stuff?'

'What makes you think there's other stuff?'

'Do me a favour,' Jane said.

The kid had realized, from quite soon after Sean's death, that her mother would need someone on whom she could lay heavy issues. There were times when she instinctively became a kind of sensible younger sister – with no sarcasm, point-scoring, storage of information for future blackmail.

'Hang on, though.' Merrily looked up. 'What time is it? The school bus'll be going without you.'

'I'm taking the day off. I have a migraine.'

'In which case, flower, you appear to be coping with the blinding agony which defines that condition with what I can only describe as a remarkable stoicism.'

'Yeah, it's a fairly mild attack. But it could get worse. Besides, when you've really sussed out the way teachers operate, you can take the odd day off any time you like without missing a thing.'

'Except you never have – have you?'

'A vicar's daughter has to be flexible. If I went to school, you'd stay up and work all day, and by the time I got home you'd be *soooo* unbearable.'

'Jane—'

'Don't argue. Just have some breakfast and bugger off to bed. I'll stick around, make a brilliant log fire – and repel all the time-wasting gits.'

Merrily gave up. 'But this must never happen again.'

Jane shrugged.

'All right,' Merrily said. 'No egg for me, thanks. My digestive system can just about cope with Marmite.'

'Right.' Jane brought the teapot to the table and sat down. 'What's disturbed it exactly?'

Merrily sighed a couple of times and watched the rain blurring the window. And she then told Jane about Denzil Joy.

Some of it.

Rain sheeted down on Dinedor Hill, the twisty road narrowing as they climbed.

Dick was clearly disappointed when they ran out of track for the massive Mitsubishi Intercooler Super Turbo-Plus he'd borrowed from Denny for the weekend. Dick was contemplating a move into four-wheel drive.

Lol unbuckled his seatbelt. 'If you go any further, English Heritage'll be down on you. It'll be in the *Hereford Times* – "City Therapist Squashes Ancient Camp".'

'You may scoff. But I *do* feel it's important to be a good citizen. We *chose* to come here – which confers responsibility.' Dick braked and reversed into something satisfyingly deep and viscous. 'Even to something that just looks like any other hill.'

'You have no soul, Dick.'

Dick squinted through the mud-blotched windcreen. 'Buggered if I'm staggering up there in this weather. What am I missing?'

'Nice view over the city. For the rest, you need a soul.'

'Imagination.' Dick leaned back in the driving seat, allowing the glass to mist. 'I have very little, thank goodness. The ancestors... Jung would have found plenty to go at, but I've never been particularly drawn to the idea of the collective-unconscious, race memories, all that. It *sounds* good, but... what do you think?'

'I'm inclined to believe it. I've got a bit in common with Moon, I suppose.'

'And you fancy her. Well, of course you do. Awfully sexy creature.'

'Yes.' Lol had been half expecting this. 'She is.'

'So what's the problem?' Dick started ticking off plus-factors on his fingers. 'You're both on your own. *I'm* her actual therapist, not you, so no ethical barriers. Do find her attractive, don't you?'

'She's beautiful.'

'But you think she doesn't fancy you – that it? Oh, I think she does, old son. I think she does.'

Lol felt awkward. 'Maybe we wouldn't be too good for each other. You don't get to laugh much around Moon.'

'Not a terrific sense of humour, no,' Dick conceded.

'Like, you want to make her happy, but you don't somehow think she'd be happy being happy.'

And that was it really: you couldn't help feeling that life with Moon was destined to end in a suicide pact.

'Lol,' Dick said, 'I realize you're a sensitive soul, but you don't particularly need to think about psychology when you're shagging someone, do you?'

'Yuk,' Jane said. 'I mean... *yuk*!'

'Quite.'

'I mean, it's awful, it's tragic, and everything. But it's also... really inconsiderate. I really think you should've walked out. Like, how were you to know these nurses weren't lying? Nobody should have to make a decision like that, with the old guy's clock running down the whole time.'

'It wasn't an actual exorcism. It wasn't much at all, in the end.'

'Sounds like that's what the older nurse wanted, though. An exorcism.'

'Possibly.' The parts Merrily hadn't mentioned included the scratching finger and other sensations. The subjective aspects.

'Face it.' Jane poured the tea. 'It's a crap deal, Mum. They send you in armed with a handful of half-assed prayers and platitudes which are supposed to cover all eventualities. You're holding a duff hand from the start.'

'Well, not—'

'It's like with these evangelical maniacs, where you like go along and you're looking a bit off-colour and in about three minutes flat they've discovered you're possessed by seventeen different demons and the next thing you're rolling around on the floor throwing up. You could really *damage* people.'

'It's a bit more disciplined than that but, yeah, I know what you mean. It *is* a minefield.'

'And it's just useless *liturgy*. Like, with all respect, what real actual practical training have you had? It's not like you've even done any meditation or yoga or anything. I mean... theological college? Does that even equal, say, two weeks at a respectable ashram?'

'I think it possibly does,' Merrily said, but wondering.

'But you're not really spiritually developed, are you? Not like Buddhist monks and Indian gurus and guys like that. Like, you can't – I don't know – leave your body or anything. You've just read the books. And yet they want you to mess with people's souls.'

'It's supposed to be God who does the actual messing. That is, we don't believe we have any special powers. We kind of signpost the way for the Holy Spirit.'

'You ever ask yourself, if the Holy Spirit is so ubi... all-over-the-place and on the ball, why does it *need* a signpost?'

'We have to invite the Holy Spirit in, you know?'

'Why?'

'Because that's one of the rules. Deep theology, flower.'

'Bollocks,' Jane murmured. 'Anyway, I wouldn't let Hunter get away with this.'

Merrily paused with the mug at her mouth. 'He's the guv'nor.'

'He's a tosser.'

'But I *will* call him. I'll have a bath and a rest and then I'll call him.'

'Maybe Rowenna could get some of the SAS cross-country guys to elbow the flash git into a deep ditch,' Jane mused. 'Muddy his fetching purple tracksuit.'

The rain was battering the barn windows, and Lol was sure there was an element of sleet to it now. But Dick was all sunshine, like his row with the boy James had never happened.

'Well, this is super.' Clasping his herbal tea to his chest. 'This is quite magnificent.'

And it was. The little barn was transformed. All the boxes had disappeared, everything put away, everything tidy. A bright coal-fire on the simple, stone hearth. Fragments of black pottery arranged on a small shelf. On the wall alongside the steps to the bedroom loft was a detailed pen-and-ink plan of, presumably, the Dinedor Iron Age community – round huts with stone bases and conical thatched roofs. Moon had made mysterious marks on it: dots and symbols – archaeologist stuff.

Ideal Homes show barn?

'You were right and we were wrong,' Dick told Moon. But he was smiling at Lol and the smile said: *I was right and you were wrong*.

Above the fireplace was a gilt-framed photograph of a smiling man leaning against a Land Rover. The man's smile was Moon's smile.

'We thought you'd be a bit, ah, cut off up here,' Dick said. 'A bit lonely? But this is your place, Moon. What are you going to do?'

'Well, I'm going back to work in the shop.' Moon wore the long grey dress, freshly washed; without mud on the hem it looked like a hostess dress. Her very long hair was in a loose, lush plait. 'For a while, anyway.'

'Playing it day by day.'

'I'm not an alcoholic, Dick.'

She didn't smile. She hadn't looked at Lol. He felt he'd betrayed her.

'What I *meant*, Moon,' Dick said, 'is that you clearly no longer feel the need to hurry – rush from one experience to another. You've been away, you've been through all kinds of changes, and now you've returned to repossess your past. *Your* past, *your* place, firm ground – it must feel wonderful.'

Moon said nothing. Dick took this as agreement, and nodded enthusiastically. It was the conclusion he wanted, the neat outcome of a very singular case. He had her all packaged up in his head: at least an article for *Psychology Today* or whatever he subscribed to. Moon was getting better. Moon was taking responsibility for herself.

So why, to Lol, had she never seemed more of an enigma? What had caused her suddenly to launch into this place like a team of industrial cleaners? As if she'd known they were coming. Or someone else? Determined that the barn should project the image of a balanced, settled academic individual.

It was a façade; it had to be.

And the picture of her smiling father disturbed him. If Dick had noticed it, he didn't comment. Lol looked closely at the photograph. When it was taken, Moon's father would have been about Denny's age – early to mid forties. He looked more like Moon than Denny did, the same smile and the same deep-sunk, glittering eyes. Something black and gnarled lay on the mantelpiece below the picture. Lol bent to examine it.

'Don't touch that!' Moon almost ran across the room, eased herself between Lol and the fireplace.

Lol stepped back. 'I'm sorry…'

'It's very delicate.'

'What is it?'

'I found it. It was only about ten yards from the barn. Someone had started digging out a pond some time ago and never finished it, and there was a heap of soil where the ground was turned over, and it was actually projecting – sticking out.'

She moved aside to let them see, now they realized they mustn't touch. It was knobbled and corroded, about ten inches long.

'Anyone else, if they didn't know about these things, they'd think it was just an old tractor part or something. I mean, nothing much has ever been found up here. A trench was once cut from the ramparts to the centre of the camp, and nothing much was found there except lots of black pottery and an axe-head.'

'It's a dagger,' Lol decided.

'A sword. Confirmation for me that this farm – not so much the house, but the *farm* – has been here since the Iron Age. It was waiting for me to find it. You see, now?'

'Fate,' Lol said hollowly.

'Oh no,' Moon said. 'Far less random than fate.'

'What's that mean?'

Moon shook her head. He thought she smiled.

'You could take it to a museum, have it cleaned up by experts.'

Moon was horrified. 'Nobody's going to touch it but me. I don't want the flow blocked by anyone else's vibrations.'

'Good for you, Moon,' said Dick. 'Look, we must have a good long chat.'

'Yes, but not today,' Moon said. 'My landlords are coming over for lunch. Tim and Anna Purefoy? From the farm?'

'Ah.' Dick nodded. 'Excellent. Getting to know the neighbours.'

'I'm meeting all the people who live around the hill – for my book. If I'm going to trace how the community's changed over two millennia, I have to examine its components. Quite a few of the newcomers here are very interested too. They're going to help me.'

'Terrific.' Dick looked like he wanted to pat her on the head. 'Can't wait to read it.'

Later, when Dick went to have fun reversing the Mitsubishi out of the morass in front of the barn where someone had once started to dig a pond, Moon came to stand next to Lol in the doorway.

'Don't bring him here again.'

'He'll hear you.'

'I don't care if he does. I don't want him here. He's an idiot. Denny only employed him to get the court off our backs.'

'*Your* back, Moon.'

'He's an idiot.'

'He means well.'

'Lol, If you come here again as Dick's assistant, I won't tell you anything in future. I don't need people around me I can't trust.'

The slanting rain plucked at the mud.

'I'm sorry,' Lol said. 'Do you want me to come back?'

She looked at him, smiling almost coyly. 'Only as yourself.'

As Merrily rolled gratefully into bed, the phone rang.

'Unplug it!' Jane screeched from the landing. 'Unplug it *now*! I'll get it downstairs.'

'Hello,' Merrily said. 'Ledwardine Vicarage.'

'Merrily? It's Sophie at the Bishop's office. Michael asked me to ring. We wondered if you'd be popping into town today and, if so, could you call in?'

'Well, I wasn't planning…' On the one hand, she very much needed to talk to the Bishop; on the other, not in this state. 'Bit tied up this morning.'

'Oh. Well, this afternoon there'll be nobody here. Better make it tomorrow, I suppose. It's just a little job – in connection with the Deliverance side of things.'

'Oh?'

'I don't imagine it's terribly urgent.'

'Good. Sophie, do all the Deliverance cases come through your office?'

'Well, it's intended that they should. I'm afraid Canon Dobbs was less organized.'

'What about the problem last night at the General Hospital?'

'At the hospital? *Was* there a problem?'

'So it didn't come through the office?'

'It didn't come through *me*.'

'If you weren't there, would the Bishop have handled it himself?'

'They wouldn't normally get through to the Bishop. Anyway he wasn't here last night. He was at his parents' home in the Forest of Dean. They thought his father had suffered another heart attack but it was a false alarm, I'm glad to say.'

'Oh,' Merrily said, 'good.'

'Did you have to go to the hospital, then, Merrily?'

'Yes, I did.' She gripped the phone tightly. If Hunter had been away, then who had directed the hospital to approach her? Who set her up for Denzil Joy's grisly farewell party?

'Merrily, are you all right?'

'Yes, I… This other job – can you tell me what that is?'

'I'm not sure I should over the phone.'

'You don't need to mention names.'

'Well, it's… a haunting. At a home for the elderly. Near Dorstone, out towards the Welsh border.'

'And where did *that* come from? Who told you about it?'

'It came from the new vicar of Dorstone, I believe. Michael had asked me to keep him informed of any reports of this nature, and when I mentioned it to him he said he'd like you to… take a crack at it, as he put it. He…' She hesitated. 'What he went on to say, if I'm not speaking out of turn, is that it would be a test of how committed you were.'

'Committed?'

'Frankly, he feels you're rather stalling. He'd expected a firm answer by now. When we spoke on the phone, he asked if I'd heard from you.'

'I see. So if I sidestep this haunting, or suggest the Vicar of Dorstone handles it himself, he'll take that as a no.'

'I may be wrong about that.'

Sophie was never wrong. Merrily felt she could almost see the hand of fate, grey-gloved in the half-light of the bedroom.

From the landing, Jane called out, 'For Christ's sake, Mum!'

In Merrily's head, the demonic Denzil Joy sat up in bed for the last time, tubes flying out of his nose in twin puffs of snot. Huw Owen's voice echoed over the Brecon Beacons. *Might as well just paint a great big bullseye between your tits.*

And, she thought, *it was Dobbs, wasn't it? It was bloody Dobbs – it has to be. Dobbs set me up.*

She felt light-headed with fatigue. She knew that later, when she awoke again, she was going to be very angry, but now the rage was still misty and distant.

So were the words she spoke, so faintly that she wasn't sure she hadn't merely thought them. 'I'll come in tomorrow then, Sophie. Ten? Ten-thirty?'

She didn't hear the reply, wasn't even aware of hanging up the phone.

There were no dreams, thank God.

14

The First Exorcist

SHE STOPPED AT the top of the gatehouse stairs, rubbing circulation back into her hands. It seemed to have become winter overnight. The waxed jacket felt as flimsy as a bin-liner. No good, she'd have to get herself a proper coat when she had time.

When she saw the office door, she didn't know whether to laugh or cry or turn around and creep quietly away.

The white panels were adorned by a single, black gothic letter. Above it, a simple, black cross.

𝕯

The Rev. Charlie Headland was chuckling softly in her head. *More like MI5...*

Too late to turn around and creep out. Sophie – grey suit, pearls, neat white bun, half-glasses on a chain – stood in the adjacent doorway.

'Merrily, good morning. Did you see a few specks of snow? I'm convinced I saw snow. Heavens, come up.'

'Do I have to sign in? Maybe pass through a detector?'

Sophie smiled wryly. 'Michael's specific instructions. In one respect I suppose it's rather elegant.'

'Sophie, it looks like the entrance to a bloody chapel of rest.'

'Oh.' Sophie looked put out. She *was* the Bishop's person, whoever the current bishop happened to be.

The new arrival on the office desk was an Apple Mac and a printer, and something Merrily took to be a scanner.

'Jesus,' she said. 'All I know how to do on one of these is type.'

'Don't worry,' Sophie said, a little cool now. 'I'm your secretary as well, for a while. Michael wants me to open a Deliverance database: filing and categorizing the various cases, and giving area breakdowns. He also wants me to arrange a meeting with the Director of Social Services, the Chief Executive of the Health Authority, charities like MIND – and also the police.'

Merrily flopped down behind the desk. 'What?'

'And you're to have an e-mail address, possibly a website.'

She looked into the blank computer screen as though it were a crystal ball, conjuring up Huw Owen's tired, rugged face. *I don't want stuff letting in. A lot of bad energy's crowding the portals. I want to keep all the doors locked and the chains up...*

Her new secretary stood by the window, hands linked demurely at the waist of her tweed skirt.

'Look... Sophie,' Merrily moistened her wind-roughened lips, 'the thing about Deliverance, it needs to be low-profile. I wouldn't go as far as to use the word "clandestine", but there's a danger of attracting time-wasters and fanatics and loonies and... other undesirable elements. The Bishop doesn't seem to have grasped this basic point.'

'Deliverance is getting a high priority, Merrily.' Sophie slipped into the visitor's chair. 'Look... I really wouldn't worry about this. Michael's a very young man to be a bishop, and he perhaps feels he's been put in place to make an impression, help push the Church firmly into the twenty-first century. He's also a very clever man, with an impeccable pedigree which he tends to underplay. Father and an uncle were both bishops... father-in-law's the Dean of Gloucester. Michael feels that if people are aware of the amount of work undertaken by the Deliverance ministry, they may be more inclined towards what you might call spiritual preventative medicine.'

'You mean what we used to call "Going to Church"?'

Sophie smiled wryly.

'I know,' Merrily said wearily. 'It all makes a kind of sense. I just wish there was less... bollocks.'

'I don't doubt that you'll cope, Merrily. You'll find the details of the Dorstone haunting on your computer, if you click on the desktop file marked *Memo*. I shall be next door if you want me.'

'Thanks.' Merrily shed her coat and switched on the computer.

And then closed the door and picked up the phone and rang Eileen Cullen at home.

'Timed it well, Merrily. Come off shift, whizz round Tesco, home to bed.' Away from the ward, Cullen's voice sounded softer. 'How are you now?'

'Bit confused.'

'Ah-ha. Well... what can I tell you? There's a palpable sense of relief on the ward. We laid him out – he made the scariest corpse I ever handled – then we fumigated the side ward. Too much to expect that he'd take his smell down to the mortuary with him.'

Almost immediately, Denzil's reptilian odour was in her head. Merrily stifled a cough.

'Oh, and later in the morning,' Eileen Cullen said, 'I'm told that the old man came in and said a prayer or two.'

'Old man?' Merrily tingled.

'I don't even know his name, but his collar was the right way round so nobody questions it.'

'His name is Dobbs,' Merrily said.

'Aye, that's the feller, I suppose.'

'He already knew about Denzil. Didn't he?'

'He must've. Though how he'd have found out the man was dead, I don't know. We've hardly got the time to put out a general bulletin to the clergy.'

'OK, look, let's not keep walking around each other – I'll explain. Canon Dobbs is the Diocesan Exorcist. I'm the one being set up to take over from him. He doesn't want to go, and he certainly doesn't want to be replaced by a woman. I'm coming round to thinking he set me up with Denzil last night to give me a taste of just how nasty and squalid the job could be. *And* why it's not a suitable job for a woman.'

After a moment Cullen said, 'That wasn't very nice of him then, was it?'

'Not awfully. So I'd appreciate just… knowing. Like, anything you can remember. Entirely off the record, Eileen.'

'Aye,' said Cullen, 'you get surgeons like that. They love to leave you holding the shit end of the stick. All right, I'll tell you what I know. He *did* know Denzil Joy. Whether this was from Denzil's life outside of hospital I wouldn't know. Probably. But he came in once – I didn't see this, I wasn't there, but Protheroe was – and they had to ask him to leave. Denzil's spitting at him, coming out with all kinds of foul stuff you don't want to be hearing from a sickbed, and it carried on that way after the priest was well out of the building. It's why we put him in solitary the past two times. Though obviously his wife lived to regret that.'

'Did anyone ask Dobbs about the incident?'

'Oh, he wouldn't talk to the likes of us – except very briefly to Protheroe. He said to let him know if we had any further trouble with Mr Joy. So, naturally, the other night, after the business with the wife, Protheroe's screaming, "Call the priest, call the priest, the man's possessed with evil." '

'And you called him?'

'I called the number she gave me and a woman answered, and I told her what it was about and she said to hang on, and then she came back and said to call the Reverend Watkins. Does that solve your problem?'

'Do you remember the phone number you rang for Dobbs?'

'Oh, I probably wrote it down and threw it away. Protheroe probably keeps it in a gold locket around her neck.'

'Well, thanks. You've been very helpful.'

'Aye.' A pause. 'How're you feeling yourself, Merrily? Like, did he do anything to you?'

'I... maybe.'

'I don't want to worry you,' Cullen said, 'but they say it comes back sometimes. Like the ache you get with the shingles, you know?'

'I've never had shingles.'

'Pray you never do,' Cullen said. 'Seems daft saying this to a priest, but if you ever want a chat about anything, you've got the number.'

'Thanks,' Merrily said. 'Thanks.'

She clicked on *Memo*.

STRICTLY PRIVATE AND CONFIDENTIAL
Mrs Susan Thorpe, proprietor, the Glades Residential Home,
Hardwicke (between Dorstone and Hay-on-Wye) requests a
discreet meeting with regard to unexplained occurrences.

Sophie's head came round the door just then, as if she'd heard the click of the mouse. 'Would you like me to call her for you? Make an appointment?'

'Just leave the number on the desk. Sophie, could you give me another bit of information?'

'It's what I'm here for, Merrily.'

'Could you tell me exactly where in the Close Canon Dobbs lives?'

Sophie removed her half-glasses. 'Ho-hum,' she said.

'The Bishop's specific instructions are to keep Dobbs and me well apart, right?'

'Michael doesn't discuss Canon Dobbs. Perhaps you could try the telephone directory?'

'Of which you know he's ex-.'

Sophie sighed. 'He moved out of the canonry when his wife died. He lives in a little terraced house in Gwynne Street.'

'That's...?'

'Less than fifty yards from where I sit – just down from the Christian bookshop. And I didn't tell you that.'

'Thank you.'

'I suppose you had to get this over at some stage.' Sophie refixed her glasses. 'Don't forget your haunting, will you?'

Frost-blackened plants dripped down the sides of a hanging basket next to the door. The green door needed painting. Paint was peeling from the wooden window ledge; the wood was rotting. The house itself rather let Gwynne Street down.

The street was narrow, almost like an alley, following the perimeter wall of the Bishop's Palace, and sloping downhill towards the river. The house was one of the lower ones, before they gave way to warehouses and garages near the banks of the Wye.

There was no bell, no knocker. Merrily banged on the door with a fist, which hurt and brought more paint flying off.

There was no answer. She peered in at the window. The curtains were drawn against her. She looked around in frustration. There was no sign of another way in. Above her, the sky was tight and dark-flecked like stretched goatskin.

'Hello, Merrily. All right, luv?'

'I don't really know.'

'Oh.' Silence on the line as Huw Owen mulled this over. 'That sounds like you took on the job. I *thought* you wouldn't back out.'

'I was actually about to turn it down.' Merrily lit a cigarette, looking out of the window into the Bishop's Palace yard. 'Then a case happened.'

'Just happened, eh?' Huw said. 'Just like that. Well, what's done's done, in't it? How can I help?'

'I don't suppose any of the others've called. Charlie? Clive?'

'Never off, lass. "Do excuse me bothering you again, Huw, but I have a teensy problem, and I'm not entirely sure if it's a *weeper* or a *breather*." '

146

Merrily blew an accidental smoke-ring. 'So I'm the first to come crying to the headmaster.'

'I always liked you the best, anyroad, luv. Charlie and Clive'll fall on their arses sooner or later, but they won't tell *me*.'

She started to laugh, picturing him sitting placidly in his isolated, Brontë-esque rectory, like some ungroomed old wolfhound.

'Let's hear it then, lass.'

She told him about Denzil Joy. She told it simply and concisely. She missed out nothing she thought might be important. *Scritch-scratch*. And then the Dobbs link. It took over fifteen minutes, and it brought everything back, and she felt unclean again.

'My,' Huw said, 'that's a foxy one, in't it?'

'What d'you think?'

'Could be a few things. Could be just a very nasty little man. Or it could be a *carrier*.'

'A carrier. Did you tell us about carriers?'

'Happen I forgot.'

'Meaning you deliberately forgot. Would *carriers* be the people who pick up *hitchhikers*?'

'You're not daft, Merrily. I said that, din't I? Provable carriers are... not that common. And not easy to diagnose. And they can lead to a lot of hysteria of the fundamentalist type. You know, if one bloke's got it, it must be contagious? And then you get these dubious mass-exorcisms, everybody rolling around and clutching their guts.'

'Just one man,' Merrily said, 'so far.'

'That's good to know. Well, a carrier is usually a nasty person who attracts more nastiness to him – like iron filings to a magnet. Usually there's a bit of a sexual kink. An overly powerful sex-drive and probably not bright. Not a lot up top, too much down below.'

'Anything I need to do now he's gone?'

'To make sure he don't come back? Sounds like Mr Dobbs has done it. Not going quietly into that good night, is he?'

147

'Clearly not.'

'Might not work, mind. That's the big irony with Deliverance – half the time it don't work. But in somewhere like a hospital it'll fade or get consumed by all the rest of the pervading anguish. You could happen do a protection on yourself periodically. Oh, and leave off sex for a week.'

'Gosh, Huw, that's going to be a tall order.'

'Oh dear,' Huw said. 'So you're still on your own, eh? What a bloody waste. God hates waste.'

Before lunch, Merrily made an appointment to meet Mrs Susan Thorpe at the Glades Residential Home at eleven o'clock the following morning. There must have been somebody in the room who didn't know about this issue, because Mrs Thorpe kept addressing her as if she were Rentokil coming to deal with an infestation of woodworm.

Sophie was meeting a friend for lunch at the Green Dragon. Merrily decided to see what was on offer at the café inside All Saints Church: a fairly ingenious idea for getting bums on pews or at least *close* to pews.

But first – *Sod it, I'm not walking away from this* – she slipped round the wall and back into Gwynne Street.

There was a weak, cream-coloured sun now over Broad Street, but Gwynne Street was still in shadow. The only point of light was in the middle of Dobbs's flaking green door.

It turned out to be a slender white envelope trapped by a corner in the letterbox flap. As she raised a fist to knock on the door and wondered if she ought to push the envelope through, she saw the name typed on the front:

Mrs M Watkins

She caught a movement at an upstairs window and glanced up, saw a curtain quiver. He was there! The old bastard had been in the whole time. He'd watched her standing here knocking more paint from his door.

And now he'd left her a letter.

The street was deserted: no cars, no people, no voices. She felt like smashing Dobbs's window. Instead she snatched the envelope out of the box and walked away and didn't look back.

She walked quickly out of Gwynne Street, past the Christian bookshop and the Tourist Information Shop, and round the corner into King Street, where she stood at the kerb and tore open the envelope. She hoped it was a threat, something abusive.

There was a single sheet of notepaper folded inside. In the centre, a single line of type:

The first exorcist was Jesus Christ.

This was all it said.

15

Male Thing

THE WOMAN BEHIND the counter was, by any standards, drop-dead gorgeous. Worse still, kind of pale and mysterious and distant, with hair you could trip over.

A woollen scarf masking her lower face, Jane watched from outside the shop window. Saturday morning: bright enough to bring thousands of shoppers into Hereford from all over the county and from large areas of Wales; cold enough for there still to be condensation on the windows, even in sheltered Church Street.

Jane had come in on the early bus, the *only* bus out of Ledwardine on a Saturday. At half-twelve, Rowenna was picking her up outside the Library. It was Psychic Fair day.

Which left her a couple of hours to kill. It was inevitable she'd wind up here at some point.

She almost wished she hadn't; this was *so* awful. Lol had written songs about creatures like this. And now he lived above the same shop. Maybe during the lunch hour the woman would weave her languorous way up some archaic spiral staircase, and he'd be waiting for her up on the landing, where they'd start undressing each other before making their frenzied...

'Jane?'

Damn. He must have come out of a side entrance. She must remain cool, show no surprise.

'So that's her, is it, Lol?'

'Who?'

He was shivering in his thin, faded sweatshirt. His hair needed attention; it had never looked the same since he'd cut it off at the back and lost the ponytail. Made him look too grown-up, almost like a man of thirty-eight.

'Moon?' Jane lowered her scarf. Inside the shop, the woman saw them looking at her and smiled absently, arranging a display of CDs on the counter. 'She's quite ordinary-looking, isn't she?'

'Almost plain,' Lol said. 'Jane, how much would it cost to make you go away and stop embarrassing me?'

'More than you've got on you. Much more.'

'How about a cappuccino?'

'Yeah, that'll do,' Jane said.

It was set in deep countryside, a kind of manor house, rambling but not very old, maybe early nineteenth-century. Squat gate-posts with plain stone balls on top, and a notice in the entrance – THE GLADES RESIDENTIAL HOME – stencilled over a painted purple hill with the sun above it. A bright yellow sun with no suggestion of it setting, which would have been the wrong image altogether.

There was a small car park in front, with a sweeping view of the Radnor hills, but a woman appeared around the side of the house and beckoned her to drive closer to her.

Merrily followed the drive around to a brick double-garage and parked in front of it, the woman hurrying after her.

'You're wearing your... uniform,' she said in a loud, dismayed whisper, when Merrily got out of the car. 'I'm sorry, I should have emphasized the need for discretion.'

Merrily smiled. 'Don't worry about that.' *Don't worry yet; we may not even paste your case on the Deliverance website.*

'It's all been very difficult,' the woman said. 'We didn't want to call in the local vicar – *far* too close – so the obvious person was Mr Dobbs, but then... such a bombshell – we won't talk about that. I'm Susan Thorpe. We'll go in this way.'

She was a big woman, dark blonde hair pushed under a wide, practical hairslide. She led Merrily through a small back door, down a short drab passage and into what was clearly her private sitting room: very untidy.

'Have a seat. Throw those magazines on the floor. I've sent for some coffee, is that all right? God, I didn't need this, I really didn't *need* this. Everything comes at once, don't you find that? Now I discover I have to find a room for my mother.'

'Must be a problem, if you run a home like this and your mother gets to the age—'

'Oh, it's not like that. Mother's fitter than me. She's lost her job, that's all, *and* her home – she was someone's housekeeper. I'm sorry, I'm afraid I've forgotten your name.'

'Merrily Watkins.'

'Merrily. And you're the new diocesan exorcist. I was in quite a quandary, Merrily, so I rang the Diocese. I said, "Could you send *anybody* but Dobbs."'

Dobbs? Merrily still had his one-liner in her bag: *The first exorcist was Jesus Christ.* Hence, Jesus must be our role model, and Jesus was not a woman. 'Why didn't you want Canon Dobbs?'

'This problem... I was very loath at first to think it *was* a problem – your kind of problem, anyway. Old people can be such *delinquents*. They'll break a teapot because they don't like the colour, wet the bed because they don't like the sheets.'

'This is a *volatile*... er, poltergeist phenomenon?'

'Oh no, the point I was making is that, when one of the staff complains of strange things happening, I immediately suspect one or other of the residents. In this case, neither I nor – so far, thank God – any of the residents have seen or heard a thing.'

'So who has?' Merrily still hadn't received an answer to her question about Dobbs. Was this another of his set-ups, another attempt to show her why she, as a woman, was unfit to follow in the footsteps of Jesus?

'Chambermaids,' said Mrs Thorpe. 'Well, domestic care-workers, actually, but we do try to make it seem like a hotel for the sake of the residents, so we call them chambermaids. The other week, one simply gave in her notice – or rather sent it by post, having failed to return after a weekend away. Gave no explanation other than "personal reasons". It was only then that my assistant manager told me the woman had rushed down-stairs one evening white as a sheet and said she wasn't going up *there* again.'

'Where?'

'To the third floor.'

Merrily tensed, thinking of her own third-floor problem, currently in remission, at the vicarage. 'Did she elaborate?'

'No, as I say, she simply left and we thought no more about it and took on a replacement, a local woman who didn't want to live in but was prepared to work nights. Well, at least *she* couldn't just bugger off without an explanation.'

'She's had the same experience?'

'We presume it was the same. Do you want to talk to her?'

'If that's possible.'

'She'll be coming in with the coffee in a minute.' Mrs Thorpe pulled a half-crushed cigarette packet from between the sofa cushions. 'Does smoke interfere with whatever it is you do?'

'I hope not. Have one of mine.'

'I'm terrible sorry – with all the persecution these days, one assumes other people don't smoke. Have you met Canon Dobbs?'

'Kind of.'

'He's going out of his mind, you know.'

'Oh?'

'Always been a very, very strange man, but it's been downhill all the way for the past year. The man ought to be in a… well, a place like this, I suppose. Not this one, though.'

'So you know him quite well then.'

Susan Thorpe lit up and coughed fiercely. 'Sorry, thought I told you: my mother was his housekeeper.'

'Dobbs's housekeeper? In Hereford?'

'For five years. When his wife died he moved out of his canonry with about twenty thousand books. Bought two houses in a nearby terrace, one for the housekeeper – and more books, of course.'

'This is in Gwynne Street?'

'That's it. Quite a nice place to live if you like cities. Mother rather wondered if he might do the decent thing and leave it to her when he shuffled off his mortal coil, but then, a couple of days ago, absolutely out of the blue, he just tells her to go, leave. Gives her five thousand quid and instructions to be out by the weekend – that's today. "Why?" she says, utterly dumbfounded. "What have I *done* to you?" "Nothing," he says. "Don't ask questions, just leave, and thank you very much." What d'you make of that?'

'Weird,' Merrily said. 'I—'

I don't understand… What have I been doing wrong? She heard the words, with their long, cathedral echo, saw a woman of about sixty, distressed, walking away in her sensible boots, her tweed coat, her…

'Mrs Thorpe, does your mother ever wear a green velvet hat, sort of Tudor-looking?'

Go away. Go away, Canon Dobbs had hissed. *I can't possibly discuss this here.*

Oh my God, Jane thought. *They are. They really are. An item!*

In the corner café, she and Lol had a slab of chocolate fudge cake each, which they had to take turns in forking up because the table had one leg shorter than the other three.

'So, like, this is serious, right? You and Moon.'

'We're just…'

'Good friends?'

'Kind of.' He seemed uncomfortable discussing Moon. She must be a good ten years younger. Not that that mattered, of course. Jane was a good *twenty* years younger than Lol, and she quite…

Anyway.

'So you're kind of looking after her flat here, while she's doing up this barn?'

'Sort of. Her family came from Dinedor Hill and she's always been keen to move back. Er... how's your mum?'

'Oh, you remember her? How *sweet*. She's OK. In fact she's actually working a couple of days a week out of an office just a few hundred yards from here.'

'Really?' He looked up.

'In the Bishop's Palace gatehouse. I haven't been there yet, but I gather it's cool.'

'What's she doing there?'

'*Not* so cool. She's been appointed Deliverance minister. You know – like used to be called exorcist? Like in that film where the kid's head does a complete circle while she's throwing up green bile and masturbating with a crucifix? Mum now gets to deal with people like that. Only, of course, there aren't many people like that, not in these parts – which is why it's such a dodgy job.'

Lol put down his cake fork. He looked concerned. 'Why would she want to do it?'

'Because she thinks the Church should be in a position to give advice on the paranormal, and there was nobody around to give *her* advice when she needed it.'

'I remember.'

'The question you should be asking is why would *they* want her to do that? And *I* think it's to put a pretty face on a fairly nasty, reactionary business. Like, for instance, they'd say that the reason there isn't much about ghosts in the Bible is that God doesn't want us to mess with ghosts, or study our own inner consciousness, that kind of thing. God just wants us to toddle off to church on a Sunday, otherwise keep our noses out.'

'That wouldn't necessarily be bad advice for everybody,' Lol said, and she could sense he was thinking about something in particular.

'That's the wimp's attitude, Mr Robinson.'

'Absolutely. And somebody's who's been banged up with mad people, and even madder psychiatrists.'

'So does that mean you'll be avoiding Mum like the plague?'

'Oh that's... not a problem. I've had the plague.'

What was on his mind? Did he still have feelings for Mum, despite the exquisite Moon? Or maybe she wasn't such a trophy.

'Lol?'

'Mmm?'

'Something bothering you?'

'Er...' Lol ate the last bit of his fudge cake. 'In the film – with the kid's head spinning round and the green bile and the crucifix? All that doesn't happen simultaneously.'

'What are you on about?'

'Those're completely different scenes – in the film.'

'Thank you, Lol,' Jane said, annoyed with him now. 'I'll tell Mum. She'll be ever so reassured.'

The care assistant's name was Helen Matthews. She lived in Hay-on-Wye, about five miles away. She was about thirty, had two young children, seemed balanced, reliable. 'It's the kids I worry about,' she said, and Merrily was reminded of the poor woman in the Deliverance Study Group video, who'd said something similar. 'I wouldn't want to go taking anything back to them, see.'

Despite having dependants and an iffy husband, the woman in the video had still killed herself – clear evidence that paranormal events could drastically affect a person's mental equilibrium.

Not a problem here. Merrily felt on relatively firm ground with this one.

'From what you say, this is what we call an *imprint*, and it usually belongs to a place. It won't follow you. It can't get into you. You can't take it away. It's like a colour-slide projected on a wall.'

'Mrs Watkins…' Helen Matthews was at the edge of the sofa. She wore a white coat, her short black hair was tied back, and her voice shook. 'You can tell yourself how it won't harm you, how it isn't really there, but when you're on your own in an upstairs passage and it's late at night and all the doors are shut and the lights are turned down and you *know* that… that something is following you, and you finally make… make yourself turn round, to reassure yourself there's nothing there… and there is… *There is.*'

She shuddered so violently it was almost a convulsion. She held on to the sofa, near tears. Even Susan Thorpe looked unnerved.

'OK,' Merrily said gently. 'Let's just be sure about this. You say all the doors were closed and the lights were dimmed. Is it possible one of the doors opened and—'

'No! Definitely not. And if it was… Well, they're all old ladies. There are only old ladies here at present. This was a *man.* Or at least a male… a male *thing.*'

'What did he look like?'

'He looked…' Helen lost it. 'He looked like a bloody *ghost.* He walked out of the wall.'

'Could you see his face?'

'I think he had a moustache. And I think he was wearing a suit. Like in the old black and white films: double-breasted, wide shoulders sort of thing.'

Merrily glanced at Susan Thorpe, who shook her head.

'Description like that, it could have been anyone who lived here over the past three-quarters of a century. We've only been here four years – moved from Hampshire to be near my mother. I mean, there were no old photo albums lying around the place, and it was a guesthouse before we came. It could be anybody.'

'Are there any stories about the house? You're fairly local, Helen. Are there any… I don't really know what I'm looking for.'

'Murders? Suicides? I don't know, but I could ask around in Hay.'

'Christ's sake, don't do that!' Susan Thorpe rose up. 'I know what it's like in Hay. It'll be all over the town in no time. This is a business we're running here. Seven jobs depend on us, so let's not get hysterical. So far, we've managed to conceal it from the residents, let's keep it that way. And anyway, *we* haven't seen anything, and no residents have reported anything in the past four years. Why should this… thing start to appear now?'

'We believe imprints and place-memories can be activated after years and years,' Merrily said. 'Sometimes it's a result of an emotional crisis or a disturbance.'

'Absolutely not! Nothing like that here at all.'

'You said yourself that old people can behave like delin-quents. Sometimes mental instability, senile dementia…'

'Any signs of dementia, they have to go, I'm afraid. We aren't a nursing home. And the only signs of hysteria have been… well, not you, Helen, but certainly your predecessor…'

'*You* didn't see it,' Helen said quietly. 'Have you ever seen one, Mrs Watkins?'

'Possibly. Put it this way, I know what it feels like. I know how frightening it is. But I don't want to overreact either. I don't plan to squirt holy water all over the place. What I'd like to do is go up there now, with both of you, and say a few prayers.'

Susan Thorpe sat up. 'Aloud?'

'Of course, aloud.'

'Oh no, we can't have that. Some of the residents will be in their rooms. They'll hear you.'

Merrily sighed.

'I think it's a good idea,' Helen Matthews said. '*I'll* come.'

'I'm sorry.' Susan Thorpe stood up, adjusted her hairslide. 'I can't have it. Can't you do it outside – out of earshot? God's everywhere, isn't He? Why can't you go outside?'

'I could, but I don't think that would have any effect.'

Helen said, 'If *I've* seen it, Mrs Thorpe, it's only a matter of time before one of the old ladies does. What if someone has a heart attack?'

Merrily thought of the video again, and what Huw had said. *Bottom line is that our man in Northampton should not have left before administering a proper blessing, leaving her in a state of calm, feeling protected.* Yes, suppose someone *did* have a heart attack?

'God,' Susan Thorpe breathed, 'this is getting beyond a joke.'

'It never is a joke,' Merrily said. 'I'm starting to realize that.'

'The problem is finding a time when that passage and all the rooms off it are empty. Look, all right... most of the residents totter off to Hardwicke Church on a Sunday morning, as people of that age tend to. What are you doing tomorrow morning?'

'I'm going to my church, Susan. I'm a vicar.'

'Oh.' Susan Thorpe was unembarrassed. 'You don't do this sort of thing full-time then?' Like this diminished Merrily – a part-timer. Susan became agitated. 'Well, look... look, there's going to be a party. One of the residents is a hundred years old; we're having a small *soirée* for her. I can tell you, old people *never* miss a party. Suppose, while it was on, we could smuggle you upstairs and you could do your little ceremony? You do work at night?'

'Your mother will be here then, I suppose.'

'I should think.'

'I'll see what I can do,' Merrily said.

It would be very interesting to talk to Mrs Thorpe's mother. Five thousand quid, and instructions to be out by the weekend? Either Dobbs really was going out of his mind, or there was something very odd here. She had to go carefully, though: mustn't appear to be checking on him. Casually running into the former housekeeper while processing an *imprint*... that would do fine.

As she left the Glades, Merrily saw that it was snowing lightly out of a sky like stone. Winter deftly gatecrashing autumn's mournful party.

16

Real Stuff

THE STALL WHICH made Jane laugh the most was the one selling something called:

The Circlet of Selene

It looked like three strands of copper wire bound together into a bangle or a necklet and secured by small curtain rings. The wording was a bit careful. It didn't actually promise you more energy, a better night's sleep and a dynamic sex life; it claimed, however, that many people had *found* that all this had *come about* after *only three weeks* of wearing the Circlet of Selene. Which cost a mere £12.75 for the bangle or £17.75 for the necklet, neither of which must have cost more than 75p to produce.

Still, people were buying them – women mostly. Well, ninety per cent of the punters here were women, in fact. The totty-quotient was pretty bloody lamentable, especially in the marquee which had been erected in a field behind the pub. Most of the blokes had stayed in the bar, as blokes were wont to do, and even that wasn't exactly crowded with intriguing, dark-eyed, gipsy-looking guys.

The marquee housed most of the stalls – crystals, incense-burners, cosmic jewellery – though it was far too cold a day for a marquee. You'd think the weather situation might have been foreseen, given the number of self-styled psychics and seers on the premises. Most had clearly taken cover in the pub, where it was warmer, but Jane hadn't felt drawn to consult any of them; they were probably all a bit pricey, too.

'Taste-lapse.' She sipped muddy coffee from a plastic cup. 'Serious, serious taste-lapse, Rowenna.'

They were in a cold corner behind a trestle table displaying lurid healing crystals and supervised by a gross middle-aged couple in matching bobble-hats. Tape-loop relaxation music was trickling out of little speakers, and it got on your nerves.

'I'm sorry.' Rowenna looked around. 'The last one I went to wasn't this bad, really. Oh, there's Kirlian Photography over there. You could have your aura photographed.'

'You ever have yours done?'

'Once. I got a picture of my hand with what looked like little flames coming out of the fingertips.'

'What does it prove?'

'That you've got an aura.'

'If you didn't have an aura you'd be dead, wouldn't you?'

'I'm glad I can't see yours today,' Rowenna said. 'It'd be all dark and negative. You having problems on the domestic front or something?'

'Not to speak of.'

'You can speak to me of anything at all, kitten.' Rowenna touched the tip of Jane's nose with a gloved forefinger. Her floaty red hair was topped by a black velvet beret. The coat she wore just had to be cashmere. She looked far too cool and upmarket for this shoddy bazaar.

'Well, I was talking to this bloke,' Jane said.

'Bloke?'

'A bloke I was sure was seriously into Mum at one time, and—'

'Oh, your mum. How do you mean *into*?'

'Well, not *into* – like not in the fullest sense. I just had it in mind that they'd be good together. He's quite insecure and vulnerable, but also kind of cool. He was a musician and song-writer when he was young – *too* young maybe – and he got led astray and into drugs, and wound up in a mental hospital.'

'The way you do.'

'It's surprising how easily that can happen. Anyway, I don't like guys who are too secure and full of themselves, do you? Like, a certain degree of pathos can be kind of sexy.'

Rowenna looked unimpressed by this. The sound of slow waves breaking on rocks cascaded serenely out of the speakers – which sounded pretty naff in a damp tent in a field near Leominster.

'So I was telling Lol that Mum was now an exorcist, like in that film where the kid gets possessed and spews green bile everywhere, and how there was no call for dealing with stuff like that around here. But like... I mean there is, you know? When you think about it, it's really like that. And, whereas in that film you had these heavy-duty, case-hardened Jesuit priests and even *they* couldn't handle it...'

' "Come into me... come into me," ' Rowenna intoned. 'And then he crashes out of the window to his death. What do you mean, it's really like that?'

'She had this mega-nasty job,' Jane said soberly. 'Nightmare stuff – and, like, no warning, you know?'

'I don't actually believe you.'

'That's all right, I'm not supposed to talk about it anyway.'

'All right, if you tell me I'll buy you a Circlet of Selene.'

'Not good enough. You have to promise never ever to buy me a Circlet of Selene.' It was probably OK to talk about this one, with him being dead and everything. 'All right. Guy in the hospital – this really awful rapist kind of slimeball, gets off on degrading women, and he's dying, OK?'

'OK by me,' said Rowenna.

'But he can't let go of his abiding obsession. You can see it glistening on his skin, like grease.' Jane shivered with a warped sort of pleasure. 'Like, she didn't tell me *all* of this, but I put it together. Anyway, the nurses, they're all like really shit-scared of this pervert, because he's got this totally tainted aura.'

'What was his name?'

'Mr Joy. Isn't that excellent?'

'You're embroidering this.'

'I so am *not*! His name was Denzil Joy, he was in the Watkins Ward, right up at the top of the hospital where it's old and spooky, and the nurses were genuinely scared of him. Takes a lot to scare nurses, all the stuff they've seen.'

'What did he do?'

'She wouldn't say, but I could tell she was still, like, trembling with revulsion hours later. Heavy trauma scenario. What I think it was... was that this man could like make you feel like you'd been raped; he could invade your body just by thinking about what he wanted to do to you. And that got all boiled together with the sickness and the frustration inside him. The nurses are convinced he was possessed.'

'Creepy.'

'The hell with creepy – this was bloody dangerous, if you ask me. And the Bishop just sends her in to sort out this evil scumbag without a second thought, on account of she's like a priest and priests know what to do. But – seriously – is she equipped for this? Does she know what she's doing? Does she hell. Occult-wise, she's probably as naive as all these idiots cooing over the frigging Circlet of Selene. Like, I feel there's probably a lot I could tell her – to help, you know – but would she listen?'

'Jane,' Rowenna said, 'listen to me. You cannot change other people – only yourself. In the end, the winners in this life are the people who go in with their eyes open and say: I'm not going to let God or Nature or the Bishop of Hereford or whoever fuck about with me. *I'm* going to call the shots.'

'Right,' Jane said. 'I suppose that's right.'

'And it's great if you can actually see that while you're still young enough to do something about it – like us, you know?'

And, of course, Jane knew it *was* right. When someone like Rowenna, who was just that bit older and a cool person too, said *this* is right, it conferred a kind of responsibility. You felt you had to do something about it.

She tossed her paper cup into a litter bucket. 'Let's get out of this amusement arcade.'

'Good idea,' said Rowenna. 'Go find the real stuff.'

'Huh?'

'This is just a front, isn't it? The real heavy-duty clairvoyants are in little back rooms in the pub.'

'You want to consult a clairvoyant?'

'Check them out, anyway – see if they're genuine. If they're not, it'll just be a laugh.'

'Cost an arm and a leg,' Jane said doubtfully.

'They usually leave the amount up to you. Hey...' Tenderly, Rowenna bent and stroked back Jane's hair and peered into her eyes. 'You're not apprehensive, are you?'

'Christ, no,' said Jane. 'Let's go for it.'

Twice Lol had been down to the shop. Once to see if Moon wanted any help; but she explained that running a record shop wasn't as easy as he might think, and shooed him away. The second time to see what she was doing for lunch; Moon had brought along two apples and a banana.

Moon insisted she was fine. Dick Lyden also said Moon was fine. If Dick was in two minds about anyone it was probably Lol, who'd claimed that Moon was living in squalor in the barn – until Dick had seen the place looking like a suburban villa, and Moon poised like she was ready to serve the canapés.

Denny also seemed a little happier when he called in, appearing at the door of the flat wearing a plaid overcoat and a big hat with a red feather, halfway to a smile.

'She's looking almost healthy,' he conceded. 'Is there something I don't know?'

Lol shrugged. What could he say to him without reference to ghosts or disembowelled crows?

'Listen, I don't mind.' Denny spread himself in the armchair. 'I think it's good. I'm glad, all right?'

'She's working on her book.'

'Book? Oh.' Denny looked uninterested, a touch pained. 'That's not really gonna happen, is it?'

'*Does* your family go all the way back to the Iron Age?'

Denny's smile shut down altogether. 'Could be.'

'Is it a Celtic name, Moon?'

'I really don't know. We weren't always called Moon. A daughter inherited the farm back in the eighteenth century, married a bloke called Moon. Look...' Denny pulled on his earring. 'There's a little something you gotta help me with here, mate.'

'Unblocking drains is not my responsibility. You are the landlord, Dennis.'

'Nothing that simple, little friend. This is a *really* distasteful job. Dick Lyden fill you in about his kid? This Bishop-for-a-day crap – the kid refusing to play along?'

Lol nodded warily. 'If they'd told me at sixteen I'd been picked for Boy Bishop, I'd've tried to get expelled first.'

'This kid attends the Cathedral School,' Denny said. 'So his father pays good money for him to be publicly humiliated in front of his peers.'

Lol brought two lagers from the fridge, as Denny spelled it out. Dick, it seemed, had resorted to bribery: if the boy James swallowed his cool for just a day, Dick would finance a professionally produced CD by James and his rock band.

Lol winced. 'What are they called?'

'Tuneless Little Twats with Fender Strats. Fuck knows, does it matter? I told him you'd do it, Lol.'

'Me?'

'Produce them. You'll get paid, of course.'

'Sod off.'

'Laurence, we're talking EP-length, that's all. Four tracks – two days' work, max. A hundred copies, which is where I make *my* profit. It's common enough these days – how I keep the studio up and running. I said you'd do it. James *knows* your stuff. James even *likes* your stuff.'

'Suppose I hate *his* stuff?'

'Good boy,' said Denny, 'I appreciate this. I said we'd give their material a listen tomorrow afternoon, OK? Good. And I'm glad about Kathy and you. I am really *glad*. God knows, I would do anything, *give* anything to get her away from there. Meanwhile, if she's not alone, that's the best thing I could hope for under the circumstances.'

Lol went still. 'What has she said?'

'I'm her brother,' Denny said. 'She doesn't have to say anything to me.'

Later, after Denny had gone, it started to snow a little.

Lol stood by the window in the dark, looking down into lamplit Church Street/Capuchin Lane, the centuries seeping away along with the colours of the day. It was snowing briskly, all the shops had closed, most of the people had gone. If he leaned into the top corner of the window he could see the blackening tower of the Cathedral. Below him, a young guy guided a young woman gently into a shallow doorway and they embraced.

Lol thought of Moon in her dusty white nightdress.

'*If she's not alone…*'

'Fucking hell, I didn't expect that.' Rowenna had gone in first, and when she came out she raised her eyebrows, pulled Jane over to the door.

'She was good?'

'She *was*, actually.'

'How much?'

'Twenty. I paid for you as well.'

'There was no need for that. I'm not—'

'Forget it. Go on, don't keep her waiting. She might hang a curse on you.'

'Shit,' said Jane.

'That was a joke.'

'Sure.'

She didn't, to be honest, like fortune-tellers one bit, and for the very reasons Rowenna had put to her earlier. Suppose the woman told her she was going to die soon? Or that Mum was? Not that they ever did; they just looked at you sadly from under their headscarves and said: *Take your money back, dearie. All of a sudden I'm not feeling too well…* And that was when you knew they were genuine and your card was marked.

'Go on,' Rowenna hissed.

The booth was just an alcove in the public bar with a wicker screen set up to hide it.

ANGELA.
TAROT READINGS.

Rowenna had opted for her because, like she'd said, she herself knew a bit about the tarot, so would be able to tell if Angela was the real McCoy.

Oh, shit. Another thing Jane didn't like was the way you were kind of putting yourself and your future in someone else's hands. Whatever they wanted to tell you, it would stay with you, colour your dreams, frame your nightmares. *Not* Jane's idea of New Age, which was about self-exploration – wasn't it?

'Jane…'

'Yeah, OK.'

No alternative, no way out. Jane squeezed behind the partition.

17

Wise Women

ANGELA SMILED.

'You look worried,' she said. 'Why is that?'

'I'm not worried.'

'There's no need to be. Have you consulted the tarot before?'

'Once or twice,' Jane lied.

Angela smiled. She was sitting at a long pub table of scratched mahogany with wrought-iron legs. Behind her was a narrow window of frosted glass; the light it shed was cold and grey. It was going rapidly dark out there.

Angela's hands were already in motion, spreading the cards and then gathering them together. Her hands were slender and supple; there were no rings. Suddenly she pushed the full pack in front of Jane.

'Pick them up.'

'Me?'

Angela nodded. She was not what Jane had been expecting: no headscarf, no big brass earrings. Jane saw a long oval face and mid-length ash-blonde hair. She wore a pale linen suit which seemed no more suited to this event than Rowenna's cashmere. Jane reached out for the cards.

'And shuffle them.'

They were quite big cards and Jane was clumsy. Cards kept sliding out as she tried to mix them up. 'Sorry.'

'It's all right, you're doing fine. Now cut the pack.'

Angela's voice was the most unexpected thing. It was warm and surprisingly cultured.

Jane cut the cards and left them in two piles.

'What I want you to understand,' Angela said, 'is that the cards are merely an aid. They form a psychic link between us.' She put the pack together and then lifted her hand sharply as though it had given her an electric shock.

'Oh!'

'What's wrong?'

'Oh, Jane…'

Christ, what's she seen?

Jane said nervously, 'How do you know my name?'

'I'm psychic.' Angela laughed lightly. 'No, your friend told me, of course.'

'What else did she tell you?'

'Well, she certainly didn't tell me how powerful you were. Has no one told you that before?' Angela began to lay out the cards, one on top of another.

'Not that I recall.' Ah. Right. She was beginning to get the picture now.

'They will,' Angela said with calm certainty.

Oh, sure. I wonder how many other people you said that to today. Jane nodded and said nothing. Now she knew it was a scam, she was no longer worried. Did Rowenna realize it was a scam? Of course she did. When she came out she'd just been taking the piss, picking up on Jane's manifest trepidation.

Angela had the cards laid out in a neat semicircle. They were beautifully coloured, and Jane started looking for the ones she'd seen pictures of on the covers of mystery novels: *Death, The Devil, The Hanged Man, The Last Judgement.* But none of these was obvious in the dim light; all the designs were unfamiliar.

Angela placed one card face-down below the others, contemplated it for a moment and then turned it over to reveal a faintly smiling woman in a long white robe, sitting on some sort of throne with mystical symbols and artefacts all around her. There were lights on in the pub, but somehow they didn't penetrate into this alcove, or at least not as far as Angela.

'Tell me something, Jane. What do you know of your ancestors?'

'Sorry?'

'I mean, are you aware of – how can I put this? – wise women, in your family?'

'I guess that depends on what you mean by wise.'

'I'm picking up a… I suppose you would say a tradition. I feel… I believe you have much to inherit. Whether it's immediate ancestry or something further back, it's hard to say, but it's there. It came up immediately, no mistaking it at all. So I double-checked and the cards are reinforcing it. There's a very strong tradition here.'

Mum? Does she mean Mum? Jane found herself holding her breath.

'Do you know what I'm talking about?'

'Well… maybe.' Mum had sometimes talked of experiences she'd had in churches, visions of a cosmic benevolence in blue and gold, the feeling that she really had to—

Don't tell her what Mum is!

Astonishingly, Angela held up a hand. 'No, you don't have to explain – as long as you understand.'

'Yeah.' Jane breathed out. *Jesus Christ.*

Angela was gazing intently at the cards, her attention locked on the layout. She was absolutely still, as though she and the cards were encased in glass. Eventually, without looking up, she said, 'It's a big, big responsibility.'

'Oh.'

'It needs to be nurtured.' Angela turned over two more cards which seemed to be in conjunction. 'Ah, now… there's been a gap in your life, I think. Someone missing. Would you…? Do you perhaps have just the one parent?'

'Yes,' Jane said awed. 'How did you…?'

171

'I don't think that's been such a big handicap for you as it might have been for others. You have reserves of emotional and psychic energy which have been sustaining you. But now that reservoir of psychic energy ought to be plumbed, or it may overflow. That can cause problems.'

'How do you mean?' Jane felt a slow excitement burning somewhere down in her abdomen. She looked at Angela's half-shadowed face and saw intelligence there. And beauty too – fine bones. Angela must be over fifty but Jane thought men would find her awfully sexy.

'Jane, I don't want to alarm you, but if one is given a talent and one fails to develop it, or allows powerful energy to go its own way, it can become misdirected and cause all sorts of problems, physical and mental – chronic ailments, nervous trouble. Quite a lot of people in hospitals and mental institutions are simply people who have failed to recognize and channel certain energies.'

Angela looked up suddenly. Jane saw her eyes clearly for the first time; they were like chips of flint. She was serious about this. She was dead serious.

She said faintly, 'What does that mean?'

Angela reached over and touched her fingers. 'Oh, I'm sorry. Please don't worry. Sometimes I'm concentrating so hard I say the first things that come into my head. It's just so rare that I get anything as clear and specific as this… I'm probably getting carried away.'

'No, please go on.'

'I don't think so.' Angela swept all the cards together. 'I've been overloading you with my own impressions, and that's not a good thing to do. Let's relax a moment and I'll tell you about some less far-reaching aspects of your life.'

She asked Jane to shuffle and cut the pack again, then did a couple of smaller layouts and told Jane a few things about herself and her future which were more in line with the stuff you expected to hear. Well, a bit more *intimate* perhaps…

172

like that she was a virgin but wouldn't be for long. That she would have more than one serious lover before she was twenty.

Jane smiled. At one time she'd have been fairly excited about that, not to say relieved, but right now it didn't seem as vital.

Angela told her that she was extremely intelligent and could have her pick of careers, but she might feel herself drawn towards communications or even performance art.

Cool.

But her main choices – Angela sighed, like she'd tried to get away from this but couldn't – would be in the spiritual realm. Other levels of existence were already becoming accessible to her.

'Other planes,' Angela said, 'other spheres. Someone who has gone before has opened the way. Does that make any sense to you?'

Jane thought at once of her old friend, the late Miss Lucy Devenish, writer of children's stories and proprietor of the magical giftshop called Ledwardine Lore, who had introduced her to rural mysteries and the mystical poetry of Thomas Traherne. And showed her that spirituality was a shining crystal, of which Christianity was only one face.

'What...?' Jane found it hard to speak, her mouth was so dry. 'What do you think I should do?'

'Don't know. It's not for me to say. This is a very personal issue.'

'You can't just leave it like that. I mean, I could buy books and things, but I already do that.'

Angela gathered up the cards. 'Have you had any personal experiences which have mystified you?'

'Maybe. Like, there was this time I kind of fell asleep in a field, and when I awoke I felt as though I'd been someone else. It's like really hard to explain, but—'

'Don't tell me. These are messages for you alone. Look, Jane, what I'm going to do is give you a telephone number. Not mine, because I don't think you should be entirely influenced by one person or feel that you're being pressed from one direction.'

Angela reached down to a handbag on the floor and pulled out a notepad and a pen. Jane felt a welling excitement and also a small, fizzing trepidation as Angela wrote.

'This is the number of a young woman called Sorrel, not far from here. You'll like her. She's very down-to-earth.'

'Who... is she?'

'Just another person with a questing spirit. She runs a health-food restaurant in Hereford and holds meetings there for people of a like mind: to share experiences and consider methods of developing their skills.'

'Sounds a bit... I mean, I'd feel a bit...'

'If you did decide to go, you could always take your friend... Rosemary, was it?'

'Rowenna.' Jane felt *much* better. 'Yeah, that'd be cool. Er... develop skills? What sort of skills do you think I might have?'

'Healing? Clairvoyance? It's not for me to say. Perhaps you can find out.' Angela tore the top page out of her notebook and placed it in front of Jane. 'It's entirely up to you now.'

'Right,' Jane said. 'Right.'

When she stood up, her legs felt cold and trembly.

Moon was pulling down the old-fashioned rollerblind over the CLOSED sign on the door.

All the lights were out except for a brown-shaded one on the counter, so that the air in the shop had a deep-shadowed sepia density. The unsaleable balalaika hung forlornly on the wall behind the till. The low-level music from the speakers each end of the single seventeenth-century beam was by Radiohead at their most suicidal: the one about escaping lest you choked.

Lol swallowed. Moon said to him, as though he'd been here for some time, 'I asked Denny to come over for supper. He said he'd really love to but he was too busy. I knew he'd say that.'

'Well, he probably is. Work's piling up in the studio.'

Moon shook her head. 'It's his wife. Maggie thinks I'm still doing dope – and I'm poison in all sorts of other ways. Plus, he just doesn't want to come to the barn.'

She came to stand next to him. She was wearing a long brown cardigan over a too-much-unbuttoned white cotton blouse and jeans. Something dull and metallic hung from a leather thong around her neck.

'Moon, you can't go home on your bike, in the dark, up that hill. It's snowing hard.'

'I've got good lights – and nothing will touch me on Dinedor.'

'I could try and get it in the back of the car. Or I could take you back in the car now, and pick you up again tomorrow.'

He felt tense – the missing element here, as usual, was lightness. In any situation, Moon was a solemn person: no humour, no banter. As if all the family's irony genes had been been used up on Denny sixteen years before she was born.

'Silly making two trips,' Moon argued.

'I don't mind, really.'

'Or you could stay,' Moon said. 'Why not stay over?'

She was very close to him. 'What exactly did Denny say to you?'

'He said… that he was glad you weren't on your own.'

Moon laughed lightly.

'What did you tell him, Moon?'

'It doesn't matter. Poor Denny.' Moon took Lol's left hand and held it between both of hers. They were slim hands but strong, hardened by delving in the earth. 'And stupid Dick. I can't believe how timid and stupid people can be. Dick and his feeble psychology; Denny hiding behind a wall against the past. And you?' She looked closely at his hand. 'Are you timid too?'

'Oh, I'm more timid than any of them,' Lol said.

'What of? What are you frightened of, Lol?'

She was standing close enough now for him to see that there was dust on her blouse. She seemed to attract dust. *Dust of ages*, Lol thought. The past had become attracted to her.

A long way away, Radiohead were playing *Karma Police*, about what you got if you messed with Us; he could hardly hear it for the drumming in his head.

'I think I'm frightened of you,' Lol whispered in shame, 'and I don't know why.'

The movements were so minimal that he'd hardly noticed her creeping into his arms, until they were kissing and his hands were in the long, long hair and something flared inside him like when you finally put a match to a long-prepared fire of brittle paper and dry kindling.

'So what are you going to do?' Rowenna asked, as they drove into Ledwardine marketplace, which had a lacing of snow.

'Stop just here for a while,' Jane said. 'You haven't even told me what she said to *you*.'

The cobbled square, with its little timbered market-hall, was lit by electric gaslamps on wrought-iron poles and brackets. Rowenna parked under one of these, and its light turned her hair into shivering spirals of rose-gold.

'She told me my spiritual progression would be very much bound up with a friend's.'

'Oh, gosh.'

There were only two cars on the square, both in front of the Black Swan. There was a light visible between the trees which screened the vicarage, and Jane thought she could see a cluster of early stars around the tip of the church steeple, but that might just have been snow. She just so much wanted this to be a magical night.

'So, are you going to phone this other woman, kitten?'

'It's a big step.'

'No, it isn't. You can check it out first, and if it sounds iffy you don't get involved.'

'*I* don't get involved?'

'All right, *we* don't.'

'What about Mum?'

'We don't have to invite her, do we?'

'You know what I mean. Right now, she would not be cool about this. She's insecure enough as it is.'

'Of course she's insecure. She's a Christian.'

'I don't think I can do it to her.'

'You're not doing anything to her!'

'I'd be lying.'

'They expect us to lie,' Rowenna said.

The snow made spangles in the fake gaslight.

'I need to think about this.'

'Well, don't think too long. Like Angela said, repressing it may seriously damage your health.'

Jane sighed. The village seemed deserted. Through the snow-flakes, the light in the vicarage looked very far away.

18

Overhead Cables Cut

'WHERE DID YOU get to, flower?'

'Oh, Hereford and places. Shopping and stuff.'

'What did you buy?'

'Nothing much. Rowenna got… some things.'

'She seems to have a lot of money,' Merrily said, heating soup at the stove. 'I suppose she's indulged quite a bit, having to be dragged around the country with her father stationed at different bases.'

'Yeah,' Jane said noncommittally. She'd arrived home about seven – looking a bit pale, Merrily thought. Outside, it was snowing quite hard and sticking impressively to the ground and the trees. November snow; it couldn't last, surely.

'Where did Rowenna live before?'

'What's this about?' said Jane.

'Just interest. You seem to be spending a lot of time with her, that's all.'

'That,' said Jane, 'is because she's interesting. They were at Malmesbury in Wiltshire. Her dad was with the Army at Salisbury or somewhere. They don't like to talk about it, the SAS, so I don't ask. Satisfied?'

Later, she said, 'I'm sorry, Mum. I'm being a pig. Tired, that's all. I think I'll have an early night.'

Merrily didn't argue; she wanted to be up early herself. She suspected there'd be a bigger congregation tomorrow than usual; people always liked going to church in the snow.

She was in bed by eleven, with a hot-water bottle. Less than ten minutes later, the phone bleeped.

'Ledwardine Vic—'

'Merrily, it's Sophie at the Bishop's office. I'm terribly sorry to bother you, but we're having a problem – at the Cathedral. I wonder, could you perhaps come over?'

Big grey snowflakes tumbled against the window. Merrily sat up in bed. It had never felt so cold in here before.

'What's happened?'

'I… it involves Canon Dobbs. I don't like to say too much on the phone.'

Merrily switched on the bedside lamp. 'Give me half an hour. Maybe forty-five minutes if the roads are bad.'

'Oh God, yes, I didn't realize. Do be careful.'

'I'll see you soon.'

When she came out of the bedroom, buttoning her jeans, she found Jane on the landing. 'I heard the phone.' She was in her dressing-gown, and mustn't have been asleep.

'Some kind of problem at the Cathedral.'

'Why should that concern *you*?'

'I don't really know.'

'Shall I come? It looks a bit rough out there.'

'God, no. You get back to bed.'

'What if you get stuck? These roads can be really nasty and the council's mega-slow off the mark – like about three days, apparently.'

'It's a big car. I'll be fine.'

'This is like Deliverance business again, isn't it?'

'To be honest, I just don't know.'

'Talk about secrecy,' Jane said, strangely wide awake. 'You Deliverance guys make the SAS seem like double-glazing salesmen.'

* * *

Why had she imagined the Cathedral would be all lit up? Maybe because that was how she'd been hoping to find it: a beacon of Old Christian warmth and strength.

But in the snow and the night, she was more than ever aware of how set-apart it had become. Once it had stood almost next to the medieval castle, two powerhouses together; now the city was growing away from the river, and the castle had vanished. The Cathedral crouched, black on white, like the Church at bay.

Merrily parked on Broad Street, near the central library. The dashboard clock, always five to ten minutes fast, indicated near-midnight. It had been a grindingly slow journey, with her window wound down to let the cigarette smoke out and the arctic air in, just to keep her awake. She'd taken the longer, wider route east of the Wye, where there was always some traffic, even the chance of snowploughing if anyone in the highways department had happened to notice a change in the weather. The road-surface was white and brown and treacherous, snow-lagged trees slumped over it like gross cauliflowers.

It all still seemed so unlikely – what would Hunter want with her at this time of night? Was he trying to turn Deliverance into the Fourth Emergency Service?

Merrily locked the Volvo, put on her gloves, pulled up her hood and set out across the snow-quilted silence of Broad Street.

No one about, not even a drunk in view. No traffic at all. The city centre as you rarely saw it: luminous and Christmas-card serene, snowflakes like big stars against the blue-black. Merrily's booted steps were muted on the padded pavement. Behind her only the Green Dragon had lights on. She felt conspicuous. There was no sign of the Bishop or the Bishop's men. Hadn't a woman once been raped in the Cathedral's shadow? Hadn't the last time she'd been called out at night...?

Christ be with me, Christ within me.

The Cathedral was towered and turreted, the paths and the green lawns submerged together in snow, a white moat around God's fortress. But no other night defences; its guardians – the canons and the vergers – were sleeping in the warren of cloisters behind. Nobody about except...

'Merrily!'

Sophie came hurrying around the building, towards the North Porch, following the bouncing beam of a torch attached to a large shadow beside her.

Merrily breathed normally again.

'Thank heavens you made it.' The Bishop's secretary lived not five minutes' walk away, in a quiet Victorian villa near the Castle Green. She wore a long sheepskin coat, her white hair coming apart under a woollen scarf. 'We were just wondering whether to call Michael, after all.'

'But I thought the Bishop—'

'He doesn't know anything about this,' Sophie said quickly. 'Do you know George Curtiss?'

'Good evening, Mrs Watkins. I, ah, think we have met.'

'Oh, yes. Hello.' He was one of the Cathedral canons: a big, overcoated man with a beard of Greek Orthodox proportions and a surprisingly hesitant reedy voice.

'George called me to ask if we should tell Michael about this,' Sophie said. 'But I suggested we consult you. This is all very difficult.'

'Look, I'm sorry... Am I supposed to know what's happening?'

'You tell her, George.'

'Yes, it's... Oh dear.' George Curtiss glanced behind him to make sure they were alone, bringing down his voice. 'It's about old, ah, Tom Dobbs, I'm afraid.'

'Merrily,' Sophie was hugging herself, 'he's virtually barricaded himself in. We think he's...'

'Drunk, I rather fear,' George said.

'What?'

'He's behind that partition,' Sophie said. 'You know, where they're repairing the Cantilupe tomb?'

'He's in there with—?'

'Chained and padlocked himself in. He won't talk to us. He's just rambling. To someone else? To himself? I don't know. Rambling on and on. Neither of us understands, but I just... well, I rather suspected you might. It's all... it's rather frightening, actually.'

'So there is a' – Merrily swallowed – 'a Deliverance context?'

What a stupid question.

'Oh, yes,' Sophie said, 'I think so. Don't you?'

George Curtiss shuffled impatiently. 'I trust we can, ah, rely on your discretion, Mrs Watkins. I know he's an odd character, but I do have a long-standing admiration for the man. As does... as does the Dean.'

'But I don't know him. I've never even spoken to him.'

'He's, ah, had his problems,' George said. 'Feels rather beleaguered – threatened by... by certain recent developments. In view of these, we'd rather avoid involving the Dean – or the Bishop – at this stage.'

'But I don't *know* him. And he—'

'But you know what he *does*, Merrily,' Sophie whispered urgently.

'Do I?'

'Mrs Watkins.' George Curtis coughed. 'We all know what he *does*, if not the, ah, technicalities of it. It's just we're a little nervous about what's... going on in there.'

'You want me to try and talk to him?'

'Just listen, I suppose.' Sophie tightened her scarf. 'Interpret for us.'

'My Latin isn't what it used to be,' George said.

'Latin?'

George dragged a long breath through the brambles of his beard, but his voice still came out weakly. 'My impression is he's talking to, ah... to, ah... to St Thomas.'

'I don't understand,' Merrily said.

Sophie almost snapped at her, 'You think *we* do?'

They followed George Curtiss and his torch around the building to St John's door, which was used mainly by the clergy and the vergers. Snow was already spattered up the nearby walls.

'We'll go in very quietly,' George said, as though addressing a party of schoolchildren – he was one of the regular tour-guides, Merrily recalled. 'I sometimes think the Dean has ultrasonic hearing.'

Merrily stepped warily inside – as if a mad-eyed Dobbs might come rampaging at them, swinging his crucifix.

Drunk? If Dobbs had a drink problem, it was the first she'd heard about it. But if the old exorcist had become a public embarrassment, the Dean could no longer be seen to support him. That way the Dean would himself lose face. And if the Bishop found out, he would make the most of it – in the most *discreet* way, of course – to strengthen his position as an engine of reform, get rid of Dobbs, and perhaps the Dean as well.

Can of worms!

Although it felt no warmer inside, Merrily unzipped her waxed coat and put a hand to the bump in her sweater, her pectoral cross.

This was because the atmosphere in the Cathedral was different.

Live?

Sophie touched her arm. 'Are you all right?'

'Yes.' Merrily remembered reading once that gothic churches somehow recharged themselves at night, like battery packs. She felt again the powerful inner call to prayer she'd experienced on the afternoon she'd emerged from the shell-like chantry to encounter Dobbs and the woman.

'I won't put on any lights,' George whispered. 'Don't want to draw undue, ah… attention.'

He snapped off his torch for a moment. The only illumination now was the little aumbry light over the cupboard holding the emergency sacrament: wine and wafers in a silver container. Merrily felt a desperate, vibrating desire to kneel before it.

There was no sound at all.

'All right.' George switched on his torch again, and they followed its bobbing beam through the Lady Chapel and into the North Transept, where the great stained-glass window reared over the temporary screening partition hiding the dismantled tomb of St Thomas Cantilupe. George shone his torch over the various posters drawing-pinned to it, telling the story of Cantilupe – a wise and caring bishop, according to the Cathedral guidebook, who stood firm against evil in all its guises.

George stopped and called out harshly, 'Thomas?' as though he hadn't intended to – as though the word had been wrenched out of him.

Merrily quivered for an instant.

Thomas? – as if he was summoning the spirit of Cantilupe.

He might as well have been. There was no response.

Merrily looked at Sophie. 'You're sure he's still…?'

George moved across and shone his torch on the plywood partition door. Merrily remembered a padlocked chain connecting steel staples on the outside.

'All this will be taken down quite soon,' George said. 'They're putting the tomb back together next week.'

The chain appeared to have been dragged inside through a half-inch crack between the ill-fitting door and its frame. Dobbs – or someone else – had to be still behind it.

Merrily said, 'Do you feel anything?'

'I feel quite annoyed, actually,' Sophie muttered. 'Why isn't he doing… what he was doing earlier? You'll think we only dragged you here on a such a dreadful night on some sort of perverse whim.'

'No. The atmosphere, Sophie – the atmosphere's somehow…
I don't know… disarranged.'

'How do you mean?'

'I don't know. I've never been in here at night before. Not like this, anyway.'

She had a feeling of overhead cables cut, slashed through. Of them hanging down now, still live and dangerous.

'Thomas?' George rapped on the plywood door. 'Thomas, it's George. Getting a bit anxious about you, old chap.'

'Something's happened,' Merrily said suddenly. 'Can you break it down?'

'Thomas!' George slapped the partition with a leather-gloved hand. 'Are you there?'

'Break it down!'

He swung round. 'This is a cathedral, Mrs Watkins.'

'Maybe you can snap the chain?'

'I can't even *reach* the chain.'

'Kick the door.'

'I… I can't.'

Merrily hurriedly unzipped her coat and slipped out of it. 'Stand back, then. I'll do it.'

'No, I… Thomas! For God's sake!' George put an ear to the crack between the door and the frame. 'Stop… wait… I can hear…'

Merrily went still.

'I can hear him breathing,' George said. 'Can you hear that?'

She turned her back to the plywood screen, steadying her own breathing. She rubbed her eyes. *Think practically, think rationally.* When she turned back, both George and Sophie were staring at her. And the air in the high transept was still invisibly untidy with snipped wires.

'All right.' Big George began to unbutton his overcoat. 'I'll do it.'

He wore fat, black boots. Doc Martens probably, size eleven at least. With equipment like that, he could bring the whole damned partition crashing down.

He gave Merrily the rubber-covered torch, which felt moist. By its light, she saw that his brown eyes were wide and scared, and a froth of spittle glistened in his beard.

'Christ be with us,' Merrily heard herself saying.

19

Costume Drama

SIREN WARBLING, BLUE beacons strobing – violently beautiful over the snow – the ambulance broke the rules by cutting from Broad Street across the Cathedral Green.

Merrily stood outside St John's door with Sophie. Feeling useless.

Even in his condition, Dobbs had reared up from the stones at the sight of her, one arm hanging limp, and his face like a waxwork melting down one side. George Curtiss had then taken charge, suggesting she and Sophie should phone for help from the office in the gatehouse.

Merrily had glanced back once before they hurried away, and had seen George fumbling at the wall under the aumbry light.

'The sacrament.' Sophie had started to shake. 'Oh, dear God, he's asked for the sacrament.'

Merrily wasn't sure Dobbs had been in any condition, at the time, to voice a request; this was probably George's own decision. Probably a wise one.

She and Sophie stood back while the paramedics brought the old man out. Multiple headlights creaming the snow and more people gathering – one of the vergers, a couple of policemen.

And the Right Reverend Michael Hunter loping towards them. The Bishop in a purple tracksuit.

'Merrily, what on earth are you doing here?'

'Michael, I sent for her,' Sophie explained at once. 'I thought—'

'That's good,' the Bishop said. 'That's fine. Entirely appropriate.'

Summoned from his bed, no doubt, by the ambulance siren, he seemed neither cold nor tired. Merrily could almost see his athlete's glow as an actual halo as he raised a palm over the two women, like a blessing.

'Poor Canon Dobbs,' Sophie said.

The Bishop nodded. 'A good and distinguished servant of God.'

Huh? Merrily recalled their discussion in the Green Dragon. *'The old man's ubiquitous. Hovering silently, like some dark, malign spectre. I'd like to... I want to exorcize Dobbs.'*

Classic episcopal hypocrisy.

'But he worked himself too hard – and for too long,' the Bishop said. 'A stroke, I gather.'

'Yes,' Merrily said, 'that's what it looks like.'

'No!' Cool, efficient Sophie started to cry. '*Two* strokes. It must have been two, don't you see? We thought he must be... must have been drinking. When we heard his voice all slurred, in fact he was simply struggling to speak after a first stroke – probably only a minor one. And then... I remember my father... Oh God, how stupid we were, how utterly thoughtless.'

'Sophie,' Merrily said, 'if it wasn't for you, he might still be lying there.'

'Perhaps it was us shouting at him to come out... perhaps all the fuss threw him into some sort of confused panic and that was what brought on the second stroke.'

'Sophie, listen.' The Bishop took his secretary by both shoulders, then eased back her scarf so as to look into her eyes. 'We all knew that Thomas was long, long overdue for retirement. His particular ministry put him under enormous pressure. Several of us, as you know, tried very hard to persuade him to give it up. I think it was becoming explicitly clear to everyone that this good man's mind was breaking down. Hey, watch yourself...'

He guided Sophie out of the path of the ambulance as it started up, preparing to bear the stricken Dobbs to the General

Hospital. George Curtiss appeared from behind it, breathing hard through his beard.

'Bishop...'

'Well done, George.'

'I'm afraid I didn't do enough.'

'I'm sure you did everything humanly possible,' Mick Hunter said – then, after a pause, 'except to inform your bishop.'

'Oh, yes. I, ah, thought... hoped... that it wouldn't be necessary to involve you – or the Dean.'

'I want to be appraised of *everything*, George. You won't forget that again, will you?'

'No.' The big canon, a good ten years older than the Bishop, looked like a chastized schoolboy. 'I'm sorry, Bishop.'

'Get some sleep. We'll talk about this tomorrow. Merrily—'

'Bishop?' She was annoyed at the way he'd spoken to George, who'd administered the sacrament to Dobbs, stayed with him, tried to make him comfortable, keep him calm.

The Bishop said, 'What was Canon Dobbs actually doing when you found him?'

'He was having a stroke, Bishop,' Merrily said wearily.

Mick Hunter was silent.

'I'm sorry,' Merrily said. 'It's been a difficult night.'

'Has it? I see. I'll talk to you on Monday, Merrily. This is obviously going to have a bearing on your situation.' He turned and walked towards the Cathedral.

'I thought for a moment he was going to say something about God moving in mysterious ways,' Merrily muttered, 'to clear the way for the new regime.'

'He's wearing trainers,' Sophie said absently. 'His poor feet must be absolutely soaked.'

'Wellies wouldn't fit the image.'

'He's more than image, Merrily,' Sophie said quietly. 'I think you know that. He's a very young man. One day he'll be a great man, I should think.'

One day he'll probably be an archbishop, Merrily thought. *But I doubt he'll be a great man.*

But she'd said enough.

'Thank you for coming,' Sophie said, 'though clearly it wasn't a terribly good idea.'

'Sophie...' Merrily glanced over her shoulder at the Cathedral, which – although someone, probably the Bishop, had put on lights – was still not the imagined beacon of old Christian warmth, not now. 'When George said Dobbs was talking to Thomas Cantilupe, what did he mean by that?'

Sophie appeared uncomfortable. 'Does that matter now?'

'Yeah, I think it does.'

'That was George's surmise. I thought he was talking to himself. Thomas, you see – both of them Thomases. It was as though he... perhaps he was already feeling ill and he was urging himself to hold on.'

'What were his words?'

'Well, like that. He did actually say that at least once: "Please God, hold on, Thomas." And then he'd lapse into mumbling Latin.'

'How did he get *in*? Does he have keys?'

'He must have.'

'Does he often come here alone at night?'

'It...' Sophie sighed. 'So they say.'

'What else do they say?'

'They say he has rather an obsession with St Thomas Cantilupe. I do know he studied the medieval Church, so perhaps he sought some sort of deeper communion with the saint, on a spiritual level. I don't like to—'

'You mean because the tomb was lying open, for the first time in over a century, he thought the saint would be more accessible? You have to help me here, Sophie. I don't understand.'

'I don't know what to say,' Sophie said. 'I don't feel it's right to talk about it now, with the poor man probably dying. I mean, George gave him the *sacrament*.'

'Sophie, just let me get this right. Are you saying you called me in because you and George thought Canon Dobbs was attempting to make contact with a dead saint?'

'I don't *know*, Merrily.' Sophie was wringing the ends of her scarf. 'Look, I just wanted to protect… Oh, I don't know *who* I wanted to protect. The Bishop? Canon Dobbs? Or just the Cathedral? In the end it all comes back to the Cathedral, doesn't it? I…' She stamped a booted foot on the snow as if to emphasize it to herself. 'I work for the Cathedral.'

'Is there something… is there a problem in the Cathedral? Is that what you're trying to say?'

Maybe she should talk to George, who was still with the two policemen beside their car at the roadside.

'Can we talk about this… again?' Sophie said.

'If I'm going to help, you've got to trust me.'

'I *do* trust you, Merrily. That's why I telephoned for you. And I feel guilty now – you look so awfully tired. Do you really have to drive back? The roads are going to be dreadful.'

'No worse than when I came. I think the snow's stopping anyway.'

'But it'll probably freeze on top. That's rather treacherous – and it's always a little warmer in the city. Look, why don't you stay with us tonight? We always keep a room prepared, and Andrew will have hot chocolate ready.'

'Well, thanks. But there's Jane at home. And tomorrow's services.'

'I do feel so guilty about bringing you here.'

'Don't worry, I won't fall asleep at the wheel. I'll smoke.'

'Hmm,' Sophie said disapprovingly.

'Good night, Sophie.'

Watching Sophie walk away towards warmth and hot chocolate, Merrily felt damp and chilled inside her thinning fake-Barbour. She saw the police car pulling away into Broad Street, and George Curtiss had already gone.

Fatigue had induced detachment. She didn't *want* to be detached. She remembered how, when she and Sophie and George had first entered the Cathedral tonight, the urge to pray had washed over her like surf, a tide of need. *Dobbs's need?*

That had gone now; her prayers weren't needed – or not so urgently. She ought to have obeyed that call, fallen to her knees, and the whole bit.

Bloody Anglican reserve. The Church of the Stiff Upper Lip.

Abruptly, Merrily went back into the Cathedral, to pray for Dobbs, before it was all locked up again. Knowing she would make for the place where George had kicked down a partition door: the Cantilupe fragments.

What did she know about Cantilupe? Bishop of Hereford in the late thirteenth century. Born into a wealthy Norman baronial family. Educated for the Church. A political career before he came to Hereford in middle age, in the reign of Edward I. A row with the Archbishop of Canterbury which got him excommunicated. Reinstatement, then death, then sainthood. Then the miracles, dozens of miracles around the shrine: the tomb that no longer had a body in it, and that was now in pieces.

The aumbry light still shone: a relic of the medieval Church, seldom needed now. Tonight another medieval relic had required the last rites.

Merrily realized she very much did not want Dobbs to die. She went down on her knees, on the hard coldness, before the aumbry light itself. *Let him live. Please God, let him survive. Build some kind of bridge between us. Throw down some quiet light. Let there be...*

Useless, incoherent – she was just too tired. She couldn't find the words to explain herself.

'Merrily.'

She opened her eyes.

'I'm sorry I was so abrupt, Merrily. It wasn't you – it was me, I'm sorry. I felt excluded.'

The late-night DJ voice, resonant, burnt-umber. She should have realized he'd still be here. Perhaps she had.

'Hello, Mick.'

The Bishop extended a hand. He was very strong, and suddenly she was on her feet again.

'You look very tired,' Mick said. 'I hear you've been working hard tonight.'

'*Finding* it hard, that's all.'

'As you're bound to.' His lean face was crinkled by a sympathetic, closed-mouth smile. He surveyed her in the mellow light. 'It's a very taxing role: social worker, psychotherapist and virtuoso stage-performer, all rolled into one.'

'Stage-performer?'

'We're all of us actors, Merrily. The Church is a faded but still fabulous costume drama.'

'Oh.'

'And, to survive, it has to be considerably more sophisticated these days. Poor Dobbs is strictly Hammer Films, I'm afraid. He should retire, if he recovers, to one of those nice rural nursing homes for ageing clerics. There to write his memoirs, don't you think?'

'I don't know what I think.'

'You're overtired,' Mick said. 'Poor baby, I'm not going to let you drive home, you realize that.'

'It's only twenty minutes.' He was offering to drive her?

'In these conditions? At least an hour – and requiring rather more attention than I suspect you'd be able to summon. Consider this an executive ruling. Come to the Palace. We've lots of spare rooms I always feel guilty about. Perhaps we should make some available to selected homeless people, what do you think?'

'I think it would be very much an unnecessary imposition on Mrs Hunter.'

'What, accommodating the homeless? Or accommodating you? Either way, not a problem. Valentina's away for a couple of days, visiting her ageing parents in the Cotswolds. Old Church, Val's father – yesterday's Church. We have endless and insoluble theological arguments, so these days I tend to plead pressure of work.'

Merrily smiled. 'Look, it's very kind of you, Mick. It's just—' She moved self-consciously towards St John's door.

'*You*' – he followed her – 'need all your strength. Just let others look after you sometimes. We can get you back in good time for tomorrow's services, if that's what you're worried about. We have a wonderful old Land Rover at our disposal.'

'There's Jane, you know?'

'Jane?'

'My daughter.'

She thought he blinked. 'She's not a child any more, is she? She must be getting quite used to your nocturnal comings and goings.'

'I suppose she is.'

'Well, then…'

He put his hands on her shoulders, as he had on Sophie's earlier. His hands were big and firm and warm.

'Merrily, you have to stop shouldering the problems of the world. Besides, it would be a good opportunity for us to talk about the future. It'll be impossible to keep this out of the papers, you know, especially if the old guy dies on us. We need to be ready, hmm?'

As Mick Hunter lowered his arms from her shoulders, his head bent quickly, and she was sure his lips touched her forehead just once, on the hairline.

'This means we can stop quietly phasing you in and officially announce the establishment of a Deliverance consultancy. We need to discuss how we're going to handle that.'

'But not tonight.'

'Oh no, not tonight. Tomorrow.' He paused. 'Over our breakfast, perhaps.'

The way he said *our* breakfast. The way he had his arms by his sides now, but had not stepped back. The way he seemed to be closer than when his hands had been on her. She felt an awful compulsion to fall forward, collapse into that strong, muscular episcopal chest.

'Up to you, of course,' he said. 'Coincidentally, we've just had a guest suite refurbished. Bathroom with shower, small sitting room – that sort of set-up. You may find you have to overnight in Hereford quite often as your role expands. Consider it available at any time. As you'll be reporting exclusively to me, it would seem like an arrangement with considerable... possibilities, you know.'

She stayed silent, giving him an opportunity to qualify that, but he didn't. He just stood there gazing at her, and after a moment he calmly folded his arms – sometimes a defensive gesture, but not this time.

No, this couldn't be? Couldn't possibly be how it sounded.

'Everything's changing, Merrily,' Mick said easily. 'This is a time of transition when traditional values, old restrictions, should be allowed to drift away. We should stop presuming to know what God wants of us.'

Merrily backed against the door, needing cold air, space.

'We should be prepared to experiment,' Mick continued calmly, 'until the waters settle and we know where we are again. For a while.'

He followed her out of the Cathedral, leaving the door for the verger to lock. Outside, an unreal mauvish mist was gathering around white roofs, over white pavements, the grey-white road. A Christmas-card Hereford, out of time. Mick Hunter, in his purple tracksuit, seemed part of the picture. Part of the illusion. Not real.

'See, no traffic at all,' he said. 'Earlier, I believe, the TV and radio stations were warning motorists not to venture out unless it was absolutely vital.'

Time of transition? In the tingling mist, Merrily felt as though she was being drawn into a developing, lucid dream and had to go with it – some of the way, at least – to see if its destination could possibly be what she was half-imagining.

Or make a wild dash across Broad Street for her car. Or…

She heard Jane saying, *It's probably considered socially OK to fuck a bishop*, and felt appalled.

'Mick, look, I actually think it's beginning to thaw. I can be home in half an hour.'

'Nonsense. Merrily, you know you don't really want to do that.'

'I have to.'

She began to walk away from him towards the road, and then stopped and turned as the Bishop spoke again with quiet insistence.

'You only *have* to do what you want to do.'

'That's not true…'

This was not the Bishop talking but the bulge in his tracksuit trousers. She closed her eyes briefly and wished him gone.

'Oh… Excuse me, miss.'

A man stepped out from behind one of the trees like some accosting beggar – one of those homeless that Mick and Val would *not* be accommodating at the Palace.

'Not now,' the Bishop told him irritably.

'Sorry, sir. Not you – the lady. Are you by any chance the lady whose daughter ordered a minicab?'

'Huh?'

'Mrs Watson?'

'Watkins.'

'Yeah, that's it.'

Mick Hunter didn't move. Merrily shrugged and gave him a bashful smile. 'I didn't know she'd done that. Kid does my thinking for me. Thanks anyway, Bishop. What time do you want to see me on Monday?'

'Eleven o'clock,' the Bishop said tonelessly, 'in the Great Hall.'

She nodded.

'Good night,' he said.

'It's this way,' said the cabbie.

Mick Hunter had vanished by the time she found out that the cabbie did not have a vehicle with him.

20

Not Good

THEY WALKED IN silence a short way along Broad Street until Merrily was sure the Bishop had returned to the Palace. Then Lol Robinson hurried her discreetly across the whitened green and into Church Street.

'Little Jane called me, about half an hour ago. Said you were heading this way and you might be able to use a cup of coffee at some stage. I've just been... hanging around.'

'So intuitive, that kid.' God, she was pleased to see him. Although, under the circumstances, anybody at all would have been a serious blessing.

'I think she was worried about you,' he said.

Merrily smiled. 'I'm sure.' She felt light-headed – glad, for the first time she could remember, to be out of the Cathedral.

'Who was that guy in the tracksuit?' Lol unlocked a recessed door in the alleyway next to the little music shop.

'That, Laurence, was the Bishop of Hereford.'

'Oh, I see.' Lol wore nothing over the familiar black sweatshirt with the Roswell alien face printed on it in flaking grey. He must be freezing. 'I had him down as some late-night jogger, who... I don't really know.'

'Thought I was a prostitute.'

'Like you always find in the Cathedral Close.' Lol grinned. 'Who was the bloke they put in the ambulance?'

'Canon Dobbs. He's had a stroke. We found him collapsed in the Cathedral.'

'Oh.' Lol shouldered the door open and turned on the light. They entered a hallway with a flight of stairs and a mountain-bike.

'They called me in,' Merrily said, 'because he was... still *is* the last diocesan exorcist. You know about all that, I suppose.'

'Well, you know, I've talked to Jane.'

'Then you know everything.'

She looked around the shapeless, lamplit room with its beams and trusses and sash windows with lots of little square panes. Lol's old guitar rested on a metal stand by the bricked-up fireplace. A stained and sagging armchair she remembered from his old cottage in Ledwardine.

'Ethel used to sleep in this,' she said.

'How *is* Ethel?'

'Ethel is fine. You get extra points for being a vicarage cat.'

Lol moved around, opening up radiators. His brass-rimmed glasses had half-misted.

'This place is better for you?' Merrily flopped into the chair without taking off her coat. 'Do you feel better here?'

'Haven't been here long enough to think too much about it. It's OK, I suppose.' He went into what was presumably the kitchen, leaving the door open, a blue-white light flickering.

'Very central. Convenient for the Cathedral.'

'Right.'

She forced herself out of the chair, and went to join him in the kitchen. It had barely room for two people. The fluorescent strip-lighting hurt her eyes, reminding her of the sluice-room next to the Alfred Watkins Ward.

'That was your idea, the taxi?'

'All I could think of at the time.' He had his back to her, filling the kettle.

'Thank you,' she said solemnly. 'You… got me out of something heavy.'

'Really?' He turned round, looking happy. 'Like you did for me and Ethel that night?'

'Oh, more than that. The way this was going, I might not have had a career.'

'Well, you know, I didn't really hear anything.'

'Yes, you did.'

'OK, I did. How many points for sleeping with a lady vicar?'

'For a bishop? I honestly can't recall a precedent. But bishops are survivors – especially this one, I suspect. Lady vicars… they're expendable. Especially ones caught in sin.'

She was startled at how easy it was to discuss all this with Lol, though they hadn't spoken for months. It might have been just this morning she last saw him. She looked around the little kitchen: plywood cupboards, a small fridge, a microwave, three mugs with hedgehog motifs on a shelf. Nothing suggestive of permanence. She was looking for a sign that Lol was out of limbo now and not finding one.

'Erm…' He turned to pull two of the mugs from the shelf. 'When you said just now that you might not have had a career, does that mean that if I hadn't shown up…?'

'What it would have meant,' Merrily said slowly, 'is that, in order to get away from him, I would probably have had to stop pretending he was simply offering me a room for the night.'

'Right.' Lol set down the mugs. His glasses had misted again. 'Jane'll be glad to know that.'

They sat and drank their coffee, Merrily in Ethel's old chair, Lol on the floor, his back to the window. She'd have to be going soon if she was going to grab a couple of hours before Holy Communion.

'Jane said you were training to be a psychotherapist.'

'Wild exaggeration. I've been helping *my* therapist. *Former* therapist, hopefully. That means I help a bit with other clients

– as a kind of therapy. Well, one other client mainly: the woman who used to live in this flat.'

'Oh,' Merrily said, 'that would be this, er... Moon? Just that Jane implied—'

'I've got a vague idea what Jane implied.'

'That kid could start wars.' Merrily stretched. 'I don't want to move.'

'So don't move.'

'I have to. Anyway, I think you'd make rather a good psychotherapist.'

'Being an ex-loony?'

'Not only that.'

'Thanks.'

'You know what I mean. You've been swallowed by the system once. You could be good at keeping other people *out* of the system.'

Lol said, 'Maybe there are too many therapists and counsellors around already, all talking different kinds of bollocks.'

'Is this Dick paying you?'

'Kind of. There's no big problem with money: the song royalties trickle in. And I might have another album – sometime.' Lol stood up. 'I, er... I was thinking of ringing you sometime, actually. What do you do if someone insists they've seen a ghost? I mean, not just any old ghost – a close relative. And so maybe they *want* to see it. To see *more* of it.'

'Well... I'd try and find out if it was a real ghost. Maybe I'd ask a psychiatrist – or a psychotherapist – for some advice.'

'And say this psychotherapist – or somebody else who knew this person well – was fairly convinced that there *was* something... unusual happening here.'

'Well...' Merrily lit a cigarette. 'I'd probably try and explain to the person that this was not a very good idea. It's not uncommon, actually, seeing relatives who've just passed on.'

'Twenty-five years ago?'

'That's *more* uncommon. A *visitor* is the loose term we, er, we tend to use for this kind of... phenomenon.'

'And it's a bad thing, is it? Even if the person is not scared by it.'

'Any prolonged contact with a... spirit, or whatever, is unhealthy. It can lead to all kinds of problems. Mental problems obviously, and also... Well, you might think that what you're seeing is your old mum, but it might be something else. I take it we're talking about this Moon?'

'Possibly.'

'Lol, you only *have* one client...'

'OK, it's Moon.'

'Who's she been seeing?'

'Her father. He died when she was two.'

'Any complications?'

'Shot himself.'

'Oh.'

'That's not good, is it?'

'That's not good at all,' Merrily said. 'Would she see me, do you think?'

'I don't know. Maybe if you weren't wearing... you know?'

'A dog-collar.'

'And I introduced you as a friend.'

'Sounds like a good idea.'

'She's working in the shop down below all week.'

'Maybe I'll call in on Monday, then,' Merrily said. 'I don't know what time yet. I'll be in the gatehouse if you want me – except mid-morning when I'm having discussions with my friend the Bishop.'

'Pity you can't see her house, really – a barn she's leasing up on Dinedor Hill. She's quite obsessive about the hill. It's where she was born, where the family have lived since the Iron Age – or so she claims.'

'This sounds awfully complicated, Lol.' Merrily yawned and forced herself out of the chair. 'Where'd I put my coat?'

'All I can say is that she's different when she's up there. A different person – half... half somewhere else.' He unhooked her waxed jacket from behind the door. 'I don't suppose... No, never mind.'

'I hate it when anyone says that.'

'Just that she left her bike here and I drove her home last night, because of the snow. So I have to pick her up on Monday morning, fetch her in to work.'

'Early?'

'Ish.'

'If you could get me back to the gatehouse by eleven, I can come up with you. What's my excuse, then?'

'Your car wouldn't start, so I'm giving you a lift somewhere? She'll buy that. This is really good of you, Merrily.'

'It's my job. We're told to work with shrinks. The Bishop would approve.'

'The shrink doesn't know,' Lol said. 'The shrink must *never* know.'

'A non-believer, huh?'

'Of the most intractable kind,' Lol said. 'You want me to drive you back now?'

'No, Lol,' Merrily annunciated carefully, 'you're – not – really – a – minicab – driver. That was for the benefit of the Bishop.'

She went smiling into the snow. She must be overtired.

At least the roads were no worse. Back in the vicarage just before five, she called the General Hospital. She gave them her name and they put her through to the ward. She just knew which one it was going to be – there was an ironic inevitability about it.

'Reverend Watkins? Not the biggest surprise of the morning, to have you ring.'

'What *was* the biggest?'

'The biggest, to tell you the simple truth,' Eileen Cullen said, 'is that the auld feller's still with us.'

'Would that be an indication he might be coming through this?'

'Ah, now, I wouldn't go taking bets on that. He knows when you're talking to him – his eyes'll follow you around the room. But he's not talking back yet.'

'Mr Dobbs is not a big conversationalist, in my experience. The room? You haven't got him—'

'Christ no. We have this other wee side ward at the far end of the main ward. If Denzil was still with us, Mr Dobbs wouldn't even be able to smell him.'

Merrily shuddered.

'So, collapsed in the Cathedral, they say?' Cullen said nonchalantly.

'Yes, that's what they say.'

'Well, I'm off home in a while, but I'm sure they'll keep you posted on any developments. I'll mention it.'

'Thanks.'

A pause, then Cullen said, 'Funny, isn't it, how things come around. Mr Dobbs arranging like that for you to have a mauling from Denzil in his death-throes, and now… You ever find out why he did that to you?'

'I never did,' Merrily said. 'Maybe never will now.'

'Well,' Cullen said, 'a patient'll talk about all kinds of things, so he will – in the night, sometimes. I'll keep my ears open.'

21

Chalk Circle

SHE KNEW THE words, of course she did, *she knew the words*. But they wouldn't come. She bent close to him – his breath uneven, his eyes closed against her, like this was an act of will. She brought the chalice close to his stony face on the hospital pillow, white as a linen altar-cloth, and tipped her hand very slightly so that the wine rolled slowly down the silver vessel and trickled between his parted lips, a drop remaining on his lower lip, like blood.

Blood. Yes. Yes, of course.

'The blood of our Lord, Jesus Christ, which was shed for you, preserve your body and soul into everlasting life. Drink this in remembrance that Christ's blood was shed for you…'

Thomas Dobbs began to suck greedily at the wine. She was so grateful at having remembered the words that she tilted the chalice again, at a steeper angle, and wine flooded between his lips and filled his cheeks, and she began to murmur the Lord's Prayer.

'Our Father, Who…'

There was a cracking sound, like splintering stone, and his eyes flicked open, shocking her. Dobbs's eyes were grey and white and, when he saw who hovered behind the sacrament, they blurred and foamed like a stream over rocks in winter.

'Hallowed be…'

Dobbs's shoulders began to quake.

'Thy kingdom...'

She watched him rising up in the metal bed, his cheeks expanding. She could not move; this was her job. She kept on murmuring the prayer. When, eyes bulging in fury, he coughed the consecrated wine in a great spout into her face, it was indeed as warm as fresh blood, and she felt its rivulets down her cheeks.

This was her job; she could not move.

His hand snaked from under the bedclothes, and when it gripped her wrist like a monkey-wrench, the green tubes were ejected from his nose with a soft popping.

She didn't scream. She was a priest. She just woke up with a whimper, sweating – after a little over an hour's sleep on the sofa, and half a minute before the alarm was due to go off.

'You look awful,' said Ted Clowes after morning service. As senior churchwarden and Merrily's uncle, he was entitled to be insulting. 'This damned Deliverance nonsense, I suppose. I've told you, I have an extreme aversion to *anything* evangelical.'

Uncle Ted, a retired solicitor, had read 'widely' (the *Daily Mail*) about the Toronto Blessing and certain churches in Greater London where parishioners with emotional problems were exorcized of their 'devils' in front of the entire congregation. He was monitoring all Merrily's services for 'danger signs'.

'In addition, there's all the time it seems to take up – time that should be spent in this parish, Merrily.'

'Ted, I wouldn't have been doing anything here in the parish in the early hours of this morning.'

'But look at the state of you! Look at the shadows under your eyes. You look as if you'd been beaten up. I tell you, these things don't go unnoticed in a village. Half of those old women are not listening to a word of your sermon; they're examining you inch by inch for signs of disrepair. Anyway, I should get some sleep for an hour or two after lunch. Put that child of yours on tele-phone duty.'

Jane was sitting in Mum's scullery-office, with Ethel on her knees and her one purchase from the psychic fair open on the desk: a secondhand copy of *A Treatise on Cosmic Fire* by Alice A. Bailey. So far, she couldn't understand how a book with such a cool title could be so impenetrable. It sometimes read like one of those stereotype fantasy sagas she devoured as a kid – well, until about last year, actually – with all these references to The Sevenfold Lords and stuff like that. Except this was for real. But wasn't there a *simpler* way to enlightenment?

In her pocket, she had the phone number Angela had given her.

Sorrel.

She took it out, then put it back. Instead she rang Lol. Mum had said very little about last night apart from Dobbs and his stroke – like, tough, but the old guy was plainly out of his tree, as well as being seriously outdated on the issue of women priests. If you had to have soul police – and no way *did* you – better someone decently liberal like Mum; Dobbs should have bowed out long ago and gone to tend his roses or something.

Jane scratched behind Ethel's left ear until the black cat twisted her neck, purred luxuriously and faked an orgasm.

Lol wasn't answering his phone. Mum said she'd had a cup of coffee with Lol, that was all. Not as good as getting completely soaked through, and having to take off all her clothes on Lol's hearthrug, but a start.

Jane hung up, closed Alice A. Bailey, put Ethel on the carpet.

She took a long, long breath and got out the piece of paper.

Denny had upgraded his studio to 24-track. 'This is it for me,' he said. '*Finito*. I think we've all been getting too techno-conscious. It's not what rock and roll's about. When I was a kid you had a two-track Grundig in somebody's garage and you were bloody grateful.'

'What on earth is a Grundig?' asked James Lyden's friend Eirion, unpacking his bass.

'Forget it,' Denny said.

The house was no more than half a mile from Dick's place, about the same age but detached and with a longish drive. Just as well, with a studio underneath. However, Denny had also allowed for major soundproofing; the creation of an anteroom and homemade acoustic walls had reduced the main cellar to about two-thirds of its original size. Four of them now stood in the glass-screened control room, with Denny's personalized mixing-board. It was a warm, secure little world.

'This was the wine cellar?' James enquired, presumably wondering what Denny had done with all his wine.

'Coal cellar,' Denny snapped.

James didn't have a Stratocaster. He had a Gibson Les Paul copy – a good one; you had to look hard to be sure. He gazed around. 'I've got a *rough* idea how this set-up operates, but perhaps you could stick around for an hour or two, before you let us get on with it.'

Lol blinked. They expected Denny to leave them here alone with his gear? But Denny wasn't listening. He was underneath the mainboard now, with a hand lamp, messing with something. Lol wondered if James actually had got the wrong idea about this, or whether he was just trying it on. He looked like the kind of kid who would always try for more.

With a fair chance of success, Lol figured. The boy looked austere and kind of patrician, and tall – a good six inches taller than Dick. A good bit slimmer than Dick, too – who would have ceased to be James's role model many years ago. Like when James was about six.

'I used to rather like those Hazey Jane albums,' he said to Lol. 'You were a pretty good songwriter. You had that melancholy feel of… what was his name? I can't remember… Mum had an album of his.'

'Nick Drake?' Through the glass, Lol could see the two non-songwriting band members erecting a drum kit down on the studio floor.

'Oh, I know… James Taylor.'

'*That's* interesting,' Lol said.

James nodded knowledgeably. His mother, as a therapist, would have told him about the young James Taylor's psychiatric problems. Which would be why he'd made the comparison. Letting Lol know he knew the history.

He smiled compassionately down at Lol. 'You did absolutely the right thing, in my view. I mean packing in when you did. If everybody stopped recording at their peak, we'd have a hell of a lot less dross to wade through, in my view. Like, someone should've shot Lennon ten years earlier.'

'That's what you think?'

'They should have shot McCartney first,' said Eirion. He was from Cardiff – one of those wealthy, Welsh-speaking families – but Eirion spoke English with an accent straight out of Hampstead or somewhere.

'Eirion reckons twenty-five,' James said. 'I say twenty-seven, giving them the benefit of the doubt.'

'Compulsory retirement age for rock musicians,' Eirion explained. 'We argue about it a lot.'

'Personally, I think semi-voluntary euthanasia's probably the best answer,' Lol said. 'When they stop playing, their health goes or they take too many drugs and become a burden on the state.'

Eirion considered this. 'They could surely afford BUPA or something, couldn't they?'

Lol heard rumbles from underneath the mixing-board. Detected sounds resembling *fucking, little* and *shits*. He was beginning to enjoy this. In fact, he felt much better today about… well, most of it. This morning the disparate pieces of a song which had been lying around for most of a month had fallen exquisitely into place.

'So how many songs you actually got, James?'

'How many, Eirion? Twenty, twenty-two?'

'Well, yes, but some of them are fairly embarrassing now, actually – things we did over a year ago.'

'That old, huh?' said Lol.

James looked sullen. 'Dad says he's only paying for four. But he can cock off. That would be a pure waste of time and manpower. Besides, we've worked seriously hard and we're pretty fucking efficient. It wouldn't take that much longer to lay down the other six.'

'An album in fact?'

'Anything less isn't worth the hassle,' said James, 'don't you think?'

'We'll see how it goes,' Lol said. 'It's this bloke's studio.'

Denny came up, red-faced, from underneath the board, his big earring swinging furiously. 'Sorted,' he announced.

'Oh, I get it.' James tucked his rugby shirt into his jeans, and strapped on his guitar. 'You're the engineer, too.'

'And the cleaner,' Denny said menacingly. 'And the teaboy.'

'No, I mean… to be tactful about this, we don't mind you guys hanging around. We do want to be produced, but we need space to experiment, yeah? We're only into being… guided, up to a point. I mean, you know, I don't want to sound arrogant or anything.'

'Perish the thought,' Lol said.

He kept wondering how he would be feeling now if, instead of meeting Merrily Watkins again, he'd spent last night in Moon's barn – in Moon's futon.

But it hadn't worked out like that, and he was so glad.

Merrily lay awake, tasting the formless dregs of a dream. With the feeling of something wrong – of loneliness. And the recurrent domestic agoraphobia of two small women sharing seven bedrooms.

You're never really alone, you know. How often had she said that to a bereaved parishioner? Whichever way you looked at Him, God was never another warm body in a cold bed on a winter's night.

The luminous clock indicated 5.40 p.m. Time to leave for Evensong – except they'd dropped it last September because so few people liked turning out in winter darkness.

She remembered the essence of her dream. Oh God, an image of the lithe and tawny Val Hunter astride Mick under some high, moulded ceiling, with all the lights on. Merrily standing in the doorway, shocked to find herself wearing a very short black nightie. Cold legs, cold feet. *Come on, Merrily!* the Bishop had shouted impatiently. *Don't be nervous. This is a time of transition. We have to experiment!* The king-size bed, a four-poster, had shiny purple sheets.

But that confrontation under the aumbry light now seemed no less unlikely than the dream of the purple sheets. Merrily slid out of bed.

Downstairs there was no sign of Jane. Ethel eyed her sleepily from the basket beside the Aga, as Merrily made herself some coffee. She thought of the night Lol had first arrived with Ethel, after the cat had been savagely kicked by a drunk. They'd examined her on the kitchen table, just there –

Where a note lay, neatly printed from the computer.

MUM: Rowenna turned up. Didn't want to wake you, so left machine on. Back by ten... swear to God.
Here's list of phone calls so far.

1. Emily Price, from Old Barn Lane, wanting to firm-up a date for wedding rehearsal.
2. Uncle Ted, in Churchwarden Mode. Didn't say what it was about – probably usual pep talk about not neglecting parish for glamour of Hereford.
3. Sister Cullen. Can you ring her at home?
   That's it. Love J.

* * *

Eileen Cullen said, 'Don't worry, the auld feller's not gone yet.'

'I was thinking of visiting him. Is he allowed visitors?'

Cullen laughed. 'Well, it's funny you should say that, Merrily. Mr Dobbs *has* had a visitor. That's why I called you. I thought you'd maybe want to know. Just the one visitor.'

'Someone I know?'

'You'll be on your own if you do.'

'You're going to spin this one out, aren't you?'

'All right,' Cullen said, 'I'll tell you. First off, I wasn't there. Young Tessa was there – you remember Tessa? Sunday-school teacher – the plucky kid holding Denzil's other hand?'

'I remember.' Like you could forget anybody there that night.

'This afternoon, all right, a man in an overcoat carrying an attaché case. A minister, he says, come to pray with Mr Dobbs. But Mr Dobbs can't speak, Tessa tells him. Doesn't matter, the priest says. They would like some peace and quiet and nobody coming in.'

'What was his name?'

'He didn't give his name. I told you Dobbs was in another wee side ward, all on his own? Well, the priest's drawn the curtain across the glass in the door. Except it's not possible to block the window fully. If you're nosy enough, you can stand on a chair and look down through the top. Which Tessa did, after she caught the light from the candles.'

'Candles?'

'We're always a bit careful, the range of religious fellers show up these days – and all quite legit, you know? Only Sister Miller's on her break and Tessa's a wee bit unsure about this, so she takes a peep. He'd about finished by then, so he had. He was picking up his wee bottles of holy water, scrubbing out his chalk circle.'

'Chalk circle?' Merrily sat down hard at the scullery desk.

'Me telling you like this, it sounds like a joke, but the child was terrified. He'd drawn a circle round the bed, if you please! Yellow chalk. Making a bit of extra room by pushing the visitor's chair under the door handle, the cheeky sod, so anyone'd have a job getting in even if they wanted to. And some bottles of water, with stoppers, placed around the circle. He also had a black book – very eerie, very frightening.'

'What did she do?'

'Went to find Sister Miller. Time the two of them got back, your man had gone. She rang me here during her break.'

'Well…' Merrily drew erratic circles on a pad. 'I'm lost. I don't understand this.'

'All *I* can say is that I was raised a Catholic, and it isn't one of our… things… our rituals.'

'Doesn't even seem like proper religion, Eileen. More like… magic. You sure this was a real priest?'

'I didn't see him. Tessa says he was wearing a dog-collar. He had a hat and scarf, so she couldn't see much of his face.'

'Did they check Dobbs over after he'd gone?'

'No change. He lies there still as corpse, so he does. Sometimes his eyes'll be open, but you never see it happen. What'll we do? Call the police, you reckon?'

'I don't know what the police could do, to be honest. But if he shows up again… would you mind calling me?'

'Merrily,' Cullen said, 'if it's me that's on when he shows, I'll be on to you before the divil's got both feet on the blessed ward at all.'

22

Edict

MONDAY MORNING, AND Jane felt good – which was rare. She lay and watched for the dawn.

She'd seen like hundreds of dawns from here now, her bed facing the east window. This was not brilliant *feng shui*-wise, but you did get to see the sun come up over the wooded hill, and that was seriously important today.

Jane replayed last night's encounter – still amazed at how *cool* Sorrel had been, inviting her and Rowenna over at once to talk about it all. Jane calling Rowenna, and Ro saying, 'Look, better not tell them we're still at school. These people worry about parents finding out and making a fuss.' That was cool – so they were office working girls. Sorrel, who looked about Mum's age, had with her an elderly woman called Patricia who was kind of the head of the group and was obviously a really heavy person and had quizzed them in this really soft, knowing voice. *How important is it to you to find the Path within yourself? Are you ready for so much hard work at a time when most girls your age are out having fun?*

That made you think. You could spend years in search of enlightenment, and still wind up disillusioned at forty or something. The answer was: give it six months and then, if it wasn't working for you, let it go.

No sign of dawn, and it was getting on for seven. Mum was

probably up already, because – *yes!* – Mum was meeting Lol later in Hereford.

She didn't know what the meeting was about, and why it was so early, but that didn't matter. Their meeting was still a major coup for Mystic Jane, who had set the whole thing up the other night. Classic, when you thought about it: Lol taking Merrily in from the cold, offering her sanctuary just like she'd done for him that time. Mum still very big on the sanctuary concept, like with all those hookers she tried to rescue when she was a curate in Liverpool.

It would be really good to have Lol around again, so cool in his vulnerable, nervous way. This Moon – she was entirely wrong for him. You could tell, just by watching her in the shop, that she was remote and self-obsessed. So, OK, she was beautiful and about ten years younger than Mum. But Mum was still sexy. Well, she *could* be sexy, if she wanted to. If the bloody Church...

Or if they'd met way back – Mum in her Goth frock and her Siouxie Sioux make-up, Lol unhappily on the road with his band, Hazey Jane. You seemed to go all tightened up and inhibited when you got older. Especially when you had your whole life hijacked by the Church. The dog-collar – it was like some sick masochism trip. The punks used to wear actual dog-collars. Had Mum once been into bondage gear, and was that a natural progression to clerical costume?

Jane was just picturing Mum in the pulpit in her Sunday surplice and half a potful of coal-black mascara, when she became aware of the frozen night sky at last beginning to brown with heat from the east. Patricia said you were supposed to wait for the big orb itself but, like, what if it didn't show until you were on the school bus or something?

She scrambled out of bed and walked slowly to the east-facing window and opened it as wide as it would go. It was absolutely bloody *freezing*.

Well, good! Jane steeled herself and flung her arms wide.

Now her first exercise. She had the words Patricia had given them written out on the back of an old birthday card, all ready, balanced on the window ledge. She pictured Rowenna standing at her own window in the big modern house in Credenhill Jane hadn't yet visited.

She pictured Patricia and Sorrel – sisters, kind of.

OK. She took a mouthful of cold air and coughed. Then she looked into the sandy sky and read aloud from the card.

'Hail to Thee, Eternal Spiritual Sun
'Whose symbol now rises in the Heavens.
'Hail to Thee from the Abodes of Morning.'

Jane lowered her arms, and stayed silent. By tomorrow, she wouldn't need the card.

She was on the Path.

This time, she was going to do it right.

Merrily dumped her waxed jacket on a front pew and went to kneel in the chancel.

Before her, the altar was a hazy-grey block under a stained-glass window, its colours still sleeping. She hadn't switched on the lamps or even lit a candle.

Unlocking the church, she'd thought what a shame it was to have to restrict the house of God to not much more than normal working hours. Ted wanted to lock it up at five each evening, but Merrily was insisting on seven at least, even if she then had to go along with her own keys. A church should really be offering sanctuary around the clock. Perhaps you could employ a sympathetic security patrol to filter out the vandals – try getting *that* one past the parish council.

Enough! Merrily knelt in silence for maybe ten minutes, letting thoughts drift away, and then began.

Her voice was hesitant, but steady. She kept it low.

'Christ be with me, Christ within me.
'Christ behind me...'

Christ and who else? A story in the *Church Times* last week had revealed two more attacks – one of them sexual – on women priests in their own churches. But you couldn't wrap yourself in cotton-wool like some religious statuette.

Equally she'd seen with the Denzil Joy incident the potential dangers of not protecting yourself before you went out on a case. And there was a lot about this Moon business she didn't like. Obsession, for a start, was always dangerous. She'd called Lol last night, while Jane was out, to get some more background. She didn't like the idea of that newly displayed photograph of the dead father in a room full of Iron Age relics. There was the possibility that this woman was drawing down pagan Celtic elements she would not be able to deal with.

Lol was right: it was necessary to go to the location on this one. To try to see it through Moon's eyes. But if there was something there, some lurking presence from way way back, would Merrily be able to sense it? While, at the same time, keeping it out?

'I bind unto myself the Name,
'The strong Name of the Trinity.
'By invocation of the same,
'The Three in One and One in Three...'

Pip-pop! The green tubes ejecting from the nostrils of dying Denzil Joy. *Pip-pop!*

Merrily cringed.

Stop!

She opened and closed her eyes and pulled the folds of blue and gold around her.

Start again.

'Christ be with me, Christ within me...'

But Merrily's visit with Lol to Moon's barn was not going to happen. Something appalling already had. Something she could not ignore.

Jane took the call while Merrily was making breakfast.

'It's some really nasty, officious-sounding bastard.'

'Not so *loud*!' Merrily took it on the cordless phone in the kitchen.

'Merrily Watkins speaking.'

'This is Major Weston, area organizer for the Redundant Churches Fund. I make no apologies for calling you before eight. I find it ridiculous that I should have to call you at all. I wanted the *local* man to deal with it. Bizarrely, the local man tells me all matters of this nature have to be referred directly to you.'

'What's the problem, Major?' She wasn't aware that the Redundant Churches Fund even had an area organizer.

'Desecration is the problem, Mrs Watkins. At the Church of St Cosmas and St Damien at Stretford. Do you know where that is?'

'Vaguely.'

'I expect you'll manage to find it. The police already have, for what *they're* worth.'

'What kind of desecration?'

'What *kind*? Satanic desecration, of course.'

Jane was furious.

'You can't do this to Lol! Whatever it was, you *promised* him.'

'I have to. It's—'

'Your job – yeah, yeah. You know what I think? I think you're empire-building.'

'Flower, it's not *me*! I didn't even know about this, but apparently every vicar or rector or priest-in-charge in the diocese has received an edict from the Bishop's office to say that anything arising in their parishes possibly related to Deliverance should be referred initially to me. Through the Deliverance office, naturally, but this Major Weston's obviously had an earful from a local vicar happy to wash his hands of it, and so the Major's made a special point of finding my home number and getting me up nice and early in the morning. What can I do?'

'You don't have to go *now*.'

'I *do* have to go now. They've got to get the place cleaned up. It's a disused church supported by this charity.'

But she *was* annoyed. Neither Mick nor Sophie had mentioned this memo going out to all the priests. Yes, it did look like empire-building, and whilst a few vicars would be secretly relieved, the majority would resent it. *She* would have resented it.

'I'll call Lol,' she said.

23

Strawberry Ice

THE MAIN ROAD was a brown channel between banks of snow. The Cathedral – usually seen at its most imposing from Greyfriars Bridge – skulked uneasily in half-lit mist.

Beyond the bridge, the car slid alarmingly towards the kerb where there was a pub called the Treacle Mine. This was not promising. The hill might still be a problem – like the other night.

White hell, then. Not ten minutes out of the city, but the snow had lain undisturbed for longer. Denny's monster Mitsubishi would, for once, have been useful. Don't even try the steep bit, Moon had said. You'll just get stuck. I can walk down from here.

Oh, it's hazardous out there, Moon. Snow-blindness. Hypothermia.

Lol, the hill's only five hundred and ninety-five feet above sea level.

Sometimes her humour-vacuum was almost endearing. Ever since they'd left the shop – Moon, in her green padded ski-jacket, snuggling into his shoulder – Lol had been thinking: *I was wrong, I'm crazy. There's nothing weird going on. All she needs is love.*

Anyway, he couldn't stop now; there was nowhere to turn the car around.

This morning, with no further snow, things were better.

Someone must have been up the hill with a tractor, perhaps even a snowplough. He made it without too much revving and sliding, as far as the little car park for visitors to the ancient camp.

The desolation of the day was getting to him. He'd been looking forward to bringing Merrily up here. But Merrily couldn't make it. Second thoughts, maybe, about loopy Moon – and loopy Lol, too. He'd misunderstood her.

From the back of the car, he pulled his wellies and his old army combat jacket. The snow around here was untrodden, lying in big drifts. Even where it hadn't drifted, it was four, five inches deep.

Lol ploughed through. The earth steps had disappeared, becoming a deceptive white ski-run. Lol stopped. He'd imagined the barn below would be winter-picturesque, but it was like a short, blackened toadstool under its snow-swollen roof. Neglected and charmless, most of its windows shrunken by snow.

On Saturday night, a gauzy moon had been nesting in the snow-bent treetops, and Moon had walked across where the patch of garden would be and looked all around like she wanted to establish a memory of how the barn and the surrounding trees looked in their moonlit winter robes.

And Lol had then thought, this is it. Dick whispering in his ear, *You do find her attractive, don't you? Think she doesn't fancy you? Oh, I think she does, old son. I think she does.* And then Denny. *I would do anything, give anything to get her away from there. Meanwhile, if she's not alone, that's the best thing I could hope for under the circumstances.*

Lol crunched carefully down the long earthen steps. It was fully light now, or as light as it was going to get. He knocked on the front door, set into the glassed-over barn bay, long curtains drawn on either side.

There was no answer. After a minute, Lol stepped back on to the snow-shrouded garden and looked around.

A big man was striding out of a wall of conifers on the other side of the barn. He stopped. 'Hello. Can I help?'

'I'm looking for Kathy Moon.'

'Yes, this is where she lives.' He had a high, hearty voice – not local. He wore a shiny new green Barbour and a matching cap. 'I'm from the farm. Tim Purefoy.'

'Lol Robinson. I'm a… friend of hers.'

'Yes, I'm sure she's spoken of you.' Tim Purefoy looked down at Lol, recognition dawning. 'I know… you were here helping Katherine move in, yes?' He ambled across to the glassed-over barn bay, squinting through a hole in the condensation. 'Bit odd – she's usually up and about quite early. Cycles into town, you know.'

Lol explained about driving Moon home on Saturday, and the bike being still at the shop.

'Well, I don't know what to say,' said Mr Purefoy. 'Gone for a stroll maybe? Perhaps she wanted to see what the hill was like under snow, before it all vanished. Bit of a romantic about this hill, as you probably know. Anyway, can't be far away. Come and wait at the farmhouse if you like, and have a coffee.'

'Actually,' Lol said, 'I don't suppose I could use your phone? It's possible her brother got worried about her being up here in the blizzard. Maybe he's collected her.'

'No problem at all. Follow me.' Tim Purefoy beat his gloved hands together. 'Like midwinter already, isn't it?'

The Dyn farmhouse was unexpectedly close – no more than fifteen yards behind the tight row of Leylandii. It was these conifers that deprived the barn of its view, but when you passed between them…

Lol almost gasped.

They were standing on a wide white lawn sloping away to a line of low bushes which probably hid the road. But it might as well have been a cliff edge.

Below it, the city – a timeless vision in the mist.

'Startling, isn't it?' Tim Purefoy folded his arms in satisfaction. 'Best view of Hereford you'll get from anywhere – except from the ramparts of the hillfort itself.'

The snow had made Hereford an island and softened the outlines of its buildings, so that the new merged colourlessly with the old. And because the city had somehow been bypassed by the high-rise revolution of the sixties and seventies, it might *all* have been seventeenth-century, even medieval, underneath. It was both remote and intimate; it made Lol feel very strange.

'See how the steeple of All Saints is superimposed on the Cathedral tower?' Tim said knowledgeably. 'That's one of Alfred Watkins's ley-lines. An invisible, mystical cable joining sacred sites – a prehistoric path of power.'

'And we're standing on it?'

'Absolutely. It goes very close to the house. We had a chap over to dowse it – the earth-energy. They're energy lines, you know. And spirit paths, so we're told.'

No wonder this guy had taken to Moon. Standing in the thin rain on the snowy lawn, Lol suddenly felt he could jump off and slide down that mystical cable from the hill to the steeple to the tower in the mist.

'Probably all nonsense,' Tim Purefoy said, 'but at sunset you can feel you own the city. Come and have some coffee, my friend.'

Lol shook himself.

The farmhouse was three-storeyed, ruggedly rendered in white. With lots of haphazard, irregular mullioned windows, it looked as old as the hill itself. How could Moon live out in that sunken, tree-smothered barn, knowing her own family had lost this house, and this view?

'Anna!' Tim Purefoy shouldered open the door of a wooden lean-to porch on the side of the house. 'Coffee, darling!' He held open the door for Lol. 'Come in, come in. Don't worry about the boots. It's a flagged floor, and the place is a damn mess this morning, anyway.'

Globular hanging lights were switched on in the vast, farmhouse kitchen. It was golden with antique pine, and had an old cream-coloured double-oven Aga which seemed actually to be putting heat into the room. Like a furnace, in fact. Lol felt almost oppressed by the sudden warmth.

'One second…' The woman kneeling at the stove wore jeans and a sackcloth-coloured apron tied over a long rainbow sweater. Her fair hair was efficiently bound up in a yellow silk scarf.

'My wife, Anna.' Tim Purefoy pulled off his cap, freeing springy white-blond curls. 'Darling, this chap's a friend of Katherine – who seems to have gone walkabout in the woods again.'

'Oh gosh. Not untypical, though.' Anna Purefoy closed an oven door, sprang up, patting floury hands on her apron. 'I'm making bread. One can buy a marvellous loaf at any one of a half-dozen places in town, but one somehow feels *obliged*, living in a house this old. Do you know what I mean?'

Lol nodded. 'Responsibility to the ancestors.'

'My God,' said Tim. 'This chap *does* know Katherine.'

'It's good to think someone does.' Anna pulled out chairs from under a refectory table. Concern put lines into her face. She was perhaps fifteen years older than she'd first appeared.

'Don't *interfere*, darling!' said Tim with affection. 'You know what we said about interfering. My wife's lost unless she can find someone to worry about.'

'There's a loaf in here for Katherine,' said Anna. 'Left to herself, she'd go days without food.'

'Oh, nonsense, Anna!'

His wife glared at him. 'Tim, I have been in her kitchen and found the refrigerator absolutely *bare*, while the girl sits there with all her books and her maps and her notes. Fascinating, what she's doing, of course, and we've learned a lot by helping her, but she's so *obsessive*, isn't she? I feel enormously guilty.'

'She thinks we twisted her arm to take on the barn.' Tim pulled off his Barbour, revealing a thick and costly cowboy shirt and a silk cravat. 'In fact, she virtually twisted ours.' He focused narrowed eyes on Lol. 'You know the history, I suppose.'

Lol nodded warily. 'I, er, know about her father.'

'Oooh.' Anna hugged herself with a shiver.

'Speaking personally,' Tim said, 'I wouldn't want to live within a hundred miles of here under those particular circumstances – but there we are. Telephone's in the hall. I say, do take off your coat, so you won't feel it so cold when you go outside again.'

From the square oak-pillared hall, Lol called the shop and got no answer. Then he called Denny at home.

Denny said angrily, 'Gone? How can she be gone?'

'So you haven't seen her? I came to pick her up here—'

'What you mean, came to pick her up?'

Lol said awkwardly, 'Denny, there's… there's nothing happening between Moon and me. There never has been.'

Denny was quiet for a few seconds, then he said, 'I don't believe this. You gay, Laurence?'

'No.'

'Then what the fuck…? I can't… She sometimes goes in to see the idiots next door… at the farm.'

'That's where I'm calling from, and they haven't seen her, either. They say she sometimes goes out for walks, but I can't see any footprints.'

'I'm coming over,' Denny said. 'Fucking stay there.'

Lol went back outside with both Purefoys.

'You, er… you still own the barn, presumably?'

'Oh yes,' Anna said. 'Katherine's indicated several times that she'd like to buy it, but we're not awfully happy about that idea. It is very near to the house, and suppose she… Well, suppose she had a change of heart or had to sell suddenly?'

Meaning, Lol guessed, suppose she was removed by men in white coats.

'*Anyone* could buy it then, couldn't they?' Tim said. 'And it's awfully close to our house.'

'So you still have keys, presumably.'

'Well, we do. But we'd never dream of going in without permission. As I keep telling Anna, it's not our place to interfere. Or to be… over curious. That is, we try not to notice what we're not supposed to notice.'

What had Moon been doing?

Lol wondered how long the Purefoys themselves would stay here, once they'd got used to that view, and over the novelty of homemade bread. Houses like this, previously occupied by the same family for centuries, might then change hands half a dozen times in the following twenty years. It was hard to settle under the weight of someone else's tradition.

And costly, too. You bought a country residence for what seemed like peanuts compared with London, and then you found out how much you had to spend just to keep it standing. Moon must have been a gift to them. They'd probably run out of money halfway through converting the barn, and bodged the rest very quickly once she came on the scene.

'Are you something to do with the little shop?' Anna asked, a scarlet parka now setting off her yellow scarf. 'That place where Katherine works?'

'Me? Not exactly, I'm just a… friend of hers. And of Denny.'

'Must be a busy man, her brother,' Tim said. 'Never seems to have time to visit her here.'

Lol tried knocking one more time, harder in case she was still asleep.

'OK if I go round the back and bang on one of the windows?'

'My dear chap, whatever you want.'

Lol pushed through bushes at one corner. Behind the barn there was, under snow, what must be a small square of lawn up against a low bank. It looked quite pretty – like a cake with pink icing.

Also, like some exotic confection, its design became more complex as he stared. Pink – but pale brown in places where the thaw had already eroded the snow. Strawberry ice-cream in the middle, sorbet round the edges, up against the back wall made of rubble-stone.

All it needed was a cherry in the middle, Lol thought in the wild surrealism of the moment. The red woollen beret Merrily used to wear, that would do. If you threw her beret into the centre of this lawn, it would lodge lusciously in the soft, wet, pink snow like a cherry.

There was a jagged hole in the snow under the nozzle of a pipe poking out of the wall about eighteen inches above the ground.

They'd bodged the plumbing, he thought. That was the overflow from the bath, and it should empty down into a drain.

Oh God!

Lol stood there remembering how completely Moon had changed once they'd reached the door of the barn. Her voice becoming sharp like the night, her eyes glittering like ice under the moon, as she pulled out her keys. She had been talking about Dick Lyden again, and what a clown he was. While separating a long black key and unlocking the door in the glass bay.

Maybe not *such* a clown, Lol had thought at the time. Confidence had seemed to click into place the minute Moon arrived back here – the strength of the old settlement around her, the child of the Hill. In Dick's terms of reference, a fantasy structure: *The way we create our destiny. The way we form fate.*

He'd moved to follow her into the barn, but she'd turned in the doorway, somehow stiffening.

She'd said, *No.*

Moon?

I've changed my mind. I don't want you to come in.

He'd stepped back.

Thank you, Moon had said. Once she had opened the door, the darkness inside seemed to suck her in and thrust him away.

Now, when Lol walked back round to the front of the barn, he was shaking.

'No luck, old chap?'

'I think we're going to need those keys, Mr Purefoy,' Lol said.

24

Last Long Prayer

THE MEDIEVAL CHURCH of St Cosmas and St Damien was almost part of a farmyard situated on the edge of a hamlet among windy-looking fields in the north of the county. Not that far from main roads but Merrily, who thought she knew this county fairly well, had been unaware of it.

The church was tiny, the size of a small barn, with a little timbered bell-turret at one end.

St Cosmas and St Damien?

'Fourth-century Mediterranean saints,' said Major Weston, 'connected with physicians and surgeons, for some reason. Local doctors hold the occasional service here. Otherwise it's disused. Absolute bloody tragedy.'

'One of all too many these days, Major.' Powdered snow blew at Merrily's legs.

'Call me Nigel,' suggested Major Weston, whose belligerence had dropped away the moment he saw her. He was about sixty, had a moist and petulant lower lip, and a costly camel coat.

Merrily followed him around the raised churchyard, pine trees rearing grimly on its edge.

'I think it was the Bishop of Lincoln,' the Major said, 'who warned that disused churches were now increasingly falling prey to Satanism. The message seems to be that if your people don't want them, the Devil's only too happy to take them on.'

'It's not that we don't *want* them.'

'I know, I know, but you don't, do you? Otherwise my Fund wouldn't exist. We maintain nearly three hundred churches at present, and the figure's going up at an alarming rate. Now, when you think what a comparatively tiny population England had when these lovely old buildings were erected…'

'Yeah,' Merrily said, 'tell me about it.'

They stopped outside the porch. She saw that the single long gothic window in the wall beside it had an iron bar up the middle. On one side lay the farm, and some houses on the other – a stone's throw away.

'If I was a Satanist, Major, I really don't think I'd feel too safe performing a black mass here. You wouldn't be able to chant very loudly, would you, before somebody came in with a torch and a shotgun?'

'That's what the police said. Must've been lunatics – but then that's what they are, aren't they? Not normal, these people. Beggars belief.'

'I've never met one. I'd rather like to.'

He peered at her. 'Would you, by God?'

'Just to try and find out *why*.'

'What they've done in here may just change your mind. Ready to go in?'

'Sure.'

'Not squeamish are you?'

'Let's hope not.' She followed him into the porch, and he lifted the latch. 'There's no lock!'

'There should be – and there will be. A new one's in the course of being made, I believe. Perhaps these scum knew that.'

'Meanwhile, the church is left without a lock?'

'You can't just put any old lock on a building dating back to the twelfth century. In you go, m'dear.'

Holding the door for her, letting her go in first. A gentleman, ha.

It was dim and intimate, no immediate echo. None of that sense of Higher Authority you had in most cathedrals, and big churches like her own at Ledwardine.

236

It was in fact fascinating, the Church of St Cosmas and St Damien. Quartered by an arcade of stone and a wooden screen with a pulpit in the middle. Two short naves and what seemed to be two chancels with two altars, although she could only see one from where she was standing – a plain wooden table without a cloth.

Against the far wall, and close to the floor, the stone effigies of a knight in armour and his lady shared that last long prayer.

Merrily didn't move. She was reminded of nowhere so much as the little stone Celtic cell where she'd had the vision of the blue and the gold and the lamplit path. Only the smell was different.

She knew the smells of old churches, and they didn't usually include urine.

Before Tim Purefoy was even back with his keys, a big vehicle was roaring up to the barn bay, sloshing through the wet snow. The dull gold, bull-barred Mitsubishi, spattered from wheels to windscreen with snow-slicks and mud, skidded to within a couple of feet of the glass wall.

Denny Moon slammed out, looking once – hard – at the barn, as though angry it was still there; not burned out, derelict, toppled into rubble. He wore an old leather jacket and a black baseball cap. Wraparound dark glasses, like he feared snow-blindness. He took in the encircling trees and the overgrown Leylandii hedge, sucking air through his teeth.

'Fucking place!'

Lol walked nervously towards the car. 'Mr Purefoy's gone for his keys.'

'Fuck that. I'll kick the door down.' Denny gave him a black stare. 'Lol, what is it? What is it you know, man?'

'We just need to get in.'

'Look at you! Something's scared you. What is it?'

Tim Purefoy appeared, holding up a long key on an extended wire ring holding also two smaller ones.

At the same time his wife came round from the back of the barn. She looked stricken. 'Call... call the police,' she stammered. 'Better call the police.'

Denny gasped and snatched the keys.

The big room was brightened by snowlight from the highest window, exposed trusses the colour of bone.

'Kathy!' Denny bawled. '*Kathy!*'

The smell of candlewax. Blobs of it on the floor.

Denny's head swivelled. 'She sleep up there?' He made for the stairs to the loft. He hadn't seen the lawn, so he wouldn't know that what they really needed was the bathroom. 'Kathy!'

Two doors behind the stairs: one ajar, through which Lol could see kitchen worktops and the edge of a cooker; the other door shut.

Lol opened it and went in.

Into the square, white, bitter-smelling, metal-smelling bathroom, quietly closing the door and snipping the catch, sealing himself in with her. Like he should have done on Saturday night – resisting the hostile thrust of the barn – when she'd said, *I don't want you to come in.*

His back against the door, he saw first, on the wall over the bath like an icon, the photograph of a smiling man standing before a Land Rover.

On the rim of the bath were pebble-smooth shards of black pottery, arranged in a line.

'No sign,' he heard Denny shout from upstairs, sounding relieved, almost optimistic, because he hadn't found her dead in her futon.

Lol saw the crusted brown tidemark on the porcelain around the overflow grille, like sloppy dinner deposits around a baby's mouth. Presumably a tap had been left running and the overflow had gulped it all down and regurgitated it on to the snowy lawn, stopping only when the primitive water tank ran dry.

'Lol?' Denny's feet descending the stairs. 'Where'd he go?'

It was dreamlike. Lol thought at first – from the position of her, the stillness of the tableau – of Ophelia in that sad, famous Pre-Raphaelite painting.

The thin pine door bulged against him as Denny tried to open it, and then battered it with his fists, making it vibrate against Lol's back until Lol almost tripped and fell forward towards the bath. And he cried out, 'Oh God!' seeing it now as it was: graceless, peaceless, sorrowless – nothing like Ophelia.

Who wouldn't have been naked or grinning like Moon was grinning, congealing in her stagnant pool of rich, scummy, pinky-brown, cold water. With eyes open, like frosted glass, and lips retracted over stiff, ridged gums and sharp white teeth.

Beautiful Moon, so defiantly disgusting now with her cunning, secret, bloodless grin and her blood-pickled fingers below her breasts – on the waterline, on the bloodline. And the wrists ripped open: not nice neat slits – the skin was torn and ruched.

'Lol!' Denny screamed, and the pressure on Lol's back eased, telling him Denny was about to hurl himself against the door.

She'd been here a long time, you could tell. This hadn't happened this morning or even last night; this had to be Saturday night, maybe only hours after he'd brought her home and meekly taken no for an answer... almost gratefully, because he'd already had the sense of something dark and soiled. He should have said: Moon, there are things we have to talk about. He should have said this long ago – after the crow. He should have gone long ago to Merrily Watkins.

Swallowing his nausea, he went closer and bent over the bath. On the bottom, between Moon's legs, lay the eroded file-like blade, ragged and blackened and scabby and old, very old.

He remembered those slender but unexpectedly hardened hands fouled by crow's blood, and turned away, and opened the door to Denny.

I'd like to sleep now, Lol.

25

Sad Tosser

SOPHIE SAID, 'WAS it *very* horrible?'

'It was, actually.'

'It's so utterly distressing.' Sophie's face creased into shadows. 'I once read a book by a reformed Satanist who said that when they break into a church and do appalling acts, it has an almost intoxicating effect. Afterwards they feel a terrible elation. Almost... sexual.'

'Well,' Merrily said, 'by the very nature of what they are, they're not going to walk out feeling disgusted and nauseous, are they?'

Sophie shuddered.

When she'd gone, Merrily rang Huw Owen.

No reply, no answering machine.

She thought about calling Lol to rearrange that chance encounter with his troubled friend, Moon, but then Sophie came through again.

'Merrily, it's Chief Inspector Howe on the line.'

'Oh. Right.'

'Ms Watkins?'

'Good morning.'

'Ms Watkins, I, er... I'd like to consult you – as an expert.'

'Me?'

'Indeed,' Howe said.

'Heavens.' What seemed likely was that the Superintendent, after a lunch with the Bishop, had strongly suggested Annie

Howe consult Merrily over something, anything. Howe would be disinclined, as *acting* DCI, to make waves.

'Ms Watkins?'

'Sorry, just swallowing one of the pills I've been prescribed for moments of overexcitement.'

Howe sighed. 'Perhaps we could meet. I gather you've been cleaning up after devil-worshippers.'

'Blanket term, Annie. I'm not convinced.'

'Good. That's what I wanted to discuss with you.'

'One o'clock? Pub?'

'No, I'll come to your office,' Annie Howe said, keeping it official, hanging up.

Sophie came back again. 'The Reverend Owen now. Take it on my phone if you like. I have to powder my nose.'

It seemed that Sophie didn't feel she was ready to hear about this incident in detail.

'Hard to get rid of the taste, in't it, lass?'

'Hard to lose the smell.'

'Number twos as well?'

'Not that I could detect, but I didn't go prying into too many dark corners.'

'Aye, well, your problem here,' Huw said, 'is deciding whether this is the real thing or just kids who think it'd be fun to play at being Satanists for an hour or so.'

'I thought you didn't get away with just playing at it.'

'In my experience you don't, but let's not worry about poor little dabblers at this stage. Tell me again about the bird.'

'Well, it was… had been a crow or a raven. Is there much difference? I don't know. It had been cut open, and its entrails spread over the altar. There are kind of twin chancels in this church, but this was the real altar, on the right.'

'Two chancels?'

'Side by side. Very unusual. Quite a special little place.'

'Let me have a think.'

Merrily looked down from Sophie's window at white roofs on cars and people hurrying. Hereford people were essentially country folk, and country folk had no great love for snow. Certainly not November snow. Never a good sign; winter was supposed to settle in slowly. What if this went on until March or April?

'Two chancels,' Huw said. 'They might see this as representing a dualism: left and right, darkness and light.'

'Actually, there was some blood on the other table, too, as if the sacrificed crow had been brought from one side to the other.'

'How do you know it was sacrificed?'

'I don't. It would be nice – nicer – to think it was already dead, and they just wanted to make a mess. Huw, the way you're talking suggests you think this was the real thing.'

'It's possible.'

'If it *was* the real thing, what would be the motive? What would they be after?'

'Kicks... a buzz... power. Or – biggest addiction of the lot – the pursuit of knowledge. Nowt you won't do to feed your craving. Ordinary mortals – expendable like cattle. Kindness and mercy – waste of energy. Love's a drain, faith's for feeble minds. Can you understand that? To *know* is all. Can you get a handle on that?'

'No. That's why I'm a Christian.' *Working towards it, anyway. Made it to the pious bitch stage.*

'Mind, a crow splattered over a country church, that still has the touch of low-grade headbangers. What are you going to do about it?'

'Major Weston was asking for reconsecration. I said that wasn't necessary, as a consecration's for all time.'

'Correct. What you proposing instead?'

'A lesser exorcism, do you think?'

'When?'

'I was thinking early evening, if we could get some people together then. I wouldn't like to think of the place getting snowed in before we could do it.'

'You want me to come over?'

'I couldn't ask you to do that.'

'Give me directions,' Huw said. 'I'll be there at five.'

'I can't keep leaning on you.'

'I like it,' Huw said. 'Keeps me off the drink.'

Merrily smiled. She saw Annie Howe, in her white belted mac, walking rapidly out of King Street carrying a briefcase. 'I... suppose you've heard about Dobbs.'

'Aye.'

'Any thoughts on that?'

'Poor bugger?'

'That's it?'

'Let's hope so,' Huw said.

Sophie pulled up an extra chair for Howe and left them in her office. The Acting DCI kept her mac on. She hated informality.

'My knowledge of police demarcation's fairly negligible,' Merrily said, 'but aren't you a bit *senior* to be investigating the minor desecration of a country church?'

'I'm not sure I am.' Annie Howe brought a tabloid newspaper from her case and placed it before Merrily, on Sophie's desk. 'You've seen this, I imagine.'

A copy of last night's *Evening News*. The anchor story:

WYE DEATH: MAN NAMED.

'Oh, this is the guy...' Merrily had scarcely given it another thought. All memories of that night were still dominated by Denzil Joy. She scanned the text.

... identified as 32-year-old Paul Sayer, from Chepstow. Mr Sayer had not been reported missing for over a week because his family understood he was on holiday abroad.
Acting Det. Chief Inspector Annie Howe, who is leading the

*investigation, said, 'We are very anxious to talk to anyone
who may have seen Mr Sayer since November 19. We believe
he may have arrived in Hereford by bus or train and...*

'No need to read the lot. It's mainly waffle. His relatives
aren't going to talk, and we ourselves have been rather economical with any information given out to the press.'

'Aren't you always.'

'Need to Know, Ms Watkins,' Howe said, 'Need to Know. Let
me tell you what we do know about Sayer.'

She brought out a folder containing photographs. Sophie,
fetching in coffee for them on a tray, spotted one of them and
made a choking noise.

'Would you mind?' Howe stood up and shut the door on
both Sophie and the coffee.

'I believe it's known as the Goat of Mendes,' Merrily said.

A colour photograph of what seemed to be a poster. Luridly
demonic: like the cover of a dinosaur heavy-metal album from
the eighties.

'We'll return to that,' Howe said. 'But this is a photograph of
Paul Sayer. He may, for all we know, have been around the city
for several days before he was killed.'

He had a fox-like face, the lower half almost a triangle. No
smile. Hair lank, looked as if it would be greasy. Though his
eyes were lifeless, he was not dead in this picture.

'Passport photo.' Annie Howe unbelted her raincoat. 'Does
look like him, though. Recognize him?'

Merrily shook her head. Howe looked openly around
the office. Merrily wished the ⅅ on the door was remov-
able for occasions like this. She felt self-conscious, felt
like a fraud.

Howe smiled blandly, her contact-lensed eyes conveying an
extremely subtle sneer. 'You're like a little watchdog at the gate
up here, Ms Watkins.'

'Look, if you're not here specifically to arrest me, how about you call me Merrily?'

'Actually, the people I call by their first names tend to be the ones I've *already* arrested. Standard interview-room technique.'

'But the suspects don't get to call you Annie.'

You might wonder if anyone did, under the rank of superintendent, she had such glacial dignity. She was only thirty-two, Merrily estimated, the same age as the man pulled out of the Wye – Paul Sayer whose photo lay on the desk.

'I expect you'll get round to explaining what this poor guy has to do with the Goat and me.'

' "This poor guy"?' said Annie Howe. 'Why do I suspect your sympathy may be short-lived?'

'He had, er, form?'

'None at all. He was, according to his surviving family, a quiet, decent, clean-living man who worked as a bank clerk in Chepstow and lived in a terraced house on the edge of the town, which was immaculately maintained. He was unmarried, but once engaged for three years to a young woman from Stroud who's since emigrated to Australia. I'll be talking to her tonight, but one can guess why the relationship foundered.'

Merrily took out a cigarette. 'Do you mind?'

'It's your office.'

'I'll open the window. Why did the engagement fall through?'

'Don't bother with the window, Ms Watkins. I'm paid to take risks. Well I suppose she must have seen his cellar.'

Cellar?

'Oh, my God, not a Fred West situation?'

'Let's not get *too* carried away. This is it.'

Six more photographs, all eight by ten. All in colour, although there wasn't much colour in that cellar.

'Christ,' Merrily said.

'So now you understand why I'm here.' Howe turned one of the pictures around, a wide-angle taken from the top of the cellar steps. 'Is this your standard satanic temple, then, would you say?'

'I've never actually been in one, but it looks… well, it looks like something inspired by old Dracula films and Dennis Wheatley novels, to be honest.'

'The altar,' Howe said, 'appears to have been put together from components acquired at garden centres in the vicinity – reconstituted stone. The wall poster's of American origin, probably obtained by mail-order – we found some glossy magazines full of this stuff.'

'Sad.'

'Yes, I admit I have a problem understanding the millions of people who seem to worship your own God, but this… How real are these people? How genuine?'

'I don't know… I'd be inclined to think the guy who built this temple is – I may be wrong – what my daughter would call a sad tosser.'

'But a dead tosser,' Howe said. 'And we have to consider that his death could be linked to his… faith.'

Merrily examined a close-up of the altar. 'What's the stain?'

'We wondered that – but it's only wine.'

'So, no signs of…?'

'Blood sacrifice? We haven't finished there yet, but no.'

'How did you find this set-up?'

'We had to break through a very thick door with a very big lock. The local boys were quite intrigued. Not that he appears to have broken any laws. It's all perfectly acceptable in the eyes of the law, as you know.'

'Makes you wonder why there are any laws left,' Merrily said. 'I've always thought Christianity would become fashionable overnight if they started persecuting us again.'

'So,' Howe gathered up the photos, 'you aren't very impressed by Mr Sayer's evident commitment to His Satanic Majesty.'

'No more than I was by the sick bastards who spread a crow over a lovely little old church, but…'

'Yes, that's the point. In your opinion, if we were to devote more person-hours than we might normally do to catching the insects who dirtied this church – which amounts to no more than wilful damage and possible cruelty to a wild bird, which is unprovable – might they be able to throw some light on the religious activities of Mr Sayer?'

'You're asking if there's a network in this area?'

'Precisely.'

'I've no idea. It *is* our intention to build up a file or database, but I'm only just getting my feet under the table, and nothing like that seems to exist at present. My… predecessor—'

'Is not going to be saying an awful lot to anyone for quite a while, from what I hear. If ever.'

'I'm sorry about this.' Merrily was desperate for another cigarette, but unwilling to display weakness in front of Howe – who leaned back and looked pensive.

'Ms Watkins, what's your gut feeling?'

'My gut feeling… is that… although there's no obvious pattern, there's something a bit odd going on. I mean, I was on a course for Deliverance priests. All of us were vicars, rectors… Nobody does this full-time, that's the point. We were told a diocesan exorcist might receive four, five assignments in a year.'

'While you…?'

'You want to see my appointments diary already – plus two satanic links within a week. Yes, you might find it worth following through on the Stretford case. I wonder if they ever return to the scene of the crime.'

'Why do you ask?'

'I'm going back tonight to do what we call a minor exorcism.'

'Interesting. If they're local, they might not be able to resist turning up.'

'That's what I thought.'

'Thank you, Ms Watkins, we'll be represented.' Annie Howe snapped her briefcase shut.

'Just one thing.'

'Hmm?'

'Could you make them Christians?'

'Who?'

'The coppers.'

'Are you serious?'

'Two reasons,' Merrily said. 'One is that, if they're not, I can't let them in. Two, a few extra devout bodies at an exorcism can only help – I understand.'

'You understand.'

'I've never done one before, have I?'

26

Family Heirloom

LOL SAT IN the flat above Church Street – Moon's 'Capuchin Lane'. He was waiting for Denny.

He'd been waiting for Denny for several hours. It was going dark again. The shop below, called John Barleycorn, had been closed all day. Denny had not yet said he was coming, but Lol knew that sooner or later he would have to.

It was Anna Purefoy who had found the photocopy, about the same time that Lol left the bathroom and Denny went in and they heard him roar, in his agony and outrage, like a maddened bull. It was Mrs Purefoy, Lol thought, who – in the choking aftermath of a tragedy that was all the more horrifying because it *wasn't* a surprise – was the calmest of them.

'Is Katherine dead?'

Lol had nodded, still carrying an image of the encrusted overflow grille. Like the mouth of a vortex, Moon's life sucked into it.

'Tim,' Mrs Purefoy had said then, 'I think you should telephone the police from our house. I don't think we should touch anything here.'

And when Tim had gone, she'd led Lol to the telephone table by the side of the stairs. 'I was about to phone for them myself, and then I saw this.' Her red parka creaked as she bent over the table. 'Did you know about this, Mr Robinson?'

It was a copy of a cutting from the *Hereford Times*, dated November 1984. It took Lol less than half a minute to make horrifying sense of it. He was stunned.

'Did *you* know about it?'

A mad question maybe. Would anybody knowing about this have bought the old house?

By then, Denny had emerged from the bathroom, and was standing, head bowed, on the other side of the stairs. After a moment he looked up, wiped the back of a hand across his lips and shook his head savagely, his earring jangling. He didn't look at Lol or Mrs Purefoy as he strode through the room and out of the barn, the door swinging behind him. You could hear his feet grinding snow to slush as he paced outside.

Mrs Purefoy said, 'Did you know her very well, Mr Robinson?'

'Not well enough, obviously,' Lol said. 'No... no I didn't know her well.'

And then the police had arrived – two constables. After his first brief interview, not much more than personal details, Lol had gone out on the hill while they were talking to Denny and the Purefoys. He ascended the soggy earth-steps to the car, freezing up with delayed horror, a clogging of sorrow and shame backed up against a hundred questions.

He'd waited by the barn with Denny until they brought the body out. Hearing the splash and slap and gurgle and other sounds from the bathroom. Watching the utility coffin borne away to the post-mortem. And then he and Denny had gone to Hereford police headquarters, where they were questioned separately by a uniformed sergeant and a detective constable. Statements were made and signed, Lol feeling numbed throughout.

He and Denny had had no opportunity to talk in any kind of privacy.

The police had shown Lol the old cutting from the *Hereford Times* and asked him if he'd seen it before, or if he was aware of the events decribed in the story.

Lol had told them he knew it had happened, but not like this. He'd always understood it had been a shotgun in the woods, but he didn't remember how he had come to know that.

Later, the police let him read the item again. In the absence of a suicide note, they were obviously glad to have it. It made their job so much easier.

ANCIENT SWORD USED BY SUICIDE FARMER

Hereford farmer Harry Moon killed himself with a two-thousand-year-old family heirloom, an inquest was told this week.

Mr Moon, who had been forced to sell Dyn Farm on Dinedor Hill because of a failed business venture, told his family he was going to take a last look around the farm before they moved out.

He was later found by his young son in a barn near the house, lying in a stone cattle trough with both wrists cut.

Dennis Moon told Hereford Deputy Coroner Colin Hurley how he found a ten-inch long sword, an Iron Age relic, lying on his father's chest.

'The sword had hung in the hall for as long as I can remember,' he said. 'It was supposed to have been handed down from generation to generation.'

A verdict of suicide while the balance of mind was disturbed was recorded on 43-year-old Mr Moon, who...

'And when you left her at the door on Saturday evening,' the sergeant said, 'how would you describe Miss Moon's state of mind?'

'Kind of... intense,' Lol had said honestly.

'Intense, how?'

'She was researching a book about her family. I had the impression she couldn't wait to get back to it.'

The sergeant had shaken his head – not quite what he'd expected to hear.

Lol sat now in Ethel's old chair, shadows gathering around him.

Sometime tonight he'd have to ring Dick Lyden – most famous quote: *I realize you're a sensitive soul. But you don't particularly need to think about psychology when you're shagging someone, do you?* He couldn't face it.

Just before four-thirty p.m., he heard a key in the lock, and then Denny's footsteps on the stairs.

It had been Merrily's plan to spend an hour meditating in Ledwardine Church before driving nearly twenty miles to meet Huw at the church of St Cosmas and St Damien, but she'd been waylaid in the porch by Uncle Ted in heavy churchwarden mode.

'Where on earth have you been? I tried to ring your socalled office – engaged, engaged, engaged. It's not good enough, Merrily.'

'Ted, I've just spent nearly two hours trying to put together a small congregation that absolutely nobody wants to join. I have one hour to get myself together and then I've got to go out again.'

'I'm sorry, Merrily, but if you haven't got time for your own church, then—'

'Ted,' she backed away from him, 'I really don't want to go into this now, whatever it is. OK? Can we talk in the morning?'

It was not too dark to see his plump, smooth, retired face changing colour. 'Were you here this morning? Someone thought they saw you.'

'Early, yes.' God, was that only today?

'What time?'

'I don't know… sevenish maybe. What—?'

'Did you notice anything amiss?'

'I just went up to the chancel to pray. Don't say—'

'Yes, someone broke in. Someone broke into your church last night.'

'Oh God.' She thought at once of a dead crow and a smell of piss. 'What did they do?'

'Smashed a window.'

'Oh no.'

'Come and look.'

She followed him into the church, where the lights were on and they turned left into the vestry, where she saw that the bulb had been smashed in its shade and a big piece of hardboard covered the window facing the orchard.

The vestry. Thank God for that. No stained glass there.

'Did they take anything?'

'No, but that's not the point, is it?'

No blood, no entrails, no urine. Merrily took the opportunity to fumble her way to the wardrobe and pull out her vestments on their hangers. She'd have to change at home now.

'Have you told the police?'

'Of course we did – not that they took much interest.'

'I suppose if nothing was taken... Look, I'm sorry, Ted. I'll have to take a proper look round tomorrow. I have to tell Jane where I'm going.'

'And where *are* you going?'

'I have to conduct a service over at Stretford. Near Dilwyn.'

'This damned Deliverance twaddle again, I suppose,' he said contemptuously. 'You're on a damned slippery slope, Merrily.'

Denny's speech, his whole manner, had slowed down – like somebody had unplugged him, Lol thought, or stopped his medication. Denny seemed ten years older. His oversized earring now looked absurd.

'You see, Dad – he'd bought this house for us to move to when he sold the farm. At Tupsley, right on the edge of the city.'

Denny had the chair, Lol was on the floor by the bricked-up fireplace. A parchment-shaded reading lamp was on.

'Far too bloody close, that house,' Denny said. 'Christ. I used to wonder, didn't he ever think about that? How Mum was gonna be able to handle living around here with his suicide hanging over us? The whole family tainted with it? Everybody talking about us? The selfish bastard!'

Lol thought of that smiling man with the Land Rover who threw a shadow twenty-five years long. Denny lit up a Silk Cut from a full packet Merrily had left behind.

'So after he... died, we flogged the Tupsley house sharpish, and moved over to the first place we could find in Gloucester. We had relatives there, see, and nobody there to blab to little Kathy about what had happened, like kids would've done if we'd still been in town – whispers in the schoolyard. Jesus, *we* never talked about it. It never got mentioned in our house – let alone how it happened. If some bloody old auntie ever let it slip, Ma would go loopy for days after. And me... she's watching me all the time in case I'm developing the symptoms.'

'Of what?'

'Schizophrenia.'

Lol sensed Denny Moon's personal fears of inheriting some fatal family flaw, some sick gene – Denny keeping the anxiety well flattened under years of bluster, laughter and general loudness.

'So we... when Kathy's five or six and starting to ask questions like how come she didn't have an old man, we told her it was an accident. His gun went off in the woods. No big deal – she never remembered him anyway. When she was older, twelve maybe, I broke it to her that he topped himself, and why. But I stuck with the gun. You know why? Cause I knew she'd make me tell her what it was like, finding him. What he looked like in that trough – like one of them stone coffins you find around old churches.'

'Yes.' Lol found himself nodding, remembering the photo of Moon in the Cathedral Close charnel pit, gleefully holding up two ruined medieval skulls like she'd been reunited with old friends. So happy, so *at home* with images of death – reaching out to the image of her dead father, feverish eyes under the flat cap she thought he might have been wearing when he shot himself.

Sick!

Denny threw him a grateful glance. 'I was fifteen. All you can do with a memory like that is burn it out of your mind – like they used to do with the stump when you lost an arm in some battle. So she leaves school, goes off to university in Bristol. I get the first shop – inherited, Mum's side. I come back to Hereford. I meet Maggie. You know the rest.'

'It never occurred to you she'd find out one day?'

'Why?' Denny croaked. 'Why should she? All those years ago, how many people remember anyway? It was *over*. And how could I ever have imagined, in any kind of worst-case scenario, that she was gonna rent this place – the same fucking barn? What kind of impossible nightmare coincidence is that? I was amazed it's still here. Like who'd want to live at a house with that abattoir right next door?'

'Somebody obviously tried hard to keep the barn out of view.' Lol thought of the wall of fast-growing Leylandii. Planted there, presumably, by the people who'd bought Dyn Farm from Harry Moon, or by the owners after that. Out of sight, out of mind, out of nightmares. 'And the Purefoys were incomers. How would they know?'

'Stupid gits.'

'You...' Lol hesitated. 'You didn't think of telling her before she moved in?'

'And what do you think that would've achieved, Laurence? You think that would've put her off?' Denny produced wild, synthetic laughter. '*Her?*'

Poor bloody Denny, who wanted to burn away his own last image of Harry Moon like cauterizing a stump – terrified of what might happen if he came up here and it all crashed back on him.

So he'd simply stayed away, paying Dick to look out for his sister, and both of them laying it on Lol. Wanting Lol to get close, move in with her. Lol imagined what Merrily would say about this – a situation so unbelievably flawed and precarious that only men could have allowed it to develop.

And in a way that was right. But Lol could see Denny's skewed logic: why he'd gone to Dick Lyden instead of a real psychiatrist, and to Dick rather than Ruth. A guy he knew from the pub – a mate, nothing formal. Someone he could talk to, without having to tell all. *He's an idiot,* Moon had said.

'That paper,' Denny said. 'That copy of the *Times* – it never even came into our house. *You* know anything about this – how she got hold of it?'

Lol shook his head. 'First time I've seen it. I don't know… Did somebody give it to her? Was she going back through the old newspaper files, part of her research, and came across it that way?'

'And just laid it out there on the table, where the Purefoy woman found it? Had it all worked out, didn't she? So bloody *happy* to join the father she couldn't even remember.' Denny began to cry. 'Happy? You think she was happy?'

Some psychologist, Lol thought… maybe even Dick in his paper for *Psychology Today*… might draw a flawed parallel with the Heaven's Gate mass-suicides, all those people in San Diego who came to believe they could hitch a ride on the Hale Bopp comet.

'I never understood her,' Lol said.

And always just a little repelled.

'All down to me,' Denny said, his voice flat and dry like cardboard. 'It's all going down to me. She suddenly learns I lied to her all those years ago; that's what they're gonna say. And that fucking sword – and the bath. You know where that bath is, don't you?' He sprang up, fists clenched at his sides. 'That was exactly where the mangers were. For winter feed and water.'

Exactly? Lol felt cold inside.

'That stone trough… it was where the bath is now, I'd swear to it. They probably used the same holes for the fucking pipes. And the sword – that fucking sword, man! I want to *scream*. It is *not* possible.'

'She said she dug it up.'

'Where?'

'Just outside. Somebody had been trying to dig a pond and given up and she saw this thing sticking out where the ground had been excavated. Unless she knew all the time about what your father really did, there's no way she would have just found this thing and made that connection.'

'Nooo!' Denny leapt up, threw his cigarette on to the hearth. 'You don't understand, do you? The police… after the inquest, they asked if we wanted it back: the fucking family heirloom. The thing he'd specially sharpened on the old scythe stone, so it'd go through f… flesh… and veins, without much sawing.'

Lol thought about the blackened relic. *She* must have sharpened that too. Must have honed the edge, testing it on her thumb maybe – rehearsing. You didn't slash your wrists sideways, you cut upwards into the vein – a fellow patient in the psychiatric hospital had told Lol that. And warm water to prevent muscle cramps and stop the blood clotting. Dreamy, otherworldly, unstable Moon hadn't done a thing wrong.

'Police said what did we wanna do with it – this valuable antique. So I took it. Ma was in no state at the time, never would be again, so *I* took it. Ma signs for it, never knew what she was signing for. I was sixteen by then – big man taking charge. I knew what to do with it. I wrapped it up in some newspaper, stuffed it in my bike bag – brought it up here, back to the old farm. Come up on the bike early one morning, and buried the fucker.'

'*You* buried it?'

'And then, many years later, my poor little mental sister comes along and digs it up – the *same* blade.' Denny hissed, 'It defies fucking *belief*.'

'You don't know that.' Lol leapt up aghast. 'You can't possibly know that.'

'Don't *know* it? It was on our wall for... I dunno, for centuries. That's why I knew Kathy wasn't talking total crap about us being in this direct line to the old Celtic village. My grandad, when I was little, he told me that artefact'd been in the family for two thousand years. Sounds balls, don't it? What family's been two thousand years in the same spot?'

'Where did you bury it?'

'In the shit.' A short, bitter laugh. 'There was this kind of slurry pit in front of here in those days. I dug down to the bottom of it. I put the sword in the shit.'

It all fitted so well. Perhaps the Purefoys or their predecessors had found the old pit, thought it was the site of a pond, so dug down – and when no water came up, they abandoned it. It all fitted so horribly well.

'You tell the police it was the same sword?'

'They never asked. They knew she'd dug up all this stuff. Far as they're concerned she was just obsessed with Dad's suicide. They're not connecting it beyond an obsession. If you were the police, would you wanner know all this shit about the ancestors? Would you want a hint of anything...' Denny drew breath and bit his lower lip. 'Anything paranormal?'

'You think that?'

'Sometimes,' Denny said, 'it's the least complicated option.'

'She said it was telling her things,' Lol said. 'She wouldn't even let me touch it. She said she didn't want the flow blocked by anyone else's vibrations.'

'Madness,' Denny said. 'Let's just call it madness.'

Lol stood up and moved to the window, looked down into Capuchin Lane, snow now in rags against the house walls after a day of shoppers' shoes. 'She just wanted to think she was in... almost physical contact with her ancestors.'

'She's with the primitive fuckers now,' Denny said sourly.

27

Protect Her This Night

THE DAY AFTER tomorrow it would be December. Amidst frozen fields, the Church of St Cosmas and St Damien, a small candle-shimmer behind its leaded windows, looked peaceful in a humble-stable-at-Bethlehem way. Or so she told herself.

Another attempt to dispel the fear.

Always make time to prepare, Huw would say. All the time she'd made, she'd blown.

An hour fending off Ted Clowes, who saw himself as her lay-supervisor, who was always credited with getting Merrily the Ledwardine living – to ease the worries of her mother, his sister in Cheltenham who was convinced that it was only a matter of time before any female curate in Liverpool was found raped and battered in the churchyard.

Ted would also dump her without a qualm if anything began reflecting badly on himself.

'I think,' he'd told her before they finally parted tonight, 'that this parish is beginning to realize precisely where it stands with you, Merrily.'

And she knew that this time he'd cause trouble. Perhaps a discreet call to the Archdeacon, a question at the parish council which would be recorded in the minutes.

It had left her less than an hour to see to the blessing and bottling of the water and to explain to Jane where she was going and why Jane, who would be more than a bit interested, could not come. The truth was, if there was anything in there, she didn't want Jane exposed to it. Kids her age were easy prey. It might even have been kids Jane's age who were behind the desecration.

But Jane seemed unconcerned, said that was OK, as she was going out anyway, to see a movie in Hereford with Rowenna.

Hardly for the first time, as she parked the Volvo at the side of the track next to a Suzuki four-wheel drive and a muddied Mondeo, Merrily wondered why Jane did not have a boyfriend.

She went round the boot to fetch her case, containing the Bibles, the prayer books, the rites of blessing and lesser exorcism that she'd hand-copied on to cards, and the holy water. She was freezing. She'd changed into her vestments before leaving, so now she put on her cowled clerical cloak of heavy-weight loden, but it did nothing for the cold inside.

Lights shone from the cottages. The church, however, was in darkness, no candlelight visible from this side.

She saw figures waiting for her at the edge of the churchyard.

'DS Bliss.' He shone a torch upwards to his own ginger-topped face. 'Franny Bliss.' Merseyside accent. 'I'm a Catholic. You all right with that, Vicar?'

'That's… fine. I'm Merrily.'

'I know. Seen your piccy in the local rag. This big yobbo's PC Dave Jones. Nonconformist, him. What was that bloody chapel of yours again, Dave?'

'Pisgah, sarge. Pisgah Chapel.' PC Jones was in plain clothes: dark anorak and a flat cap. 'Not been back in years, mind.'

'I just love to hear him say it,' Bliss said. 'Now, just so's you know, Merrily, we've gor another lad hanging out by the farm. We don't talk about him – many years lapsed. That's why he gets to stay in the cold. Anyway, we're the best the DCI could put together in the time. Where do you want us?'

'I don't know how you want to handle it.' Merrily stood on the parapet surrounding the churchyard, looking out at the bare fields gleaming silver under a sizable moon. The wind plucked at her cloak. 'This could be a wild-goose chase for you.'

'Like most of our nights, that is,' said bulky Dave.

Merrily gathered the cloak around her. She was scared – and had been since changing into her priestly things. Under her cloak, the cassock had begun to feel clammy, the surplice stiff.

'For a start, who else knows about this?' Franny Bliss asked.

'Well, I told Major Weston, and made a courtesy call to my colleague at Dilwyn. Left a message on his machine, anyway. I also rang the farm here and got the numbers of about half a dozen people living in the area, giving them the opportunity to come along if they felt strongly about it.'

'Or if they fancied watching an exorcism?'

Merrily sighed. 'Unfortunately, yes. But I said the number allowed inside the church would be limited. And definitely no children.'

'Would it be all right if we talked to a few of the locals? In areas like this, people hear things.'

'Afterwards, though.'

'We'll ask them to hang on. And we'll pay particular attention to anyone who doesn't want to. I do feel quite strongly about it meself. It's only wilful damage, but if they can do this, they're capable of a lot of other stuff carrying stiffer sentences, you know what I mean?'

'I had a chat with Inspector Howe.'

'And your Bishop's had a chat with our Divisional Super. It's about community relations at the highest level.'

'Ah, I'm sorry about that.' The Bishop had been hard to pin down, and tonight's ceremony had, in the end, been cleared with him on his mobile via Sophie.

'Not that we wouldn't be here anyway,' Franny Bliss said, 'but maybe not *three* of us. Still, get *these* lads, and even if we don't get a line on the body in the Wye, we might get something else.'

'Might get possessed, sarge,' PC Jones said heavily.

'Merrily'll protect us, Dave. Won't yer, Merrily?'

There was nothing essentially *wrong* with Christianity, Patricia said. It promoted a useful, if simplistic, moral code. But it was an import. When it was introduced, it was revolutionary and brash and sometimes brutal and crass. It trampled over ancient wisdom.

Jane saw Rowenna's glance. None of the rest of the group knew her mother was a vicar. They thought she was a teacher. And they thought Jane was eighteen and working as a secretary.

Blinds were down over the window. A small brass oil lamp burned on a high table. Seven of them sat in a vague semicircle around Patricia, on mats and dark-coloured pillows. There was a faint scent, musty-sweet, perhaps from the oil in the lamp. It was mysterious but also cosy.

'And Christianity has always been used as a prop for prejudices,' Patricia continued, 'creating the myth of the cloven-hoofed devil and demonizing black cats, which were tortured and slaughtered in their hundreds.'

Jane thought about Ethel and seethed.

'So many of these things are forgotten now,' Patricia said.

Patricia had the look of someone much older than she possibly could be, someone who'd been soaking up wisdom for like *centuries*. She was the elder of the circle and the others deferred to her. Jane wasn't sure how many others there were in the group. They came from a wide area on both sides of the Welsh border. All women: a couple of old-hippy types – long skirts and braided hair – but mainly the kind you thought of as school-teacherish. Thank heavens none of their own teachers were here.

She and Rowenna were the youngest. The women called themselves 'the Pod', after the café itself.

Patricia was saying: 'It's the basis of many of our exercises that human beings are the central nervous system of the Earth.

Thus we can receive impulses and also send them out. We can effect changes with our minds, and this is a responsibility not to be taken lightly.'

That was the definition of magic, wasn't it? Effecting change with the mind – Mum's lot would say that only God could effect changes. Which, from where Jane was sitting, was bollocks basically – all this Serving the Will of God stuff. Like the wholesale slaughter of black cats? The Spanish Inquisition?

But was the Pod a *pagan* thing? Because, OK, she was entitled to find her own spiritual path, but it would be better if it was like *parallel* to Mum's. She wasn't particularly looking for confrontation and heavy-duty domestic strife.

She just wished someone would explain simple things like that.

'It's about consciousness.' Patricia looked suddenly at Jane, as if she'd picked up her thoughts, her uncertainty.

Jane shivered. She was a little scared of Patricia, with her smoky-grey dress and her tight, parchment-coloured hair. She wanted to ask exactly what Patricia meant by 'consciousness'. But this was only their second meeting, and she didn't want to seem stupid. The nature of consciousness was something on which she'd be expected to meditate – she was establishing a special corner for that in her sitting-room/study, next to a big yellow rectangle on one of the Mondrian walls. She'd bought a little incense-burner but hadn't used it yet.

It was all a little bit frightening – therefore, naturally, wonderful.

Jane glanced up. Patricia was looking directly at her. In the gloom, Patricia's eyes burned like tiny torchbulbs.

Jane gulped, suddenly panicked. Christ, she'd been rumbled. They'd found out that her mother was an Anglican priest. They thought she was some sort of Church spy. She looked across at Rowenna, but Rowenna was staring away into the darkness. The others were gazing placidly down into their laps. She didn't really know any of them; Angela, the tarot lady, had not been present at either of the meetings.

Jane had expected all kinds of questions before she was admitted to the circle, but it hadn't been like that. It was only when you got here and experienced the electric atmosphere – as if this little room was the entrance to an endless tunnel – that you instinctively wanted to keep quiet about yourself. At least, you did if your old lady was a vicar.

'Don't worry, Jane,' Patricia said suddenly. 'We're here to help you.' The woman smiled thinly.

The wind whined in the rafters and the flame of the oil lamp shrank back, as though it was cowering.

Cool!

The church was now lit by two oil lamps supported on brackets, three candles and a hurricane lantern on the central pulpit. It looked deceptively cosy. Huw Owen was there with a curly-haired, jutting-jawed, youngish minister, who backed away from Merrily in her cloak, as if she was a vampire, throwing up his hands in mock defence.

'Mrs Watkins, I *beg* forgiveness.'

'From me?'

'I'm Jeffrey Kimball, from Dilwyn. Major Weston approached me this morning, to perform the necessary, and I'm afraid I threw a tantrum and gave him your home number, which I looked up in the telephone book. It was pure pique on my part after that memorandum from the Bishop on the subject of Deliverance, and I'm sorry to have taken it out on you.'

'I can understand your—'

'To be quite honest, Mrs Watkins, I tend to object to more or less anything this particular bishop does. I do so *hate* blatantly political appointments of any kind. Absolutely *everyone* thought Hereford should have gone to Tom Armstrong – a canon at the Cathedral for five years before he went to Reading as Dean... *Immensely* able man... and they used a very minor heart problem as an excuse to give it to Hunter. I make no secret of my feelings, and I realize you—'

'Happen you can save that till after, lad,' Huw Owen said.

'Oh.' The Rev. Kimball let his arms fall to his sides. 'Yes, of course. I should have thought.'

'Merrily needs a bit of quiet,' Huw said.

'Yes, I shall leave you alone and go out to contemplate the moonlight on the snow.'

'Aye, give us quarter of an hour, there's a good lad.'

'I know his type,' Huw said as the latch dropped into place behind Kimball. 'Gets to the age when the bishops are looking younger. How are you, lass?'

She hugged Huw. It was the first time they'd been together since the Deliverance course. He wore what looked like an air-force greatcoat and a yellow bobble-hat.

'You all right for this, Merrily?'

'Sure.' She looked around, sniffed the air, could only smell disinfectant.

'Who cleared it up?' Huw asked.

'I did. Couldn't ask anybody else, could I? Buried the… remains… just over the wall. Little ceremony.'

'Hands and knees wi' a scrubbing brush, eh? What you got in mind for tonight?'

'We're looking at minor exorcism.'

'Never go over the top.'

'A cleansing. Holy water.'

'Go right round it, I would. Take one of them coppers with you. Never had a copper at one of mine. Right, make a start? You want to pray together first?'

'That would be good.'

They sat side by side on the pew nearest the pulpit. 'I'll keep it simple,' Huw said, 'then we'll have a bit of quiet. Lord, be with us in this tainted place tonight. Help this lass, Merrily, to repossess it, in Your name, from whatever dark shadows may still hang around it. Protect her this night, amen.'

'Amen,' Merrily added.

And, during the ensuing period of quiet, she felt nothing – at first.

When she closed her eyes, she saw neither the blue nor the gold, nor the lamplit path. She saw nothing but a swirling grey untinged by the lamps and the candles.

She was not comfortable on the strange, sloping pew. Found she was squirming a bit, her cassock feeling clammy again. She was actually sweating; she felt damp down her spine. *Come on, calm down.* She undid the cloak, let it slip from her shoulders. Opened her eyes, but lowered the lids, letting them relax. Shifted position again, and was aware of Huw's brief sideways glance.

Lamplight flushed the sandstone faces of the knight and his lady, raised only inches above the floor to her left. They were believed, she now knew, to be John and Agnes de la Bere. The de la Beres were lords of the manor for much of the Middle Ages. John wore armour and carried a shield; his wife was gowned and wimpled, slim and girlishly pretty. Another knight, probably John's father, Robert, lay in the sub-chancel in front with his wife Margaret. Some effigies were terrifying, but these were courtly and benign and truthful. John de la Bere was stocky, had narrow eyes and a big nose.

In other words, she felt OK about them. And about the church. So why was she so uneasy?

She closed her eyes again, pressed her hands formally together, like the hands of John and Agnes de la Bere, and murmured *St Patrick's Breastplate* in her mind. She smelled the pine disinfectant she'd borrowed from the farm, and ignored the slow-burning itch which occurred in the palm of her left hand and then the right, as though transmitted from one to the other.

Huw was watching her openly now. She was absolutely desperate for a smoke. She shifted again. The itch in her hands was worse; she couldn't ignore it, had to concentrate hard to stop herself pulling her hands apart and rubbing her palms on the edge of the pew.

When she could bear it no longer and yearned for relief, she was at last given some help.

Scritch-scratch.

The tiny bird-claw, the curling nail on a yellow finger. The smell of disinfectant had grown sweet and rancid, and was pulled into her nostrils like thin string and down into her throat.

Cat faeces and gangrene.

A rough cough came up like vomit. Merrily began to cough and cough and couldn't stop. She folded up on the pew, arms flailing, eyes streaming. She felt Huw's arms around her, heard him praying frantically under his breath, clutching her to him, and still she couldn't stop coughing and slid down his legs to the stone floor, and he pulled away from her and she heard him scrabbling about.

'Drink,' he said urgently. Then a hard ring of glass pushing at her lips, chinking on her teeth.

She gripped it and sucked and Huw held it there.

Merrily fell back against the pew, holy water dribbling down her chin, the lamps and candles blurring into a blaze. Huw brought her gently to her feet and put her cloak around her shoulders.

'Out of here, lass,' he said mildly. 'Don't come back, eh?'

28

Crone with a Toad

LOL SAW THAT Dick Lyden had become aware of deep waters and was now backing into the paddling area. Dick poured Glenmorangie for Lol and himself. He still looked shaken: not terribly upset exactly, more like unnerved. Almost certainly this was the first time a client of his had taken her own life.

An unexpected minefield then, psychotherapy.

Dick sat down behind his desk lamp, some art-deco thing with a cold blue shade. It created distance.

'And the police, Lol... the police are saying what?'

'Keeping the lid on it. No crime, no guilty parties. Probably doing their best to disregard the bizarre bits.'

Dick had finally got through on the phone, demanding Lol should come round at once. Needing to know, for his peace of mind and his professional security, everything that had happened and how it might rebound on him.

This was no longer jolly old Dick revelling in his newfound status as analyst, delightedly knitting strands of experience together into some stupid woolly jumper.

Lol said, 'As I understand it, they don't particularly want to *know* if it's the same sword, basically.'

'That's quite understandable. A suicide is not a murder. This... this wrist-cutting is still not uncommon, I gather, in an age of subtler methods. Not a difficult way to go. More distressing, perhaps, for whoever finds the body. And the weapon?

An important symbol for Moon, no doubt, under the regrettable circumstances, but irrelevant as far as the police are concerned. But what the hell was Denny doing sitting on this information? Would I have supported her plan to move into that place if I'd known her father had done it in that actual same... When's the inquest?'

Meaning: *Will I be called? What am I going to say?*

'Going to be opened tomorrow, but that's just so Denny can give formal identification of the body and they can release her for burial. It'll then be adjourned for weeks – maybe months – while they put the medical evidence together.'

'They haven't been to see me yet.'

'Maybe you don't matter, Dick,' Lol said coldly.

He'd hate to think that Dick was counting on the inquest being economical with the facts, so there'd be more unpublicized material available for his own psychological paper on Moon's case. He'd really *hate* to think that.

But the inquest was going to get it all wrong, wasn't it?

Just that Lol couldn't see through to the truth either.

'Look... ahm...' Dick leaned back, well behind his blue lamp. 'Lol, I don't want you to blame yourself for this. You tried to get close to her and it didn't work out. Perhaps that was a mistake, but we'll never know. We must accept we'll never know, and... and... and let it go.'

A subtle restructuring of history here: like it had been Lol's sole decision to try to get close to Moon, with Dick's tentative, guarded approval.

'Well,' Dick stood up, 'thanks for coming over. Ahm... this won't affect the boy's recording, will it? Denny... well, obviously something creative to occupy his mind.'

Tuneless Little Twats with Fender Strats.

'I'm sure it's exactly what he needs,' said Lol.

'Good man,' Dick said. 'The boy, you see... the boy's been very difficult and uncommunicative, and when he does communicate, it's with an unpleasant teenage sneer. Goes out every night now, pushing it as far as he can get. When he's not with his band, he's with some girl. Some girl's got her hooks into him, so I would rather he was with the band in Denny's studio. At least until after Sunday.'

'Why Sunday?'

'His enthronement as Boy Bishop in the Cathedral, during evensong. By the actual Bishop, and before a packed Cathedral. Just let's get that over with.'

'You still think he might back out, right?'

'Not if the little shit knows what's good for him,' Dick said through his teeth. Then he laughed at his own venom. 'Look, Lol, Moon was ill – more ill than any of us knew. Delusional. Shouldn't have been on her own there. We're all to blame for that – Denny, you, ah... me, and the Health Service. All I'm saying... the police are right. Let's not overcomplicate things, or see things that might not be there. That's how myths are created.'

'Right,' Lol said. A small fury ignited inside him.

'Good man.' Dick clapped him on the shoulder.

It was thawing at last. Clouds crowded the moon as Lol crossed the main road towards the refashioned ruins of the city wall.

This CD would be his last work for Dick Lyden. He hadn't been to his psychology night-class for over a fortnight.

The city wall glistened in the moonlight.

So the version of Moon's death which the inquest would establish would be untrue. The verdict – unless the post-mortem threw up something unexpected – would be a straightforward Suicide While the Balance of Mind was Disturbed. And no blindingly obvious warnings from the coroner afterwards; there was nothing anyone else would learn from this.

And when you left her at the door on Saturday evening, how would you describe Miss Moon's state of mind?

Kind of... intense. She was researching a book. About her family. I had the impression she couldn't wait to get back to it.

It was true. When he'd left her, there was no indication at all that she might—

If you were the police, Denny had said, *would you want a hint of anything paranormal?*

Why had Denny said that? It was the first time he'd ever mentioned the paranormal in connection with Moon, or indeed any connection at all. But how well did he really know Denny? Only well enough to know now that Denny had been putting up a front to conceal unvoiced fears. Perhaps if he'd told Denny, rather than Dick, about the crow and about Moon seeing her father…

Oh, hell!

Lol stood on the medieval bridge, gazing over the parapet into the Wye, numbed by a quiet panic. He didn't know what to do, which street to go down. Directionless. Working with Dick, while it hadn't felt exactly *right*, at least had been a new rope to hold on to.

Very soon he would reach the main road again, having walked in a complete circle. He felt like some aimless vagrant – or worse, closer to the truth, a mental patient returned to the care of the community. He turned abruptly, moved back up Bridge Street, past the off-licence and Peter Bell's Typewriter Shop, the snow on the pavement reduced to slivers of slush.

Two young women walked out of a darkened doorway about five yards ahead of him and he saw, by an all-night-lighted shopfront, that one of them was Jane Watkins. Perhaps she noticed him; she turned sharply away and hurried on, slightly ahead of her companion.

The doorway belonged to Pod's, a healthfood café. He'd been in there just once: it was dark and primitive and woody, with secondhand tables and rickety chairs – people who opened healthfood restaurants were into recycling and no frills. On the whitewashed walls, in thin black frames, he remembered, were reproductions of drawings by Mervyn Peake: twisted figures, spindly figures, bulbous figures, in gloomy landscapes. Lol recalled eating a soya-sausage roll under one showing a crone with a toad. He hadn't stayed long.

When she got in, she put out some food for Ethel and went up to the bathroom, which was still like a 1950s public lavatory, with black and white tiles and a shower the size of an iron streetlamp. She sat on the lavatory, head in hands, her stomach churning. She heard Jane's key turn in the door, but it was quite a while before Merrily could go down.

'You're ill,' Jane said. Looking up from the omelette mix in the pan. The sight of the yellow slop made Merrily want to throw up.

She shivered damply inside her dressing-gown. 'I'm sorry, flower, I can't eat... anything. I'm really sorry.'

'I'd better stay off school tomorrow and look after you,' Jane said promptly, 'if you're no better by then.'

'No, thank you... I mean, certainly not.'

'How long have you been in?'

'Not long.' Merrily leaned against the Aga rail next to her daughter.

'How did it go?'

'All right, I think.'

'Did you feel ill *then*?'

'Yes. In fact, I... couldn't do it. But Huw was there. Huw did it.'

Jane sniffed, her eyes narrowing. 'You've been drinking.'

'Hey, what is this? I called into a pub for something to settle my stomach.'

Everybody trying not to stare at the cloaked figure with the bottom of her cassock showing: the first female whisky-priest in the diocese.

'Hmm,' Jane said, 'why don't you go to bed? I'll bring you a drink up.'

'Thanks, flower.' She thought she might be about to cry.

Again.

She took up a hot-water bottle, dumped her cassock and surplice in the wash-bin, lay between the sheets and sweated.

She'd been here before: a panic-attack at her own installation service at Ledwardine Church. And hallucinations...

But what kind of sick, warped mind conjures up the filth of Denzil Joy?

Dear God.

Franny Bliss and his colleague had watched her hobble to the car, perhaps waiting to see her safely back to the church of St Cosmas and St Damien, but she hadn't returned. *Out of here, lass.*

It was all over. Finished.

Jane brought her hot chocolate.

'There's a drop of brandy in it.'

'You'll have me at the Betty Ford Clinic, flower.'

Jane smiled wanly.

'Where did *you* go tonight?'

'Just... you know... to see a couple of friends.'

'They could come here sometime. Lots of room.'

'Yeah,' Jane said. 'Maybe sometime.'

Merrily sank back into the sweat-damp pillow and slithered into a feverish sleep. At times she heard bleeps and voices – which might have been on the answering machine or in her hot, fogged head – like satanic static.

Just before midnight, the bedside phone bleeped.

'Huw?' she said feverishly.

'You were asleep, Merrily?'

'Yes. Hello, Eileen.'

'Your man's back,' Cullen said, 'with his candles and his bottles.'

'Oh.'

'I said I'd call you.'

She clawed for consciousness. 'It's not... visiting time, is it?'

'Jesus, you *must* have been sound asleep. Being as Mr Dobbs is in a side ward, *any* time is visiting time, within reason. This is not exactly within my idea of reason, but the visitor's a very plausible feller. Whatever the hell kind of weirdness he's getting up to in there, I have to say I quite took to him.'

'You... talked to him?'

'He was very apologetic. Said he'd have come earlier but he had some urgent business to see to... Are you still there, Merrily?'

'What did he look like?'

'Oh... late fifties. Longish, straggly grey hair. He had a bobble-hat and he was in this auld blue airman's coat. Talked like... who's that feller? Alan Bennett? But a real auld hippy, you know?'

'Yes.'

'He's still in there, doing his stuff around Mr Dobbs with his candles. Probably be gone by the time you get here. I could try to keep him talking, if you like...'

'No,' Merrily said bleakly, 'it's all right now, Eileen. I don't think I want to see him.'

29

Fog

At first it felt like the start of a cold: that filthy, metallic tainting of the back of the throat. And then she was fully awake – knowing what it was, panting in terror.

He's here!

Rolling out of bed, breath coming in sobs, rolling over and scrambling on to her knees, she began to mutter the *Breastplate*, groping on the carpet for her pectoral cross.

> '*... by invocation of the same*
> '*The Three in One and One in Three.*
> '*Of whom all nature hath creation.*
> '*Eternal Father, Spirit, Word...*'

And she fell back against the bottom of the bed, gulping air. *Gone? Perhaps.*

After a while she sat up, before reaching instinctively for the cigarettes and lighter, pulling herself to her feet, into the old woollen dressing-gown and out of the cold, uncosy bedroom.

She ached. The light from the landing window was the colour of damp concrete. The garden below looked like her head felt: choked with fog. She stood swaying at the top of the stairs, dizzy, thought she would fall, and hugged the newel post on the landing, the cigarette dangling from her mouth. Repeatedly scraping her thumb against the Zippo, but the light wouldn't come. Sweating and shaking with panic and betrayal.

'Mum?'

What?

'Mum!'

The kid stood at the bottom of the stairs, looking frightened.

Merrily heard a single letter dropping through the box. The postman.

Normality.

She began to cough. *No such thing.*

Because there was no light, as such, penetrating Capuchin Lane, Lol overslept and awoke to the leaden grind of a harmonium from the shop below, a deep and doomy female voice.

Nico. Mournful, sinister old Nico songs from the seventies. Unshaven, Lol made it down to the shop, past Moon's lonely mountain-bike, and found Viv, the new manager: a sloppy-hippy granny, old friend of Denny's.

'Do you like Nico, Lol?'

'Sometimes,' Lol said.

'I love her,' Viv said. 'I know she's not to everybody's taste. But it's Moon's funeral on Friday: a mourning time.'

'That's three days away.' He didn't know whether Moon had ever even liked Nico; it was not unlikely.

'I thought I'd play it for an hour every morning, to show that we're in mourning,' Viv promised. 'There's a letter for you, from London.'

Lol opened it over his toast in the corner café. Ironically it promised money – money, as usual, for nothing. The revered Norma Waterson wanted to use one of his songs on her next solo album. It was 'The Baker's Lament', the one about the death of traditional village life.

He was depressed. By James Lyden's rules, he should have been dead now for at least ten years. On the other hand, unless folk singers were exempt, Norma Waterson should have been dead for over twenty-five. He stared through the café window into the fog. There was nothing in the day ahead for him. It had come to this.

Whereas Moon, so excited by her research, so driven... had just simply ended it.

He could not believe that what she'd discovered had led her to the conclusion that the only way of repairing the broken link with her ancestors was by joining them.

He'd heard nothing more from Merrily.

Lol finished his toast, walked back to the shop. A customer was coming out, and Lol heard that endless dirge again through the open door. It sounded – because Nico was also dead – like an accusation from beyond the grave, a bony finger pointing.

Sophie was saying into the phone, 'Have they double-checked? Yes, of course, I'm sorry. But it seems so...'

Merrily pulled off her coat, tossed it over the back of her chair, slumped down into it. She was going to miss Sophie, and even the office with ₪ on the door – almost a second home now, with none of the complications of the first.

Sophie put down the phone, tucking a strand of white hair behind one ear. 'It's bizarre, Merrily, quite bizarre. That was George Curtiss. The Dean's absolutely furious. You know the Cantilupe tomb was due to be reassembled this week, in time for the Boy Bishop ceremony on Sunday? But, would you believe, there's a piece missing.'

'A piece?'

'One of the side panels. You know the side-panels with the figures of knights? Knights Templar, someone suggested.'

'I know.' She remembered the knights, blurred by age, their faces disfigured.

'Well, one had broken away from the panel. Maybe through age or stone-fatigue. It was due to be repaired, but now it's vanished!'

'Someone pinched a slab of stone?'

'So it seems. When the masons were sorting out all the segments it just wasn't there. It's not huge – about a foot wide, eighteen inches deep – though heavy obviously.'

'Not easily shoved in your shopping bag,' Merrily said. 'But safely locked up behind that partition, surely?'

'That's the point.' Sophie looked worried. 'About the only time its removal could have happened was when we were all fussing over Canon Dobbs, after his stroke.'

'They suspect one of us?' *Maybe*, she thought insanely, *I could resign under suspicion of stealing a chunk of Cantilupe.* It would be easier, less complicated.

'This Dean will suspect anyone connected with the Bishop,' Sophie said with rare malice. 'He's already calling for a full inquiry. No, I don't for a minute think they suspect one of us. They just think we might have been more... I don't know... observant.'

'Who'd want to nick a single medieval knight not in terrific condition? And what for – a bird-table?'

'Don't joke about it in front of the Dean, whatever you do.'

'I never seem to meet the Dean,' Merrily said.

'Personally I *never* joke in front of the Dean.' The Bishop had appeared in the doorway. The Bishop at his hunkiest, with the possibly-Armani jacket over a denim shirt and jeans. The only purple now was a handkerchief carelessly tucked into his breast pocket. 'Good morning, Sophie. Merrily, how did it go last night? Nothing over the top, one trusts. Restraint is our new watchword.'

She said, 'You haven't heard?'

'What should I have heard?'

'Mick, look...' She came slowly to her feet. 'I need to talk to you.'

'Oh yes,' Sophie said quickly, 'the blessing at Stretford. I gather you weren't very well, Merrily.'

'Who told—?'

'She really shouldn't have turned out, Michael,' Sophie said. 'You can see how terribly pale she is.'

'Merrily?' The Bishop moved into the office, turned his famous blue eyes on her. 'Lord, yes, you don't look well at all.'

'Fortunately,' Sophie said, 'Huw Owen was present and able to take over and conduct the service, so that was all right.'

Merrily stared at her. *What are you doing?*

'Owen?' The Bishop's face stiffened with outrage. 'Who the *hell* invited Owen?'

'I did,' Merrily said. 'I'm sorry, I should have told you, shouldn't I?'

'Yes, you should. The man's from outside the diocese. He's *Church in Wales.*'

'It's my fault,' Sophie said quickly. 'Merrily told me she'd asked the Reverend Owen to come in as…'

'Hand-holder,' Merrily said. 'It was my first serious exorcism. As it was to be in a church, I didn't want to make a mistake.'

'Well, I should have been told,' the Bishop said almost peevishly. 'I realize he was your course tutor, Merrily, but I've appointed *you*, not him. In fact, if I'd known more about Owen at the time, we might not have sent you on that particular course.'

'I'm sorry?'

'Let's just say' – the Bishop's eyes were hard – 'that his roots are planted in the same general area as Dobbs's.'

'Oh, Michael…' Any further discussion of the dangers of medievalism was forestalled by Sophie informing the Bishop about the missing Cantilupe knight, apparently smuggled out of the Cathedral.

'And that's all they took?' The Bishop slowly shook his head, half-smiling now. 'Admittedly, we don't want opportunist tomb-robbers cruising the Cathedral, but it's hardly cause for a major panic. Surely our guys can construct a temporary substitute if they need to put the shrine together in a hurry. Reconstituted stone or something. Who, after all, is going to know?'

'Reconstituted stone?' Sophie said faintly.

'Poor old boy's bones are already widely scattered,' the Bishop said reasonably. 'It's not as if those knights have anything to guard any more, is it? Sophie, Val and I shall be leaving earlier for London than planned.'

'I'm sorry,' Sophie spun towards her office, 'I thought the reception was tomorrow.'

'Well, there's going to be a dinner now, tonight – with Tony and Cherie. And other people, of course.' He laughed. 'One can hardly reschedule these things according to one's personal convenience. We'll need to get off before lunch. So... Merrily,' turning his attention on her like a loaded shotgun, 'I want you to think about something.'

He stepped back and surveyed her – critically, she thought – in her black jumper and woollen skirt, flaking fake-Barbour over the back of the chair.

Whatever it is now, she thought, *not today.*

'Ironic that the question of Dobbs and Owen should arise. Traditionalism – I want all this to be raised at the next General Synod, and I want you, Merrily, to give some thought to producing a paper on what, for want of a better term, I'm officially calling New Deliverance.'

She stared at him. 'Me?'

'Very definitely you. I think I may be looking at the very *face* of New Deliverance.'

'Bishop, I don't know what you mean about "New". Surely the whole point of—'

'You know very well what I mean, Merrily. Think back to our discussion in the Green Dragon. Anyway, I don't have time to expand on it now. We'll talk again before Christmas, yes?'

She couldn't reply.

'Excellent,' the Bishop said crisply. As he left, Merrily's phone rang.

'Merrily. Frannie Bliss. Remember? How are you?'

'I'm... OK.'

'You don't sound all that OK to me. You should've said something – us keeping you talking outside in the cold all that time. Not that it was much warmer inside. Sorry you had to go off like that, but you probably did the best thing. He's a card, that Huw, isn't he? Turned out well for us, anyway.'

'It did?'

'I'm not gonna bore you with the run-up to this, but we finally had a chat with two very nice elderly ladies: sisters, churchgoers, and active members of the Royal Society for the Protection of Birds. They put us on to a lad called Craig Proctor, lives out near Monkland. Now young Craig, for reasons you really don't want to know about, especially if you're not feeling well, is an expert at trapping wild birds. These old ladies've been after him for months, but he's clever is Craig – or he thought he was. Anyway, after a long and meaningful exchange at Leominster nick this morning, Craig has told us he was approached by a chap he didn't know, and given a hundred and fifty pounds to procure one live carrion crow.'

'Christ.'

The fog outside was like a carpet against the window.

'Yeh,' Frannie said. 'Now, what's that say to you, Merrily?'

'It says you're not just looking for a bunch of kids who've seen some nasty films.'

'The real thing, eh?'

'Yes, though I don't know what I mean when I say that. Did you get a description out of him?'

'Young guy – motorbike, moustache, hard-looking. That's not much help. Craig's never seen him before, he claims.'

'You arrest him?'

'No. He knew we'd no evidence and he wasn't gonna confess.'

'You made a deal.'

'We don't make deals, as you well know, Merrily. Just have a little think about why somebody would blow a hundred and fifty on setting up some grubby little sacrifice in a church nobody uses.'

'And taking a considerable risk too,' Merrily said. 'Stretford itself might be a bit lonely, but the church is hardly lonely *within* Stretford.'

'That too.'

'Have you asked Huw?'

'Well, yeh, I did call Huw, to be honest, but he wasn't there.'

'He's a busy man,' Merrily said quietly.

Sophie had gestured to her something about popping out for a while. Merrily considered waiting for her to return, needing to find out how she'd learned about last night's disaster, and why she'd been so quick to cover up in front of the Bishop.

But, by lunchtime, Sophie had not come back, so Merrily switched on the computer and typed out the letter.

It had already been composed in her head on the way here. It was formal and uncomplicated. That was always best; no need for details – not that she felt able to put that stuff on paper.

Dear Bishop,

After long consideration and a great deal of prayer and agonizing, I have decided to ask you to accept my resignation from the role of Diocesan Deliverance Consultant.

I do not doubt that this is – or will become – a valid job for a woman. However, events have proved to me that I am not yet sufficiently wise or experienced enough to take it on. Therefore I honestly think I should make a discreet exit before I become a liability to the Church.

I would like to thank you for your kindness and –

albeit misplaced – confidence in me. I am sorry for
wasting so much of your very valuable time.
    Yours sincerely,
    Merrily Watkins

It hung there on the screen and she sat in front of it, reading
it over and over again until she saw it only as words with no
coherent meaning.

She could print it out and post it, or send it through the
internal mail. Either way, he would not see it before he and Val
left for London. Or maybe e-mail it immediately to the Bishop's
Palace? That would be the quickest and the best, and leave no
room for hesitation.

She read it through again; there was nothing more to say. She
looked up the Palace's e-mail address and prepared to send. It
would be courteous, perhaps, to show it first to Sophie. Perhaps
she'd wait until Sophie returned, perhaps she wouldn't. What
she would *not* do was ring Huw Owen about it.

As often, the only certainty was a cigarette. Her packet was
empty, so she felt in her bag for another, and came up with a
creamy-white envelope, the one pushed through the letterbox
while she was shivering on the landing. She'd stuffed it into her
bag, while arguing with Jane that she was perfectly fit to go to
work – no, she did not have flu. *It's mental, flower. I'm coming
apart and torturing myself with sick, sexual, demonic fantasies.
God's way of showing me I'm not equipped to take on other
people's terrors.* But she hadn't said any of that either.

She opened the letter, postmarked Hereford and addressed
to The Reverend Mrs Watkins. It came straight to the point.

Dear Reverend Watkins,

You should know that your Daughter has been seen
brazenly endangering her Soul, and yours, by
mixing with the Spiritually Unclean.

Ask her what she was doing last Saturday
afternoon at the so-called PSYCHIC FAIR at
Leominster. It is well known that such events
attract members of Occult Groups in search of
converts. Ask her how long she has been
consorting with a Clairvoyant who uses the Devil's
Picturebook.

Many people have always been disgusted that
your Daughter does not attend Church as the
Daughter of a Minister of God ought to. Now we
know why.

If it is true that you have been appointed
Exorcist then perhaps you should start by
cleansing the Filthy Soul of Your Own Daughter.

It was unsigned. Quite expensively done, judged by the
standards set by these creeps. Usually the paper was cheap and
crumpled, and whereas most of them were pushed into a letterbox, either here or at the church, this one had come by post.

Surprising how many anonymous letters you got. Or perhaps
male ministers didn't get so many – quite a few of these letters
muttered that you should stop pretending to be a priest and go
out and get yourself a husband like ordinary, decent women did.
One or two of them also offered to give her what ordinary, decent
women were getting, but she evidently wasn't. She picked these
ones up by one corner and washed her hands afterwards.

Some of them she felt she ought to file, or give to the police
in case other women were receiving similar messages and the
sender ever got nicked. Some she really didn't want to take to
the police, in case anyone at the station suspected there was no
smoke without fire.

But most of them got burned in the grate or the nearest
ashtray.

Merrily flicked the Zippo. It would be true, of course. Jane
had laid it on the line that altogether fateful afternoon in the

coffee lounge at the Green Dragon. *The Church has always been on this kind of paternalistic power-trip, doesn't want people to search for the truth. Like it used to be science and Darwinism and stuff they were worried about. Now it's the New Age because that's like real practical spirituality.*

Psychic fairs were where people went in search of 'Real Practical Spirituality'. Merrily didn't doubt that what the letter said was essentially true. It would explain a lot of things, not least the allure of Rowenna.

She knew the Devil's Picturebook was the tarot – a doorway.

Et tu, flower. She felt choked by acrid fog. Her head ached.

No option now.

She sent the Bishop his e-mail, walked out of the office and down the stone stairs.

PART THREE

PROJECTION

30

Self-pity

SHE FELT COLD, and dangerously light inside, as though a dead weight had rolled away, but releasing nothing. She stepped through a tide of pensioners, a coach party heading towards the Cathedral. The sky was overcast. Nobody seemed to be smiling any more. One of the old men looked a bit like Dobbs.

She should tell Dobbs that it was OK now. That he could go ahead and recover. She'd do that, yes. She'd go to the hospital at visiting time and tell him. *Jesus Christ was the first exorcist; the pattern is unbroken.* This would draw a final line under everything.

Unless Huw was there, the bastard, with his holy water and his candles.

Jesus!

The city swirled around her in the fog, undefined. She mustn't look back at the Cathedral. It was no part of her life now. She should go back to her own parish and deal with the church break-in. Head Ted Clowes off at the pass. At Ledwardine – her home.

Or not?

Sweat sprang out on her forehead. She felt insubstantial, worthless. She had no home, no lover, no spiritual adviser, no...

Daughter?

Failed her. Too bound up in your own conceits. Sending her into the arms of New Age occult freaks, a reaction to living with a...

Pious bitch?

Her dead husband Sean had been the first to call her that. After a day quite like this, a headachy day, the desperate day when she'd found out just how bent he was, and screamed at him for his duplicity and his greed, and he'd screamed back: *I was doing it for you, you pious bitch.*

She hated that word. Don't ever be *pious*. Smoke, curse, never be afraid to say *Jesus Christ!* in fury or astonishment – at least it keeps the name in circulation. Strive to be a good person, a good priest, never a *pious* priest.

Once, up in Liverpool, she'd conducted a youth service wearing a binliner instead of a cassock. It was half a generation too late; some of the kids were appalled, others sneered. Not so easy not being *pious*.

Merrily found herself back on the green, watching the Cathedral placidly swallowing the coach party. The fog was lifting, but the sky behind it was darkening. She had no idea which way to go next.

Suppose she'd backed away from the lamplit path and supported Sean, had said, *Let's fight this together*? Would he have made the effort for her, found some fresh, uncorrupted friends, a new but much older secretary? Would he, in the end, have *survived*? Might she have saved his life by not following the Path of the Pious Bitch into the arms of God?

She stood at the barrier preventing cars turning into Church Street. She was panting, thoughts racing again. Wasn't it true that having women in the priesthood was creating a new divide between the sexes – because men could love both God and their wives, but no truly heterosexual woman could love both God and a man with sufficient intensity to make both relationships potent? Was it all a sham? Was it true that all she was searching for in God were those qualities lacking in ordinary men? Or, at least, in Sean.

Oh *Christ*. Merrily flattened herself against a brick wall facing the side of the Cathedral. The headache had gone; she wished it was back, she wanted pain. Fumbling at her dog-collar, she took it off and put it in her bag. A cold breeze seemed to leap immediately to her throat, like a stab of admonishment.

She zipped up her coat, holding its collar together, turned her back on the Cathedral and walked quickly into Church Street.

Lol saw Merrily from his window, through the drifting fog: gliding almost drunkenly along the street, peering unseeingly into shop windows newly edged with Christmas glitter.

He ran downstairs, past the bike, past Nico's sepulchral drone and the very interested gaze of Big Viv.

'Merrily?' Close up, she seemed limp, drained.

'Oh,' she said. 'Hi.' And he was shocked because she looked as vague as Moon had often been, but that was just him, wasn't it – his paranoia?

But paranoia hadn't created the shadows and creases, the dark hair all mussed, dark eyes moist, make-up escaping.

He looked around. Not the flat now – it had been too awkward there the other night, as if foreshadowed by the death of Moon.

She let him steer her into the corner café where he and Jane had eaten chocolate fudge cake.

There was no one else in the back room. A brown pot of tea between them. On the wall above them was a framed Cézanne poster – baked furrowed earth under a heat haze.

The letter lay folded on the table, held down by the sugar bowl, revealing only the words 'known that such events attract members of Occult Groups in search of converts'.

'But surely,' he said, 'they mainly just attract ordinary people who read their daily horoscopes. It doesn't mean she's sacrificing babies.'

But he thought of seeing Jane and the other girl coming out of Pod's last night, long after it was closed. And Jane pretending, for the first time ever, not to have seen him.

'If this was London,' she said, 'I could get away with it. Or if Jane was grown-up and living somewhere else. If she'd even been up-front about it, I could have—'

'Merrily, it means nothing. I can't believe you've just quit because of this. It's the Bishop, isn't it?'

'Sorry?'

'He made another move on you, right?'

'No.' She smiled. 'He's been… fine. And anyway I might have taken that the wrong way: late at night, very tired. No, I'm just… paranoid.' She held up her half-smoked cigarette as though using it as a measure of something. 'Also I have filthy habits and a deep reservoir of self-pity.'

He nodded at the cigarette. 'What are the others, then?'

Merrily tipped it into the ashtray. He saw she was blushing. She had no filthy habits.

'Just… tell me to pull myself together, OK?'

'I like you being untogether. It makes me feel responsible and kind of protective – sort of like a real bloke.'

She smiled.

'So what are you going to do now?'

'Go back to my flock and try to be a good little shepherd. The Deliverance ministry was a wrong move. I thought it was something you could pick up as you went along. I didn't realize… I'm a fraud, Lol. I don't know what I'm doing, let too many people down. I even let you down. I said I'd go and see your friend, Moon…' She looked vague. 'Was that yesterday?'

'Mmm.'

'I mean, I could still see her. I'm still a minister, of sorts.'

'She's not there now,' he said too quietly.

'Lol?' She looked directly at him for the first time since sitting down at the table.

'She died.'

Her face froze up behind the smoke.

'No!' He put up his hands. 'She was dead long before you could've got there. There was nothing you could have done.'

And he told her about it: about the Iron Age sword... about the old newspaper report... why Denny had concealed the truth – why Denny *said* he'd concealed the truth... why Dick thought they should let it lie.

She kept shaking her head, lips parted. He was relieved at the way outrage had lifted her again.

'Lol, I've never heard anything so... There is something deeply, deeply wrong here, don't you think?'

'But what can you do about it? We can't bring her back. And we can't find out what was in her mind.'

'What about this book she was supposed to be writing?'

'Supposed to be, but I don't think she'd written a word. But if there is anything lying around, Denny will find it. And if it says anything he doesn't like, he'll destroy it without telling anyone.'

'Will you be called as a witness at the inquest?'

'I expect so. I was the first to... the first to enter the bathroom.'

'And what will you say?'

'I'll just answer their questions. That should cover about *half* of the truth.'

'And the rest of it *can't* be the truth, because it has no rationality.' She looked down into her cup as if there might be a message for her in the tea-leaves. 'I'm so sorry, Lol.'

The point at which people say, *Ah well, one of those things.* Except this wasn't.

After a while, she said, 'What if all your working life is concerned with things that three-quarters of the civilized world now consider irrational?'

'That could be stressful,' he said. There were lights on in the café now, but they didn't seem to reach Merrily. *What* was she not telling him?

297

She said, 'You know why some vicars busy themselves constantly with youth work and stuff like that? It's so that if, at any point, they realize there's no God, they can think: *Well, at least I haven't been wasting my time.*'

'Cynical.'

'Rational. For the same reasons, some Deliverance ministers prefer to think of themselves as Christian psychologists.'

'Psychology is wonderful,' Lol said grimly. 'Look how much it helped Moon.'

'Perhaps she had the wrong therapist.'

'We must get her a better one next time. I think *you* could have helped Moon. I wish to God I'd told you about her earlier. And I think... I think there must be a lot of other people you could help.'

'Thanks, but you're being kind.' She dropped the cigarettes and lighter into her bag, then folded up the anonymous letter very tightly.

This was not good: nothing had been resolved. He sensed that when she returned to her flock she would be different: a sad shepherd exiled, unfulfilled, into a community that wasn't a community any more. None of them were; village life, like he'd said in his song, was no more than a sweet watercolour memory. She'd grow old and lined, and end up hating God.

'Listen.' Lol lowered his voice to an urgent whisper. 'My life is pathetic. I'm a failed performer, a mediocre songwriter, an ex-mental patient who can't keep a woman. My sole function on this earth at the present time appears to be producing an album for a semi-talented, obnoxious little git who's blackmailing his father. Three days ago, a woman I couldn't love but needed to help just... shut me out in the snow. And then slashed both her wrists. Now somebody who I care about is holding out on me in exactly the same way. What does this tell me?'

Mega self-pity, he thought as she sat down again. *Occasionally it works.*

Merrily said, looking down at the table, 'Sometimes I think you're the only friend I have left.'

'Friend,' he repeated sadly.

She met his eyes. 'It's a big word, Lol.'

He nodded, although he knew there were bigger ones.

Outside, it was already going dark, and the fog had never really lifted.

31

Old Tiger

JANE STOOD ON the vicarage lawn, Ethel the cat watching her from inside the kitchen window. There was fog still around, but a paler patch almost directly overhead; the moon was probably just there, behind layer upon layer of steamy cloud.

Right, then.

She'd been told that it was OK to do this from the inside of the house, but she didn't feel quite right about that. Not with the moon, somehow. And it *was* a vicarage. Whereas the garden bordered the old and sinister orchard which, though it belonged to the Church, had been here, in essence, far longer. Pre-Christian almost certainly.

The night was young but silent around Jane. You could usually hear some sounds from the marketplace or the Black Swan, but not many people seemed to have ventured out tonight. Also, the fog itself created this lovely padded hush. It lined the hills and blocked in the spaces between the trees in the dense woods above Ledwardine, as if the whole valley had acquired these deep, resonant walls like a vast auditorium.

She wondered if Rowenna was outside in *her* garden, too. The problem was that there were doubtless other houses over-looking that one, and Rowenna had younger brothers who would just take the piss, so she was probably now in her room – searching for the same moon.

Jane looked up, cleared her throat almost nervously. Probably Mum felt like this in the pulpit. *Don't think about Mum. This is nothing to do with her.*

She drew in a long, chilled breath, imagining moonbeams – unfortunately there weren't any – also being drawn down, filling her with silken, silvery light. And then she called out – not *too* loud, as villages had ears.

> *'Hail to Thee, Lady Moon,*
> *'Whose light reflects our most secret hopes.*
> *'Hail to Thee from the abodes of darkness.'*

Something about that *abodes of darkness* making it more thrilling than the sun thing in the morning. Especially in this fog.

And it did work, this cycle of spiritual salutation. It put the whole day into a natural sequence. It deepened your awareness of the connectedness of everything, and your role as part of the great perceiving mechanism that was humanity.

Jane felt seriously calm by now and not at all cold – like she was generating her own inner heat. Or *something* was. She looked up into the sky again, just as this really miraculous thing began to happen.

The moon appeared.

First as just a grey imprint on the cloud-tapestry. Then as this kind of smoke-wreathed silver figurine: the goddess gathering the folds of her cloud-robes around her.

And finally… as a core of brilliant white fire at the heart of the fog.

Winter glory.

Oh, wow! She heard me.

Jane just stood there and shivered in amazement and delight, like totally transported.

Cool!

Like really, really, *really* cool.

* * *

302

'Visiting time's not for another hour,' Sister Miller said. 'It's teatime and the patients have to eat. You'll need to come back.'

Sister Miller was all nurse: tough and ageless. Merrily concentrated on her seasoned face, because the view along Watkins Ward was dizzying and oppressive. It would have been hard to come up here alone tonight, any night.

She told Sister Miller that Sister Cullen had said visiting hours were less strict if the patient was in a side ward.

'Which one?'

'Canon Dobbs.'

'That old man?' said Sister Miller. 'Are you relatives?'

'I'm a... colleague.'

'Because my view is that he doesn't need to be here now, no matter what Dr Bradley says. Why can't someone look after him at home? He's just taking up a bed.'

'You mean he's recovering?'

'Of course he's recovering. I've been in nursing for nearly forty years. Mr Dobbs was walking perfectly well this morning. He can also feed himself. I believe he could also talk, if he wanted to.' Sister Miller turned on Lol. 'Have *you* any idea why he's refusing to talk?'

Lol thought about it. 'Perhaps he's just impatient with routine questions like "How are we today?".'

'You have ten minutes and no longer,' said Sister Miller.

It was like praying over a tomb. He lay on his back, as still as an effigy. Eyes shut. You were not aware of him breathing. He looked dead.

Just a short prayer, then. Nothing clever. Someone else having seen to all the smart stuff. Afterwards, Merrily brushed her knees and sat in the bedside chair.

'Hello, Mr Dobbs.'

He didn't move. He was like stone. Could he possibly be awake?

'We haven't spoken before, as such. I'm Merrily Watkins.' Keeping her voice low and even. 'I've come to say goodbye.'

On the other side of the door's glass square, Lol smiled. OK, that was not the most tactful thing to say in a hospital.

'By which I mean that I've now decided not to accept the Deliverance... role. I just wanted you to know that. We never met formally, and now there's no reason we ever should.'

The side ward enclosing Dobbs was like a drab chapel. A faintly mouldy smell came from him – not organic, more like the miasma of old books in a damp warehouse.

'I'm sorry that you're in here. I'm sorry we didn't get to you sooner in the Cathedral.' She half-rose to pull the bedside chair a little closer and lowered her voice to below prayer level. 'I'm even sorrier you didn't feel able to tell any of us what you were doing there.'

She leaned her face forward to within six inches of his. They'd kept him shaved, but stubble had sprouted under his chin like a patch of sparse grass on a rockface.

'It doesn't matter to me now – not professionally. I'm out of it, feeling a little humiliated, rather slighted. I *know* Jesus Christ was the first exorcist, but also that half the world's population is female, and rather more than half the people with problems of psychic disturbance – or so it seems to me – are female too. I believe that one day there *will* be a female exorcist in this diocese, without the fires of hell burning in High Town. I just wanted you to know that too.'

No reaction. Yet he could apparently walk and feed himself. She felt angry.

'I probably felt less insulted, but more puzzled, when I heard you'd been avoiding *all* women. Dumping your housekeeper – that wasn't a terribly kind thing to do. Why are you scared of women?'

Her hand went instinctively to her throat. She still wasn't wearing the dog-collar.

'I don't know what makes you tick, Canon Dobbs. I've been trying to forgive you for setting me up for that final session with Denzil Joy.'

She felt tainted just uttering the name, particularly here. Too much like an invocation?

'If you wanted to scare me off, show me how unpleasant it could be, you very nearly succeeded. But that wasn't, in the end, why I decided to quit.'

She stood up. On his bedside table she placed two pounds of seedless grapes and two bottles of Malvern water.

'Maybe you could share these with Huw Owen – next time he comes with his candles, and his holy water, and his magic chalk.'

She waited. Not a movement. She took a last look at him, but he remained like a fossil.

When she reached the door, she stopped, noticing that Lol's eyes had widened. She resisted the urge to spin around.

Once out of the door, she turned left towards the ward entrance, refusing even to glance back along Watkins to the top side ward where Denzil Joy's spirit had left his body.

And gone where?

The sudden shudder ripped up her spine like a razor-blade.

'OK, he opened his eyes,' Lol informed her, outside the hospital. 'As soon as you turned your back and walked away, his eyes snapped open. Then closed again when he saw me standing on the other side of the glass.'

Merrily's Volvo was parked in a small bay near a little park. By the path to the Victoria footbridge over the Wye. They leaned against it.

'He heard it all, then?' she said.

'Every word. His eyes were very bright, fully aware – and mad as hell when he saw me.'

'Good. My God!'

'Mmm.' Those eyes had spooked Lol. They were burning with the hard, wary intelligence of an old tiger. But the effect of this news on Merrily he found exciting.

The cold had lost its bite and the fog had thinned. He could see the three-quarter moon as through a lace curtain.

Merrily said, 'Could we go for a short walk? I need to clear my head.'

It was *very* short. He followed her through the patch of parkland to a kind of viewing platform overlooking the still dark Wye and the suspension footbridge.

'Last time I stood here, Inspector Annie Howe was showing me where a body had been found.'

'What exciting times you have, Merrily. Such drama.'

'Too much drama.' She stood with her back to the river, beside an ornate lamp standard. 'Well, this suggests Dobbs was an active participant in Huw's ritual, doesn't it? Or maybe even directing it?'

'You're the expert.'

'Obviously not, or I'd know what this was about.'

'And this Huw going behind your back, that's the reason you resigned?'

She shrugged.

'I still don't see it.'

'Lol, he was my course tutor: the Deliverance man. He's the nearest I've had or wanted to have to a spiritual adviser. I rated the guy. I really *liked* him.'

'I see.'

'No, you don't. A father-figure, just about. But, more important, the person you trust to guide you through the... through the hinterland of Hell, if you like. But what if there's something iffy about what they were both doing?'

'Iffy?'

'I don't know.'

'And you want to?'

306

'Yeah.' Her dark hair shone in the lamplight.

'More than a professional interest?'

'I don't *have* a professional interest any more. I am just so angry. That *shit*.'

'Excellent.'

'Huh?'

'I'm happy you're mad. When I first saw you in Church Street you were about as animated as Mr Dobbs back there. I worry easily.'

She smiled, shaking her head. 'Lol…'

'Mmm?'

'I said some stupid things, all right? Things that weren't necessarily true.'

'Which in particular?'

'You choose,' Merrily said. Her face seemed flushed.

He thought for a moment. 'OK, I've chosen.'

'Don't tell me.'

'Why not?'

'Because…'

'Because little Jane doesn't know where you are?'

'Little Jane doesn't bloody care.'

'I think she does, Merrily. And it's not my place to say so to a professional good person, but if you take this out on her before you've gone into it properly, you might regret it.'

'You mean I should take steps to find out what she's doing – and who with?'

'I can… help maybe, if you want.'

'Why are you doing this, Lol?'

'A number of possible reasons.' Lol stood close to her but looked across the river to the haze of misted lights on the fringe of the city. 'You choose.'

Merrily sighed. 'I can't go to bed with you, you know.' And, naturally, she looked soft-focus beautiful under the lamp. 'Not the way things are.'

'God,' Lol said sadly. 'He has a lot to answer for.'

'It isn't God,' Merrily said.

'Oh.' He wanted to roll over the rail into the black river. 'That means somebody else.'

'Yes.'

She turned away from him and from the light. In the moment before she did, he saw her eyes and he thought he saw a flash of fear there, and he thought there was a shudder of revulsion.

But he *was* paranoid. Official!

'I'll take you back now,' Merrily said.

32

Fantasy World

JANE THREW OPEN the bedroom window, and the damned fog came in and she started to cough. It was like being with Mum in the scullery-office on a heavy Silk Cut night.

Down on the lawn the last rags of snow had gone. Snow was clean, bright, refreshing. Fog was misery. It was December today, so only three weeks to Midwinter, the great solstice when the year had the first gleam of spring in its eye.

Always darkest before the dawn. This, Jane thought, was like a midwinter of the spirit. She cleared her throat.

'Hail to Thee, Eternal Spiritual Sun.
'Whose visible symbol now rises from the Heavens.'

That was a bloody laugh.

'Hail unto Thee from the Abodes of Morning.'

It had been so brilliant last night out in the garden. Maybe she was a night person. Maybe a moon person. And yet the bedtime exercise had not gone too well, the great rewinding of the day.

Before you go to sleep, make a journey back through the day.
Starting with the very last thing you did or said or thought,
then going back through every small event, every action,

every perception, as though you were rewinding a sensory
videotape of your day. Consider each occurrence impartially,
as though it were happening to someone else, and notice how
one thing led to another. Thus will you learn about cause
and effect. This reverse procedure also de-conditions your
mind from thinking sequentially – past, present and future –
and demolishes the web of falsehood you habitually weave to
excuse your wrong behaviour.

It was impossible to stay with it. You got sidetracked. You
thought of something interesting and followed it through. Or
something bad, like Mum being ill, which could plunge you
without warning into some awful Stalinist scenario at Gran's in
Cheltenham: *As long as your mother is in hospital, Jane, you are*
under my roof, and a young lady does not go out looking like
THAT. Or you remembered seeing some cool male person and,
despite what Angela had foretold, you were into the old dying-
a-virgin angst. Rowenna never seemed prey to these fears; had
she *no* hormones?

Gratefully, Jane closed the window. Mum had not looked too
bad last night. Quiet, though: pensive.

'You're not OK! You're not! You look like sh—'
'Don't say it, all right?'
'It's true.'
And, Jesus, it *was* true. That ratty old dressing-gown, the cig
drooping from the corner of her mouth. A vicar? Standing on
the stairs, she looked like some ageing hooker.
'It's the weather,' Mum said.
'It so is *not* the weather! Maybe you should see a doctor. I
don't know about exorcist; you look like completely bloody
possessed.'
For a moment, Mum looked quite horrible, face all red and
scrunched up like some kind of blood-pressure situation. And
then...

'STOP IT! Don't you ever *ever* make jokes about that, do you hear?'

'And, like whatever happened to the sense of humour?' Jane backed away into the kitchen, teetering on the rim of tears.

They ate breakfast in silence apart from the bleeping of the answering machine: unplayed messages from last night. 'Aren't you going to ever listen to that thing?' Jane said finally at the front door.

'I'll get around to it, flower,' Mum said drably, turning away because, for less than half a second, Jane had caught her eyes and seen in them the harsh glint of fear.

No, please.

Standing desolate on the dark-shrouded market square, as the headlights of the school bus bleared around the corner, Jane thought, suppose it's not flu, nor even some kind of virus; suppose she's found symptoms of something she's afraid to take to the doctor.

Oh God. Please, God.

The only time Jane ever reverted to the Old Guy was when it was about Mum.

Bleep.

'*Merrily, it's Sophie. I'm calling at seven o'clock. Please ring me at home.*'

Bleep.

'*Ms Watkins. Acting DCI Howe, 19.27, Tuesday. I need to talk to you. Can you call me between eight-thirty and ten tomorrow, Wednesday. Thanks.*'

Bleep.

'*This is Susan Thorpe, Mrs Watkins, at the Glades. Could you confirm our arrangement for tomorrow evening? Thank you.*'

Bleep.

'*Merrily, it's Sophie again. Please call me. You must realize what it's about.*'

311

Bleep.

'Hello, lass. Time we had a chat, eh?'

Merrily didn't think so.

Lol said, 'Viv, *you* know the Alternative Hereford – I mean, most of the people on that side of things.'

'My love,' Big Viv laughed throatily, 'I *am* the Alternative Hereford. Just don't ask me to point you to a dealer.'

'What happens over that healthfood café in Bridge Street?'

'Pod's?' Viv gave him a sharp look. He saw she had two tight lip-rings on this morning. 'Well, they used to do a good cashew-burger, then they got a different cook and it wasn't so good. You won't meet anybody there.'

'Uh-huh.' Lol shook his head gently. 'I'm not looking to score anything chemical.'

He collected another hard look. 'What then?'

'I don't know. Mysticism?'

'You won't score that either. Not at Pod's.'

He didn't know whether to be relieved or disappointed.

'Wrong gender, Lol. It's a woman thing there. I can put you on to a few other people, if you like, depending what you're into. Wicca... theosophy... Gurdjieff...?'

'I'll tell you the truth,' Lol said. 'It involves a friend of mine. She thought her daughter might be involved in something possibly linked to Pod's, and she'd like to know a bit about it. It's a peace-of-mind thing.'

'What's her name?'

'Jane. Jane Watkins.'

'Don't know her.' Viv went to sit behind the till. 'All right, I went there a few times, but it got a bit intense, yeah?'

'What was it into?'

'Self-discovery, developing an inner life, meditation, astral-projection, occult-*lite* – you know?'

'You manage to leave your body, Viv?'

'No such luck, darling. The best teacher they had just dropped out, then they got very responsible. A bit elitist – no riff-raff, no dopeheads. Like an esoteric ladies' club, you know? That was when I kicked it into touch. Life's too short.'

'For what?'

'For taking seriously. Plus, it was inconvenient. They started meeting in an afternoon on account of the kind of women they were attracting didn't want their oh-so-respectable husbands to find out. Anyway, it was all a bit snooty and bit too sombre.'

Lol wondered how sombre was too sombre for a Nico-fan.

'This is a very intense, intellectual kid, Lol?'

'Not how I'd describe her. Well… not how I *would* have described her.'

'They change so fast, kids,' Viv said.

The only call Merrily returned was Susan Thorpe's. A care-attendant answered: Mrs Thorpe had left early for Hereford Market. Merrily said quickly, before she could let herself back out, 'Could you tell her the arrangement still stands.'

She felt really unsure about this, but she very much wanted to speak to Susan Thorpe's mother – wanted every bit of back-ground she could get on Thomas Dobbs.

And it was only an *imprint*: a redirection of energies. She could handle that – couldn't she? – if she protected herself.

'That's fine,' the woman said. 'Thank you, Mrs Watkins.'

'OK.'

She lit a cigarette and pulled over the phone book. This was something she should have done days ago.

Napier. Surprisingly, there were three in Credenhill. Would it say Major Napier? Colonel Napier? She didn't even know Rowenna's father's rank. A serving officer in the SAS would, anyway, be unlikely to advertise his situation. Might even be ex-directory. She called the first Napier – no reply. At the second, a woman answered, and Merrily asked if this was where Rowenna lived.

The woman laughed, with no humour. 'This is where she sleeps' – London accent? – 'sometimes.'

There was the sound of a morning TV talk-show in the background, a studio audience programmed to gasp and hoot.

'Is that Mrs Napier?'

'No, it's Mrs Straker.'

'Would it be possible to speak to Mrs Napier?'

'I wouldn't know, dear. Depends if you can afford long-distance.'

Merrily said nothing.

'I'm Rowenna's aunt,' Mrs Straker continued heavily, like she'd had to explain this a thousand times too many. 'I look after the kids for Steve. He's my younger brother. He and Helen split up about four years ago. She's in Canada now. If you want to speak to Steve, you'll have to call back tonight.'

'I'm sorry. I didn't know any of this. My name's Merrily Watkins. From Ledwardine. My daughter, Jane… she seems to be Rowenna's best friend, at school.'

No reaction. This wasn't what she'd expected. She wanted a warm, concerned parent, delighted to hear from little Jane's mother.

'I don't know any Jane,' Mrs Straker said. 'See, Mrs…'

'Watkins. Merrily.'

'Yeah. See, since her dad bought her that car we never know where she is. I wouldn't have got it her, personally. I don't think she should have a car till she's at college or got a job, but Steve's soft with her, and now she goes where she likes. And she don't bring her girl friends back here. Or the men either.'

Merrily sat down, her picture of Rowenna and her family background undergoing radical revision.

'Sometimes,' Mrs Straker was saying, 'I think I should be bothering more than I do, but when she was here all the time it was nothing but rows and sulks, and this is a very small house for the five of us. Where we were before, down in Salisbury, things was difficult, but it was a bigger place at least, you know what I mean?'

'I suppose your brother has to go away a lot.' In the SAS, Merrily had heard, you could never rely on not having to be in Bosnia or somewhere at a day's notice.

'No,' said Mrs Straker.

'He *is* a... an Army officer, isn't he, your brother?'

Mrs Straker laughed. 'That's what she told you, is it?'

'Not exactly,' Merrily said. It was Jane who'd told her.

'Steve's a corporal. He works in admin.'

'I see.'

'That's not good enough for Rowenna, obviously. She lives in what I would call a fantasy world. Steve can't see it, or he don't want to. I dunno what *your* daughter's like, Mrs Watson.'

'Impressionable.' Merrily's stomach felt like lead. 'She's been out a lot lately, at night, and she doesn't always say where. I'm getting worried – which is why I rang.'

'You want to watch her,' Mrs Straker said. 'Keep an eye on her, that's my advice.'

'Why would you... advise that?'

Mrs Straker made a pregnant humming noise. There was a lot she could say, would enjoy relating, but she apparently wanted more encouragement.

Merrily said, 'It's a bit difficult for me to keep an eye on Jane all the time, being a single mum, you know? Having to work.'

'Divorced?'

'Widow.'

'Yes, I'm a widow too,' Mrs Straker said. 'It's not easy, is it? Never thought I'd end up looking after somebody else's kids, even if they are my own brother's. But I can't watch that girl as well – I told Steve that. Not now she's got a car. What do you do?'

'Yes, I can see the problem.'

'No, what do *you* do? What's your job?'

The front doorbell rang.

'I'm, er… I'm a minister in the Church. A vicar.'

The line went quiet.

'Oh dear,' Mrs Straker said, 'that's not what I expected at all. That's very funny that is.'

The doorbell rang again, twice, followed by a rapping of the knocker.

'Why is that so funny?'

'That's your front door, dear,' Mrs Straker said. 'You'd best go and get it. Ring me back, if you like.'

'Why is that so funny, Mrs Straker?'

'It's not funny at all, Mrs Watson. *You* won't find it funny, I'll guarantee that.'

33

Wrong Number, Dear

ANNIE HOWE STOOD on the step, young and spruce and clean, fast-track fresh against the swirling murk.

'Ah, you *are* there, Ms Watkins. I was driving over from Leominster, so I thought I'd call.' Her ash-blonde head tilted, taking in the dressing-gown – and the blotches and the bags, no doubt. 'You really *aren't* well, are you?'

'Not wonderful.'

'Flu?'

'No, it's OK to come in,' Merrily said. 'You won't catch anything.'

'I seldom do. Is this nervous exhaustion, perhaps?'

'That might be closer.'

Howe stepped into the kitchen, with a slight wrinkling of the nose. Her own kitchen would be hardwood and stainless-steel, cool as a morgue. She sat down at the table, confidently pushing the ashtray away.

'Ms Watkins, it's the Paul Sayer thing again.'

Merrily filled the kettle. 'That seemed to have gone quiet?'

'That's because we're still choosing not to make too much noise about it. I'm wondering if we ought to.'

'You want me to discuss it in a sermon?'

Howe smiled thinly. 'Perhaps a sarcasm amnesty?'

'Sure. Sorry, go on.'

So what did she do about this? If Howe knew she was in the process of shedding the Deliverance role, this conversation would never reach the coffee stage. Difficult, since she was unable to square it with the Bishop until his return from London. OK, say nothing.

'You heard from DS Bliss, I believe,' Howe said.

'He told me about the supplier of crows. Did you get any further?'

'Unfortunately not. They appeared to have paid their money, taken their crow, and melted back into their own netherworld. But, as you agreed with Bliss, the fee suggests that the people involved in this are not the usual... how shall I say—?'

'Toerags.'

'Quite.'

'So, let me get this right – have you actually said publicly that Sayer was murdered yet?'

Howe shook her head. 'We're staying with the phrase "suspicious circumstances". The situation is, as you must realize, that we could doubtless get widespread national publicity if we told the press about Sayer's hobby.'

'Especially if you gave them the pictures.'

'Of course. But apart from producing an unseemly double-page spread in the *Daily Star*, I can't see that it would help. I'm no longer sure the people we want to talk to would ever read a tabloid. Yes, it's possible, Sayer *may* simply be a wanker. We've found some videotapes under a floorboard which seem to show ritual activities, but we don't know if these are events that Sayer was personally involved in or sado-pornographic tapes he acquired for his own gratification. They're quite explicit.'

'Not commercial films?'

'Oh, no, the quality's not good enough. Lots of camera shake and the picture itself is so poor it seems to have been recorded with either old or very cheap equipment – which suggests it's not simulated.'

'What kind of ritual activities?'

'You can view them if you like.'

'I'd rather you just told me.'

'Well, one shows a man penetrating a woman on an altar. She's wearing a blindfold and a gag, and it looks like rape. The man's face is not hidden, but well covered by long hair and a beard. In the background are several people whose faces are even less distinguishable. What does that sound like to you?'

'Any suggestion of location?'

'Possibly a church. And then there's the inevitable passing-round-the-chalice sequence.'

'Black Mass?'

'Someone drinks from the chalice, and there's residue on the mouth suggestive of blood. But, as I say, the quality is appalling.'

'You see, on the one hand,' Merrily said, 'the Black Mass is the best-known of all satanic rituals, and probably the easiest to carry out if you're just idiots with a warped idea of fun. You just do everything in reverse – say the Lord's Prayer backwards, et cetera. And you pervert everything – urinate in the chalice or... use blood instead of wine. Blood is the aspect which could, on the other hand, mean serious business. Blood represents the life-force, and it's seen as the most potent of all magical substances. If you want to make something happen, you use real blood.'

'Of course, we have no way of knowing whether *this* is. It looks too thin for ketchup, but it could be soy sauce or something.'

'I'm not being much help. Am I?'

'It's more a question of what help you might be in the future,' Howe said. 'We've failed to identify a single person who's been involved in any... any activity with Sayer. Or, indeed, with serious satanic activity of any kind. That's not including the self-publicists, of course.'

'When did you ever see a serious, heavy-duty, *educated* Satanist stripped off in the *News of the World*?'

'You mean – as with organized crime – the big operators are the outwardly respectable types you'd never suspect?'

'I suppose that's a good parallel.'

'It's also largely a myth,' said Howe. 'The Mr Bigs of this world are very rare, and we *do* know who they are. But I'm still interested. Do you personally believe there are high-powered practitioners with big houses and executive posts?'

'How would I know? I'm only a village vicar. But if Sayer *was* just a wanker, perhaps he was playing out of his league.'

'You mean, if he was regarded by some serious and outwardly respectable practitioner as a potential embarrassment…'

'Or he was getting too ambitious. Or he angered some rival… group. I'm told there's a lot of jealousy and infighting and power-struggling among certain occult sects.'

'Who told you that?'

'It was discussed during a course I was sent on. Is this what you wanted to hear?'

'Go on.'

'We were told that there are basically two classes of Satanist – what Huw, our tutor, calls the headbangers who are just in it for the experience or whatever psychic charge they can get; and the intellectuals. These are people who came out of Gnosticism and believe that knowledge is all, and so anything is valid if it leads to more knowledge.'

'Including murder?'

'Probably. Although they'd be as reluctant as the rest of us to break the law. Satanists, basically, are the people who hate Christianity. And they hate us because they see us as irrational. They despise us for our pomp and our smugness. All these great cathedrals costing millions of pounds a year to maintain, all the wasted psychic energy… to promote what they see as the idiot myth that you can get there by *love*.'

'I see.'

'Why do I get the feeling you also think it's an idiot myth?'

'Because I'm a police-person,' Howe said. 'Love is something we seldom encounter.'

When Howe had left, Merrily phoned Mrs Straker back four times, and never got an answer. Her own phone rang three times; she didn't pick it up, but pressed 1471 each time. The calls were from Sophie, Uncle Ted and Sophie respectively.

She owed Sophie an explanation, but couldn't face that now. And anyway, when Mick returned tomorrow, she'd have to talk to *him* – at length, no doubt. Before then, she wanted to have lost this… virus.

In the afternoon, she filled a plastic bottle with tapwater and took it across to the church and into the chancel, where she stood it before the altar. In the choir stalls, she meditated for almost an hour. *Blue and gold. Lamplit path.*

She went into the vestry and changed into the cassock and surplice she'd worn at St Cosmas and St Damien, since washed and replaced in the vestry wardrobe. She walked, head bowed, along the central aisle, back to the chancel, and stood before the altar.

'Lord God Almighty, the Creator of Life, bless this water…'

Back in the vicarage, she went up to her bedroom and sprinkled holy water in all four corners. Then across the threshold and at the window, top and bottom.

She went down on her knees and prayed that the soul of *our brother Denzil* might be directed away from its suffering and its *earthly obsessions* and led into the Light.

Filtered through fog, the fading light lay like a dustsheet on the bedroom.

Jane felt uncomfortable on the school bus home. Increasingly so, as more and more students got off. The buses had arrived early at the school, on account of the fog which was getting worse; classes had been wound up twenty minutes ahead of time.

The bus was moving very slowly, in low gear. It must be like driving through frogspawn. Jane just hoped to God that Mum was feeling better – was not going to be *really* ill.

Ledwardine was near the end of the line. Dean Wall, legendary greaseball, knew that, so there was no need at all for him to dump his fat ass on the seat next to Jane. He was on his own tonight, his mate Danny Gittoes off sick, supposedly.

'Just wanted to make sure you didn't miss your stop in all this fog. Seein' as how you en't much used to buses these days.'

Very funny! Jane gathered her bag protectively on to her lap. 'Don't worry about me. I have a natural homing instinct.'

The bus was crawling now. She had no idea where the *hell* they were.

'Only tryin' t'be helpful, Watkins.' Dean Wall shoved his fat thigh against hers, leaned back and stretched. The fat bastard clearly wasn't going to move. 'Goin' out tonight?'

'Probably not.'

'Off with some bloke tonight, then, is she?'

'I wouldn't have thought so.'

Wall's big fat lips shambled into a loose smile.

'Look, just sod off, OK?' Jane said.

'I wouldn't worry, Watkins – you'll still get yours. Er's likely bisexual.'

'Will you piss *off*?'

'You don't know nothin', do you? You're dead naive, you are.'

Jane gazed out of the window at dense nothing. 'Stop trying to wind me up.'

'I'm tryin' to put you *right*, Jane. You wanner talk to Gittoes, you do. 'Cept he en't capable of speech right now – still recoverin', like. His ma's thinkin' of gettin' him plastic surgery to take the smile off his face.'

'I don't want to know!'

'I bet you do.' Dean Wall leaned a little closer and Jane shrank against the streaming window. Dean lowered his voice. ''Er give Danny a blow job, back o' the woodwork building.'

She spun and stared at him.

'Listen, I en't kiddin', Jane.' He threw up his hands like she was about to hit him. 'Gittoes was pretty bloody gobsmacked himself, as it were.'

'You totally disgusting slimeball.'

''Er needed a favour, see.'

'I want you to sit somewhere else, all right?' Jane said. 'I'm going to count to five. If you haven't gone by then, I'll start screaming. Then I'll tell the driver you put your hand up my skirt.'

'Mrs Straker?'

'Yes?'

'Who's this?'

'It's Merrily Watkins again. I've tried several times to call back, but I suppose you had to go out.'

'Who'd you say you were?'

'Merrily – it's Jane's mum. She's Rowenna's friend. We spoke earlier.'

'I think you've got the wrong number, dear.'

'We spoke about an hour and a half ago. You said there was something I should know about Rowenna.'

You won't find it funny. I'll guarantee that.

'You must be thinking of somebody else,' Mrs Straker said. 'I've never spoken to you before in my life.'

She couldn't talk, Merrily decided. Someone had come into the house who shouldn't hear this. Or someone she was afraid of.

'Is there somebody with you? Has Rowenna come back? Is Jane with her? Could you just answer yes or no?'

'Listen,' Mrs Straker hissed, 'I don't know who you are, but if you pester me again I'll call the police. That clear enough for you, dear? Now get off the fucking line.'

She lay awake that night for over an hour, a whole carillon of alarm bells ringing.

It was the first evening this week that she and Jane had eaten together. Afterwards, they made a log fire in the drawing room and watched TV, all very mellow and companionable. Later they put out the lamps and moved out of the draughts and close to the fire, sipped their tea and talked. And then she got around to telling Jane about Katherine Moon.

'Dead?'

So she hadn't known. It was hard to tell how Jane really felt about this; she seemed to have assumed Moon and Lol had been, at some stage, an item. When Merrily came to Moon's use of the Iron Age knife – this kind of stuff never seemed to upset Jane particularly, as long as no animals were involved – the kid nodded solemnly.

'Sure. The later Celtic period, coming up to the Dark Ages, that was like this really screwed-up time.'

'It was?' Merrily curling her legs on to the sofa.

'Bad magic. The Druids were getting into blood sacrifices and stuff. If your family was rooted in all that, you're quite likely to get reverberations. Plus, who knows what *else* happened on the site of that barn? I mean way back. It could be really poisoned, giving off all kinds of mind-warping vibrations. If you don't know how to handle these things, it could go badly wrong for you.'

'That's very interesting,' Merrily had said mildly. 'Where did you learn all that, flower?'

'Everybody knows that,' Jane said inscrutably. She was sitting on a big cushion at the edge of the hearth. 'So this Moon was bonkers all along?'

'She had a history of psychiatric problems.'

Which led to a long and fairly sensible discussion about Lol and the kind of unsuitable women into whose ambience he seemed to have been drawn, beginning with his born-again Christian mother, then the problem over a fifteen-year-old schoolgirl, when he himself was about nineteen but no more mature than the girl, and then some older woman who was into drugs, and later Alison Kinnersley who'd first drawn him to Herefordshire for entirely her own ends.

'How's he taken it?' Jane set her mug down on the hearth and prodded at a log with the poker.

'He thinks he should have known the way things were going, which is what people always say after a suicide. But in this case people were *trying* to help her. It's very odd. It doesn't add up.'

'So, like, Lol… was he in love with her?'

'I really don't think so, flower.'

And at this point the phone had rung and she'd waited and dialled 1471, finding it had been Lol himself. She called him back from the scullery-office, still answering monosyllabically, because Jane was sometimes a stealthy mover. So she never did learn how he'd discovered the kid had become involved with something called the Pod, which met above a café in Hereford. It could be worse, however, Lol said: women only, nothing sexual. Self-development through meditation and spiritual exercises. Progressing – possibly – to journeys out of the body.

Oh, was *that* all?

When she went back to the drawing room, Jane had put on the stereo and it was playing one of the warmest, breathiest, Nick Drake-iest songs on the second and final Hazey Jane album. The one which went, *Waking in the misty dawn and finding you there.*

Merrily lay on the sofa and listened to the music, her thoughts tumbling like water on to rocks.

During the remainder of the evening, the phone rang twice. Merrily said the machine would get it, although she knew it was still unplugged.

The last caller, she'd discovered from the bedside phone, was Huw Owen. She fell asleep trying to make sense of him and Dobbs.

She lay there, half awake for quite a while, dimly aware of both palms itching, before the jagged cold ripped up her, from vagina to throat, and then she was throwing herself out of bed and rolling away into a corner, where the carpet was still damp from holy water, and she curled up dripping with sweat and terror and saw from the neon-red digits of the illuminated clock that the time was four a.m., the hour of his death in Hereford General.

Across the room, with a waft of cat's faeces and gangrene, a shadow sat up in her bed.

34

A Party

THE BULKHEAD LIGHT came on and the back door was tugged open.

Somewhere deep in the stone and panelled heart of the Glades a piano was being plonked, a dozen cracked sopranos clawing for the notes of what might have been a hymn.

'Ah.' Susan Thorpe stepped out in her Aran sweater, heathery skirt, riding boots. 'Splendid. We were beginning to think you weren't going to venture out.'

No 'How good of you to turn out on a night like this'. Mrs Thorpe appeared to think Deliverance was the kind of local service you paid for in your council tax.

The singing voices shrilled and then shrank under a great clumping chord.

'I can never say no to a party,' Merrily said.

She shed her fake-Barbour in the hall. Underneath, she wore a shaggy black mohair jumper over another jumper, her largest pectoral cross snuggling between the two layers. Susan Thorpe looked relieved that she wasn't in a surplice. But her husband Chris obviously thought she ought to be.

'This is a *proper* exorcism, isn't it?' He was extremely tall, with a shelf of bushy eyebrow and a premature stoop.

His wife glared. 'They aren't *all* bloody deaf in there, you know.'

'Let's get this clear,' Merrily said. 'It isn't going to be an exorcism at all. An exorcism is an extreme measure only normally used for the removal of an evil presence.'

'How d'you know it isn't that?'

'I don't know *what* it is yet, Mr Thorpe.' *Yet* – that was optimistic. 'If it does turn out to be, er, malevolent, we shall have to think again.'

Believe me, if you had real malevolence here, you would know...

'Always believed in belt and braces, myself,' Chris Thorpe said gruffly. 'Go in hard. If you've got rats, you put down poison, block all the holes.'

Merrily smiled demurely up at him. 'How fortunate we all are that you're not an exorcist.'

'Let it go, Chris.' Susan Thorpe pushed him into the passage leading to the private sitting room, held open the door for Merrily. 'The truth is, my husband's a sceptic. He teaches physics.'

'Oh, where?'

'Moorfield High,' Susan said quickly. Oh dear, a mere state school. The Thorpes were no more than late-thirties, yet had the style and attitudes of people at least a generation older. You couldn't imagine this was entirely down to living with old people. More a cultivated image over which they'd lost all control.

The sitting room was gloomily lit by a standard lamp with an underpowered bulb, but it was much tidier tonight – possibly the work of the plump woman who sat placidly sipping tea. On her knees was a plate with a knife on it, and cake crumbs.

'This is my mother, Edna Rees. This is Mrs Merrily Watkins, Mother. She's Dobbs's successor.'

The former housekeeper to the Canon had raw red farmer's cheeks and wore her hat indoors; how many women did that these days? She put down her cup, and studied Merrily at length, unembarrassed.

'You seem very young, Mrs Watkins.'

'I'm not sure which way to take that, Mrs Rees.'

'Oh, I think you are, my dear.' Mrs Rees's accent was far more local than her daughter's – Hereford-Welsh. 'I think you are.'

Merrily smiled. *How do I get to talk to her in private?*

Susan Thorpe frowned. 'I don't know how long this operation normally takes you, Merrily. But our venerable guest of honour is usually in bed by ten.'

'So there's going to be nobody on that floor until then?'

'Nobody living,' said Mrs Rees blandly.

Chris Thorpe glanced at Merrily's shoulder-bag. 'You have some equipment?'

'We don't have to be near any power points, if that's what you mean.'

'Chris, why don't you go and do something else?' Susan said through her teeth.

'It's my house. I've a right to be informed.'

'But I don't feel you really believe it's going to achieve anything,' Merrily said. 'It's just that normally we like to do this in the presence of people who are a bit sympathetic – a scattering of actual Christians. I mean, *are* there any practising Christians around? What about the woman who saw... him? Helen?'

'Supervising the party,' Susan said. 'Making sure it doesn't get too rowdy. Anyway, she doesn't want to be involved. Christians? No shortage of *them* but they're the ones we're trying not to alarm. You're on your own, I'm afraid, Merrily. Can I offer you a fortifying cigarette?'

'Thanks. Afterwards, I think. If you could just point me at the spot.'

'Don't fret.' Mrs Rees put down her cup and saucer. 'I'll go with you.'

Excellent.

'Did you ever go with Canon Dobbs, Mrs Rees?'

329

'Oh no.' Mrs Rees stood up, shaking cake crumbs from her pleated skirt. 'Wasn't *woman's* work, was it?'

Jane and Rowenna ordered coffee and doughnuts at the Little Chef between Hereford and Leominster. Jane nervously stirred an extra sugar into hers. 'I didn't even tell her I was going out tonight. It's come to this: separate lives.'

Rowenna was unsympathetic. 'You're a woman now. You live by your own rules.'

'Yeah, well...' Jane looked through the window at the car park and a petrol-station forecourt. She kind of liked Little Chefs because they sold maps and stuff as well, giving you a feeling of being on a *journey*. They weren't travelling far this time, however.

Only to the pub where the psychic fair had been held – there to meet with the gracious Angela. Jane felt like Macbeth going for his second session with the Weird Sisters. Like, face it, the first meeting had changed Jane's life.

She hadn't seen much of Rowenna over the past couple of days. Then, this morning, the lime-green Fiesta had slid into Ledwardine market square while she was waiting for the bus.

She'd immediately wondered whether to tell Rowenna what Dean Wall had said. If somebody was spreading that kind of filth about you, you had a right to know. But the minute she got in, Ro was like: 'Guess who called *me* last night?'

Jane abandoned half her doughnut, pushed the plate away.

'Don't look so worried.'

Rowenna wore a new belted coat of soft white leather; Jane was wearing her school duffel coat. People must think she was like some hitchhiker this genteel lady had picked up.

'Is she going to give us a reading?'

'I don't know,' Rowenna said. 'You scared of that?'

'I was so pissed off when I got up, I forgot to do the sun thing.'

'So what's she going to do about that?' Rowenna said quite irritably. 'Give you detention? Lighten up, these people are not like…' With a napkin over her finger, she dabbed a crumb from the edge of Jane's mouth. 'Listen, you know what your problem is? Your mother's dreary Anglicanism is weighing down on you. So *gloomy,* kitten. You spend your whole life making sacrifices and practising self-denial in the hope of getting your reward in heaven. What kind of crappy deal is that?'

'Yeah, I know.'

'Going to waste her whole life on that shit – and they get paid peanuts, don't they? I mean, that great old house and no money to make the most of it? What's the point? She's still attractive, your old lady. It's understandable that it pisses you off.'

'I can't run her life.'

'No? If it was me, I'd feel it was my responsibility to kind of rescue her, you know? She's obviously got talent, psychic-sensitivity, all that stuff, but she's just pouring it down the drain.'

Jane laughed grimly. 'Oh sure, I walk in one night and I'm, like: "Look, Mum, I can get you out of this life of misery. Why don't you come along to my group one night and learn some cool spiritual exercises?" '

'You underrate yourself, Jane. You can be much more subtle than that,' Rowenna said. There was something new about her tonight: an aggression – and a less-than-subtle change of attitude. Remember *Listen to me. You cannot change other people. Only yourself.* How many days ago did she say *that*?

'Come on,' Rowenna said, 'let's go.'

A bulb blew.

Merrily's right hand slid under her top sweater to grip the pectoral cross. A bright anger flared inside her.

The lights were wall-mounted: low-powered, pearlized, pear-shaped bulbs, two on each dusty bracket, the brackets about eight feet apart along the narrow passage. This was the one furthest away, so that now the passage – not very bright to begin

331

with – was dimmed by new shadows and no longer had a visible end. Easy, in this lightless tunnel, to conjure a moving shadow.

Edna Rees chuckled. She was sitting in a pink wicker chair pulled out from a bathroom. Merrily was kneeling on the top-most of three carpeted steps leading up to the haunted east wing.

This was the third floor, and once was attics.

This was a stake-out.

Because you didn't simply arrive and go straight into the spiel. *Spend some time with it*, Huw Owen said. *Let it talk to you. No, of course they seldom actually* talk. *And yet they do.*

Could she trust anything Huw Owen had told her?

They'd been here twenty minutes. Downstairs, Susan Thorpe would be glaring at her watch. *Always take your time*, Huw said. *Never let any bugger rush you. Where some of these customers come from, there is no time. Don't rush, don't overreact, don't go drowning it in holy water.*

Merrily's bag contained only one small bottle of holy water, for all the use that was. Her only other equipment was a Christian Deliverance Study Group booklet of suitable prayers, most of which she knew off by heart anyway.

She was just going through the motions, with no confidence that it would work.

It doesn't always work – Huw's truest phrase. It should be printed on the front of the Deliverance handbook.

It should be the *title* of the Deliverance handbook.

And where was she really? How far had she come since the four a.m. horror? Since the fleeing of her bedroom, the vomiting in the kitchen sink, the stove-hugging, the burning of lights till dawn and the *Oh Christ, why hast thou forsaken me*?

There was then the Putting On A Brave Face Until The Bus Takes Jane Away interlude. She'd had the time – hours – to wash and dress carefully, apply make-up. To stand back from the mirror and recoil at the sight of age and fear pushing through like a disease.

Then the staring-at-the-phone phase. The agitated For God's Sake Ring, Huw moments. *He keeps calling you. He wants to explain. So you should call him back. It doesn't matter that he and Dobbs conspired against you. It doesn't matter what he did. You need him. You need him to take it away. You need to call him now and say, Huw, I am possessed. I am possessed by the spirit of Denzil Joy.*

Yet it was not like that. She might look rough in the mirror, but her dull, tired eyes were not the sleazed-over eyes of Denzil Joy. She didn't feel his greasy desires. She didn't *know* him.

Was not possessed by him.

Haunted, though – certainly that. Useless to paper it over with psychology; she was haunted by him. He followed her, had become her spirit-stalker. Because she'd failed, that night in the General, to redirect his malignant energy, its residue had clung to her. She'd walked out of the hospital with Denzil Joy crawling and skulking behind her like some foul familiar. He was hers now. No one else had caught his disease.

And she'd been unaware of it until – once again insufficiently prepared – she had been collecting herself for the assault on the crow-killer of St Cosmas. Collecting her energy. Then into the cocktail had seeped his essence.

Was that what happened? Had yesterday's holy-water exercise been a failure because it had been directed only at the bedroom – making the *room* safe – rather than herself?

Because she was the magnet, right? She'd *invited* him – sitting by his bedside, holding his kippered hands. The female exorcist attracting the incubus, just as the priest-in-charge had invoked the lust of the organist who'd flashed at her from a tombstone.

Today, she'd concentrated on cleansing herself. Leaving the answering machine unplugged, she'd set out on a tour of churches, a pilgrimage on the perimeter of Hereford. A full day of prayer and meditation.

Finally, parking in a back street near the Cathedral School, and slipping discreetly into the Cathedral, sitting quietly at the back for over an hour while tourists and canons she didn't know flitted through.

She had not called Huw, or Sophie. Had resisted the impulse to enter Church Street and find Lol. She had left the answering machine unplugged. At four p.m., she'd returned to the vicarage and fed the cat and made a meal for Jane and herself. Then one more visit to the church before the drive – leaving plenty of time – to the Glades.

It was not about proving herself as an exorcist any more. That was over. This was about saving her ministry.

And her sanity?

Leave sanity out of this. Sanity is relative.

Edna Rees looked along the passage, without apparent apprehension, to where the bulb had just blown. 'Surely that's not the first time it's happened to you, my dear?'

Merrily said nothing.

Edna shifted comfortably in her wicker chair. 'Regular occurrence, it was, in Gwynne Street. Wherever he lived, it happened. So I learned.'

'Bulbs blowing?'

'Might've put me off if I'd known before I took the job, see. But you get used to it.'

Merrily glanced along the line of bulbs. The loss of one seemed to make all the others less bright, as though they were losing heart. There was probably a simple scientific explanation; she should ask Chris Thorpe.

'One week we lost five,' Edna said. 'I said, you want to charge them for all these bulbs, Canon. Well, expensive they are these days, bulbs. We tried those economy things – cost the earth, take an age to come on, but they're supposed to last ten years. Not in that house, they didn't.'

'What else happened?'

'Some nights...' Edna pulled her skirt down over her knees, '... you just couldn't heat that place to save your life, even with all the radiators turned up, the living-room fire banked all day. Wasn't even *that* cold outside sometimes, see. And yet, come the night, just when you'd think it'd be getting nicely warmed up...'

Cold spots?

This passage had five doors, all closed. Closed doors were threatening. Doors ajar with darkness within were terrifying. Merrily guessed she just didn't like doors. Otherwise, there was no sense of disturbance, no cold spots – and certainly nothing like the acrid, soul-shrivelling stench which had gathered around...

Stop!

She turned briskly to Edna. 'Are you saying that he... brought his work home?'

Edna looked at Merrily from under her bottle-green velvet hat. Her eyes were brown and shrewd, over cheeks that were small explosions of split veins.

'My dear, his work *followed* him home.'

She froze. 'He told you that?'

'He never talked about his work,' Edna said. 'Not to me; not to anyone, far as I know. But when he came back sometimes, it was like Jack Frost himself walking in.'

'What did he do about that?'

'Not for me to know, Mrs Watkins.'

'No,' Merrily said, 'obviously not. I... saw you with him the other week, in the Cathedral.'

'Yes,' Edna said calmly, 'I thought it was you.'

'He was telling you to go away. He said there was something he couldn't... couldn't discuss there.'

'Sharp ears you have.'

'Is it none of my business?'

'You must think it is.'

'Why "here"? Why did he want to get you out of the Cathedral?'

335

'For the same reason he wanted me out of his house, Mrs Watkins.'

'Which is?'

'Why are you asking me these questions?'

'Because I can't ask him. Because he's lying in hospital apparently incapable of speech. Or at least he doesn't speak to the female nurses.'

Edna smiled.

'Any more than he'd speak to me before his stroke. He froze me out, too, on the grounds that I wasn't fit to do his job. His sole communication with me was a cryptic note saying that Jesus Christ was the first exorcist. There. I've told you everything, Edna.'

It was what she wanted.

'Merrily... Can I call you Merrily?'

'Please do.'

'Merrily, this began... I don't know exactly *when* it began, but it did have a beginning.'

'Yes.'

'I started to hear him praying, very loud and... anguished. I would hear him through the walls: sometimes in what sounded like Latin – the words meant nothing to me. He would shout them into the night. And then, backwards and forwards from the Cathedral he'd go at all hours, in all weathers. I would hear his footsteps in the street at two, three in the morning. Going to the Cathedral, coming *from* there – sometimes rushing, he was, like a man possessed. I don't mean that in the...'

'I know.'

'And this was when he began cutting himself off: from men too, but especially from women. Would not even see his own sister. He would put her off – *I* was made to put her off – when she wanted to visit. He would not even speak to her on the telephone. Or to his granddaughters – he has two grand-daughters. One of them brought her new baby to show him. He saw her coming down the street and made me tell her he was away. It made no sense to me. He'd been married for forty years.'

'Does it make sense now?'

'I have been reading,' Edna said, 'about St Thomas of Hereford.'

'Thomas Cantilupe?'

'He would not have women near him, either.'

She fell silent.

'But that was *then*,' Merrily said. 'That was the Middle Ages. Cantilupe was a Roman Catholic bishop. They weren't *allowed* to have…'

'I know that, but where did the Canon go when he went into the Cathedral? Where did he have his stroke?'

'Cantilupe's tomb.'

'I can't tell you any more,' Edna said. 'You had better do what you came for.'

In fact, the routine for this kind of situation usually involved blessing the entire house, room by room, starting at the main entrance, the blessing thus extended to all who passed in and out. But Susan Thorpe was hardly going to permit that.

If you couldn't tie down a haunting to a specific incident in the history of the house, then you at least should ask: What's causing it to happen *now*? Is it connected to the present function of the house, the kind of people living here? Old people feeling unwanted, neglected, passed-over? Confused, their senses fuddled…? Yet Susan Thorpe wouldn't accommodate that kind of client. *Any signs of dementia, they have to go. We aren't a nursing home.*

You could spend days investigating this, and then discover it was a simple optical illusion. Merrily moved a little closer to the dead bulb's bracket.

'I don't know what your son-in-law expected, but—'

'Stuffed-shirt, he is,' Edna said. 'I hope I die, I do, before I have to go into a place owned by people like them.

Pretend-carers, they are.' Out of her daughter's earshot, Edna's accent had strengthened. 'Poor old souls. Grit my teeth, I will, and stay here until I can find a little flat, then you won't see me for dust.'

'Good for you,' Merrily said.

It was quiet. No wind in the rafters. They stood in silence for a couple of minutes and then Merrily called on God, who Himself never slept, to bless these bedrooms and watch over all who rested in them.

35

Sholto

HER HANDS TOGETHER, head bowed.

Even the piano was inaudible up here, and in the silence her words sounded hollow and banal.

'... and ask You to bless and protect the stairs and the landings and the corridors along which the residents and the workers here must pass to reach these rooms.'

She was visualizing the old ladies gathered around the piano two floors below, so as to draw them into the prayer.

'We pray, in the name of Our Lord, Jesus Christ, that no spirit or shade or image from the past will disturb the people dwelling here. We pray that these images or spirits will return to their ordained place and there rest in peace.'

This covered both *imprints* and *insomniacs*, although she didn't really think it could be an *insomniac*. There'd surely be some sign, in that case, some pervading atmosphere of unrest.

'Amen,' Edna said.

Merrily held her breath. It had been known, Huw Owen had said, for the spirit itself to appear momentarily, usually at the closing of the ritual, before fading – in theory for ever – from the atmosphere.

Mind, it's also been known to appear with a mocking smile on its face and then – this is frightening – appearing again and again, bang-bang-bang, in different corners of the room...

Although it was hard not to flick a glance over her shoulder, Merrily kept on looking calmly in front of her under half-lowered eyelids, her body turned towards the darkness at the end of the passage. From which drifted a musty smell of dust and camphor which may not have been there before.

She waited, raising her eyes to the sloping ceiling with its blocked-in beams, and the filigree pouches of old cobwebs over the single curtained window. She straightened her shoulders, feeling the pull of the pectoral cross.

It was darker – well *seemed* darker. As though there'd been a thirty per cent decrease in the wattage of the bulbs. Possibly something was happening, something absorbing the energy – something which had begun as she ended her first prayer. A mild resistance was swelling now.

Merrily began to sweat, trying not to tense against the ballooning atmosphere. She wondered if Edna was aware of it, or if she herself was the only focus, her lone ritual beckoning it. When she spoke again, her voice sounded high and erratic.

'If there is a… an unquiet spirit… we pray that you may be freed from whatever anxiety or obsession binds you to this place. We pray that you may rise above all earthly ties and go, in peace, to Christ.'

That sounded feeble. It lacked something. It was too bloody *reasonable*.

Belt and braces, said the awful Chris Thorpe, stooped like a crane and sneering.

Yes, OK, there was something. Now that she was sure of that, there should perhaps be a Eucharist performed for the blessing of the house. It could be conducted by the local vicar, held under some pretext where all the residents could be invited. Those who were churchgoers would accept it without too many questions.

The atmosphere bulged. She felt a sudden urgent need to empty her bladder.

'May the saints of God pray for you and the angels of God guard and protect you…'

Either the air had tightened or she was feeling faint. Resist it. She fumbled at the mohair sweater to expose the cross. As she pulled at the sweater, her palms began to—

'Mrs Watkins.'

Merrily let go of the sweater; her eyes snapped open. Edna Rees was pointing to where, at the top of the three shallow steps, a figure stood.

'Please, there's really no need for this,' it said.

Angela turned over six cards in sequence and then quickly swept the whole layout into a pile.

But not before Jane had seen the cards and recognized three of them: *Death… The Devil… The Tower struck by lightning.*

'I can't do this,' Angela said. 'I'm afraid it's Rowenna's fault.'

It was the same pub where the psychic fair had been held, but this time they were upstairs in a kind of boxroom. Pretty drab: just the card table and two chairs. Rowenna had to perch on a chest of drawers, her head inches from a dangling lightbulb with no shade.

'I'm sorry, Angela,' she said. 'I really didn't realize.'

Angela looked petite inside a huge sheepskin coat with the collar turned up. She also looked casually glamorous, like a movie star on location. But she looked irritated, too.

'I suppose you weren't to know, but it's one of my rules in a situation like this to know only the inner person. I don't like to learn in advance about anyone's background or situation, because then, if I see a problem in the cards, I can know for sure that this information comes from the Source and is not conditioned by my personal knowledge, preconceptions or prejudices. I'm sorry, Jane.'

Jane heard the rumble of bar-life from the room below.

'Angela,' she said nervously, 'that's not because you turned up some really bad cards and you don't think I can take it?'

341

Angela looked cross. 'Cards have many meanings according to their juxtaposition.'

'Looked like a pretty heavy juxtaposition to me,' Rowenna said with a hint of malice. Angela had already done a reading for Rowenna – her future was bound up with a friend's, needing to help this friend discover her true identity – something of that nature. Rowenna had seemed bored and annoyed that the emphasis seemed to be on Jane.

Jane said, 'What was it Rowenna told you?'

'I told her what your mother was, OK?' Rowenna said. 'On the phone last night. It just came out.'

Priest or exorcist? Jane was transfixed for a moment by foreboding. 'That reading was telling you something about me and Mum, wasn't it?'

Angela straightened the pack and put it reverently into the centre of a black cloth and then folded the cloth over it. 'Jane, I'm not well disposed towards the Church. A friend of mine, also a tarot-reader, was once hounded out of a particular village in Oxfordshire because the vicar branded her as an evil infuence.'

'Vicars can be such pigs,' Rowenna said.

'However,' Angela looked up, 'I make a point of never coming between husbands and wives or children and parents.'

'Please, will you tell me what—?'

'Jane.' Angela's calm eyes held hers. 'When I look at your inner being, I sense a generous and uninhibited soul. But if your mother's burden is to be constrained by dogma and an unhappy tradition, you really don't *have* to share it.'

'Well, I know, but… mostly we get on. Since Dad died we've supported each other, you know?'

'Admirable in principle.'

'Like, she's pretty liberal about most things, but she's got this really closed mind about… other things.'

'All right, my last word on this…' Angela began to exude this commanding stillness; you found you were listening very hard.

'It might be wise, for both your sakes – your own and your mother's – for you to keep on walking towards the light. Don't compromise. Don't look back. Pray… I'm going to say it… pray that she follows in *your* wake.'

'You mean she needs to get out of the Church.'

'These are *your* cards, Jane, not hers.'

'Or what? What's going to happen to her if she stays with the Church?'

'Jane, don't put me in a difficult position. Now, how are things going at the Pod?'

The shadow on the stairs spoke in a surprising little-girly voice.

'Aren't you going to introduce me to your friend, Mrs Rees?'

'This,' Edna said with an overtone of resignation, 'is Miss Anthea White.'

'Athena!'

'Miss Athena White. Why aren't you at the party, then, Miss White?'

'At the piano with all those old ladies? One finds that sort of gathering *so* depressing.' Miss White moved out of the shadows. She was small, even next to Merrily, wearing a long blue dressing-gown which buttoned like a cassock.

Very tiny and elflike. Not as old as you expected in a place like this – no more than seventy.

'This is Mrs Watkins,' Edna said.

Miss White inspected Merrily through brass-rimmed glasses like the ones Lol Robinson wore, only much thicker. 'Ah, *there* it is. You keep the clerical collar well-hidden, Mrs Clergywoman. I say, you're very very pretty, aren't you?'

'Thank you,' Merrily said.

'One had feared the new female ministers were all going to be frightful leather-faced lezzies. Come and have a drink in my cell.'

'Now,' Edna said, 'you know you're not supposed to have alcohol in your rooms.'

'Oh, Mrs Rees, you aren't going to blab to the governor, are you? It's such a *frightfully* cold night.' Light seemed to gather in her glasses. '*Far* too cold for an exorcism.'

'Perhaps you could excuse me,' Edna said.

'Oh, do you *have* to leave?'

'I rather understand that I do,' Edna said tactfully.

'How did you guess?' Merrily asked, feeling tired now.

'Oh, don't be ridiculous.' Miss White handed her an inch of whisky in what seemed to be a tooth glass. 'You were hardly here to conduct a wedding.'

Her room was an odd little grotto up in the rafters, with Afghan rugs on the wall, an Aztec-patterned bedspread. And a strange atmosphere, Merrily sensed, of illusion. Twin bottles of Johnnie Walker lurked inside an ancient wooden radio-cabinet. There were several free-standing cupboards, with locks. The room was lit by an electrified pottery oil-lamp on a stand.

Athena White went to sit on the high wooden bed, her legs under her in an almost yogic position, her dressing-gown unbuttoned upwards to the waist. No surgical stockings needed here. Merrily was sitting uncomfortably on a kind of camping stool near the door. It put her head on a level with Miss White's projecting knees. Miss White seemed relaxed, like some tiny goddess-figure on a plinth.

'Now then,' she said. 'What are you trying to do to Sholto?'

She let the name hang in the air until Merrily repeated it.

'Sholto?'

A mellower light gathered in Miss White's glasses. 'Weren't you able to see him?'

Merrily made no reply.

'Come on, young Mrs Clergyperson, either you did or you didn't.'

'Let's say I didn't.'

'That's a shame. Perhaps you were erecting a barrier? That's what your Church does though, isn't it? Very, very sad

– throwing up barriers, wrapping itself in a blanket of disapproval. And yet' – Miss White's head tilted in mild curiosity – 'you are afraid.'

'I don't think so.'

'Oh yes, I can always detect fear. You're not afraid of Sholto, are you?'

'Am I to understand Sholto is your ghost?'

'How perceptive of you to apply the possessive,' said Miss White. 'I must say, it's an awful job you have, Mrs Clergyperson. I never thought to see a woman doing it.'

'Why not?'

'Is it a specialist thing, or have you simply been commandeered as Thorpe's prison chaplain?'

'Miss White—'

'Your Church is like some repressive totalitarian regime. Everyone has a perfectly good radio set, but you try to make sure they can only tune in to state broadcasts. Whenever the curtains accidentally open on some sublime vista, you rush in and snap them shut again. *That's* your job, isn't it?'

'The soul police,' Merrily said. 'You should meet my daughter.'

'Ye gods, are you old enough to have a daughter?'

'Let's drop the flattery, Miss White. What are you trying to tell me?'

'What I *am* telling you' – Miss White turned full-face to Merrily, and the light in her glasses became twin pinpoints – 'is to leave him alone.'

'Sholto?'

'Have you *any* idea what it's like in one of these places, where all is grey and faded, and romance resides solely in one's memory?'

'This room's hardly grey and faded.'

'You like my eyrie?'

'It's very cosy.'

'Cosy!' said Miss White in disgust. 'Pah!'

'But to get back to Sholto – that's your name for him, is it?'

'That, my dear clergyperson, *is* his name.'

'You know his history? Some things about him?'

'There's nothing I *don't* know about him. He's a randy sod sometimes, and a frightful lounge lizard, but very, very charming. A look of Ronald Colman, but I suppose you're too young—'

'No, I've seen some of those old films. And you… have seen him, I take it.'

'What a stupid question.'

'And the other residents?'

'Well, I can't speak for *all* the hags. Sholto's quite choosy – won't pinch the flabbier old buttocks.'

'What?'

'Oh, for heaven's sake, don't look like that, girl. He was a man of his time. Men *used* to pinch bottoms.'

'I'm sorry.' Merrily was feeling cramped on the stool. 'But what exactly are we talking about here? Who… what exactly do you think Sholto is?'

'What do I think he is?' A vaguely malevolent elf now, white light spearing from her glasses. 'What do *you* think he is?'

An imprint? An insomniac? A volatile? This is the terminology of the Deliverance Age, Miss White.

'I'll tell you what he *isn't*, Mrs Clergygirl.' A finger wagging, the face narrowing, and the eyes almost merging behind the glasses. 'He isn't doing any harm. So you should go away and forget about him. In this museum of memories, Sholto is necessary.'

Merrily drank more whisky to moisten her mouth. 'Would you mind if I had a cigarette?'

'Certainly I would! Pull yourself together. If you don't realize the importance of willpower in *your* job…' Miss White's neck extended, birdlike. 'What *is* the matter with you, child?'

Willpower.

Merrily went cold. 'It was you, wasn't it?'

'I beg your pardon.'

'Something was trying to stop me administering the blessing. That was you, wasn't it? Exercising your... *willpower*.'

'Oh, what nonsense!' Miss White sniffed, delighted.

'Please,' Merrily said wearily, 'no more bullshit, Athena.'

A self-satisfied smile escaped beneath a little portcullis of teeth. 'Why don't you just ask yourself... What's your name, by the way?'

'Merrily.'

'Well, ask yourself, Merrily, was what you were doing appropriate? Was it polite?'

'Sorry?'

'Did you ask permission? No, you didn't. It was like a police raid: the way they always go in at dawn and bash someone's door down. It's disgraceful – we're not criminals, even if we are in prison. And what has Sholto done wrong?'

'Well, he... he's dead. He shouldn't *be* here.'

Miss White's magnified eyes glowed.

She's mad, Merrily thought. 'Look,' she said reasonably, 'shouldn't he be free to move on? That's what matters. And what keeps him here – that matters, too. Because if what keeps him here is only—'

'The undying pull of the flesh, one presumes. Perhaps we're part of his karma. Broke a lot of young hearts in his time, I'd guess. Now all he has to amuse him is a bunch of raddled old bags with their tits round their waists. For him, that's Purgatory, to use your terminology. But we're all of us far too old to be corrupted. Sholto is needed here to feed people's fantasies. He's not only harmless, he's essential, and that's an end to it. I'll keep him in order, don't worry. You can tell Thorpe you've got rid of him. Now... let's examine your own problem, which I would guess is a good deal less benign. What *are* you carrying around with you?'

'What?'

'Look at you, all hunched up against the cold. You're cowering.'

Merrily instinctively straightened as best she could on her camping stool.

'Oh, stop it! You're cowering *inside*. You can't hide that from me. Come here.'

Merrily found herself standing up.

'Come and sit on the bed. Come on, I'm not going to touch you up!' Athena White slid from the bed and leaned, in her tubular robe, over Merrily, peering closely into her eyes. 'Ye gods, you *are* buggered up, aren't you?'

Merrily's legs felt suddenly quite weak.

'Don't struggle,' Miss White said.

'This is not right.'

'It's not right at all. Look at me – no, *focus* on me, girl. That's better. I want to see the *inner* person. I feel you're normally quite strong, but he's certainly depleted you.'

'Who?'

'You tell me. Go on. Tell me his name.'

'I don't know what you—'

'Tell me his name: that ball of spiritual pus that's attached itself to you. What is his *name*?'

'Denzil Joy.'

'That's better,' said Miss White.

36

Crow Maiden

By 9:30, James Lyden and his band had been ejected from the cellar studio in Breinton Lane. Lol got out of there, too, before Denny's rage could do some damage. By the time the band had been packed into their Transit in the driveway, he was making his excuses – there was someone he needed to call.

Which was true.

'You can do it from here, man.' Denny's bald head was shining with angry sweat.

'I can't.' Lol was backing away out of the drive, pulling on his army-surplus jacket. No way he wanted to discuss this with Denny until he had some background.

'You…' Denny was stabbing at the fog. 'You know more than you're letting on. Where's this come from? What's this crow shit?'

'I'll call you tomorrow.'

'And you can tell that fucking Lyden he's finished!' Denny bawled after him down Breinton Lane.

The Transit van had reversed, and was alongside Lol now, James's Welsh friend, Eirion, at the wheel. It stopped.

'Mr Robinson,' Eirion shouted, 'for heaven's sake, what have we done?' He sounded shocked and frightened.

'Get your cocking head back in here, Lewis,' Lol heard James say lazily. 'The old man will sort it.'

'I'm sorry,' Eirion said, as the van pulled away. Lol wondered what his chances were of talking to Dick before James did.

'How old are you, Merrily?'

'Thirty-six.'

She sat at the bottom of the bed, feeling a little unconnected, slightly not-quite-here. She felt guilty because that was not unpleasant. Maybe the whisky...

Or not?

'When I was your age, I knew nothing,' Miss White said. 'Indeed, I knew very little even when I retired from the Civil Service. You would have been only a child then. I, however, was very high-powered in those days, or so I thought. In reality I knew nothing. It was only when I left London that I began to study in earnest.'

She unlocked one of the cupboards, threw open its double doors.

Merrily thought: *Oh... my... God...*

Books. Hundreds of books – many stored horizontally on the shelves, so as to stuff more in. Madame Blavatsky, Rudolph Steiner, Israel Regardie, Dion Fortune: recent paperbacks wedged against yellowing tomes on meditation, astrology, the Qabalah. If the other cupboards were similarly stocked, there must be several thousand books in this attic.

A lifetime's collection of esoteric reading. A witch's cave of forbidden literature. You wouldn't have prised Jane out of here this side of breakfast time.

'They know I have books in my cupboards,' Miss White said, 'but I rather imagine they consider me a subscriber to the lists of Messrs Mills and Boon.'

Merrily thought how wary she herself used to be of Jane's guru: the late folklorist, Lucy Devenish. God only knew what *this* old girl got up to when the lights were out.

One thing puzzled her.

'Miss White, I can't… What are you doing in a place like this?'

'Ah, yes… why not the bijou black and white cottage? Why not the roses round the door and the Persian cat in the window?'

'Something like that.'

'Because then, my little clergyperson, one would be obliged to prune the roses and feed the cat, to shop for food and employ workmen to preserve the ancient timbers. How much more space there is here… *inner* space, I mean. As well as beautiful hills to walk in, should one be overtaken by the need to commune with nature.'

'But how can you…? I don't know how to put this.'

'Be surrounded by twittering biddies, patronized by the dreadful Thorpe? That is simply the outer life. The Thorpes suspect I have enough money to buy the whole place, so they don't pressure me. All right, when one gets very, *very* annoyed with them, one can be… mischievous…'

'I bet.'

'… while at the same time' – Miss White smiled almost seraphically – 'giving one's fellow inmates a welcome, nostalgic *frisson* once in a while.'

His name drifted serenely in the air between them.

'Sholto,' Merrily said eventually.

'A-ha.'

'How did you do it?'

Miss White selected from the bookshelves what turned out to be a stiff-backed folder, and took out a yellowing photograph pasted on card.

'This is him?'

He wore a pinstriped suit with wide lapels. His hair was dark and kinked, his moustache trimmed to a shadow.

'I bought him in a print shop in Hay,' said Miss White. 'I liked his little twist of a smile. No idea who he is or where he came from – there's no name on the photo. I thought he rather looked like a Sholto.'

Merrily said, 'I'm not going to ask you how you did this.'

'Good, because I should refuse to tell you. You could find out easily enough, if you studied. It's a very well established technique.'

'He isn't a ghost at all.'

'He's a projection. Do you know what I mean by that?'

Merrily said, 'Can I think about it?'

Projection?

Psychic projection, psychological projection – a grey area. Come on, Huw, what are we dealing with here?

We don't fully understand this, but if we assume, to put it simply, that an imprint exists on a sensory wavelength or plane parallel to our own, then it follows that some people are capable of tuning into that wavelength, sometimes allowing the imprint to be transmitted in a way that renders it visible to others. They may be able, consciously or unconsciously, to lend it the energy it needs to manifest. They may even create their own imprint, projecting it like a hologram. If you come across one of these, you're unlikely to be able to get rid of it through prayer or ritual alone. You've got to stop the person from doing it.

Merrily imagined, in the part of the passage where the bulb had blown, turning it into a black tunnel, a man in a double-breasted suit bringing a match to his cigarette, exhaling the smoke towards her – smoke which rose in a V, a grey, sardonic smile – before shrivelling up into his own vapour like a silently bursting balloon.

'You're thinking, is this devilry – aren't you?' The light through Miss White's glasses was intense and focused, like when as a kid you used the sun through a magnifying glass to burn a hole in a newspaper.

'I suppose I am.'

'Would you settle for *naughty*?'

'I'd love to, but I don't think I'd be allowed to. You see, the problem – as I see it – is that you've created an energy form separate from yourself, but possessing a few atoms of your transferred… intelligence?'

'Perhaps.'

'How far is that from it acquiring a level of existence of its own? A primitive level, perhaps, but then other – possibly negative – energies might be attracted to it. And then you could have trouble that's not so easy to control: a *volatile* – a poltergeist. Or worse.'

'Yes.' Athena White sat down next to Merrily. 'I follow your argument. It's unlikely, though, especially if *I'm* here.'

'But… I'm sorry, Athena, but you're not always going to be here, are you?'

'He'll die when I die.'

'You reckon?'

'Oh, you *are* a pain, Mrs Clergyperson. All right, I'll consider it. But it'll be a frightful wrench – for all of us.'

'I'm sure he'll live on in all your memories.'

'I've said I'll *consider* it,' Athena snapped. 'Now tell me about Denzil Joy.'

There was a rapping on the door, and Susan Thorpe said, 'Miss White, is there a woman in there with you?'

'I'm here, Susan,' Merrily said. 'Miss White's been helping me.'

'I hope she can keep her mouth shut.'

Miss White said loftily, 'You may, for once, count on it, Thorpe. Now leave us.'

'You know I can't drag the party out much longer.'

'Well, tell your husband to take his clothes off.'

'Oh!' said Susan Thorpe. They heard her footsteps recede.

'That makes me feel quite queasy,' Merrily said.

'Wait till you're as old as they are.' Mrs White stood up. 'Merrily, I'm very disturbed by this. I think he's feeding off you.'

'Don't.'

'If one doesn't face these things, one can't take remedial action. I suspect you haven't been yourself for some days. Tired? Depleted? Prone to emotional outbursts?'

'Well, yes, since you ask. And also flu-like symptoms: vaguely sore throat, blocked nose, temperature. I put it down to stress.'

'Losing the will to fight it?'

'Half the time I just want to run away. I mean... Well, to be quite honest, this was going to be my last job as Deliverance consultant... diocesan exorcist.'

'You were giving it up?' An eyebrow rose above the spectacles. 'While, under different circumstances, that is a decision one might wish to applaud—'

'I felt I couldn't cope. I felt under attack from all kinds of different directions.'

'As you may well be. This could be precisely what's happening. How many people know of your appalling experience with this man?'

'I don't know. The nurses involved... my daughter, Jane... my Deliverance course tutor. And Canon Dobbs, of course.'

'As he appeared to have arranged it for you? The sheer *ignorance* of the clergy dumbfounds me. Who else?'

'There's no one else I've told, I don't think. It's not something I enjoy talking about. What's the significance of that, anyway? If I mishandled the job in the hospital, and I've let him in, that's not their fault.'

'Admittedly, the idea of an unhappy spirit desperately clinging at the moment of death to a living person is not unknown, particularly in a sexually charged situation. But I think you must also consider the possibility of psychic attack by person or persons unknown. Which is far *far* more common than most people would imagine. Merely thinking ill of someone is its most basic form, but we may be looking at something more complex in this instance. If I were to lend you my copy of Dion Fortune's *Psychic Self-Defence...*'

'What are you trying to do to me? I'm a Christian.'

'As was Fortune herself, after her fashion. Merrily, how soon after the incident at the hospital did this unclean presence make itself apparent?'

'I felt tired afterwards, but that was natural; I'd been up all night. But I don't think I really became aware of it until I was called in to cleanse a desecrated church.'

'Interesting. This was during your service?'

'Well, I didn't actually... It was *before*.'

'When you entered the church?'

'I...' Merrily remembered standing outside the church talking to the policemen – with a stiffness and a clamminess in her vestments. Had she felt that in the car on the way there? Possibly.

'Think back, Merrily. Who were you with when you first experienced something amiss?'

'Policemen? I don't know, can't think. I'm mixed up and a bit anxious because I'm sitting here, a minister of the Church, unburdening myself to a practising occultist who, by force of willpower, has created a haunted house.'

'Who would you normally go to for spiritual help?'

'Huw, my course tutor, who was in the church with me when I exhibited what must have seemed to him like many of the symptoms of demonic possession.'

'In which case, why the blue blazes—?'

'It's complicated.'

'All right.' Athena White placed a hand on Merrily's knee. It didn't feel like a cloven hoof. 'Go home, pull your bed into the centre of the room, and draw a pentacle...'

'You have *got* to be joking!'

'All right, a circle – in salt, or even chalk – around the bed. Perform whatever rite your religion allows, but supplement it, when you're lying in bed, by visualizing rings of bright orange or golden light around you and above you, so that you are enclosed in an orb of light. Keep that in your mind constantly until you fall asleep. If you awake in the night, visualize it at once, intact. This should bring you unmolested to the morning.'

'A circle?'

'Don't be afraid of it. There is but one God. Consider it heavenly light – angelic.'

Huw and Dobbs? Merrily frowned. She always knew it had to be something like this.

'Secondly, take the robes – vestments – you were wearing in the church when you were spiritually assaulted and burn them. You could try to bless them or sprinkle them with holy water, but it's really not worth it. Get rid of them.'

Merrily supposed this made sense.

'But that is not enough, and you know it, Merrily. Until you trace it to its source and eradicate it, you're always going to be a magnet for the obscene advances of this earthbound essence. This Denzil Joy. One can almost see him now, bloating your aura. You absolutely cannot afford to rest – indeed, you will *not* rest because of who you are – until you put *him* to rest.'

'Yes, I was going to ring you,' Dick Lyden said, agitated. 'The boy's back already, and he's not terribly happy.'

'*He's* not happy...' Lol dragged the phone over to the armchair.

Dick said, 'Laurence, it was my understanding that Denny's studio was a proper professional operation – not some Mickey Mouse outfit. You know what this is costing me, don't you?'

Lol assured Dick that, while this was not the biggest studio around, it was one in which he personally would be delighted to record.

Dick said, 'As long as it didn't bloody well blow up, presumably.'

It didn't blow up, Lol told him. *Denny* blew up, pressured beyond reasonable resistance by the song they were laying on him. When Denny had heard enough of it, wires became detached.

'I'm not paying the man to be a bloody critic,' Dick said. 'I don't like *any* damned song they do either, and I haven't even heard them.'

Lol said, 'Do you and Ruth talk about your work much, over the family supper, comparing notes, that kind of thing?'

'What the hell has—?'

'For instance, did you talk much about Moon in front of James?'

Dick's voice dropped like it had been fast-faded. 'What are you saying?'

Lol said, 'James, as you may have gathered, isn't satisfied with an EP – he wants an album. Denny and me, we were a bit underwhelmed by the quality of what we'd heard so far. We suggested the boys run through the rest of their material, so we'd know what we were looking at. Most of it wasn't wonderful either.'

To be fair, it wasn't badly played, and the harmonies were as neatly dovetailed as you might expect from newly retired cathedral choirboys. It was the material – derived from the work of second-division bands which were already derivative of other second-division bands twenty years earlier – that didn't make it. Denny had, in reality, told Lol – behind the protection of thick glass – that they would make a recording of such pristine quality that the deficiencies in the area of compositional talent would stand out like neon.

'Well, James's mate Eirion isn't entirely insensitive.'

'Really?' Dick said. 'His old man runs Welsh Water.'

'Eirion can tell Denny isn't impressed, so after about three routine power-chord numbers he gets the band into a huddle, and then he and James sit down with acoustic guitars and they go into this quiet little ballad which James introduces as "The Crow Maiden". Perfect crystal harmonies – you could hear every word.'

'Get to the point.'

'I tend to remember lyrics – remembered the last verse, anyway, so I wrote it down.' Lol began to unfold a John

Barleycorn paper bag. 'It's really subtle, as you can imagine –
still you'll probably get the drift. You ready?'

'Oh, for heaven's sake—'

Lol held up the paper bag, and recited:

'Found your refuge in the past
'You hid beneath its shade
'And when you knew it couldn't last
'You took your life with an ancient blade.
'CROW MAIDEN
'CROW MAIDEN
'YOU'RE FADIN'
'AWAY...'

'Would you like that again?'

You could hear Dick's hand squeezing the phone.

'The little shit,' Dick said.

37

Faeces and Gangrene

FRIDAY MORNING, SIX a.m. A cold morning moon through new glass. And a smell of putty in the vestry at Ledwardine, where Merrily stood before the wardrobe, frozen with indecision.

She had the Zippo. The Zippo would do it.

What are you waiting for?

She hadn't slept well, but she *had* slept until five, with – all right, yes – the bed in the middle of the room inside a circle of salt. All of which she'd swept into a dustpan before she left the vicarage, in case she didn't return before first light and Jane came looking for her, popped her head around the bedroom door and – God *forbid!*

She was half ashamed, half embarrassed – and had, as soon as she arose, knelt before the window and apologized to God, if He had been offended by the circle and the salt. But she was, in the end, helplessly grateful. For the first time in days, she had not awakened feeling ill, congested, soiled, or worse.

Grateful to whom, though? She'd prayed for a peaceful night, prayed for the soul of Denzil Joy. But it was, to her disquiet, the orange-gold orb of Athena White which had coloured her dreams.

Was she balancing at the top of the slippery slope into New Age madness? Into Jane country? And if she burned the cassock and surplice?

Last night, in her state of compliance at the Glades, half hypnotized by the extraordinary Miss White, this had seemed entirely logical. This morning, she'd been dwelling on it with increasing horror – a bonfire of these vestments was wholly sacrilegious, the most explicit symbolic rejection of her vows.

She'd prayed hard over this one, kneeling under the window, summoning the blue and the gold. *Oh Jesus, give me a sign that this is acceptable in Your eyes.*

Please God, don't take it the wrong way. Infantile? God listened to your heart.

You will not rest – until you put him *to rest.*

Oh, Miss White, so plausible. This career civil servant – *very high-powered* – who had committed herself to an old folks' home to develop her inner life. *Damned woman,* Susan Thorpe had said afterwards, *I could have sworn she was downstairs with the others. But you did manage to complete your exorcism?* No problem, Merrily had assured her. Miss White was a surprisingly devout believer. *One God. Angelic light.*

A dabbler? A minister of God was following the advice of a mad dabbler all the way to New Age hell?

Now Merrily stood in the vestry, with no lights on and her torch switched off – after Sunday night's break-in, Ted probably had vigilantes watching out for signs of intruders. She felt like a thief: the taking and destruction of priest's vestments… wilful damage… and worse.

Burn them.

Where? On the drawing-room fire? In the garden, like a funeral pyre of her faith?

It was well meant. She had no bad feelings at all about Athena White as a human being. And the advice was… well meant.

And it was insidiously irresistible last night, after Jane had gone to bed, and Merrily had been standing at the sink, filling her hot water bottle and contemplating the night ahead… smelling *his* smell, feeling *his* fingers – *scritch-scratch*… hearing the ratchet wrench as *his* body snapped upright in its deathbed, the tubes expelled, *pip-pop!*

And now remembering how Ethel the cat – who, until this week, had habitually slept at the bottom of Merrily's bed – had once again padded discreetly and faithlessly up the stairs after Jane.

It was then that she'd reached into the cupboard for the drum of kitchen salt. Taking it with her into the scullery-office, where she'd followed the mad woman's next instruction – *Trace it to its source* – and called the Alfred Watkins Ward to ask Eileen Cullen for the address of the widow Joy.

And Eileen, puzzled, asking her, 'Is there a problem there, Merrily, you think? Would it not be a case of blessed relief for the poor woman?'

'Sometimes it doesn't work like that,' Merrily had said. 'She may even be feeling guilt that she wasn't there at the end.'

'That was my fault, so help me, for not telling the poor cow until it was over. All right, Merrily, whatever your secret agenda is, you made a good case. You know your way to Bobblestock district?'

She'd find it. As soon as Jane was off the premises, she would go and find Mrs Joy. She would take the whole Deliverance kit, and fresh vestments in the car boot.

But not these vestments.

She opened the wardrobe and pulled them down. They'd been washed, of course, since the night at St Cosmas. She hung the cassock and surplice over the arm that held the torch, still not switched on. She opened both doors wide and felt around to make sure she'd taken the correct garments.

Which was when she found the man's suit.

What?

She pushed the torch inside the wardrobe and switched it on. The suit was on a hanger, pushed to the end of the rail so that it was not visible if you opened only one door.

Merrily pushed her head inside to examine the suit. It was dark green, with a thin stripe of light brown, made of some heavyweight material, and well worn. She touched it. It felt damp.

Or moist, more like.

Merrily screamed. She now had her sign.

She stood, retching, in the moon-washed vestry.

The thin smell the suit gave off had reminded a doctor at the General Hospital of cat faeces and gangrene.

It was around eight, cloudy but fog-free, when Lol spotted the boy in Cathedral School uniform lurking below in Church Street. He went down, and the boy came over: a stocky dark-haired boy with an unexpectedly bashful smile. It was Eirion Lewis, son of the boss of Welsh Water.

'Hoped you might be about, Mr Robinson. I just… didn't really feel like going to school until I knew where we stood, you know?'

'Come on up,' Lol said.

Once inside, Eirion went straight to the guitar. 'Wow, is that a Washburn? Could I?'

Lol handed Eirion the Washburn and the boy sat down with it, picking out the opening riff to 'The Crow Maiden'.

'I have to play bass in the band because James is rather better on this than me.'

'Like McCartney,' Lol recalled.

'Really?'

'He was the worst guitarist in the band, so he wound up on bass.'

'Brilliant bass-player, actually. I… You know, I didn't mean what I said about how he should have been shot. You feel you've got to keep up with James's cynicism sometimes. Like, he's younger than me, you know?'

'Right,' Lol said.

'I… Mr Robinson, I really don't have much time. I just sort of…' Eirion hung his head over the guitar. 'I don't know what we did, but we did *something*, didn't we? I mean, this is really important to me, this recording. I don't want to blow it. You know?'

'Well, it was that song,' Lol said.

'*This* song? "The Crow Maiden"?'

'Which of you actually wrote it?'

'We both did. I do the tunes, James does the words. Like, he gives me a poem or something and I work a tune around it – or the other way about. You know?'

'It's a bit more, er, resonant than the other stuff, isn't it?'

'Yes, it is.'

'James tell you where he got the idea?'

'I assumed he made it up – or pinched it from some ancient Fairport Convention album or something. Actually, you know, what can I say? I mean… James is a shit, isn't he?'

'Oh?' Lol tilted his head. 'Why?'

'He just is, isn't he? He kind of tells lies a lot. Enjoys getting up people's noses. Does kind of antisocial things for the hell of it. Well, lately, anyway. God, this is stupid of me; you're his dad's mate, aren't you? You used to kind of work with him, right?'

'Oh, well, that's over now,' Lol said. 'Nothing you say will get back to James's old man, OK. "The Crow Maiden", it's about Denny's sister.'

'Sorry?'

'She committed suicide last weekend. She cut her wrists with an ancient blade.'

Eirion's fingers fell from the frets.

'Mmm,' Lol said, 'I can see you didn't know that.'

At the front door, Jane sniffed. 'What's burning out there?'

'I can't smell anything, flower. It's probably from the orchard. Gomer's been clearing some undergrowth.'

'Right.' Jane inspected her mum in the first bright daylight of the week. 'You're looking better.'

'Thanks.'

'Pressure off now?'

'Maybe. You're going to miss the school bus.'

Jane said casually, 'You know, if things have loosened up a bit, Mum, you really ought to take the opportunity to think about your long-term future.'

'It's not a problem, flower. I'll be going to heaven.'

'God,' said Jane, 'you Christians are so simplistic. 'Bye.'

'Work hard, flower.'

When the kid was out of sight, Merrily went around the side of the house to check out the garden incinerator. The vestments were ashes. She made the sign of the cross over them.

Then she burned the suit.

Merrily called directory enquiries for the Reverend Barry Ambrose in Devizes, Wiltshire. She rang his number.

'I'm sorry, he's just popped round to the church,' a woman said pleasantly. 'He'll be back for his breakfast any minute. I'm Stella, his long-suffering wife. Can I get him to call you?'

'If you could. Tell him I really won't keep him a minute.'

'That's no problem. He's talked a lot about you, Merrily, since you were on that course together. He thinks you're awfully plucky.'

'Well, that's... a common illusion. Has Barry done much in the way of Deliverance so far?'

'Only bits and bobs, you know. He's still quite nervous about it, to be honest. And you?'

'Still feeling my way,' Merrily said.

Waiting for Barry Ambrose to call back, she went to the bookcase in the hall where they kept the local stuff. She plucked out one she'd bought in the Cathedral shop: *St Thomas Cantilupe, Bishop of Hereford: Essays in His Honour*. She hadn't yet had time to open it.

I have been reading, Edna Rees had said, *about St Thomas of Hereford.*

In the book, several historians explored aspects of the saint's life and the effect he'd had on Hereford – enormous apparently. Merrily began to read about Cantilupe's final months, in 1282, after his dispute with the Archbishop of Canterbury, John Pecham.

This seemed to be a bureaucratic argument about one going over the other's head, further fired up by a clash of temperament. It had ended with Cantilupe being excommunicated and travelling to Italy to appeal personally to the Pope. On the way back, exhausted, he'd collapsed and died – at dusk on 25 August – while still in Italy. As was the custom (*Really? Christ!*) the body was boiled to remove the flesh from the bones. The flesh was buried at the monastery church of San Severo, the heart and bones were brought back to England by Cantilupe's steward, John de Clare. The heart was then kept at Ashridge, in Buckinghamshire, at a college of canons, while the bones came back to Hereford.

Where they began to attract pilgrims – thousands of them. When news of the miracles spread – cures of the crippled and the blind – it became the most important shrine in the West of England. And it made this comparatively remote cathedral very wealthy.

Although several of the bones seemed to have been removed as relics before this, it was not until the shrine was destroyed in the Reformation, on the orders of Henry VIII, that they were dispersed. The book recorded, without further comment, a story that during the journey from Italy the 'persecuted bones' had bled.

Barry Ambrose called back. She liked Barry: he was inoffensive, hamsterish, an old-fashioned vicar.

'Hey, Merrily… you heard about Clive Wells?'

The lofty old-money priest who'd sneered at Huw. 'Should I have?'

'He's packed it in,' said Barry.

'What, Deliverance?'

'The lot. He's apparently planning to emigrate to Canada with his family. Had some experience he wouldn't talk about to anybody – now he can't even go into the church. Can't even *pass* a church without going to pieces, so they say.'

'God.'

'Makes you think, doesn't it, Merrily. What can I do for you?'

It was, she admitted, a long shot. 'There's a girl moved into this area from Wiltshire... Salisbury.'

'Oh, they're very doubtful about me in Salisbury. You know what it's like.'

'Yeah. No, it's just... if you happened to hear anything. I don't even know what I'm looking for. This girl's called Rowenna Napier. They left the area earlier this year. It was suggested to me that there was something funny in her past which might not seem very funny to a church minister. I'm sorry, that's it, I'm afraid.'

Barry was unfazed. 'Well, I've got a name – that's a start, I suppose. I can only roll it along the Cathedral Close and see if anybody picks it up.'

'Could you?'

'Give me a day or two. So, how's it going, Merrily – really?' She heard the boxy sound of him covering the mouthpiece. 'I tell you, it scares seven shades out of me sometimes.'

'Thank God you said that, Barry. Stella gave me the impression you hadn't been doing too much.'

'All *she* knows,' Barry said with an audible shudder.

Viv arrived at the shop with a *Hereford Times*.

'Not too much about Moon, thank Gawd. They haven't picked up on her father's suicide, so that's a mercy. Maybe nobody's worked there long enough to remember.'

Or else Denny had refused to talk to them, Lol thought, and they were sitting on it till it all came out at the full inquest.

Viv said, 'Oh, yeah, I talked to my friend who still goes to the Pod. It's bizarre, but these two girls turn up out of nowhere: your friend's kid and an older one, right? Patricia, who is like mother superior in the group, says to make this Jane feel at home, she's a special person, they have to take care of her, she's got problems at home – this kind of stuff.'

'Problems *at home*?'

'I only mention this... like maybe you don't know as much as you think. You got something happening with the mother, is that it? Was that her the other day, when you ran outside?'

Lol didn't answer. Viv had tossed the *Hereford Times* on the counter, and he'd just noticed the lead headline.

CROW SACRIFICED IN COUNTY CHURCH HORROR

He snatched up the newspaper...

38

Nevermore

'Do you *know* how many messages I have left on your machine in the past two days?' Sophie demanded angrily. 'Surely, even if you were ill…'

Ill? Yes, she'd been ill. She saw that now. Merrily sat at the desk in the office with the ☩ on the door. Nothing had altered and yet everything had. The white winter sun lit the room. There were things to do.

'I'm very sorry, Sophie. I've behaved very badly.'

It could have been entirely psychological. If her vestments were tainted, however slightly, with Denzil's insidious musk, it would have a subliminal effect: expanding at moments of high emotional stress or extreme sensitivity – like the build-up to an exorcism in a country church – into a near manifestation. And it would then take root, and arise again at times – like emerging from sleep – when the subconscious was in free-flow.

Whatever, someone out there had tried to break her. But now, deep in her solar plexus, she was feeling the warm, pulsing thrill of redemption.

Sophie wore a royal-blue two-piece woollen suit. Her white hair was tightly bunned. She looked angry and perhaps over-tired, but her eyes also displayed a small sparkle of hope. She'd become like a mother, Merrily realized.

'Merrily, about your resignation e-mail…'

'Oh, yes. Has the Bishop received that yet?' She heard the unconcern in her own voice. It didn't really matter any more whether or not she was the official Deliverance consultant. That was a spurious, manufactured title which conferred no special powers. It was just a beacon for the rat-eyes in the dark.

'The Bishop doesn't read his e-mail,' Sophie said. '*I* read his e-mail, and print out the relevant items and put them on his desk. This is yours, I think. What would you like me to do with it?'

She placed in front of Merrily a sheet of A4.

Dear Bishop,

After long consideration...

Merrily saw what Sophie wanted – how she could make Sophie much happier. 'Could you wipe it?' she said easily. 'I wasn't really myself, was I?'

Sophie gripped the desk tightly, and then let go.

'Sophie?' Merrily stood up, took her arm.

'I didn't want you to go, and leave me alone here.' Sophie swallowed. 'Sometimes I feel I'm going mad.'

'That doesn't sound like you.'

'I know. Capable, reliable old Sophie – total commitment to the Cathedral. That's the *problem*, isn't it?'

'What is?'

'Something in the Cathedral's going wrong, and I'm afraid Michael...'

Merrily sighed. 'Might as well say it, Sophie. He can't see it, can he? He wouldn't feel it because he has no basic faith or spirituality? Isn't that what you're saying: that the Cathedral's not safe in Mick's hands?'

Treason.

'Sophie?'

Sophie brought a finger to her brow, as if to halt a fast-escaping thought. 'We have to talk, Merrily.'

The phone rang on her desk in the other office.

'Sure,' Merrily said. 'Whenever.'

She went in search of Lol. In John Barleycorn, the large, tribal-looking woman regarded her with some interest.

'You must be Jane's mum.'

'You *know* Jane?'

'Not personally,' the big woman said with an enigmatic smile. 'But I've got daughters, so I know the problem.'

'*Is* there a problem?' What the hell had Lol been saying? Merrily rocked inside with a blinding urge to wipe away all the rumours and gossip and deceit that had gathered in the days of the fog.

And, oh, there was so much to say to Jane and so much to bring out, after a week in which Merrily had felt so scared of her own daughter that the only way she'd been able to approach this issue was behind the kid's back.

The shop woman smiled to herself, heavy with superior knowledge.

'Where's Lol?' Merrily snapped.

'Oh.' The woman recoiled. 'I think he's over in the central library. That's where he said he was going.'

'Thank you.'

The day had taken a sharp dive into December dusk. She became aware, for the first time, of Christmas lights. Little golden Santas racing across Broad Street on their sleighs, and the warm red lanterns winking a welcome to wallets everywhere.

Christmas in three weeks: goodwill to all men... school Nativity play in the church... afternoon carol service... midnight eucharist. The churchwardens beadily monitoring those big festive collections. Courtesy visits: *Glass of sherry for the vicar, Celia. Not too much – don't want you falling out of the pulpit, ha-ha.*

And the core of cold and loneliness at the heart of it all. The huddling together, with drunken bonhomie and false laughter to ward off the dark.

She stopped outside the library, the lights still blinking universal panic over parties unorganized, presents unbought. For Merrily they emphasized a core of darkness in the little city of Hereford, deep and intense. She stood amid the rush-hour shoppers and she felt it in her solar plexus, where the ghost of Denzil Joy – the ghost that *wasn't* – had formed an interior fog. And now it was clear.

Lol was coming down the library steps, with a big brown book under his arm.

'Merrily!' Santa-light dancing across his gold-framed glasses.

Lol, she wanted to shout, *I'm all right. I'm clear.*

And rush into his arms.

And I still can't go to bed with you. We priests don't do that kind of thing.

'We have to talk, Merrily.'

Suddenly everybody wanted to talk.

'Me too,' she told him, still on that strange, sensitive high. 'Let's go to church.'

The vicar of All Saints had a bigger, more regular congregation than the Cathedral's.

This was because they'd cleared a big space at the rear of the medieval city-centre church and turned it into a restaurant. A good one too. It might not work in a village like Ledwardine, but it had worked here. This church was what it used to be in the Middle Ages, what it was built to be: the centre of everything. It was good to hear laughter in a church, see piles of shopping bags and children, who maybe had never been in a church before, gazing in half-fearful fascination down the nave towards the secret, holy places.

They carried their cups of tea to a table. Lol still had the big brown book under his arm. 'That's the Holy Bible, isn't it?' Merrily said. 'Go on, I can take it. Excite me.'

'Not' – Lol put down the book – 'exactly.'

On the spine it said, black on gold:

ROSS: pagan celtic Britain

'Damn,' Merrily said. 'So close.'

'The crow,' Lol said.

'What?'

'You didn't tell me about the bloody crow they spread all over the altar at that little church.'

'Should I have?'

Lol opened the book. 'Didn't anyone give a thought to why they would sacrifice a crow?'

'Lol, we just want to keep the bastards out. We're not into understanding them. Maybe you should talk to the social services.'

'Crows and ravens,' Lol said. 'Feared and venerated by the Iron Age Celts. Mostly feared, for their prophetic qualities. But not like the you're-going-to-win-the-lottery kind of prophecy.'

' "Quoth the raven, *Nevermore.*" '

'Right. *That* kind of prophecy – harbingers of darkness.'

'Being black. The persecution we still inflict on anything or anybody black, how bloody primitive we still are.'

'In Celtic folk tales, it says here, crows and ravens figured as birds of ill-omen or… as a form taken by anti-Christian forces.'

Merrily sat up.

'There's a story in here,' Lol said, 'of how, as late as the seventeenth century, a congregation in a house in the north of Scotland that was used for Christian worship… how the congregation was virtually paralysed by the appearance of a big black bird sitting on a pillar, emanating evil. Nobody could leave that house for over two days. They became so screwed up that it was even suggested the householder's son should be sacrificed to the bird. This *isn't* a legend.'

'Then why, if it inspires so much primitive awe, would anyone dare to sacrifice a crow?'

'Possibly to take on its powers of prophecy, whatever. That's been known to happen.'

'This makes me suspicious,' Merrily said. 'You're doing my job for me. Why are you doing my job?'

'Because of something that happened with Moon.'

And he told her about the disturbed woman standing on the Iron Age ramparts at Dinedor, with her hand inside a dead crow.

Merrily, thinking, drank a whole cup of tea, then poured more. She stared down the nave into the old mystery.

Lol said, 'The way she died – I don't believe she would have killed herself like that. I can't believe in the *reasons*. Like the psychological answer, that she was locked into this fatal obsession, so when she found out how her father died it all came to a head. Or the possible psychic theory that maybe Denny's been turning over in his mind: some lingering dark force which periodically curses his family with madness, and the only way you can make sure of avoiding it is to stay the hell away from Dinedor Hill.'

'That can happen, Lol. We believe that can happen. Psychology and parapsychology are so very close. But I don't necessarily buy a connection between what happened to Moon and the crow sacrifice at St Cosmas.'

'No,' Lol said, 'maybe you're right. Maybe I just saw the headline in the *Hereford Times* at the wrong time. Crows were on my mind then.' He closed the book. 'You look better, Merrily. Tired, but better.'

'Tired? I suppose I must be. I didn't realize. I've been dashing about. Oh, I took back my letter of resignation.'

'Figured you might.'

'Something… gave.'

'Like, you found out about this guy Huw and old Dobbs.'

'No, I… still don't know about that. But I will, very soon.'

'And Jane?'

'Inquiries are in hand.'

Lol said, 'I've had Viv in the shop looking into the Pod.'

'Ah… that explains *her*.'

'Apparently – you might find this interesting, not to say insulting – the women were told to look after Jane. That she was a special person with, er, a problem background.'

Merrily stiffened. 'A special person? She said that? *A special person with a problem background?* Where did that come from? Who told these women all this?'

'Don't know.'

Merrily breathed out slowly.

That night, Lol dreamed he awoke and went into the living room and stood at the window gazing down into Capuchin Lane, which was murky with pre-dawn mist, no lights anywhere.

He knew she was there, even before he saw her: grey and sorrowful, the dress meeting the mist in furls and furrows, her eyes as black as the eyes of the crumbling skulls she held, one in each hand.

I'd like to sleep now, Lol, she said. But the tone of it had changed; there was anguish.

He awoke, cold and numb, in Ethel's chair. He didn't remember going to sleep there.

39

One Sad Person

SHE SLEPT THROUGH, incredibly, until almost ten, without any circles of golden light. Without, come to think of it, any protective prayers, only mumbles of gratitude as she fell into bed.

'Why didn't you *wake* me?'

'Because you were like mega-knackered,' Jane said. 'You obviously needed it.'

Merrily registered the toast crumbs. Jane had breakfasted alone. There was weak sunshine, through mist. It looked cold out there.

'Nobody rang?'

'Nobody.'

'Not even Ted? Not Huw Owen?' She'd called Huw four times last night, to keep herself in line for last-caller if he should try 1471.

'Uh-huh.' Jane shook her head. 'You need a new dressing-gown, by the way. You look like a bag-lady.'

'Not Annie Howe either?'

'The ice-maiden of West Mercia CID? You can't be that desperate for friends.'

'We commune occasionally.'

'Jesus,' said Jane, 'it'll be girls' nights out at the police social club next. And guest spots on identity parades.'

'Jane.'

'What?'

Merrily pulled out a dining chair. 'Sit down.'

'Why?'

'Because we need to talk.'

'I can't. I'm meeting Rowenna in town.'

'When?'

'For lunch at Slater's, then we're going Christmas shopping. But I wanted to get into town a couple of hours early because I haven't got *her* anything yet, OK?'

'You're spending a lot of time with Rowenna, aren't you?'

'Meaning like more than with you.'

'Or even boys,' Merrily said lightly.

Jane's eyes hardened. 'That's because we're lesbians.'

'You going to sit down, flower?'

'I have to *go*.'

'Sit *down*.'

Jane slumped sullenly into the chair. 'Why do you hate Rowenna?'

'I don't *know* Rowenna. I've only met her once.'

'She's a significant person,' Jane said.

'In what way?'

'In a way that I'd expect you to actually understand. Like she has a spiritual identity. She seeks wisdom. Most of the people at school, teachers included, think self-development is about A-levels and biceps.'

'Rowenna's a religious person?'

'I think we've had this discussion before,' Jane said loftily. 'Religion implies *organized* religion.'

'Anything else, therefore, must be *dis*organized religion.'

'Ah' – a fleeting faraway-ness in the kid's eyes – 'how wrong can you get?'

'So *tell* me.'

Jane looked at her, unblinking. 'Tell you what?'

'Tell me how wrong I can get. Tell me why I'm wrong.'

'Again?' Jane raised her eyes. 'It has to be a personal thing,

378

right? You have to work at it. Make a commitment to yourself. I mean, going to church, singing a couple of hymns, listening to some trite sermon, that's just like, Oh, if I do this every week, endure the tedium for a couple of hours, God'll take care of me. Well, that's got to be crap, hasn't it? That's the sheep mentality, and when you end up in the slaughterhouse you're thinking: Hey, why didn't I just get under the fence that time?'

Merrily felt shadows deepening. 'So you're under the fence, are you, flower?'

Jane shrugged.

'Only I had this anonymous letter,' Merrily said.

'Was it sexy? Was it from one of those sad old guys who want to get into your cassock?'

'I'll show it to you.' Merrily went over to the dresser, plucked the folded letter out of her bag, handed the letter to Jane. Glimpsing the words brazenly endangering her Soul, as the kid unfolded it.

' "Brazenly endangering her soul and yours," ' Jane said, ' "by mixing with the Spiritually Unclean." Well, well. Unsigned, naturally. When exactly did this come?'

'Few days ago.'

'So you've been kind of sitting on it, right?'

'I've had one or two other things to think about, as you well know.'

Jane held the letter between finger and thumb as though it might be infected. 'Burn it, if you like,' Merrily said.

'Oh no.' Jane carefully folded the paper. Her eyes glowed like a cat's. 'I don't think so. I'm going to hunt down this scumbag, and when I find out—'

'I think,' Merrily said, more sharply than she intended, 'that you're missing the point. You went to this so-called psychic fair without even mentioning it.'

'Why? Would you have wanted to come along?'

'Maybe I would, actually.'

'Yeah, like some kind of dawn raid by the soul police.'

'I accept' – Merrily kept her temper, which would have gone out of the window long ago if they'd been having this discussion last night – 'that most of the self-styled New Age people at these events' – selecting her words like picking apples from an iffy market stall and finding they were all rotten – 'are perfectly nice, well-meaning...'

'... deluded idiots!'

'Jane—'

'I can't believe this!' Jane leapt up. 'Some shrivelled-up, po-faced old fart sends you a poison-pen letter and you secrete it away in your bag and save it up, probably sneaking the occasional peep to stoke up your holier-than-every-bastard-for-miles-around righteous indignation—'

'Sit down, flower.'

'No! I *thought* you were behaving funny. You're bloody terrified, aren't you? It's not, like: How dare this old fart point the finger at my daughter? Oh, no, you're crapping yourself in case this gets back to *Michael* and you get, like, decommissioned from the soul police! Jesus, you are one sad person, Mother.'

'Jane...' Merrily steadied herself on the Aga rail. 'Would you come back and sit down? Then we can talk about this like... adults?'

'You mean like priest and sinner. I don't think so, Merrily. I'm going upstairs to my apartment. I'm going to light some candles on my altar and probably offer a couple of meaningful prayers to my goddess. Then I'm going out. I'm not sure when I'll be back.'

'Light a couple of candles? I see.'

'Maybe four. They say it's always so much more effective,' Jane said, 'coming from a vicarage.'

'Really?'

Jane turned away and opened the door to the hall.

'That's what they say at the Pod, is it?' Merrily said.

* * *

380

The phone rang in the kitchen just then, and half a second later in the scullery-office. And it went on and on, and Merrily didn't dare answer it because she knew Jane would be out of the room before she reached the receiver.

'You'd better get that. It might be Annie Howe,' Jane said, and Merrily could see she was trembling with rage. 'She must... she must've already taught you everything she knows. About spying on people, undercover investigations... The soul police will never look back – you fucking nosy bitch.'

'Right! That's it!' Merrily bounced off the stove and into the middle of the room. 'You think you're incredibly cool and clever and in control of your own destiny, and all this crap. The truth is you're either a complete hypocrite or you're unbelievably naive, and has it never entered your head that the only reason this little... sect is interested in you is because of me and what I—'

'Me! *Me*, me, *me!*' Jane screeched. 'You are so arrogant. You are *soooo* disgustingly ambitious that you can't see the truth, which is that nobody gives a *shit* for your Church or the pygmies strutting around the Cathedral Close, not realizing what a total joke they are. Your congregations are like *laughable*. In twenty years you'll all be preaching to each other. You don't *matter* any more. You haven't mattered for years. I'm just like *embarrassed* to tell anybody what you do, you know that? You embarrass me to death, so just get off my back!'

The phone stopped. 'Get out,' Merrily said.

'Fair enough.' Jane smiled. 'I may be away some time.'

'Whatever you like. In fact, maybe you could go and stay at Rowenna's for a few days. I'm sure there are lots of spare bedrooms in Colonel Napier's mansion.'

Jane paused in the doorway. 'Meaning what?'

'Only that you may not know as much about your very best friend as you thought you did.'

'You've been investigating her too? You've been checking up on *Rowenna*?'

Tears spurted into Jane's eyes, and Merrily took a step towards her. 'Flower, please—'

'You keep away from me. You keep *away*. You don't care how low you sink, do you, to protect your piddling little reputation?'

'Get a life, Jane.'

Jane's smile was horribly twisted. 'Oh, I will. I will certainly get a life.' She was whispering now. 'You see, there's no way I could ever trust you again, and if you can't trust somebody, what's the point? I don't have to stay at Rowenna's. There are loads of places I can live. I know lots of people now – like really *good* people.'

'That would be really stupid. You're sixteen years old.'

'That's right, at least you can count.'

'And these are not good people.'

'What the fuck would you know, Merrily?' Jane prodded a finger at the air between them. 'I'll tell you something. I'd rather sell my soul to the Devil than spend one more night in this mausoleum.'

'All right,' Merrily said. 'Stop right there. I don't care what you say about me, but don't ever say *that*. Just don't... ever... say it.'

Jane shrugged. 'Like... come and get me, Satan?'

She tossed back her hair, which wasn't really long enough to toss, and went out into the hall and Merrily heard her snatching her coat from the peg and then the creak and judder of the front door.

Merrily stood in the centre of the kitchen. After a while, she was aware of Ethel, the black cat, mewing pitifully at her feet. She picked up the cat, and saw that the mist outside was thickening.

The phone rang again.

She'd been hoping the first call would be from Huw. But now she hoped it was Lol. She needed to tell somebody.

'Merrily? It's Barry Ambrose.'

'Oh… Hello, Barry.' She sat down at her desk in the scullery-office, hoping, just at this moment, that he was calling to say he hadn't found out a thing.

'I found out about that girl, Merrily.'

'Rowenna?'

'I hope she's not too close to you, that's all,' Barry said.

PART FOUR

SQUATTER

40

Dark Hand

THE FOG WAS worse in Leominster, which was why the bus was late, the driver explained. Fog, just when you thought you'd got rid of it!

Then again, if the bus hadn't been late, Jane would have missed it – thanks to the Reverend Bloody Watkins.

She slumped down near the back and felt sick. That was it, wasn't it? That was really *it*. There was no way she could go back there tonight. Outside the bus windows, the hills had disappeared, the view of fields extended about fifty yards, and then all you saw were a few tree-skeletons.

Why had she done this to herself? Why hadn't she just sat it out, mumbled a few apologies about going to the psychic fair and… but that wouldn't have worked, would it? Mum knew about the Pod. How the *hell* did she find that out? Was the Pod leaky? Had it been infiltrated by Christians?

This was just like so totally *unfair*. Jane felt sad and shabby in her old school duffel coat – hadn't even had a chance to find something else. If you're storming out, you had to do it, like, *now*! You couldn't blow the whole effect by going up to your apartment to change into your tight black sweater and your nicer jeans, or collect your new fleece coat.

Ironic, really. This morning, doing her salute to the *Eternal Spiritual Sun*, she'd thought: What is this really achieving? And thinking of the women in the Pod, how basically sad most of them looked. And yet the fact that they *were* so sad completely discredited Mum's crap about them only being interested in Jane because her mother was this big-time Church of England exorcist.

This was all so mega-stupid. If the bitch hadn't been so totally *offensive*, the two of them could have sorted this out. That remark about Jane having no boyfriend, that was just, like, well out of order. Boyfriend like who? Dean Wall? Danny Gittoes? The really humiliating aspect of this was that Mum herself – not long out of leather pants and tops made out of heavy-duty pond-liner – had been pregnant at nineteen, so presumably had been putting it about for years by then.

Life was *such* a pile of shit.

When they crawled into the bus station behind Tesco, Jane didn't want to get off. She had her money with her, but she didn't feel like shopping. Especially while walking around with Rowenna in all her designer items, and Jane in her dark-blue school duffel. What was she going to buy Rowenna, anyway, that wouldn't cause mutual embarrassment?

She made her way out of the bus station and across the car park, hoping there was nobody from school around – which was too much to hope for on a Saturday close to Christmas. Everybody came into Hereford on Saturday mornings – where else was there to go?

The fog was cold and she didn't even have her scarf. Tonight it would probably be *freezing* fog. Suppose Rowenna couldn't organize her a room, what would happen then? It was a lie, natch, that Jane knew loads of people; she didn't know anyone in the Pod well enough to beg a bed. Worst-case scenario, some shop doorway in the Maylords Orchard precinct? Or did they have iron gates on that? And then at two a.m. some dopehead comes along and rapes you.

OK, if it came to it, she probably had enough money to get a room in a hotel. Not the Green Dragon obviously, maybe something between that and the pubs where the junkies went to score. Funny how homely old Hereford took on this new and dangerous aspect when you were alone, and destined to stay alone, possibly for ever.

She turned down where the car park dog-legged and the path led through evergreen bushes to the archway under the buildings and into Widemarsh Street... and then Rowenna laughed lightly and said, 'Why don't we do it here? We'd be hidden by the fog. That would be pretty cool.'

Huh?

Jane stopped. There were cars parked fairly tightly here, with thick laurel bushes just behind them.

You could tell there were two people in the bushes, standing up, locked together. Jane backed up to the edge of the main car park. Vehicles were coming up out of the tunnel from the underground part, and one of them hooted at her to get out of the way. So she moved to the edge of the undergrowth and flattened herself against the wall.

They probably would never spot her from the bushes, as she couldn't see them properly either. She wouldn't have known it was Rowenna but for the voice. She could see the guy better, because he was pretty tall, and from here it looked like most of his tongue was down Rowenna's throat.

'Don't you think this has appalled me too?' Dick Lyden was raking his thick, grey hair. 'I can only offer you my profoundest apologies and assure you that it won't happen—'

'It fucking *has* happened,' Denny snarled, his back to the door of Lol's flat, as if Dick might make a break for it. 'It's done. It exists. If I hadn't been listening to the words – which I usually don't – *I'd* be down as producing it!'

'Denny, don't do this to me,' Dick pleaded.

'Don't do it to *you*?'

Lol was sitting on the window ledge. He had no meaningful contribution to make to this.

'How old is *your* boy?' Dick said to Denny.

'Eleven – and a half.'

'I'd like to think you didn't have this to come, Denny, but at some stage in his adolescent years you'll wonder what kind of monster you've foisted on the world – as well as trying to think what you did to become the object of his undying hatred.'

Sensing that Dick was actually close to tears, Lol said, 'Did you find out how he came to write that song?'

'Oh, well,' Dick escaped gratefully into anger, 'an artist... an *artist* gathers his inspiration wherever he may find it. Art is above pity. Art bows to no taboos. You know the kind of balls they spout at that age. I don't... I don't actually know what's the matter with him lately. He's become remote, he's arrogant, he sneers, he does small spiteful things. A complete bastard, in fact.'

Lol said, 'That's your professional assessment then?' and Denny finally smiled. 'The point is,' Lol continued, 'that the song isn't going to be heard any more, because Eirion Lewis says he'll refuse to play it. He's not a bad kid, it seems.' He glanced apologetically at Dick. 'A bit older than James, so perhaps he's come *through* the bastard phase.'

'In the final analysis,' Dick said, 'this is *my* fault. Ruth and I discuss cases, and quite often the boy's pottering about with his Walkman on and one thinks he's not interested. Little swine was probably making notes. It's a... I suppose a diverting tale, isn't it?'

'It's a family tragedy,' Denny growled.

'Denny, I *have* learned a lesson.'

'But the crows, man – how the fuck'd he know about the crows?'

'It's an old Celtic harbinger of death,' Lol said quickly, because he'd never actually told Denny about the crow.

Denny looked dazed for a second, then shook himself like he was trying to shed clinging shreds of the past. He moved away from the door, his earring swinging less menacingly. 'All right, I'll let them back in, so long as Lol turns the knobs.'

Dick looked at Lol.

'OK,' Lol said. Puzzled about what Denny had meant – *how the fuck'd he know about the crows?* – and still wondering how James could have been so crazy as to sing that song blatantly in Denny's face. Like the boy needed to see how far he could go, how much he could get away with, how badly he could hurt.

'Thanks,' Dick said humbly. 'Thank you both. You know I… This is going to sound a bit cranky coming from a shrink, but I *am* a *Christian* sort of shrink, and I feel that becoming Boy Bishop will somehow help to straighten the lad out.'

'What *is* this Boy Bishop balls, anyway?' Denny said. 'You hear about it, read bits in the *Times*, but I never take much notice.'

'More people ought to take notice or we'll lose it, like so many other things. It's a unique example of the Church affirming Christ's compassion for the lowly.'

'But it's always a kid from the Cathedral School,' Denny pointed out. 'How lowly is that?'

'It's symbolic – dates back to medieval times. The boy is Bishop until Christmas, but doesn't do much. Gives a token sermon on his enthronement, makes the odd public appearance – used to be taken on a tour of churches in the county, but I think they've dropped that. It also illustrates the principle of the humble being exalted. It's about the humble and the meek… something like that.'

'The humble and the meek?' Lol said. 'That's why they chose James?'

'All right, I know, I know. I suppose they chose James because he was a leading chorister. And he's a big lad, so the robes will fit. And, of course, he, ah, rather looks the part.'

'Like I said,' Denny shrugged, 'it's basically balls, isn't it?'

'I see it as a rite of passage,' Dick persisted. 'I don't think you can do something like that without experiencing a man's responsibility.'

Lol thought this was not the best time to talk about a man's responsibility in front of Denny.

But Denny didn't react. 'Listen,' he said. 'Tell the kid I can maybe do the studio Monday. I'll feel better tonight when the funeral's over.'

When Dick had gone, he said to Lol, 'I'm still looking for somebody else to blame for Kathy. He just got in the way.'

Lol nodded.

'I'm closing this shop, by the way,' Denny said.

'This afternoon – for the funeral, Viv said.'

'For good. We close at lunchtime, we don't open again.'

'Ever?'

'I'm shifting the records to the other place tomorrow. And big Viv, too. Extending the shop space into a store-room. If you're selling hi-fi, it makes sense to have a record department on the premises. This one was never big enough to take all the stock you need to really get the punters in. It was just… Kathy's shop. I don't ever want to come here again.'

'And this flat?'

'It won't affect you unless I can't manage to let the shop on its own, in which case I'll maybe sell the whole building. Sorry to spring it on you, mate, but nothing's permanent. You're not a permanent sort of guy anyway, are you?'

Lol forced a smile.

'See you at the crem then,' Denny added. 'There won't be a meal or nothing afterwards. Won't be enough people – plus I'm not into that shit.'

'Denny,' Lol said, 'when you said to Dick, how did he know about the crows, what did you mean?'

'Leave it.' Denny opened the door. 'Like you said, it was nothing, a coincidence. Just the way some things cause you to remember other things. Some memory pops up, and you put it all together wrong.'

'What memory?'

'You don't let go of things, do you, Lol?'

'Some things won't let go of me. It's guilt, probably.'

'You didn't like her, did you?' Denny said.

'I liked her more towards the end.'

'You wouldn't fuck her because you didn't *like* her. That's the truth, isn't it?'

'I don't know.'

'That's kind of honourable, I suppose.'

'No, it isn't. Tell me about the crows.'

Denny came back in, shut the door. 'When she was a kid, they used to put her in her pushchair in the farmyard, to watch the chicks and stuff, yeah? And the crows would come. Crows'd come right up to her. They'd land on the yard and come strutting up to the pushchair. Or they'd fly low and sit on the roof, just over the back door. Sit there like vultures when Kathy was there. Only when she was there.'

Lol thrust his hands in the pockets of his jeans and stiffened his shoulders against the shiver he felt. 'How long did this go on?'

'Until the old man shot them,' Denny said.

'Do you remember Hilary Pyle?' Barry Ambrose asked her.

'I don't think so. Who was she?'

'He,' Barry said. 'It was in some of the papers, certainly the *Telegraph*, which always seems to splash Church crises. But they didn't know the whole story. Even I... I didn't know that was her name until this morning. Where's she now, the girl you asked about?'

'She's at my daughter's school.'

'Oh dear,' said Barry. 'But then people do sometimes change, don't they?'

'If they want to,' Merrily said, 'they have to *want* to. So what happened to this Hilary Pyle?'

'*She* did. He was a canon at the Cathedral, forty-five years old, married, with kids. I didn't know him particularly well, but I assumed he was a sound bloke. Certainly not the kind you'd imagine taking up with a schoolgirl.'

'Rowenna?'

'Soldier's daughter. Wasn't named in the papers – I think she was underage – in fact I'm sure she was. Fifteen or something. Also there was some question of rape when they first arrested Hilary, so the girl couldn't be named in the press, but he certainly was.'

'*Now* I remember. About two years ago? But he—'

'Yes. Poor bloke hanged himself in his garage. Leaving a note – rather a long note. Do you remember that? It was read out at the inquest – he'd apparently requested that.'

'Remind me.' Merrily felt a stab of foreboding.

'It was a rather florid piece of writing; he kept quoting bits of Milton. He said the girl was sent by the Devil, and this caused a bit of amusement in the press. Just the sort of thing some clergyman *would* say to excuse his appalling behaviour. "Sent by the Devil." She was a pale little thing, they said, but she knew which levers to pull, if you'll pardon the, er…'

Merrily found she was writing it all down on her sermon pad.

'You said there was more… other things that didn't get into the press.'

'Oh, yes, I'm frankly amazed it didn't get out. But I suppose the people who knew about it realized what the bad publicity could do. I think it was probably as a result of this that I, of all people, was asked to take on the Deliverance ministry here. They wanted an outsider, someone previously unconnected with the Cathedral. You see, it's so easy for a panic to spread. Look at Lincoln and the Imp. Look at Westminster. There are always people who'll look for the dark hand of Satan, aren't there?'

'Not us, of course.'

'Quite.'

'So what happened?'

'After Hilary committed suicide, two other canons confessed to the Bishop that they'd also had relations with this girl.'

'Jesus!' She hadn't been expecting that.

'It was thought there was another one, but he kept very quiet and survived the investigation. Not a *police* investigation, of course.'

'Did anybody talk to the girl herself?'

'Quite frankly, I don't think anybody in the Cathedral was prepared to go anywhere *near* the girl. What happened, I believe, was that the Army arranged for her father to be based somewhere else. Hereford, obviously, though no one here knew where they'd gone – nor wanted to. It cast quite a shadow for a while. Perhaps it still does: I know a number of previously stable marriages have gone down the tubes since then. Poor Hilary's suggestion of something evil had gathered quite a few supporters before the year was out.'

'Barry, I don't know how to thank you.'

'I don't know what you're going to tell your daughter, Merrily,' Barry said, 'but if she hangs around with Rowenna Napier she might start growing up a little too quickly, if you see what I mean.'

'I owe you one,' Merrily said.

Now she was frightened.

41

Take Me

IN SLATER'S, BEHIND Broad Street, Jane had a deep-pan pizza and stayed cool – reminding herself periodically about Dean Wall, the slimeball, on the school bus in the fog, and what he'd said about Rowenna and Danny Gittoes.

Gittoes was Dean's best friend, and slightly less offensive, but the thought of Rowenna's small mouth around whatever abomination he kept in his greasy trousers was still pretty distasteful, especially when you knew it could be true.

'Calm down, kitten.' Rowenna had a burger with salad, mayonnaise all over it – *oh, please*.

'I just lost it completely.' Jane was sitting with her back to the door and the front windows, watching the cook at work behind a counter at the far end. The problem with Rowenna was that she was so incredibly charming; she gave you her full attention and you felt so grateful she wanted you as a friend.

'What did you say to her?'

'I slagged off the Church, rubbished everything that means anything to her. Said she was ambitious and arrogant – and that I'd rather sell my soul to the Devil than spend another night there. I guess this was not what Angela had in mind when she talked about leading Mum towards the light.'

Rowenna laughed. 'And you didn't mean a word of it, right?'

'I meant it at the time.' Jane cut another slice of pizza. 'She also said *we* were spending too much time together. She suggested I should be going out with boys, can you believe that?'

'That's uncommon,' Rowenna said. 'They're usually terrified you're going to get pregnant.'

'Like... there's nothing wrong with me,' Jane said experimentally. 'I don't have problems in that area. I've had relationships. It's just there aren't any guys around right now that I could fancy that much.' It occurred to her they'd rarely talked about men.

'The choice is severely limited.'

'Almost nonexistent.'

'Sure.'

'Like, I travel on the bus every day with Wall and Gittoes.'

'Don't,' Rowenna said. 'I may vomit.'

She grinned, shreds of chargrilled burger on teeth that were translucent like a baby's. *Come on*, Jane thought, *it might not have been her at all by the car park. It might not.*

'Could we perhaps lighten up now?'

'I keep thinking of those tarot cards,' Jane said seriously. 'You said it seemed like a pretty heavy layout, right?'

'Kitten, it's ages since I even looked at a tarot pack. You forget these things.'

'You don't forget. Those are like archetypal images. They're imprinted on your consciousness.'

'That guy in the denim jacket fancies you.'

'He's looking at *you*. He's just wondering how to get me out of the way. Death – that was the first of them.'

'Yeah, but the Death card can also just mean the end of something before a new beginning.'

'The Tower?'

'It's been struck by lightning. There's a big crack, with people falling off. That speaks for itself really: some really horrendous disaster, something wrenched apart.'

'Shit.'

'Or it could just mean a big clear-out in your life: throwing out the stuff that isn't important.'

'Like, if I don't get away, I'll go down with the Tower?'

'Say the Tower, in this instance, represents your mother's faith in this cruel Old Testament God, and you've got to help shatter it.'

'It could have been a prediction of what began this morning, though, couldn't it? Everything quiet, right? Me getting ready to go out. *She's* had this decent night's sleep for once – well rested, looking much better. And then like, out of nowhere, we're into the worst row for like… ages. It just blew up out of nothing – like the Tower cracking up. And then I say that thing to her about the Devil. It just came out; I wasn't thinking. And that… that was the *third* card.'

'Don't panic.' Rowenna put down her knife and fork. 'The Devil isn't always negative either, you know. The Devil was invented by the Christians as a condemnation of anybody who thought that they, the Christians, were a bit suspect. But actually the Devil's vital for balance in this world.'

'You reckon?'

'Living with a vicar, you're bombarded with propaganda. But when you look at the situation, all the Devil represents is doing what *you* want, not what you're told. Satan is just another word for personal freedom. So maybe Satanists are just people who don't like rules.'

'That's a bit simplistic, isn't it?'

'No, it's not.'

'OK, what about the low-lifes who killed that crow in the church?'

'So?'

'Well, that's got to be evil.'

'OK,' Rowenna said. '*One*, there's nothing to say they killed the crow. *Two*, it was a church nobody uses – a redundant church, right? *Three*, what's the difference between that and any normal protesters who disagree with what something stands for and go in and trash the place? Suppose these are just people who are seriously pissed off at how rich the Church of England is – and how totally useless, like the House of Lords… a complete con to keep people in order.'

'Well… maybe.'

'There's no *maybe*. That was your subconscious talking. Your inner self crying out to be free by coming out with the most outrageous thing possible in a vicarage, right?'

'Or I just wanted to get up her nose.'

'You're back-pedalling. You didn't plan what you wanted to say before it came out, so it has to be an expression of your innermost desire to be free. Listen, do it.'

'Are you crazy?'

'There you go again. Put up or shut up. So do it: give yourself to the Devil. You just stand up and open your arms, and you breathe, in your most seductive voice: *Lord Satan, take me…*' Rowenna giggled. 'It's just words, so it can't harm you… but it's also an invitation to your inner self to throw off the shackles. I reckon if you actually said that in a church, you'd get this *amazing* buzz.'

'No thanks.'

'See' – Rowenna pointed her knife – 'you're just completely indoctrinated. You will never escape.'

Jane was uncomfortable. She'd felt cool and superior when she'd first come in, but now Rowenna had turned the tables. She was a wimp again, a frightened little girl.

'Ro,' she said. 'Any chance of sleeping at your place tonight? I can't go back, can I?'

'Sure you can go back. Take Satan with you. By which I mean, go back with your head held high, with a new attitude.'

'It would just be one night.'

'Oh, kitten…' Rowenna sighed. 'That could really be a problem. We have this diplomat from the Middle East staying with us. I'm not supposed to even tell you this, because there are a lot of people want this guy dead. It's a security job – and we're the safe-house, you know what I mean? Armed guys in vans parked outside all night? It's really, really tedious.'

'Oh.'

'It happens to us quite often. It means that anybody wants to stay with us, they have to be vetted weeks in advance in case something crops up.'

'What am I going to do?'

Rowenna leaned over and squeezed Jane's wrist. 'You know your problem? You worry too much. You still have this deeply constricted inner-self. OK, the Pod will help sort that eventually – and I mean *eventually*.'

'What's wrong with the Pod?'

'Nothing. It's fine as far as it goes. It's merely a reasonable outlet for bored housewives too timid to have an affair. You must have realized that by now.'

'I thought it was quite heavy, actually.'

Rowenna smiled sympathetically. 'Listen, I have to go now. Go on, ask me where. You're gonna like this.'

'Huh?'

'The Cathedral.'

'I thought we were going shopping!'

'Yeah, me too,' Rowenna said ruefully. 'I just forgot what day it was. I have to meet my cousin, who—' Rowenna looked up. 'Who's this?'

'Where?'

'Guy looking at you through the window.'

'You tried that one earlier,' Jane said.

'He's not bad actually, if you're into older men. He's wearing black. He's *all* in black. I think he's coming in.'

'Yeah, I know.' Jane bit off a corner of pizza. 'It's fucking Satan, right?'

'He is. He's coming in for *you*.'

A draught hit the back of Jane's ankles as the door to the street opened.

* * *

401

Just when Merrily was in no mood to talk to him, Huw rang.

'How are you, lass?'

'I'm OK.'

'I've rung a few times,' Huw said. 'I've prayed, too.'

'Thanks.'

'What's been the problem?'

As though they'd spoken only last night and parted amicably.

'Rat-eyes,' Merrily said, 'probably.'

'Oh aye?' No change of tone whatsoever.

She told him calmly that she had been the subject of what seemed to be a psychic attack. She told him it had now been dealt with.

'This was what came with you into St Cosmas?' Huw said.

'I believe so.'

'And it's dealt with?'

'Yes.'

'You're clean, then?'

'I believe I am. How about you?'

Huw left a pause, then he said, 'About the hospital – I went in last night and I got a bollocking from an Irish nurse with a very high opinion of you. I said I shared that, naturally.'

'And explained to her why you and Dobbs were shafting me?'

'I assured her I would explain the situation fully to you at the earliest possible opportunity. Which is why I'm ringing. Can I meet you tonight?'

'I don't know,' Merrily said. 'I have other problems.'

'Happen I can help.'

'Happen I don't want you to.'

'Merrily…'

'What?'

'We have a crisis.'

'Who's *we*?'

'You, me, your Cathedral – the C of E.'

402

'Do you want to come here?'

'We'll meet in your gatehouse at six. We'll be alone then?'

'All right,' she said.

Lol held open the passenger door of the Astra for her. He slammed it shut and got in the other side.

Jane stared at him, coming down off her high. 'Where are we going?'

He started the engine, put on the lights, and booted the ancient heap out into the traffic. 'To a funeral, I'm afraid.'

'You're kidding.'

'Yeah, I'm kidding. I always wear a black suit on Saturdays.'

'Oh, Christ,' Jane said. 'It's Moon, isn't it?'

Lol turned right, towards Greyfriars Bridge. She was making a point of not asking him why he'd just swanned into the restaurant like that – looking quite smooth, for Lol. It had been cool, anyway, to play along. Cool, too, that the extreme warmth of her welcome appeared to have shocked him a little.

She grinned. 'I frightened you, didn't I?'

'There's effusive,' Lol said, 'and there's *effusive*.'

'Darling, as it happens I was glad to see you.' There was no way Lol would let her spend the night in C & A's doorway. 'What was her face like?'

'Whose?'

'Rowenna's. I couldn't see, could I? I was busy expressing my delight at your arrival.'

'Yeah,' he said, 'I can still taste the mozzarella.'

'So how did she react?'

'She looked surprised.'

'Excellent,' Jane said.

Lol crossed four lanes of traffic at the lights, foot down. He must be running late. She suspected there were aspects of Lol's relationship with Moon she didn't fully understand. Of course, the problem here was that if he'd taken time to come and find her, in his funeral suit, that suggested he was acting on specific instructions from the Reverend Watkins. In the end you couldn't get away from her, could you?

'You weren't just passing, were you, Lol?'

'Your mum told me where you were having lunch.'

'Great,' Jane said dully.

'She said you'd had a row.'

'It was a minor disagreement.'

'Like between the Serbs and the Croats.'

'What else did she say?'

'She said a lot of things I'm inclined to let her explain to you personally.'

'Look,' Jane said, more harshly than she intended, 'tell her to fax it or something. I'm not going back.'

'You bloody are, Jane.'

'You can't make me do anything I don't want to.'

Lol turned left into the crematorium drive. 'You're right.' He sighed. 'I probably can't even trust you to stay in the car while I go inside.'

God, he looks so kind of desolate.

'Yes, you can,' she said. 'I'm sorry, Lol.'

Denny had been wrong. The modern crematorium chapel was at least half-full. Distant relatives, he explained to Lol – nosey bastards whose faces he only half remembered. Also, a pair of archaeologist friends of Moon's from Northumberland, where she'd lived for a couple of years. And Big Viv and her partner, Gary. And the Purefoys, Tim and Anna. And Dick and Ruth Lyden.

And Moon, of course. Moon was here.

Denny had booked a minister. 'Though she'd probably have preferred a fucking druid,' he said, seeming uncomfortable and aggressive. He wasn't wearing his earring; without it he looked less amiable, embittered. He looked like he wanted to hit people. His wife Maggie was here, without the children. She was tall, short-haired and well dressed, and talked to the relatives but not much to Denny. He must be difficult to live with right now.

The minister said some careful things about Moon. He said she was highly intelligent and enthusiastic, and it was a tragic loss, both to her brother Dennis and his family and to the world of archaeology.

Denny muttered and looked down at his feet. Anna Purefoy wept silently into a handkerchief. They sang two hymns, during which Lol gazed at the costly oak coffin and pictured Moon inside it, with her strange, hard hands crossed over her breast. To intensify the experience in this bland place, to make it hurt, he made her say, *I'd like to sleep now, Lol.*

It hurt all the more because he knew that was wrong. She couldn't sleep. He kept thinking of his dream of the mist-furled Moon in Capuchin Lane, holding the broken heads of the ancestors as she'd held the crow. A dream... like the dreams she'd had of her father. Moon had joined not the ancestors but the grey ranks of the sleepless. When the curtains closed over the coffin, there were tears in Lol's eyes because he could not love her – had not even been able to help her. It was a disaster.

And it was not over.

Outside, in the foggy car park, Dick Lyden said to Lol, 'Never seen you in a suit before, old chap,' then he patted Denny sympathetically on the arm. Denny looked like he wanted to smash Dick's face in. Lol found the slender, sweet-faced Anna Purefoy at his side.

'I feel so guilty, Mr Robinson. We should have positively discouraged her. We should have seen the psychiatric problems.'

'They aren't always easy to spot,' Lol said.

'I taught at a further-education college for a year. I've seen it all in young women: manic depression, drug-induced psychosis. I should have *seen* her as she really was. But we were so delighted by her absorption in the farm that we couldn't resist offering her the barn. We thought she was perfect for it.'

'You couldn't hope to understand an obsession on that scale,' Lol said. He realized it was going to be worse for the Purefoys than for anyone else here, maybe even for Denny. They would have to live with that barn. 'What will you do with it now?'

'I suspect it will be impossible to find a permanent tenant. We'd have to tell people, wouldn't we? Perhaps we could revert to our original plan of holiday accommodation. I don't know, it's too early.'

'Well, good luck,' Lol said. He wondered if Merrily might be persuaded to go up there and bless the barn or something. He watched the Purefoys walk away to their Land Rover Discovery. Denny's wife, Maggie, was chatting to an elderly couple, while Denny stood by with his hands behind his back, rocking on his heels. A lone crow, of all birds, flew over his head and landed on the roof of the crematorium, and stayed there as though it was waiting for Moon's spirit to emerge in the smoke, to accompany it back to Dinedor Hill.

But nobody could *see* the smoke in this fog – and the way to Dinedor would be obscured. He imagined Moon alone in that car park, after everyone had gone. Moon cold in the tatters of her medieval dress – bewildered because there was nobody left. Nobody left to understand what had happened to her.

The Astra was parked about fifteen yards away. As he approached, Jane's face appeared in the blotched windscreen, looking very young and starved. He tried to smile at her; she looked so vulnerable. It was cold in the car as he started the engine.

She said, 'Lol, that woman you were talking to...'

'Mrs Purefoy?'

'The blonde woman.'

'That was Moon's neighbour and landlady, Anna Purefoy.' He drove slowly out of the car park on dipped headlights.

Jane said, 'You mean Angela.'

'I thought it was Anna. I could be wrong.'

'Moon's neighbour?'

'On Dinedor Hill. They own the farm where she died.'

After a while, as the car crept back into the hidden city, Jane said, 'Help me, Lol. Things have got like horribly screwed up.'

42

The Invisible Church

THE GOLDEN SANTAS drove their reindeer across a thick sea of mist in Broad Street. The lanterns glowed red like fog warnings. In the dense grey middle-distance, the Christmas trees twinkling above the shop fronts were like the lights of a different city.

And Merrily, alone in the gatehouse office, with the Cathedral on one side and the Bishop's Palace on the other, felt calmer now because Lol had called her before she left. Because Jane was with Lol in the flat above John Barleycorn, not three minutes' walk away, and maybe Lol would now find out how far it went, this liaison with the wan and wispy Rowenna, serial seducer of priests.

Scrabbling about under Sophie's desk, she found an old two-bar electric fire with a concave chrome reflector, plugged it in and watched the bars slowly warm up, with tiny tapping sounds, until they matched the vermilion of the lanterns outside.

Merrily stood by the fire, warming her calves and watching the lights. They were all part of Christmas, but anyone who didn't know about Christmas would not see them as linked.

She thought about that devil-worshipper pulled from the river not half a mile from here... the strings of crow-intestine on a disused altar... the inflicted curse of Denzil Joy... the old exorcist lying silent, half-paralysed – or faking it – in a hospital bed inside a chalked circle. And, inevitably, she thought of Rowenna.

Linked? All of them? Some of them? None of them?

After a while she spotted the untidy man – in bobble-hat, ragged scarf, RAF greatcoat – shambling out of the fog, with his exorcist's black bag, and wondered how many answers he could offer her.

Jane had decided to clean up Lol's flat: ruthlessly scrubbing shelves, splattering sink-cleaner about, invading the complexity of cobwebs behind the radiators.

A purge, Lol thought.

Just as they were hitting the city centre, she'd asked if they could go somewhere: the village of Credenhill, where the poet Traherne had been vicar in the seventeenth century. Where the SAS had, until recently, been based. And where, just entering dusk, he and Jane had found the perfectly respectable but undeniably small Army house where Rowenna's family lived. Until the last possible moment, Jane had been vainly searching for some rambling, split-level villa behind trees.

She'd stood for a long time at the roadside, looking across at the fog-fuzzed lights of the little house with the Christmas tree in its front window. 'Why would she lie? Why would she think it mattered to me if she lived in a mansion or bloody tent? Why does she *lie* about everything?'

On the way back, Lol considered what Merrily had said on the phone about Rowenna's sexual history. It had made him look quickly – but very hard – at the girl over Jane's shoulder in Slater's. Rowenna was pale, appeared rather fragile – fragile like glass.

Once they were back in his flat, he'd told Jane about the events in Salisbury.

Jane had listened, blank-faced, silent. Then she stood up. 'This flat's in a disgusting state.'

Lol sat with Anne Ross's *Pagan Celtic Britain* open on his knees, and let Jane scrub violently away at the kitchen floor and her own illusions. In the book, he read that crow-goddesses invariably forecast death and disaster.

At last, Jane came back from the kitchen, red-faced with exertion and inner turmoil.

Lol put the book down.

'I'm not going to be able to live with any of this,' Jane announced.

'But you still shafted me.'

Merrily was feeling her fury reignite – reflected in the red glow of the tinking electric fire, the sparky glimmerings from the Santas over Broad Street.

Trust in God, but never trust a bloody priest.

'You claimed you hardly knew him.'

Huw had taken off his scarf, but left his woolly hat on. They were sitting at opposite ends of Sophie's long desk under the window. Huw was just a silhouette with a bobble on top. You had to imagine his faded canvas jacket, his shaggy wolfhound hair.

'I *don't* know Dobbs,' Huw said, 'and I never tried to shaft you.'

She shook her head and lit a cigarette, staring out of the window. It was after six now and the traffic was thinning out. A granny and grandad kind of couple were walking a child down Broad Street towards All Saints, the child between them hopping and swinging from their hands under the decorations.

'I'm trying to explain,' Huw said. 'I want to give you a proper picture, as far as I can see it. They didn't want me to tell you, but there's no way round that now, so balls to them.'

'Who didn't?'

'The canons, the Dean's Chapter – well, not officially. None of this is *official*.'

'No kidding.'

'Two fellers came to see me. No,' raising a shadowy hand, 'don't ask. But they're honourable blokes.'

'As Mark Antony once said.'

411

'Jesus!' Huw thumped his forehead with the heel of his hand. 'Merrily, there is *no* conspiracy. These lads are scared. They didn't know what Dobbs was at, but it put the wind up them. Give us one of them cigs, would you?'

She slid the packet across the desk to him. 'Didn't know you did.'

'You know bugger all about me – nor me about you, when we cut to the stuffing. Ta, lass.' Huw shook the packet, extracted a cigarette with his teeth. 'The Devil, what's *he* like these days?'

'What?'

'The Devil, lass.'

Merrily said, 'Forked tail, cloven hooves, little horns – deceptively cuddly. And we invented him to discredit the pagan horned god Cernunnos. This is what Jane tells me, over and over.'

'Canny lass.' Huw extended his cigarette towards her Zippo, and in its flare she saw his grainy bootleather features flop into a smile. 'Like her mam.'

'Thank you.'

And then the smile vanished. 'So…' He drew heavily. 'What do *you* believe?'

'I do accept the existence of a dark force for evil,' Merrily said steadily.

Huw nodded. 'Good enough.'

When he had first arrived, she'd told him about the projection of the fouled phantom of Denzil Joy: how they'd done it, how well it had worked. She'd told him about the burning of the vestments, and the eucharist she planned for Denzil and Denzil's mute, abused wife. She was telling him because she needed him to know she was clean, able to deal with things.

Huw started now to talk about evil in its blackest, most abstract form. Evil, the *substance*. How it was always said that the deepest evil was often to be found in closest proximity to the greatest good. How Satanists would despoil churches for the pure intoxication of it, the dark high it gave them.

'And does that explain St Cosmas?'

'I don't know. I've not told Dobbs about that. He smelled it on me, mind, that night. Knew I'd just done an exorcism. Happen that's what got him talking.'

'Ah,' Merrily sat up, 'so Dobbs *has* talked to you.'

'Only in bits, till last night. The other times he were weighing me up, getting the measure of me. See, what he's done is he's shut himself down, boarded himself up, put himself into a vacuum. Working out whether he was going to snuff it or be fit enough to go back. I figured it was my job to give him the space he needed. To see he wasn't pestered – you know what I'm saying?'

'You sealed him into a kind of magic circle.'

'*Protective* circle: the invisible church. Magic is where you use your willpower to bring about changes in the natural pattern, to rearrange molecules. *We* ask God to do it, if He thinks it's the right thing – which is subtly different, as you know.'

'Protecting him from what? The Devil? What, Huw?'

'I wanted to bring you in on it, Merrily, honest to God I did. I *hated* going behind your back. But the Dean's lads are saying no way, no way. It's the last thing Dobbs'd want. They don't like the Bishop and you're the Bishop's pussycat.'

'Terrific.'

'You know that's not what I think, so stuff the Dean. Let's talk about this; I really don't know how much time we've got. I've not come across it before in any credible situation.'

'*What?*'

A shadow had dropped over the room, like a cloth over a birdcage. Merrily saw that a line of golden Santas had gone out over Broad Street.

'We think there's a *squatter* in the Cathedral,' Huw said.

* * *

So, like, how could she go back to that school on Monday and be in the same room with the lying slag? The same building?

How?

Lol said, without much conviction, that maybe it was best not to leap to too many conclusions.

'Yeah?' Jane collapsed on to the rug. 'Like which particular conclusions is it best to avoid, Lol? Should I maybe like hang fire on the possibility that Rowenna wants to be my best friend for reasons not entirely unconnected with my mother?'

'No, that's valid.'

'Is she real, Lol? Is she psychotic? Is there a word for women who need to shag priests?'

'Janey, if we were merely talking about a psychological condition, it would make it all so much simpler. She hasn't been anywhere near Merrily, has she?'

'Just the once.'

'All right,' Lol said, 'let's go back to when you first knew her. This must be before your mum became an exorcist. When did she make the first approach?'

'She didn't. It was me. This was when she first started at the school, right? Before her, the last new girl there was me, and I know what it's like when you come in from out of the area and they're all kind of suspicious of you. I went over to talk to her, and we just got on. That's it.'

'Did she know about Merrily?'

'Pretty soon she did. See, one of her most… attractive qualities is she likes talking about *you*. She listens, she asks questions, she laughs at the things you say. She's sympathetic when you've got problems at home. *You* are the most interesting person in the world when you're with Rowenna.'

'You tell her everything.'

'Yeah,' Jane said gloomily. 'You tell her *everything*.'

'How soon before the psychic things, the New Age stuff?'

'I don't know. It just happened. You're talking all through the lunch hour, then you discover she's got her own car, so she gives you a lift home. But, yeah, when I found out she was interested in like otherwordly pursuits, that was the clincher.

Soul-mates! It's just like so brilliant when you find somebody you can talk to about that stuff, and they're not going: *Yeah, yeah, but where do you go on Saturday nights?* It just never occurs to you to be suspicious, you're so delighted. And when she says, *Hey, there's this psychic fair at Leominster,* you don't go, *Oh, I'd better ask my mum,* do you?'

'What happened at the psychic fair?'

'We met Angela.'

'Mrs Purefoy?'

'If you say so. Although, when I look back, was she really *doing* the psychic fair? How do we know she read anybody *else's* cards? See, it was Rowenna who first mentioned the fair. It was Rowenna who, when we'd been there a while and it was getting cold and boring, suggested we consult a clairvoyant in the nice warm pub. It was Rowenna who said she'd had a call from Angela wanting to see us again. I will struggle for a long time against things I don't want to believe, Lol, but when the cracks start to appear…'

'What was Angela like?'

'Really, really impressive – not what you were expecting. Very smooth, very poised, very articulate and kind of upper-class. Like, you felt she had your best interests at heart at all times. And, of course, you believed every damn word she said.'

Lol smiled.

'She said I had extraordinary abilities.'

'Which, instinctively, you knew.'

Jane scowled.

'I suppose she recommended you should develop them.'

'She put me in touch with a group called the Pod.'

'Meeting over the healthfood caff in Bridge Street.'

'It *was* you then. I thought you hadn't spotted me.'

'If you'd been your usual friendly little self,' Lol said, 'I probably wouldn't have thought anything of it. So what happens at the Pod?'

'It's good actually. It's just about building up your awareness of like other realms.'

'Nothing heavily ritualistic?'

'Not at all. In fact – here we go – Rowenna's already suggesting it's kind of low-grade stuff. God, it's so transparent when you start seeing it from another angle.'

'It's not really. It seems quite sophisticated to me. They introduce you into a group full of nice, amiable women who mother you along, don't scare you off...'

'So the Pod are part of this?'

'I don't know. They seem fairly harmless. Somebody apparently suggested you'd be an asset. That's what I was told.'

'Because of Mum? What *is* all this?'

'It's just about women clerics, I think,' Lol said. 'They're still new and sexy, and it's the biggest and most disruptive thing to happen in the Church for centuries. Angela's involved with the Pod, right?'

'I don't actually think so. She's never's been to a meeting in the short time I've been going.'

'She mention your mum?'

'She said Rowenna'd told her. She said she was annoyed about that because she thought it was ethically wrong – some bullshit like that – to know things about people you were doing readings for. And, yeah, she's like, "Oh, I can't tell you anything tonight after all, I've probably got it all wrong" – until I'm begging her. And then all this stuff that I have to tease out of her and Ro, about needing to lead Mum into the light. And they're dropping what now seem like really broad hints that if I don't, some disastrous situation will develop. They just want to like... corrupt her, don't they?'

'I suppose so,' Lol said. 'And Merrily's right: they're getting at her through you. Whatever you might think, you're the most important thing in her life. That must be obvious to them – you being the only child of a single parent.'

'Who's them?'

'I don't know. The idea of all these evil Devil-worshippers targeting priests, it just sounds so... and yet...'

'We have to do something, Lol. I'm just like so boiling up inside. It's like I've been raped, you know? We...' Jane sprang up. 'Hey! Let's go and see *Angela*! Now we know who she is, let's just turn up on her doorstep and, like, demand answers.'

'No!'

'Why not?'

'Not yet, anyway.'

'*Why* not?'

'I've got to think about this.'

Jane frowned. 'This is about Moon again, isn't it?'

43

Deep Penetration

HUW LIFTED HIS black bag up on to the desk, switched on the lamp, and took out a fat paperback.

Merrily recognized it at once. *The Folklore of Herefordshire* (1912) by Ella Mary Leather had been, for several months, Jane's bible, introduced to her by the late Lucy Devenish, village shopkeeper, writer of fairytales for children and a major source of the kid's problematic interest in all things New Age. It was a formidable collection of customs and legends, gathered from arcane volumes and the county's longest memories.

Huw opened it.

SECTION IV
SUPERNATURAL PHENOMENA
(1) WRAITHS

Visitors, it would have said now, in Huw-speak.

Mrs Leather revealed that all over Herefordshire it was accepted – at least in 1912 – that the wraith of a person might be seen by relatives or close friends shortly before or just after death. The departing spirit was bidding farewell to the persons or places most dear to it; this was stated as a matter of fact. It seemed amazing that it had taken less than a century for believers in ghosts to be exiled into crank country.

Huw turned the page and pushed the book directly under the desk lamp for Merrily to read. He said nothing.

(3) DEMONS AND FAMILIAR SPIRITS
A Demon in the Cathedral

A very strange story of the appearance of a demon in the Cathedral is told by Bartholomew de Cotton. The event is supposed to have happened in AD 1290.

An unheard of and almost impossible marvel occurred in the Cathedral Church of the Hereford Canons. There a demon in the robes of a canon sat in a stall after matins had been sung. A canon came up to him and asked his reason for sitting there, thinking the demon was a brother canon. The latter refused to answer and said nothing. The canon was terrified, but believing the demon to be an evil spirit, put his trust in the Lord, and bade him in the name of Christ and St Thomas de Cantilupe not to stir from that place. For a short time he bravely awaited speech. Receiving no answer, he at last went for help and beat the demon and put him in fetters; he now lies in the prison of the aforesaid St Thomas de Cantilupe.

She looked up. 'Who was Bartholomew de Cotton?'
'No idea.'
'Where's the prison of St Thomas?'
'Don't know. Bishops *did* have their own prisons, I believe.'
'So what does it all mean?'
'I don't know,' said Huw. 'It could be an allegorical tale to put the knife in for one of the clerics. Could simply be some penniless vagrant got into the Cathedral and nicked a few vestments to keep himself warm, and it got blown up out of all proportion.'
'Or?'

'Or it could be the first recorded appearance of the *squatter*.'

Merrily became aware of a thin, high-pitched whine nearby. Possibly the bulb in the desk lamp, a filament dying.

She realized fully now why Huw used all these bloody silly words: *visitor, hitchhiker, insomniac*. It was because the alternatives were too biblical, too portentous.

And too ludicrous?

'So a *squatter*,' Merrily said, 'is your term for a localized demon – an evil spirit in residence.'

'If I were trying to be scientific I'd cobble summat together like *potentially malevolent, semi-sentient forcefield*. Or I might've called it a *sleeper*, but that doesn't sound noxious enough. You know what a sleeper is, in espionage?'

'It's a kind of deep-penetration agent, isn't it? Planted in another country years in advance, to be awoken whenever.'

Deep-penetration, Huw liked that. Made it sound, he said, like dampness. And it was *very* like that – in so deep, it was almost part of the fabric. It could be lying there for centuries and only the very sensitive would be aware of it.

'Like an *imprint*,' Merrily suggested.

'With added evil. Evil gathers *around* a holy place, like we said. The unholiest ground, they used to say, is sometimes just over the churchyard wall. But if it gets *inside*, you'll have a hell of a job rooting it out. It's got all those centuries of accumulated devotional energy to feed on, and it'll cause havoc.'

'But if you accept that this was an evil spirit, how could this canon beat it and put it in fetters? That argues for your first suggestion – that the canon caught some vagrant who'd stolen the vestments.'

'Or the entire story's metaphorical. It suggests he was able to bind this evil by ritual and the power of the Lord, and also…'

'St Thomas Cantilupe.'

'Aye,' said Huw, 'there we have the link – the key to it all.'

The whining in the bulb was making her nervous. It was like a thin wire resonating in her brain.

'Thomas Cantilupe.' Huw leaned back, and his chair creaked. 'Tommy Canty – now *there* were a hard bastard.'

The Norman baronial background, the years in government, the initial ambition to be a soldier. 'And you could still think of him as one,' Huw said. So he already had the self-discipline and, on becoming a bishop of the Church, had taught himself humility – and chastity.

'He went to Paris once and stayed wi' a feller, and the feller's wife – a foxy lady – contrives to get into bed wi' Tommy. Tommy rolls out t'other side, pretends he's still asleep. Next morning she asks him how he slept and he tells her he'd have had a better night if he hadn't been tempted by the Devil.'

Merrily thought of Mick Hunter under the aumbry light. And then she thought of herself and Lol: how close she'd come, in her near despair, to slipping into Lol's bed.

'Tommy Canty,' said Huw. 'No sleaze. No risks. Warrior for the Lord. What would your lad Hunter have made of him?'

Both fast-track, Merrily thought. Cantilupe had come straight in as bishop. No weddings and funerals for him, presumably. But, yes, in spite of that they'd probably have hated each other's guts.

'But think what Cantilupe did for this town,' Huw said. 'Most of the religious establishments along the border were well into debt during that period. After St Thomas's day, Hereford Cathedral never looked back. They were adding bits on to the building, all over the place. Pulling power of the shrine meant thousands of pilgrims, hundreds of accredited miracles, cripples brought in droves.

'If you were too sick to get to Hereford, you were measured on a length of string and they brought that instead. I don't know how it worked, but it did. You believe in miracles, Merrily, don't you? I bet Hunter doesn't.'

'Who can say? Look, the demon story – how long had Cantilupe been dead by then?'

'About eight years. And the shrine's power was near its peak.

How could that demon get in? Was it brought in by one of the pilgrims? Was it already there and something activated it?'

'Like a *sleeper*?'

'Aye, exactly. But, thank God, the unnamed medieval canon, and the power of Christ channelled through the Cantilupe shrine… they contained it. *Imprisoned* is the word. Not killed or executed, but *imprisoned*.'

Merrily experienced one of those moments when you wonder if you're really awake. Mrs Straker, the aunt, had said Rowenna Napier lived in what she would call a fantasy world. But what would she call this? Where was it leading?

'Tommy Canty' – Huw liked saying that, maybe a Northerner's need for familiarity, as if he and the seven-centuries-dead St Thomas wouldn't be able to work together unless they were old mates – 'guardian and benefactor of Hereford. Must have been a mightily good man, or there'd be no miracles. Now his bones have all gone, but he's there in spirit. His tomb's still there' – Huw suddenly leaned towards her, blocking out the lamplight – 'except when it's *not*…'

'Oh.' She felt a tiny piece of cold in her solar plexus.

'Know what I mean?'

'Except when it's in pieces,' she said.

And the image cut in of Dobbs lying amid the stones, arms flung wide, eyes open, breathing loud, snuffling stroke-breaths.

'I want to show you something else.' Huw bent over the bag, his yellowing dog-collar sunk into the crew-neck of his grey pullover. He brought out a sheaf of A4 photocopies and put them in front of Merrily. She glanced at the top sheet.

HEREFORD CATHEDRAL: SHRINE OF ST THOMAS CANTILUPE
Conservation and Repair: the History

'You know what happened when he died?'

'They boiled his body, separated the bones from the flesh. And the heart—'

'Good, you know all that. All right, when the bones first arrived in Hereford, they were put under a stone slab in the Lady Chapel. You know about this, too?'

'Tell me again.'

'That was temporary. A tomb was built in the North Transept and the bits were transferred there in the presence of King Edward I – in, I think, 1287. The miracles started almost immediately, and petitions were made for Tommy to be canonized, but that didn't happen until 1320. That's when he got a really fancy new shrine in the Lady Chapel – which, of course, was smashed up during the Reformation a couple of centuries later, when the rest of the bones were divided and taken away.'

'So the present one is… which?'

'It appears to be the original tomb, which seems to have been left alone. According to this document, one of the first pilgrims wrote that he'd had a vision of the saint, which came out of the "image of brass" on top of the tomb. We know there *was* brass on this one, because the indent's still visible. Now, look at this.'

Huw extracted a copy of a booklet with much smaller print, and brought out his reading glasses.

'This is the 1930 account of the history of the tomb, and it records what happened the last time it was taken apart for renovation, which was in the nineteenth century. Quotes a fellar called Havergal, an archaeologist or antiquarian who, in his *Monumental Inscriptions*, of 1881, writes… can you read this?'

Merrily lifted the document to the light. A paragraph was encircled in pencil.

This tomb was opened some 40 years ago. I have an account written by one who was present, which it would not be prudent to publish.

Huw's features twisted into a kind of grim beam. 'You like that?'

'What does "not prudent" mean?'

'You tell me. I'd say the person who wrote that account was scared shitless.'

'By what they found?'

'Aye.'

'But the bones had all gone, right?'

'People aren't frightened by bones anyroad, are they? Least, they wouldn't be in them days.'

'You're presuming some… psychic experience?'

'The *squatter*,' Huw said. 'Suppose it was an apparition of the *squatter* in all his unholy glory.'

'Oh, please…' Merrily shuddered. 'And anyway, nothing happened when they opened it this time, did it?'

'No. And why didn't it?'

'How can I possibly…? Oh, Huw… Dobbs!'

And backwards and forwards from the Cathedral he'd go, at all hours, in all weathers, said Edna Rees. *I'd hear his footsteps in the street at two, three in the morning. Going to the Cathedral, coming from there, sometimes rushing, he was like a man possessed.*

'Dobbs exorcized this thing?'

Huw shrugged. 'Contained it, he reckons – like that canon in the thirteenth century – with the help of St Thomas Cantilupe in whose footsteps *our* Thomas had so assiduously followed. Until he was struck down.'

Memories of that night snowballed her. Sophie Hill: *He's just rambling. To someone. Himself? I don't know. Rambling on and on. Neither of us understands. It's all rather frightening…* George Curtiss: *My Latin isn't what it used to be. My impression is he's talking to, ah… to Thomas Cantilupe.*

And the atmosphere in the Cathedral of overhead wires or power cables slashed through, live and sizzling.

'Dobbs modelling himself on his hero, Tommy Canty,' Huw

425

said. 'Keeping his own counsel, thrusting away all temptation… keeping all women out of his life? Making sense now, is it, lass?'

The whining from the lamp was unbearable now, like the sound of tension itself. She was afraid of an awful pop, an explosion. Although she knew that rarely happened, she felt it would tonight.

'He fired his housekeeper of many years, did you know that? She didn't know what she'd done wrong.'

'Strong measures, Merrily, measuring up to Tommy Canty. Very strict about ladies – not only sexually. He kept *all* women at more than arm's length, with the exception of the Holy Mother. See, what you have, I reckon, is Dobbs inviting the mighty spirit of Cantilupe to come into him. Happen he thought they could deal with it together.'

'That's what he told you?'

'In not so many words. Not so many words is all he can manage.'

'You're saying that when it emerged that the Hereford Cathedral Perpetual Trust had finally managed to put enough money together to renovate the tomb, Dobbs was immediately put on his guard, suspecting something had happened when the tomb was last opened.'

'He *knew* it happened. He told me exactly where to find this document. He told me where to look in Mrs Leather's book. All right, it's not much, and that's the end of the documentation, but just because that eye-witness account was never published doesn't mean it hasn't been passed down by word of mouth.'

'Which is notoriously unreliable. All right, what *did* happen when they opened the tomb this time?'

Huw smiled. 'When you've been with that owd feller a while, you learn he doesn't like talking. And when he does, there are words he won't use. Me, I'll ramble on about *squatters* and *visitors* and the like, but Dobbs'll just give you funny looks.'

'Helpful.'

'I don't know, Merrily. I don't know that he's prepared to even think, at the present time, about what it was gave him the stroke. It's part of shutting down.'

'So who contained the' – she couldn't bring herself to use the word *demon*, either – '*squatter*, last century?'

Huw shook his head. 'Don't know. But if you carry on with this theory, you've got two explanations. *One* is that the then exorcist, or *somebody* at least, was ready for it. *Two* is that all you had was a single terrifying manifestation; that there wasn't sufficient energy around on that occasion for it to take up what you might call serious occupation.'

'So why should it now? What's changed?'

'Jesus Christ, Merrily, *you* can ask me that?' He held up a hand against the window, and began counting them off on his fingers. '*One*, the recent Millennium: two thousand years since the birth of Our Lord, and a time of great global religious and cosmic significance. *Two*, the appointment of a flash, smart-arse bishop who doesn't believe in anything very much...'

'You can't say that!'

'Have you questioned the slippery bastard in any depth, lass? Has anybody? *Three*—'

Merrily could stand it no longer and clicked off the whining lamp, dipping them back into reddened darkness. Outside, she noticed, a third row of golden Santas had gone out – as if the whole of this end of town was suddenly beset by destructive electrical fluctuations because of what they'd been discussing.

Madness! Stop it!

'And *three* is...'

Huw paused.

'You,' he said.

427

44

A Candle for Tommy

'I KNEW SHE was going to be trouble,' Sorrel said to Lol.

Patricia would have been the best, but Jane had no idea where she lived, didn't even know her last name. Sorrel was the one they got because there weren't many Podmores in the phone book. Sorrel who lived at Kings Acre, in the suburbs, but wouldn't let Lol come to see her there. She hadn't wanted to see him at all, until he mentioned police.

'How old *is* she?' Sorrel had finally agreed to meet him at the café in Bridge Street. They sat at one of the rustic tables, with the window blinds down. They sat under the Mervyn Peake etchings of thin, leering men and the fat witch with the toad.

'Thirteen,' he said, just to scare her.

Sorrel was plump and nervous. She closed her eyes on an intake of breath. 'We didn't know – no way we knew that. She said she was working. We thought she was seventeen at least.'

'Does she really look seventeen?'

'Oh God, I'm sorry.' Sorrel threw up her hands. 'This should not have happened. We're a responsible group. We have a strict rule about children.' She looked hard at Lol. 'You're Viv's friend, aren't you – the songwriter? She said—'

'And a friend of Jane's mother's,' Lol said. 'Her mother the vicar.'

Sorrel paled. Lol was starting to feel sorry for her.

'This could cause a lot of damage if it got out,' Sorrel said. 'I mean damage to the business. You know what people are like.

They don't understand about these things. They'll think we're using children for weird rituals. It could close us down – I mean the café.'

'Mmm.' Lol nodded.

'I mean, I've got kids myself. And my husband, he doesn't… It's got out of hand, you see. They started calling it the Pod only because they were meeting here. It just grew out of healthy eating and Green issues. I'm not really that involved, but the name's linked now, and it's very hard for me to… to…'

'Look,' Lol said, 'I realize this is not your fault. You had pressure put on you, right?'

Sorrel didn't answer.

'So maybe it's whoever put on the pressure I need to talk to.'

'Please' – she was actually looking scared now – 'can't you just leave it?'

'I wish I could, but her mother's in the clergy. Things are difficult enough for women priests.'

'How did she find out?'

'An anonymous letter.'

'Bastards,' Sorrel said.

'You know what I think, Sorrel? I think you suspected Jane was quite young, but somebody else put the arm on you to take her into the group, and you weren't in a position to refuse. Who would that have been?'

Sorrel bit her lip.

'Was it Angela?'

'I don't know any Angela.'

'Anna Purefoy?'

'Oh Christ.' Sorrel stood up and walked to the counter, picked up a cloth and began scrubbing Today's Specials from a blackboard, her back turned to Lol.

He stood up. 'I gather she's not actually in the group.'

'She doesn't need to be.'

'Why's that?'

She turned to face him. 'Because they own this building.'

'The Purefoys?'

'The building came up for sale when our lease had only about six months to run. The chemists next door were going to buy it to extend into, so it would've been… over for us. Then suddenly the Purefoys bought it. They knew one of our members…' Sorrel began to squeeze the cloth between her hands. 'Mr Robinson, I don't want to talk about this. I really do need this café. My husband's about to be made redundant, we've got a stupid mortgage… I'm sorry about Jane, but she's not been with us long, there's been no harm done. Nothing to interest the police, really.'

'Quite a bit to interest the press.'

'What do you *want*? I've said I'm—'

'How well do you know Rowenna?'

'I don't. No more than I know Jane. All right, a bit more. She's picked up messages here and things.'

'From whom?'

'We have a notice-board, as you can see. People leave messages.'

'And some that aren't on the board, maybe?'

'There are no drugs here,' Sorrel said firmly.

'I never thought there were. I don't even assume the Pod gets up to anything iffy. What I think is that maybe Jane will meet other people who aren't regular members, and she'll get invited to – I don't know – interesting parties. And Rowenna makes sure she goes to them, and at these parties there are maybe some slightly off-the-wall things going on, and before you know it her mother receives some pictures of Jane, well stoned and naked on a slab. Just call me cynical, but I used to be in a band.'

'That's ridiculous.'

'You know it's not.'

Sorrel threw the cloth down. 'So what do you… *want*?'

'I want to know about Anna Purefoy.'

'I don't know anything about her.'

431

'OK.' Lol stood up and moved towards the door. 'Thanks for all your help.'

'But I… I know somebody who might help you.'

He turned and waited.

'She used to be our teacher – before Patricia. When she heard the Purefoys had bought this building, she stopped coming. She may or may not need some persuading. But I can tell you where to find her.'

'In Hereford?'

'About twenty miles out,' Sorrel said. 'If she's still alive, that is.'

By the time they left the gatehouse, half the street's Santas and lanterns seemed to have gone out. You felt as though you were on the bridge of a ship leaving port at night, gliding slowly away from the lights.

'I'm sorry, lass,' Huw said, 'but think about it. What does the smart-arse iconoclast new Bishop do first? He breaks a two-thousand-year convention by appointing a female exorcist. In a city which history has shown to be periodically in need of a good guard dog, he…'

'Swaps his Rottweiler for a miniature poodle?'

'I've gone far enough down that road, luv. Don't want me throat torn out. All I'm saying is that the combination of all these factors – and maybe others we don't know about – could be felt to be having a dissipating effect. And a weakened body invites infection. Well, I'm telling you how Thomas Dobbs sees it.'

They walked across the green towards the huge smudge of the Cathedral.

'And you,' Merrily asked him, 'what do you believe?'

'Wait till we're inside.'

She was struck, as always, by the hospitality of the place: the stones of many colours, almost all of them warm; the simplicity of the arcade of Norman arches; the friendly modern glitter of the great corona, which always seemed to be hanging lopsided, although it probably wasn't. She knew nothing about medieval architecture, but it just felt right in here.

Ancient centre of light and healing.

They went directly to the North Transept, deserted except for one of the vergers, a tubby middle-aged man in glasses who looked across, suspicious, then relaxed when he saw Huw's collar and recognized Merrily.

He raised a hand to them. 'Anything I can do?'

'I've got a key, pal.' Huw indicated the partitioned enclosure. 'We'll be about ten minutes.'

'I'll have to stay in the general vicinity,' the verger said, 'if you don't mind. The Dean's been a bit on edge since that slab was reported stolen.'

Huw stopped. 'What was that?'

'I'd forgotten all about it,' Merrily said. 'A chunk of one of the side-panels, with a knight carved on it – it's missing.'

'Oh no,' the verger said, 'it isn't missing. Somebody must have made a mistake – miscounted. When the mason was in here this morning, he confirmed everything was there. Quite a relief, but it did make us think a bit more about security.'

Huw said, 'Do you know which piece it was? Which knight?'

'No idea, sir. The masons will be back on Monday. They'll now be able to put St Thomas together again. Too late, unfortunately, for the Boy Bishop ceremony. It'll be the first time he won't be able to pay his respects.'

'Boy Bishop?'

Merrily briefly explained about the annual ceremony and its meaning, while Huw unlocked the padlock with what apparently were Dobbs's keys. She saw where rudimentary repairs had been carried out since George Curtiss had kicked his way in.

Huw surveyed the dismantled tomb, looking more or less as it had the afternoon Merrily and Jane had stood in here with

Neil, the young archaeologist. Segments of a stone coffin; knights in relief, with shields and mashed faces. 'What happens at this Boy Bishop ceremony then, lass?'

'Never been to one. Harmless bit of Church pageantry, I'd guess.'

'Is it?'

'Harmless? Any reason why it shouldn't be?'

'Everything worries me tonight.' Huw shoved his hands into the pockets of his greatcoat. 'Especially this missing stone business. First a stone's missing, then it's not. Church masons don't miscount.'

'Which means it's either still missing…'

'Or it's back. In which case, where's it been meanwhile?'

She wondered for a moment if he meant that the stone had been somehow dematerialized by the demon. Then she realized what he *did* mean.

'Hard to comprehend, especially seeing it like this,' he trudged around the rubble, 'that this box was once the core of it all. If you try and imagine the amount of psychic and emotional energy – veneration, desperation – poured into this little space over the centuries…'

'You can't. *I* can't.'

'And then imagine if – while it was away – that same stone had hot blood and guts spilled on it.'

'Huw!'

'And then it was brought back?' He shrugged. 'Just a thought.'

Merrily looked up at the huge, lightless, stained-glass window, and saw the dim figure of a knight pushing his spear down a dull dragon's throat.

'All right, what would happen if the balance tilted – if the dominant force in here was the force of evil?'

'Even a bit of evil goes a long way. Take all the aggro they've had over at Lincoln Cathedral. Terrible disruption, hellish disputes, and bad feeling and bitterness among the senior clergy. And consider the number of people who put all that down to evil influences emanating from this little old carving in the nave known as the Lincoln Imp. A thousand sacred carvings in that place – and one imp, know what I mean?'

'Yes.' Merrily was wondering what damage had been caused at Salisbury by Rowenna's sexual forays into the canonries.

'Had a few rows here too, mind,' Huw recalled. 'You remember – could be this was before your time – when the first contingent of Hereford women priests staged a circle-dance here in the Cathedral?'

'I read about it. They were supposed to have been gliding around trancelike, caressing the effigies on bishops' tombs, which some fundamentalists thought was a bit forward and rather too pagan.'

'Bloke who organized it, he said it were simply to introduce women to the Cathedral as an active spiritual force for the first time in its history. So as to make their peace with the old dead bishops. The Bishop at the time, he went along with it, but Dobbs went berserk, apparently. It were said he went round from tomb to tomb that night, like an owd Hoover, removing all psychic traces of the she-devils.'

'Devils?'

'I exaggerate.'

'*You* have a problem with circle-dancing?'

'Not especially. But I don't rule out there might *be* a problem. Cathedrals are just not places you bugger about with, without due consideration. You walk carefully around these old places.'

Merrily found herself wondering what a demon would look like. She tried to imagine one in canon's clothing, but all she could conjure was the crude cartoon image of a grinning skull, its exposed vertebrae vanishing into a dog-collar. What *was* the image with which Dobbs – if only in his own mind – had been confronted in the seconds before his stroke?

She thought of the lightning impression of Denzil Joy ratcheting up in her own bed. What if she'd been old, with a heart condition?

435

'What are we fighting here, Huw? Your *malevolent, semi-sentient forcefield* – and what else? Who else?'

'I wish I knew. But if Dobbs knew the significance of the dismantled tomb – and it's been in the newspaper enough times, so other folk did too. And we're not just talking about the headbangers now.'

He looked at Merrily.

'Who, then?' she asked.

Huw scratched his head. 'Happen the ones with knowledge, and seeking more. *Higher* knowledge – the knowledge you can't get from other men. And you won't get it from God or His angels either, on account of you're not meant to have it. But demons are different: you can *command* a demon if you're powerful enough. Or you can bargain with it.'

'They found one headbanger floating in the Wye,' Merrily said. 'That's not been released by the police yet, so don't, you know… but a man whose body was found in the Wye, with head injuries, kept a satanic altar in his basement. With a big poster of the Goat of Mendes, and American stuff, dirty satanic videos, all that.'

'When was this, lass?'

'Couple of weeks ago. He was from Chepstow. The police are trying to identify his contacts in satanic circles – without conspicuous success.'

'Where in the Wye?'

'Just along the river from here, near the Victoria Bridge. Any relevance, do you think?'

He shook his head. He didn't know any more than she did. She needed to stop regarding Huw as the fount of wisdom, and start thinking for herself. If the possibility of arousing the demon of Hereford Cathedral had already become an occult cause célèbre, perhaps Sayer had been in here that night.

Merrily was cold and confused. This was all getting beyond her comprehension, and the sight of the empty, segmented tomb was starting to distress her.

She was glad when Huw said, 'Let's light a candle for Tommy,' and they moved out of the enclosure.

There was a votive stand which had previously been sited next to the tomb when it was intact. All its candles were out, so she passed Huw her Zippo and he lit two for them. The little flames warmed her momentarily.

He touched her elbow. 'Let's pray, eh?'

She nodded. They knelt facing the partition and the ruins of the shrine. One of the candles went out. She handed Huw the Zippo again, and he stood up and relit the candle. Merrily put out a hand, feeling for a draught from somewhere. No obvious breeze.

As Huw stepped back, the second candle went out.

He waited a moment then applied the lighter to the second candle. As the flame touched the wick, the first candle went out.

A thin taper of cold passed through Merrily, and came out of her mouth as a tiny, frayed whimper.

Outside, in the fog-clogged and freezing night, Huw said, 'Watch yourself.'

Merrily was shivering badly.

'What I'm saying is, don't feel you've got summat to prove.'

'Li… like… like what?'

'You know *exactly* what. If anything happened, and you thought the sanctity of the Cathedral was at risk, you might just be daft enough to go in there on your own, to call on Tommy Canty and Our Lord to do the business.'

'I don't think I w… would have the guts.'

She felt naked, as though the fog was dissolving all her clothing like acid. She wanted Jane to be with her, and yet didn't want Jane anywhere near her.

'Listen to me: it were playing with us, then. It's saying, *I'm here. I'm awake.* You asked me what I believe. I believe there's an active squatter in there.'

'Suppose it was subjective… Suppose… the c… candles… Suppose that was one of us?'

'Then it was acting *through* one of us. You'll need extra prayers tonight, you know what I mean?'

'But what do we do, Huw?'

'A negative presence in the Cathedral itself? We might well be looking at a major exorcism, which in a great cathedral would require several of us, probably including – God forbid – the Bishop himself. Meanwhile, my advice to you, for what it's worth, is not to go in there alone.'

'Huw, I—'

'Not by night nor day. Not *alone.*'

Her forehead throbbed. She thought of what Mick Hunter had said that seemingly long-ago afternoon in the Green Dragon. *I NEVER want to hear of a so-called major exorcism. It's crude, primitive and almost certainly ineffective.*

She wished, at that moment, that Huw had taken the advice of the Dean's Chapter, and left the Bishop's pussycat well out of this. She felt she would never have the nerve to light a candle again.

'You know what you've got to do now, don't you, Merrily?'

'Go and talk to Mick.'

He put his big hand on her shoulder. 'He likes you. You're his favourite appointee. Tell him what's squatting in his Cathedral. Tell him what's got to happen.'

45

All There Is

FOR THE FIRST time, it looked like a real palace. There were many lights on, hanging evenly and elegantly in the foggy night. Several cars were parked tightly up against the deep Georgian windows.

Merrily hesitated.

Well, of course she did.

She remembered the end of day three of the Deliverance course in the Brecon Beacons – the lights in the chapel going off, the video machine burning out. Odd how all these power fluctuations seemed to occur around Huw.

First law of Deliverance: always carry plenty of fuse wire.

She'd wanted him to come with her to the Palace. *Got to be joking, lass. A lowly rural rector from the Church in Wales creeps on to Hunter's patch and diagnoses a demonic presence in the man's own Cathedral? That would get me a big row, and a stiff complaint to the Bishop of Swansea and Brecon. And certainly no action. That would be the worst of it – no action at all. Best he doesn't know about me. That way, if he doesn't get involved, happen I can organize something on the quiet. Be a bit of a risk, mind, but it's a critical situation.*

She'd wanted Huw to come and stay the night at Ledwardine vicarage, but he'd said he had to think. First put some mountains between himself and Hereford, then think and meditate – and pray.

She'd watched him walk away under the darkened Santas, into the fog, winding his scarf around his neck. And she wondered...

Fourth one in two years, Huw had said as she'd looked into the scorched mouth of the ruined video. *It's a right difficult place, this.*

And *It were playing with us*, he'd said just now, as the serial snuffing of votive candles threw shiver after shiver into her, convincing Merrily, without a second thought, of his claim that there was a squatter in the Cathedral.

She stood cold and doubt-haunted on the lawn before the Palace, her shopping bag full of supporting documents lying on the grass by her feet. The night seemed as heavy as Huw's greatcoat around her.

Suppose it was *him*? What, after all, was a priest but a licensed magician?

And where did this squatter story have its origins? Dobbs, perhaps – the man who had made a point of never once speaking to her directly; who had sent her that single cryptic note; who had made her a little present of Denzil Joy. A man, too, with whom Huw had spent long hours. Had they talked about Merrily? Huw hadn't said – but how could they have avoided it?

She looked up to where the sky began, below the tops of the chimney stacks.

Help me!

She was only aware that she must have shouted it aloud into the unyielding night when the white door opened, and there, against the falling light was...

'Merrily? Is that you?'

The Bishop himself, in tuxedo and a bow-tie of dark purple.

'Merrily!'

'I...' She started forward. 'Can I see you, Bishop?'

'Mick,' he reminded her softly. 'Come in, Merrily.'

She felt the pressure of his hand between her shoulder blades, and found herself in the chandeliered splendour of the Great Hall. Doric pilasters, a domed ceiling at the far end, like God's conservatory. She was blinded for a moment, disoriented.

The Bishop blurred past her to a table, pulling out two velvet-backed chairs.

'No,' she said, her nerve gone. 'This is terrible. I'm interrupting something. Could I come back early tomorow, perhaps? Oh, God, tomorrow's Sunday…'

'Merrily, relax. It's a perfect, timely interruption of a terminally tedious dinner party with some oleaginous oafs from the City Council and their dreary wives. Val will sparkle all over them until I return. Sit. You look terribly cold. A drink?'

'No, please…' She sat down, feeling like a tramp next to the Bishop, with his poise and his elegance. 'I just need your help, Mick.'

He listened without a word. Twenty minutes and no interruptions.

She talked and talked – except when she dried up.

Or fumbled in her bag for Mrs Leather – a book of local folklore: collected nonsenses.

Or for the report by the late Mr Havergal on the opening of the Cantilupe tomb in the mid-nineteenth century, an eye-witness description of which it had been considered imprudent to publish.

Or for her cigarette packet, which she gripped for maybe ten seconds, as though the nicotine might be absorbed through her stimulated sweat glands and made to flow up her arm, before she let it drop back into her bag.

It was an impromtu sermon given before an expert audience. A dissertation combining medieval theology with the elements of some Hollywood fantasy-melodrama. An exercise in semi-controlled hysteria.

'I can't… won't… ask you to believe the unbelievable. But I'm trying to do the job that you asked me to do… although… it's… led in directions I could never have imagined it would. Not so soon, anyway. Probably not ever, if I'm honest. But it's a job where you have to rely on instinct, where you never know what is truth and what's…'

Tests. Lies. Disinformation.

'And I'm reporting back to you in confidence, because those are the rules. And you're probably thinking what's the silly bitch doing disturbing me at home on a Saturday night, with dinner guests and…'

Looking up at him, wanting some help, but getting no reaction.

'You must wonder: is she overtired? Has she gone bonkers? The bottom line' – looking up at the twinkling chandelier, half wishing it would fall and smash into ten thousand crystal shards; that *something* would happen to make him afraid – 'is that I believe we should do this cleansing. And that you should be there. And the Dean, too. And as many canons as you feel you can trust.'

The Bishop's expression did not alter. He neither nodded nor shook his head.

'It could be carried out in total secrecy, late at night or, better still, early in the morning, at four or five o'clock. It would take less than a couple of hours. It's… Consider it a precaution. If nothing happens, then either it was successful or it wasn't necessary. I don't care if people say later that it wasn't necessary. It doesn't matter that…'

A door opened and Val Hunter stood there in black, dramatic. 'Michael?'

'Five minutes.' He lifted one hand.

With a single, long breath down her nostrils, Val went away without even a glance at Merrily.

The Bishop waited until his wife's footsteps had receded, then he spoke. 'Have you finished, Merrily?'

She nodded, dispirited.

'Who was it?' he said. 'Come on, it's either Dobbs, or the Dean – or, more likely, Owen. Who put you up to this?'

All three, she thought miserably. 'Circumstances,' she said at last. 'A lot of individually meaningless circumstances.'

He gave a small sigh. 'But I'd rather you didn't list them.'

'All I can say is I believe my suggestion is valid. We can't afford to take any risk.'

'Risk of what?'

'Of the Cathedral being contaminated.'

'Tell me, Merrily, who would conduct this major exorcism?'

'That would be your decision.'

'Ah,' he said, 'of course.' He shifted position, looking out through the long windows to the floodlight beams across the lawns, turned to milk chocolate by the fog. 'May I list once again your items of evidence? From the felling of Thomas Dobbs in the North Transept, to the apparently supernatural extinguishing of two votive candles.'

'I never said any of that was evidence.'

'Of course you didn't. You were merely reporting to me. The decision must be mine – on the advice of my female exorcist, the appointment of whom I was strongly advised against.'

'At the time, I didn't know that.'

'You didn't? You really didn't? Oh come, Merrily…'

'Silly of me. Arrogant, perhaps.'

'Yes,' the Bishop said, 'that's certainly how it's going to look when someone leaks to the media that, within weeks of your appointment, you advised me to have my cathedral formally exorcized.'

'I know.'

'If you want to go the whole hog, why not have the ceremony conducted entirely by – and in the presence only of – women priests? Obviously, that wouldn't offend *me*, being a radical.'

'Mick, you know there's nothing political—'

'Nothing political? Are you quite serious? Tell me, Merrily, do you *want* to become the subject of a hate campaign in the diocese, as well as receiving an unflattering profile in the *Observer* and any number of politely vitriolic letters to the *Church Times*? Do you *want* to move, quite quickly, to a new and challenging ministry on the other side of the country?'

'No.'

'And do you want to damage me?'

Silence. A dismal, head-shaking silence.

Merrily said, 'So you'd like me to resign?'

Mick Hunter grinned, teeth as white as the Doric pilaster behind him. 'Certainly not. I'd far prefer you to go home, have a good night's sleep, and forget this ill-advised visit ever occurred. It isn't the first time something like this has happened to me, and it won't be the last time it happens to you. Let it serve to remind you that people like us will always have opponents, enemies, within the Church.'

'Mick, don't you think this is far too complicated and too... bizarre to be a set-up?'

'Oh, Merrily, I can see your experience of being set up is really rather limited. My advice, if you're approached again by the source of this insane proposal, is that you tell him you questioned the wisdom of informing me and decided against it.'

'Making it *my* decision to say no to an exorcism.'

'It's a responsible role you now have, Merrily. Learning discrimination is part of it. Or you could go ahead with it, without informing me – which would, of course, were I or anyone else to find out, be very much a matter for resignation. But I don't think you'd do that, because you don't really believe any of this idiocy any more than I do. Do you, Merrily?'

'I don't know.' She put her face in her hands, pulling the skin tight. 'I *don't* know.'

Mick stood up and helped her to her feet. 'Get some sleep, eh? It's been a difficult week.'

'I don't know,' she repeated. 'How can I know?'

'Of course you don't know.' He put an arm around her shoulders, peered down into her face, then said, as if talking to a child, 'That's what they're counting on, Merrily, hmm? Look, if I don't go back and be pleasant to the awful councillors, Val will... be very unhappy.'

At the door, she sought out and held his famous blue eyes.

'Will you at least think about it?'

'I've already forgotten about it, Merrily,' he said. 'Good night. God bless.'

The fog seemed to be lifting, but the grass was already stiff with frost. The Cathedral was developing a hard edge. She crossed the green and walked into Church Street. The door in the alleyway beside the shop called John Barleycorn was opening as she reached it.

'Hi.'

'Hello, flower.'

Jane stood outside in the alley, no coat on, her dark hair pushed back behind her ears. Face upturned, she was shivering a little.

'I lied.'

They stood about five feet apart. Merrily thought: *We all lie. Especially to ourselves.*

'I don't have anywhere else to sleep,' Jane said. 'I don't actually know many people at all. I, uh, don't even know the people I thought I knew. So... like... the only friends I have are Lol and you. I... I hope...' She began to cry. 'I'm sorry, Mum. I'm really, really, really...'

Merrily's eyes filled up.

'I think there must be a whole load of things,' Jane snuffled, 'that I haven't even realized I did, yet. Like all the time I was doing this stuff – selling you up the river. I told the bitch everything. I told her about *everything*. And when I said that to you about selling my—'

'You didn't,' Merrily said very firmly. 'I didn't hear you say anything, flower.'

As they clung together on the already slippery cobbles, she thought: *This is all that matters, isn't it? This is all there is.*

46

The Turning

SHE WAS LIKE an elderly bushbaby in some ankle-length mohair thing in dark brown. She was waiting for him in the residents' lounge, where they were now alone – all the others at church, she said, 'bargaining for an afterlife'. She did not want to know anything about him.

'Waste of time at my age, Robinson; it's all forgotten by lunchtime.'

Lol didn't think so. Her eyes were diamond-bright behind round glasses a bit like his own.

'Anyway,' she said, 'I prefer to make up my own mind.' And she peered at him, eyes unfocusing. '*Oh*, what a confused boy you are. *So* confused, aren't you? And blocked, too. There's a blockage in your life. I should like to study you at length, but you haven't the time, have you? Not today. You're in a *frightful* hurry.'

Lol nodded, bemused.

'Slow down,' she said. 'Think things out, or you'll land in trouble. Especially dealing with the Purefoys. Do you understand me?'

'Not yet.' Presumably Sorrel Podmore had given her the background over the phone. Which was good: it saved time.

She'd collected all the cushions from the other chairs and had them piled up around her. She was like a tiny, exotic dowager.

'What do you know about the Purefoys?'

'Virtually nothing.'

'That's a good place from which to start. It's a very, very unpretty story.'

Jane had stood at the bedroom window for a long time, still feeling – in spite of everything – an urge to salute the Eternal Spiritual Sun.

Without this and the other exercises, without the Pod, there was a large spiritual hole in her life. She wasn't sure she was ready for Mum's God. Although part of her wanted to go to morning service, if only to show penitence and solidarity, another part of her felt it would be an empty gesture – hypocrisy.

And, anyway, she was, like, burning up with anger, and if the Eternal Spiritual Sun – wherever the bastard was these days – could add fuel to that, this was OK by Mystic Jane.

While Mum was conducting her morning service, Jane pulled on the humble duffel and walked into still-frozen Ledwardine, across the market square where, at close to midday, the cobbles were still white and lethal. She moved quickly, did not slip, fury making her surefooted. Rage at what they were trying to do to Mum – and what they'd already done.

They? Who? Who, apart from Rowenna?

With whom there was unfinished business.

Jane walked down to the unfashionable end of the village, where long-untreated timbers sagged and the black and white buildings looked grey with neglect.

She and Mum had sat up until nearly two a.m., hunched over this big, comfort fire of coal sweetened with apple logs. Like old times together, except it wasn't – because Mum was dead worried, and you could understand it. She'd talked – frankly, maybe for the first time – about the dilemmas constantly thrown up by Deliverance. The need to believe and also disbelieve; and the knowledge that you were completely on your own – especially with a self-serving, hypocritical bastard of a bishop like Mick Hunter.

But she wasn't alone now, oh no.

Jane stopped outside the Ox. The pulsing oranges and greens of gaming machines through the windows were brighter than the pub sign outside. This was as near as Ledwardine came to Las Vegas.

Jane went in. She was pretty sure they would be here. They'd been coming here since they were about thirteen, and they'd be coming till they were old and bald and never had a life.

There was just one bar: not big, but already half full. Most of the men in there were under thirty, most of the women under twenty, dregs of the Saturday-night crowd. Though the pub was old and timbered, the lighting was garish. A jukebox was playing Pearl Jam. It was loud enough, but the voice from halfway down the room was louder.

'WATKINS!'

Right.

Wall and Gittoes were at a table by the jukebox, hugging pints of cider. Jane strolled over to the fat, swollen-mouthed slimeball and the bony, spotty loser who had once, she recalled, expressed a wish to have unholy communion with her mother.

'I want to talk to you, Danny – outside.'

Danny Gittoes looked up slowly and blinked. 'I'm drinking. And it's cold out there.'

Jane took a chance. She'd gone to sleep thinking about this and she'd woken up thinking about it. If she was wrong, well... she just didn't bloody *deserve* to be wrong.

'Must have been cold in the church, too,' she said.

'What *are* you on about, Watkins?' Gittoes had this narrow face, dopey eyes.

Dean Wall rose and tucked his belly into his belt. 'If the lady wants to go outside, let's do it.'

'Siddown, Wall,' Jane snarled, indicated Gittoes. 'Just... *that.*'

'Got no secrets from Dean,' Gittoes said.

'I believe you.' Jane put on her grimmest smile. 'Rowenna and I, we don't have secrets either. For Christmas, I'm buying her a whole case of extra-strength mouthwash.'

'Fetch me a map,' demanded Athena White. 'There's a stack of them in the hall. Fetch me an OS map of Hereford. I want to locate this Dinedor Hill.'

Miss White seemed much happier now she knew precisely what this was about. And what *he* was about. The process of knowing him – and where he'd been and what made him afraid – had taken all of ten minutes. It would take Dick Lyden maybe four full sessions to get this far.

Lol was impressed – also disturbed. He sensed she could be, well, malevolent, when she wanted to. There was something dangerously alien about Athena White: unmoving, sunk into her many cushions, but her mind was darting; picking up the urgency of this.

Telling her about Katherine Moon had been the right thing to do.

He brought her the map. 'Spread it out on the floor,' she commanded. 'Move that perfectly awful table, there. Oh, dear, it's what one misses most stuck out here. The seclusion, the study time, yes, but there are things *going on* that one misses. OK, Dinedor Hill. Why Dinedor Hill? Put your finger on it, Robinson. Can't make out the damned map, but I can at least see your finger. Now give me your other hand.'

He found himself kneeling on the map, with the forefinger of one hand on Dinedor Hill, while she held his other hand, both of her small hands over his. They were frail and bony and very warm.

'Look at it, Robinson, look at the hill… no, not on the map, you fool. Picture it in your mind. Feel yourself there. Feel the wind blow, feel the damp, the cold. Think about Moon being there. She's coming towards you, isn't she? Now, tell me what you're seeing.'

'I'm seeing the crow,' he said at once. 'Her hand inside the crow. We're standing right at the end of the ramparts, with the city below us and the church spire aligned with the Cathedral tower.'

'Good.'

In the moments of quiet, he could hear crockery clinking several rooms away. Footsteps clumped outside the door, the handle creaked and Athena White let out a piercing squeak. 'Get away from that door! Go away!'

And the footsteps went away.

Miss White said, 'She killed that crow, you know.'

'I wondered about that.'

'I think she would have brought the crow down and killed it.'

Brought it down how?

Crow Maiden, he thought. *And the crows would come, Denny had said. Crows'd come right up to her.*

Lol opened his eyes. Through the window, the Radnor hills were firming up as the mist receded; you could see the underside of the sun in the southern sky.

'You see, it doesn't really work unless the blood is still warm,' Athena White explained.

Jane and Danny Gittoes stood in the alley alongside of the Ox. There were men's toilets here, the foul-smelling kind, and she was starting to get pictures of Danny Gittoes and Rowenna.

'Jane, I'm sorry, all right. I'm sorry about your mother's church, but I didn't take nothing, did I? And it was her idea, all of it.'

'Yeah, tell that to the police. "I did it for a blowjob, officer." Real mitigating-circumstances situation, that is. The magistrates will really like you for that, Gittoes.'

'I'll pay for it, all right? I'll pay for the window.'

'Tell me about the suit.'

'What about it?'

'What did she say about the suit?'

'She said it was a joke – on you and your ma. I didn't twig it. She had the suit in the back of her car, in one of them plastic suit-bags like you get from the cleaners, and I had to keep it inside the bag till I'd got it in the wardrobe – then take it out of the bag.'

'Did she go in with you?'

'She waited outside with the torch. She shone the torch in and she told me where to put the suit, and to make sure it was out of sight. Look, Watkins, this is between you and her, right? This en't nothing—'

'You're going down for it, Gittoes.'

'Nobody goes down for breaking a window.'

'It gets in the paper, though, and then everybody knows how pitiful you are. Everybody sees this redhaired stunner, and then they look at you. It does kind of test the imagination, doesn't it, Danny? It'll like follow you around for years – Beauty and the Sad Git.'

'What about *her*?'

'You really think she cares what anybody thinks? Hey – wow, I forgot.' Jane stepped away from him and began to smile. 'Isn't your stepfather up for a vacancy on the parish council?'

'Fuck you, Watkins.'

'Not even in your dreams.'

'What do you want? What you want me to do?'

'Tell me what happened when she first approached you. Was she on her own?'

'Course she was on her own.'

'I bet you thought she actually fancied you, didn't you?'

Gittoes blushed.

'Don't worry, she's good at that,' Jane said. 'Come on, don't stand there like a bloody half-peeled prawn. Talk to me.'

'I dunno what you *want*!'

'What do you know about her?'

'She's *your* friend!'

'Cooperate,' Jane hissed, 'or the first thing that happens – like tonight – is word gets to reach your stepfather.'

'*Please*… what you wanner know? You wanner know where she goes when you en't with her? You wanner know who her real boyfriend is? Cause I followed her – all right? – on the motorbike. Yeah, I thought I was in with a chance – how sad is that? I followed her around. I can give you stuff to, like, even the score… if you'll leave me alone.'

'Keep talking, hairball,' Jane said.

For quite a long time, Miss White continued, she did not really understand what a Satanist was. For a start, nobody would ever admit to being one. You had this absurd American self-publicist, La Vey, with his Church of Satan, following a poor variation of Crowley's Do What Thou Wilt philosophy. But that was a misnomer: there wasn't that quality of pure, naked hate which Satanism implied.

Black magic? Ah, not quite the same thing. Black magic was simply the use of magic to do harm. And, yes, Miss White had been tempted, too – was *often* tempted. Aware, of course, of the easy slope from mischief to malignity, but she had done worse things without the need for magic – hadn't everyone?

Miss White had practised ritual magic for a number of years before the robes and the swords and the chalices had begun to seem rather unnecessary and faintly absurd. It was during this period that she first encountered Anna Purefoy, or Anna Bateman as she was then.

'We were both civil servants at the time. Anna worked at the Defence Ministry – secretary to an under-secretary, quite a highly paid post for a girl her age. She never hid her interest in the occult – neither did I. There are a surprising number of senior civil servants practising the dark arts – by which, of course, I do *not* mean Satanism. To the vast, *vast* majority of ritual magicians, the idea of worshipping a vulgar creature with horns and halitosis is absolute anathema.'

The change came with Anna's persecution by Christians in the person of a junior Defence minister with a rigid Presbyterian background. A far more senior civil servant had been linked by a Sunday newspaper to an offshoot of Aleister Crowley's magical foundation, the OTO. In the resulting purge, Anna's resignation had been sought and bitterly given.

'I suppose her resentment and loathing of the Christian Church began there,' Miss White said, 'but it really developed when she met Tim.'

Timothy Purefoy: already a rich man and getting richer.

'Tim, like Anna, was blond and rather beautiful. Terribly charming and infinitely solicitous. Especially to elderly ladies in the area of Oxfordshire where he plied his trade. For in Tim's hands it was indeed a trade.'

'What did he do?' Lol asked.

'He was a minister of the Church of England, of course. First a curate and then a rector. I think he'd risen to Rural Dean by the time he was thirty. A throwback in many ways: what they used to call a "hunting parson": field sports and dinner parties, frightfully well connected, etc. And so he often got named – along with the Church itself, of course – in the published wills of wealthy widows. This is common practice, and the Church seldom bats an eyelid as long as it gets its share as well. Timothy was always terribly careful like that. Probably be a bishop by now, if he hadn't become fatally attracted to Anna, then reduced to a comparatively lowly post with Oxfordshire County Council.'

Miss White assumed that by this time Anna's bitter resentment of the Church, its prejudices, and the hold it retained on the British establishment had almost certainly become obsessively bound up with her continuing magical studies. The Church had destroyed her promising career, so she felt driven to wound the Church at every opportunity.

Lol was picturing the gentle, sweet-faced woman with flour on her apron in that mellow farmhouse kitchen. Then, later, dabbing her eyes at Moon's funeral.

'The destruction, humiliation or corruption of a priest is a great satanic triumph,' Miss White said. 'Everyone knows that.

But the greatest triumph, the ultimate prize, is the defection, the *turning*, of an ordained minister.'

'Does that really happen?' He thought of big, bluff, jovial Tim Purefoy in his shiny new Barbour and cap. *Come to the farmhouse... have a coffee.*

'I don't know how often it actually happens,' said Miss White. 'Perhaps some of them remain ministers while practising their secret arts. How many churches have been clandestinely dedicated to the Devil – how can anyone know? What I do know is how very, very much it must have appealed to Anna, as an ex-MOD person – the idea of *turning* Tim. The Cold War was at its height, former British agents like Philby flaunted by the Soviets, so how wonderful, how prestigious – among her circle – to convert a priest to Satan? Especially such a recognizably establishment figure as Tim Purefoy.'

Of how it happened, Miss White had no specific knowledge.

'But one can imagine the Rural Dean's slow-burning obsession with the sensational blonde in the little cottage... those long, erotic Sunday interludes between Matins and Evensong. The subtler arts of sexual love come naturally to a magician,' she said enigmatically.

'But if he'd got such a good thing going, milking widows and being accepted by the county set, why would he give that all up?'

'Well, he didn't, of course – not voluntarily.'

Athena believed it was a new curate, some earnest evangelical practising an almost monastic self-denial, who blew the whistle on both of them. It was revealed that Anna had been giving regular tarot readings to villagers, in a cottage in the very shadow of Tim's parish church. And also once – famously – at the parish fête. It was Anna who was driven out of the village first, by a hate campaign drawing support from fundamentalist Christians for miles around.

'And meanwhile Tim was photographed leaving her cottage late at night. It rather escalated from there, but it never became a *very* big scandal, because the Church kept the lid on it. I don't know whether Tim was dabbling in Satanism by then, or whether that came later – but it did come. By which time both held a *considerable* grievance against the "witchhunting" Church itself. And the annexing of his spiritual baggage, no matter how corrupted it already was, due to his weak and greedy character, must have been an enormous boost for her own influence among her peers.'

Through the window, Lol could see a platoon of elderly ladies advancing up the drive.

'Damn,' Athena said. 'First they'll head off to their rooms to freshen up, if that's a suitable term, then they'll all come twittering in.'

'How did the Purefoys carry on making a living?'

'When a minister defects, he is treated – just like Philby in Moscow – as a great celebrity. He is presented at Court, as you might say.'

'What do you mean by "Court"?'

'Oh, Robinson, even *I* don't know who most of these people are. Very wealthy, very evil – actual criminals some of them. Certainly the narcotics trade, whatever they call it these days, has a very large satanic element, and has had for decades. The Purefoys had capital, they had contacts, they had a very *English* charm. With their patronage and advice, lucrative property deals followed, leading, for instance, to the purchase of that building in Bridge Street housing the Pod. I then simply could not continue working with that group any more, which was a great pity, as it did get me out of here once a week – they always sent a car for me. No, I knew what was going to happen, you see.'

'What?'

'They would use the Pod as – what do you call it? – a front. Anything from an innocent reception centre to a kind of spiritual brothel. Podmore already told me about your friend's daughter – but I want to ask you something about that. This friend herself wouldn't, by any chance, be Merrily Watkins?'

'How did you know that?'

'Ha! This clarifies certain small mysteries. Oh, *what* a target that woman must be for the Purefoys and their ilk. A *female* exorcist – and *such* a pretty girl.'

'Yes.' Lol began to fold the map.

'Ah,' said Athena calmly, 'I see.'

'Where've you been? I mean where *have* you been?' The kid just staring back at her, and Merrily taking a deep breath, gripping the Aga rail. 'I'm sorry. Christ, what am I *saying*?'

'I don't know, Mum.'

'I close my eyes in church, I see that lime-green Fiesta reversing into our drive. I come back from church, and you're not here. I'm sorry. There is no reason at all you have to be here all the time.'

'No, you're right,' Jane said. 'It was thoughtless of me.'

'Ignore me, flower. I'm badly, badly paranoid. Previously, I see a stranger in the congregation, and I think: *Yes. Wow. Another one!* Now, when I glimpse an unfamiliar face, I'm watching for a little sneer at some key moment; I'm watching their lips when we say the Lord's Prayer. I go round afterwards and sniff where they sat. Jesus, I shouldn't be saying this to you – you're only sixteen.'

'Yes, I am,' Jane said mildly. 'And I've just been to see Danny Gittoes. Rowenna gave him, like, oral sex in return for breaking into the church and contaminating your cassock with Denzil Joy's suit. Just thought you should know that.'

Merrily broke away from the Aga.

'Also – and I'm not qualified to, like, evaluate the significance of this – but Rowenna's been seeing – euphemism, OK? – *seeing* a young guy by the name of James Lyden. He goes to the Cathedral School and apparently tonight he's going to be enthroned in the Cathedral as something called – vomit, vomit – Boy Bishop. Does this mean anything to you?'

47

Medieval Thing

She called Huw, but there was no answer. She didn't know his Sunday routine. Perhaps he drove from church to church across the mountains – service after service, until he was all preached out. If he had a mobile or a car-phone, it wouldn't work up there, anyway.

She next called Sophie at home. Sophie, thank God, *was* home. Merrily pictured a serene, pastel room with a high ceiling and a grandfather clock.

'Sophie, are you going to the Boy Bishop ceremony tonight?'

'I always do,' Sophie said. 'As the Bishop's lay-secretary, I consider my role as extending to his understudy.'

'That's not quite the right word, is it? As I understand it, the boy is a symbolic replacement – the Bishop actually giving way to him.'

'Well, perhaps. Should I explain it to you, Merrily?'

'Please.'

She listened, and made notes on her sermon pad.

'Shall I see you there?' Sophie asked.

'God willing.'

'I should like to talk to you. I've delayed long enough.'

An hour later, Merrily called Huw again, and then she called Lol but there was no answer there either, and no one else to call. When she put the phone down, she said steadily to herself, 'I shouldn't need this. I shouldn't need help.'

Jane, coming into the scullery with coffee, said, 'You can only ever go by what you think is right, Mum.'

'All right, listen, flower. Sit down. I'm going to hang something on you. And you, in your most cynical-little-bitch mode, are going to give me your instinctive reactions.'

Jane pulled up a chair and they sat facing one another, side-on to the desk.

'Shoot,' Jane said.

'It's a medieval thing.'

'Most of Hereford seems to be a medieval thing,' Jane said.

'In the thirteenth century, apparently, it was a fairly wide-spread midwinter ceremony in many parts of Europe. Sometimes he was known as the Bishop of the Innocents. It was discontinued at the Reformation under Henry VIII. The Reformation wasn't kind to the Cathedral anyway. Stained-glass windows were destroyed, statues smashed. Then there was the Civil War and puritanism. In most cathedrals, the Boy Bishop never came back, but Hereford reintroduced it about twenty-five years ago, and it's now probably the most famous ceremony of its kind in the country. The basis of it is a line from the Magnificat which goes: *He hath put down the mighty from their seat and hath exalted the humble and meek.*'

'That's crap,' Jane said. 'I don't know anybody my age who is remotely humble or meek.'

'How about if *I* tell you when to come on with the cynicism. OK, back to the ceremony. After a candlelit procession, the Bishop of Hereford gives up his throne to the boy, who takes over the rest of the service, leads the prayers, gives a short sermon.'

'Would I be right in thinking there aren't a whole bunch of boys queuing up for this privilege?'

'Probably. It's a parent thing – also a choir thing. The Boy Bishop is almost invariably a leading chorister, or a recently retired chorister, and he has several attendants from the same stable.'

'So, what you're saying is, Hunter symbolically gives up his throne to this guy.'

'No, it isn't symbolic. He actually does it. And then the boy and his entourage proceed around the chancel and into the North Transept, where he's introduced to St Thomas Cantilupe at the shrine.'

'Or, in this case, the hole where the shrine used to be.'

'Yes, I understand this will the first time since the institution of the ceremony in the Middle Ages that there's been no tomb.'

'Heavy, right?'

Merrily said, 'So you're following my thinking.'

'Maybe.' Jane pushed her hair behind her ears.

Merrily said, 'If – and this is the crux of it – you wanted to isolate the period when Hereford Cathedral was most vulnerable to... shall we call it spiritual disturbance, you might choose the period of the dawning of a millennium... when the tomb of its guardian saint lies shattered... and when the Lord Bishop of Hereford...'

She broke off, searching for the switch of the Anglepoise lamp. The red light of the answering machine shone like a drop of blood.

'Is a mere boy,' Jane supplied.

'That's the final piece of Huw's jigsaw. Is that a load of superstitious crap or what? You can now be cynical.'

'Thanks.'

'So?' Merrily's hand found the lamp switch and clicked. The light found Jane propping up her chin with a fist.

'How long do we have before the ceremony starts?'

'It takes place during Evensong – which was held in the late afternoon until Mick took over. Mick thinks Evensong should be just that – at seven-thirty. Just over three hours from now.'

'Oh.'

'Not very long at all.'

461

'No.' Jane stood up, hands in the hip pockets of her jeans. 'Why don't you try calling Huw Owen again?'

'He isn't going to be there, flower. If he is, it would take him well over an hour to get here.'

'Try Lol again. Maybe he can put the arm on James Lyden's dad.'

'The psychotherapist?'

'Maybe he can.'

'All right.' Merrily punched out Lol's number; the phone was picked up on the second ring.

'John Barleycorn.' A strange voice.

'Oh, is Lol there?'

'No, he's not. This is Dennis Moon in the shop. Sorry, it's the same line. I'm not usually here on a Sunday, but Lol's not around anyway. Can I give him a message if he shows before I leave?'

'Could you ask him to call Merrily, please?'

'Sure, I'll leave him a note.'

'Face it,' Merrily said, hanging up. 'This guy is not going to pull his boy out of the ceremony – thus forcing them to abort it.'

'I suppose not. Actually, it does seem quite scary. What if something did happen and we could have prevented it? But, on the other hand, what *could* happen?'

'Well, it won't be anything like thunder and lightning and the tower cracking in half.' She saw Jane stiffen. 'Flower?'

'Why did you say that?'

'What?'

'About the tower cracking in half.'

'It was the first stupid thing I thought of.'

'That's the tarot card Angela turned up for me: the Tower struck by lightning. It's just… Sorry, your imagination sometimes goes berserk, doesn't it?'

'Look.' Merrily stood up and put an arm around her. 'Thunder is not forecast, anyway. You don't get thunder at this

462

time of the year, in this kind of weather. That tower's been here for many centuries. The tarot card is purely symbolic. And even if something like that *did* happen…'

'It did in 1786.'

'What did?'

'We did this in school. They had a west tower then, and it didn't have proper foundations and the place was neglected, and on Easter Monday 1786 the whole lot collapsed.'

Merrily moved away, looked down at the desk, gathering her thoughts. 'Look, even if it *was* likely, it's still not the worst disaster that could happen.'

'You mean the collapse of spirituality,' Jane said soberly.

'Whatever you say about the Church, flower, there's no moral force to replace it.'

'OK,' Jane said. 'So suppose all the people jumping off the Tower Struck By Lightning are the ones, like, abandoning Christianity as the whole edifice collapses. Suppose the final disintegration of the Church as we know it was to start *here*?'

Merrily said, 'Would you care?'

48

Blood

THE CROW.

As the crow flies: a straight line.

Dinedor Hill… All Saints Church… Hereford Cathedral… and two further churches, ending in…

'What's this place, Robinson? Can't make it out.'

'Stretford.' For a moment it stopped his breath. 'This… is the church of St Cosmas and St Damien.'

'Oh, Robinson,' Athena White said. 'Oh, yes.'

Once the old ladies had begun to gather in the lounge, she'd beckoned Lol away and up the stairs. In Athena's eyrie, with the Afghan rugs and all the cupboards, the OS map of Hereford had been opened out on the bedspread, and the line from Dinedor drawn in.

Athena's glasses were white light. 'It was in the *Hereford Times*, wasn't it? Was that last week, I can't remember? The crow… *the crow*. Why does one never see what is under one's nose?'

'They happened the same night. The crow sacrifice, and Moon's death… and a minister called Dobbs had a stroke in the Cathedral.'

'Yes!'

It all came out then, in strands of theory and conjecture which eventually hung together as a kind of certainty.

Tim Purefoy had said: *That's one of Alfred Watkins's ley-lines. An invisible, mystical cable joining sacred sites. Prehistoric path of power. They're energy lines, you know. And spirit paths. So we're told. Probably all nonsense, but at sunset you can feel you own the city.*

Now, Athena White said, 'It doesn't matter whether it's there or not, Robinson. It's what the magician *perceives* is there. The magician uses visualization, driven by willpower, to create an alternative reality.'

Moon had said: *The line goes through four ancient places of worship, ending at a very old church out in the country. But it starts here, and this is the highest point. So all these churches, including the Cathedral, remain in its shadow. This hill is the mother of the city. The camp here was the earliest proper settlement, long before there was a town down there.*

'When the first Christian churches were built, Rome ordered them to be placed on sites of earlier worship, places already venerated, so as to appropriate their influence. But you see, Robinson, the pre-Christian element never really went away, because of the continued dominance of Dinedor Hill. So, if your aim was to destabilize the Cathedral and all it symbolizes, you might well decide to cause a vibration in what lies *beneath*.'

And Lol had said to Merrily – ironically in the café in the All Saints Church, on the actual line from St Cosmas to Dinedor Hill: *In Celtic folk tales, crows and ravens figured as birds of ill-omen or... as a form taken by anti-Christian forces.*

'At one end of the line,' Athena said, 'a crow is sacrificed. At the other – at the highest point – is your crow maiden.'

Lol said, 'Sacrificed?'

'Oh, yes.'

'They killed her?'

'Or helped her to take her own life? Probably, yes. I'm sorry, Robinson, I don't know if this is what you wanted to hear.'

'It's just... are you sure about this?' *She's an old woman*, he thought. *She lives in a fantasy world.* 'You have to be sure.'

'And yet,' she said, 'these two deaths are so different. Calm down, Robinson, I won't let you make a fool of yourself. You see, as Crowley once pointed out, a sacrifice was once seen as a merciful and glorious death, allowing the astral body to go directly to its God. This essentially means a quick death, a throat cut... the way the crow presumably died. But your friend's blood was let out through the wrists. Not quick at all – a slow release...'

' "Crow maiden, you're fadin' away..." '

'What did you say?'

'Just a line from a song.'

Athena White's clasped hands were shaking with concentration. 'Robinson, have we discussed the power of blood?'

On the way back from the Glades, Lol kept glancing at the passenger seat – because of a dark, disturbing sensation of Moon sitting beside him.

I'd like to sleep now.

'I know,' he said once. 'I know you can't sleep. But I just don't know what to do about it.'

At the lectern in Ledwardine Church, with the altar behind them, candles lit, Merrily took both Jane's hands in hers, and looked steadily into the kid's dark eyes.

'You all right about this?'

'Sure.'

Merrily had locked the church doors – the first time she'd ever locked herself in. A church was not a private place; it should always offer sanctuary.

Merrily gripped the kid's hands more firmly.

'Christ be with us,' she said, 'Christ within us.'

'Christ behind us,' Jane read from the card placed in the open Bible on the lectern. 'Christ before us...'

'Hello, Laurence,' Denny said tiredly.

The shop was all in boxes around his knees. Despite the possible implications for his own domestic future, Lol had forgotten about Denny's decision to shut John Barleycorn for ever. The walls were just empty shelves now, even the balalaika packed away. The ochre wall-lamps, which had lit Moon so exquisitely, did her brother Denny no favours. His face was grey as he wiped his brow with the sleeve of his bomber jacket.

'I haven't been totally frank with you, Lol. Another reason for all this is that I'm going to need all the money I can get' – he looked away – 'to pay Maggie off.'

Lol remembered the distance between them at Moon's cremation. 'You and Maggie…?'

'Aw, been coming a while. I won't explain now. Kathy's death could have saved it. At least, that's what *she* thought – Maggie. But the very fact she *thought* that…' Denny smashed a fist into a tall carboard box. 'That made it unfucking-tenable.'

'I'm sorry,' Lol said awkwardly, the urge welling up in him to tell Denny what he believed had really happened to Moon. But could Denny, in his present state, absorb this arcane insanity? 'What about the kids?' he said instead.

'She'll have them.' Denny taped up the flaps of a box full of CDs. 'I'm hardly gonner fight *that*.' He looked across at the door to the stairs. 'Do something for me, Laurence. The bike.'

'Moon's bike?'

'Take it away, would you? It's oppressive. I dream about it.'

'How do you mean?'

'I *dream*. I have these fucking dreams. It starts with the bike and then it turns into this, like, cart with the same big wheels… like some old war chariot. I want to get into it, and I know if I do, it's gonner take me up there again. No fucking way.'

'To the hill.'

'No way, man. So, would you do that? Would you get rid of the bike? Somebody's gonner buy or lease this place, see, and then they'll make me take the bike out. I'm not touching it – it's like that fucking sword, you know? Take it away. Flog it, dump it… somewhere I don't know where it is.'

'All right. I'll do that tomorrow.'

'Thanks. Oh yeah, a woman rang for you. Mary?'

'Merrily?'

'Probably. She said could you call her. Look, Lol… I tried to use you to compensate for my brotherly inadequacies. I regret that now – along with all the rest.'

'There wasn't a lot you could do, Den. In the end, Moon's fate was in other hands.'

'No.' Denny's eyes narrowed. 'I don't buy this shit, Lol. I'm not buying any more than that she was sick. I'm not having anything else unloaded on me. I won't go down that road.'

Lol nodded. So he himself would have to go down that road alone.

'Hello, this is Ledwardine Vicarage. Merrily and Jane aren't around at the moment, but if you'd like—'

Lol put down the phone and went to sit down for a while in Ethel's chair, once-insignificant details crowding his mind.

Like the sword. The sword she'd just happened to find in a pit where it looked as though the Purefoys had been digging a pond. The sword sticking up for her to find – like it was meant. They'd put it there, hadn't they?

Perhaps they'd found it where Denny had buried it, or perhaps it wasn't the same sword at all – Denny's own memory refashioning it to fit the circumstances.

At the funeral, Anna Purefoy had said: *We were so delighted by her absorption in the farm that we couldn't resist offering her the barn. We thought she was perfect.*

Moon was perfect for them because – according to the tenets of Anna Purefoy's occultism – Moon's obsession was a passage to the heart of the hill's pagan past. By stimulating a resurgence of the once-dominant pagan energy, they were attempting to induce a spiritual reversion. Using the Celtic tradition of vengeful crow-goddess and blood ritual to link that holy hill with the pre-medieval Church at the terminus of the ley-line alignment. Thus feeding something old and corrupt inside the Christian Cathedral.

Belief was all, Athena White had said. It didn't matter how real any of this was, so long as *they* believed it. They hadn't even had to bend Moon to their will. She was already halfway there. But had they actually killed her? Had they used the Celtic sword as a sacrificial blade to cut her wrists? Because, if they hadn't done anything physical, it was an unprovable crime, bizarrely akin to euthanasia. Perhaps not even a crime at all.

He called Merrily again.

'*Hello, this is Led—*'

He put the phone down, then lifted it again and redialled, waiting for the message to end. 'Merrily,' he said. 'Look, I've got to tell somebody. It's about Moon and... and your desecration thing at the little church...'

He talked steadily about crows and sacrifice. After three minutes, the bleeps told him his time was up. He waited for a minute, then called back, waited again for the message to finish. This time he talked about projections. He knew why he was doing this: he had to hear himself saying it, to decide if he could believe it.

Moon's father: not a ghost but a *projection*, a transferred image. Transmitting a *projection* – Athena looking rather coy at this point – was not terribly difficult. Especially if the Purefoys had a photograph to work with. Photographs and memories, half-truth and circumstance – and the power of the ancestors, usurped.

'By some combination of projection, hypnosis, psychic-sug-gestion – maybe you have better words for this – they may have steered her to suicide.'

When the bleeps started again, he didn't call back. He took up his habitual stance at the window, looking down into Christmas-lit Church Street/Capuchin Lane. Moon's agitated shade was misting the periphery of his vision – Moon with her medieval dress and her rescue-me hair.

What did you do with information like this? What could you do but take it to the police, or try to get it raised at the inquest?

But the man to do this was Denny, the brother. At some stage, Denny – who wanted none of it – would have to be told. Lol went downstairs.

In the shop below, Denny was sitting, his back to Lol, on the last filled box. John Barleycorn was no more.

'Destroying something can be a very cleansing thing.' Denny had his hands loosely linked and he was rocking slowly on the box, his earring swaying like a pendulum: tick... tick... tick.

'You, er... you want to go for a drink?'

'Nah, not tonight, Laurence.'

'Only, you were right,' Lol said, 'about needing to talk.'

'Couldn't face it now, mate.' Denny stared out of the window. 'Anyway, you wouldn't wanner be with me tonight.' He heaved himself down from the box and grinned. 'I'll be off. You look a bit shagged-out, Laurence. Get some sleep. It'll all seem much clearer in the morning.'

'It will?'

'Maybe.' Denny looked around the skeleton shop. 'Good night, mate.' He turned in the doorway. 'Thanks.'

There was a full moon. They hadn't seen it coming because of the fog, but tonight was a flawless, icy night and the moon hung over Broad Street – and the Christmas Santas couldn't compete, Jane thought.

Hail to Thee, Lady Moon,
Whose light reflects our most secret hopes.

Her only secret hope tonight was for Mum to come through this with everything intact: her reputation, her mind...

Hail to Thee from the Abodes of Darkness.

There won't *be* any darkness, Jane thought, willing it and willing it. There *won't*.

They stood together on the green, watching people file into the Cathedral. The usual Evensong congregation, plus whatever audience the Boy Bishop ceremony pulled in with its pre-Christmas pageantry and extra choral element.

Mum had come in her long, black cloak – the winter-funeral cloak – wearing it partly because you couldn't turn up for a ceremony at the Cathedral in a ratty old waxed jacket. And partly because it was so much better for concealing—

Oh, please, no…

—the foot-long, gilt-painted, wooden cross she'd taken from Ledwardine Church, prising it out of the rood-screen with a screwdriver, then immersing its prongs in holy water.

The whole bit! The complete, crazy Van Helsing ensemble. And Merrily had no plan. If the worst happened, if there was some indication of what she called *infiltration*, she was just going to, like, walk out, holding the cross high and shouting the magic words from the Deliverance handbook.

Madness? At the very least, professional suicide. Church of England ministers did not behave like this. She would be making her entire career into this minor footnote in ecclesiastical history, right under the bit about the female priests who circle-danced around the Cathedral touching up dead bishops.

And that was what you wanted, wasn't it? You always thought it was a wasted life.

No! Uncomfortable, Jane turned away from her mother. She didn't know. She didn't know any more. She began to feel helpless and desperate. They needed help and there was none.

She looked up at the Cathedral, warm light making its windows look like the doors in an advent calendar. She was aware of the timeless *apartness* of the place, even though it was surrounded by city. She thought about its possible future as a tourist attraction, or a carpet warehouse, or something. A rush of confused emotions were creating a panic-bomb, just as a woman came towards them. She wore an expensive suede coat and a silk headscarf – Sophie Hill, the Bishop's secretary and Mum's secretary too. Sophie who, Mum explained, didn't need a secretary's job, but *did* need to be part of the Cathedral. Sophie was looking apprehensive.

'Oh, hello, Jane,' she began awkwardly.

Which was like *Goodbye, Jane*. Mum said, 'Why don't you go in, flower, and find us a discreet pew with a good view – but not too near the front.'

'Sure,' Jane said meekly. She was wearing her new blue fleece coat and a skirt. Respectable. As she slipped away, the panic-bomb began to tick.

Walking quickly down towards the Cathedral porch, when she was sure they couldn't see her, she diverted along the wall and back across the green, running from tree to tree, to the access path, and down into Church Street. Seeing this big, bald guy come out of John Barleycorn and – *Thank you, thank you, God!* – Lol Robinson behind him in the doorway.

She started waving frantically at Lol as the bald guy vanished down the alley towards High Town.

'Jane?'

He looked seriously hyped up, nervous, but grateful to see her – all of those. With the overhead Christmas greens and reds strobing in his glasses, his hands making fists, and his mouth forming unspoken words – like he was full of stories that just had to be told.

But as Jane said, 'Oh, Lol, Mum is in such deep shit,' and her tears defused the panic, reduced it to mere despair, he just listened. Listened to all the stuff about what Mum and this loopy Huw called 'the Squatter'. And about the Boy Bishop, who was the weak point, like the fuse in an electric circuit.

This was when Lol finally cut in. 'How long? How long before the Boy Bishop gets…?'

'Enthroned?'

'Yeah. How long?'

He was out in the street now, pulling the shop door closed behind him, shivering in his frayed sweat-shirt.

'I don't know. I don't know where in the service it comes. In half an hour? Maybe only ten minutes.'

She was asking him if he could get to this Dick Lyden first, and make him stop his son from going through with it, but Lol was just shaking his head, like she knew he would, and then he was pushing her away, up the street.

'Go back, Jane. Stay with her.'

'What about you?'

'I'm going to... going to do what I can.'

'You know what's going to happen, don't you? Lol, I want to come with you.'

'You can't.'

'You really *know* what's going to happen, don't you? At least, you have an idea?'

'I don't *know* anything, Jane. I just—'

'Lol...' She stumbled on the iced-up cobbles, clinging to his arm. 'Dobbs stood up against it, Dobbs put himself in the way – and he wound up as this paralysed, dribbling...'

'Dobbs was an old man in poor health.' He held her steady. 'Go back to her, Jane.'

'He was also...' Jane broke Lol's grip and spun to face him. 'He was also this really experienced exorcist. He knew all about this stuff; he'd been planning for ages. He knew exactly what he was facing, while Mum's just—'

'She wouldn't thank you for saying she was just a woman.'

'Oh, for God's sake, it's more than that.'

'Yes,' he said.

'Lol, who can we call? We can't raise Huw Owen. The Bishop's a total tosser. All those guys in dog-collars in there are just like... administrators and wardens and bursars and accountants. All this dark energy gathering, and...'

She flattened herself against a shop window as a bunch of young guys came past, hooting and sloshing lager at each other out of cans. They were lurching up the ancient medieval straight path to Hereford Cathedral – all huge and lit up like the *Titanic* – and none of them even seemed to notice it.

'Nobody really gives a shit, any more, do they?' Jane said.

49

Costume Drama

WHEN JANE REACHED the green again, Mum and Sophie were gone. Into the Cathedral, presumably. She looked behind her, hoping Lol would be there, that he'd changed his mind and would take her with him wherever he was going. But the night was hard and bright and empty; even the cackling lager crew had vanished.

She was alone now, with the frost-rimmed moon and the feeling of something happening, around and within the old rusty stones, that none of them could do a damned thing about.

She walked very slowly down to the Cathedral, hoping that something meaningful would come to her. But all she experienced was a stiffening of her face, as though the tears had frozen on her cheeks.

Should she pray?

And, if so, to whom? She reassured herself that all forms of spirituality were positive – while acknowledging that the Lady Moon looked a pitiless bitch tonight.

Jane went into the porch, and turned left through an ordinary wooden and glazed door into the body of the Cathedral. Always that small, barely audible gasp when you came out into the vaulted vastness of it. You were never sure whether it was you, or some vacuum effect carefully developed by the old gothic architects.

The organ was playing some kind of low-key religious canned music. Jane found herself on the end of a short queue of people. They were mostly middle-aged or elderly.

Which made Rowenna kind of stand out amongst them.

He remembered the last time he'd been up here at night, in the snow, with Moon beside him. *I've changed my mind. I don't want you to come in.*

What if he'd then refused to take no for an answer? What if he'd gone into the barn with her? What if he'd resisted the pushing of the darkness against him?

The pushing of the darkness? As he drove and fiddled vainly with the heater, he tried to re-experience that thin, frigid moment. There was a draught through a crack in the door, more chilling than blanketing cold outside. It felt like the slit between worlds.

He wished Denny was with him. Denny already had no love for the Purefoys – for taking advantage of Moon's fantasies so as to unload their crappy, bodged barn conversion. Incomers! Stupid gits! He needed the heat of Denny's honest rage. He needed this bloody heater to work – having run to the car without his jacket, because going back for it would have wasted crucial minutes.

Crucial minutes? Like he knew what he was going to do. Like only time might beat him: little four-eyed Lol, expsychiatric patient, shivering.

Ice under the wheels carried the Astra into the verge, the bumper clipping a fence post. Denny owned a four-wheel drive, had once done amateur rallying. But Denny wasn't here, so Lol was alone – with a little knowledge, a sackful of conjecture, and the memory of the draught through a thinly opened door.

He came to the small parking area below the Iron Age camp, and killed his headlights. There were no other vehicles there, but what did he expect – black cars parked in a circle, customized number plates all reading 666?

You know what's going to happen. Don't you?

Lol got out of the Astra and followed the familiar path. Big, muscular trees crowded him. Between them, he could see a mat of city lights – but none around him, none up here. None here since damp, smoky firelight had plumed within the cluster of thatched huts where families huddled against the dark beating of the crow-goddess's wings.

He'd never felt so cold.

Only the incense is missing, Merrily thought.

The warm colours of the soaring stone, the rolling contours of the Norman arches, the suspended corona – its daytime smiley, saw-tooth sparkle made numinous by the candles around it. And the jetting ring of red in the bottom of a giant black cast-iron stove near the main entrance.

Now a candlelight procession of choirboys singing plain-song, in Latin. One of the choirboys, the tallest of them, wore robes and a mitre, with a white-albed candle-bearer on either side.

There were about two hundred people in the congregation – not enormous, but substantial. They looked entirely ordinary, mostly over fifty, but an encouraging few in their twenties. Dress tending towards the conservative, but with few signs of the fuss and frothy hats such a service would once have produced.

Sophie sat next to Merrily, just the two of them on a rear central pew. Sophie's gloved hands were tightly clenched on her lap. What she'd said outside, her face white and pitted as the moon, had been banished to the back of Merrily's mind; not now, *not now*.

Her hands were underneath the cloak, clasped around the cross. She prayed it would never have to be revealed. She prayed that, in less than an hour's time, she and Jane would be walking out of here, relieved and laughing, to the car, where the cross would be laid thankfully on the back seat.

But where the hell *was* Jane? Not in the nave. Not *visibly* in the nave – but there were a hundred places in here to sit or stand concealed. But why do that?

Merrily studied James Lyden. He was a good-looking boy, and he clearly knew it. Could she detect an insolence, a knowing smirk, as the choirboy voices swirled and ululated around him? Perhaps not, though. It was probably James's idea of 'pious'.

And then there were two...

Here was Mick Hunter on a low wooden seat under the rim of the corona. It was not the first time she'd seen Mick in his episcopal splendour. He wore it well, like some matinée idol playing Becket. *We're all of us actors, Merrily. The Church is a faded but still fabulous costume drama.* She noticed the medieval touches, the fishtail chasuble, the primatial cross instead of the crozier; Mick was not going to be upstaged by a schoolboy. Sad, Jane would comment, wherever she was.

As the plainsong ended, the Boy Bishop turned his back on the congregation and knelt to face Mick Hunter on his throne.

Merrily's fingers tightened on the stem of the cross.

Jane had hidden in the little chantry chapel, where the stone was ridged like a seashell. She crouched where she supposed monks had once knelt to pray – though not ordinary monks; it was far too ornate. The medieval chant washed and rippled around her, so calming.

She must *not* be calm.

Rowenna stood not ten feet away, leaning against a pillar. Rowenna wearing a soft leather jacket, short black skirt, and black tights.

How would she react if Rowenna was to walk in here now?

Go for her like a cat? Go for her eyes with all ten nails?

Uh-huh, better to keep quiet and watch and listen. Whatever was going to happen here, Rowenna would be central to it. She wasn't just here to watch her boyfriend

– who would not be her boyfriend at all if he hadn't been the chosen as Boy Bishop.

And Jane suddenly remembered yesterday's lunch in Slater's, and Rowenna saying, *Listen, I have to go. Go on, ask me where. You're gonna like this... the Cathedral.* Then Jane expressing surprise because she'd understood they were going shopping, and Rowenna going, *I just forgot what day it was. I have to meet my cousin* – breaking off at this point because Lol had appeared. But it was obvious now: Rowenna would have gone with James to his dress rehearsal, so she'd know exactly...

The evil, duplicitous, carnivorous slag! Jane didn't think she'd ever hated anyone like she hated Rowenna right now.

But it was wrong to hate like this in a cathedral. It had to be wrong. She emptied her mind as the Bishop's lovely deep, velvet voice was relayed to the congregation through the speaker system. What Mum had once called his late-night DJ voice – so, like, *really* sincere.

'James, you have been chosen to serve in the office of Boy Bishop in this cathedral church. Will you be faithful and keep the promises made for you at your baptism?'

In the silence, Jane heard a small bleep quite close. It was such an un-cathedral noise that she flattened herself against the stones, and edged up to the opening and peeped out just once.

The Boy Bishop said, in a kind of dismissive drawl, 'I will, the Lord be my helper.'

Jane saw Rowenna slipping a mobile phone into a pocket of her leather jacket.

Mick Hunter said, 'The blessing of God Almighty – Father, Son and Holy Ghost – be upon you. Amen.'

Silence – as Jane held her breath.

The choir began to sing.

She relaxed. It was done. James Lyden was Boy Bishop of Hereford.

And nothing had happened.

Had it?

Amid the cold trees, below the cold moon, was a panel of light.

Lol stopped on the ice-glossed earthen steps. He thought at first it must be the farmhouse, and that he was seeing it from a different angle, seeing behind the wall of Leylandii.

But it was the barn.

The glazed-over bay was one big lantern.

Lol moved down the frozen steps and saw, behind the plate-glass wall, tall candles burning aloft on eight or ten holders of spindly wrought-iron.

A beacon! You would see it from afar, like a fire in the sky laying a flickering path towards the Cathedral tower.

It shocked him into stillness, as if the same candles had been burning on Katherine Moon's coffin. Behind their sombre shimmering, he was sure shadows were moving. All was quiet: not an owl, not a breath of wind. A bitter, still, rock-hard night.

He was scared.

Calm down, Robinson, Athena White said from somewhere. He ran from the steps to the rubble-stone barn wall and edged towards the lit-up bay. Rough reflections of the candlelight were sketched on to the ridged surface of a long frozen puddle, the remains of the pond-excavation where Moon had said she'd found the Celtic sword.

When he reached the front door, he realized it was lying open. He backed away, recalling the darkness pushing against him – the slit between worlds.

Tonight, however, the door was open, and – perhaps not only because he was so cold – the barn seemed to beckon him inside.

Merrily murmured to Sophie, 'What happens now?'

A hush as the Boy Bishop and his two candle-bearing attendants faced the high altar. Choristers were ranked either side, poised for an instant on a single shared breath.

482

As Mick Hunter walked away, smiling, the choir sailed into song, and the Boy Bishop approached the altar.

'Later,' Sophie whispered, 'the boy will lead us in prayer, and then he gives a short sermon. He'll say how important the choir's been to him, and that sort of thing. But first there'll be a kind of circular tour, taking in the North Transept.'

'The shrine?'

'I don't know quite how they're going to cope with that this time – perhaps they won't. What are you doing, Merrily?'

'I'm going to watch.' She edged out of the pew, holding the cross with one hand, gathering her cloak with the other.

'Are you cold, Merrily?'

'Yes.'

'Me too. I wonder if there's something wrong with the heating.'

The candle-led procession was leaving the chancel, drifting left to the North Transept. Merrily paused at the pew's end. She felt slightly out of breath, as if the air had become thinner. She looked at Sophie. 'Are you *really* cold, as well?'

Behind her, there was a muffled slap on the tiles.

Sophie rose. 'Oh, my God.'

Merrily turned and saw a large woman in a grey suit, half into the aisle, her fingers over her face, with blood bubbling between them and puddling on the tiles around her skittering feet.

50

Abode of Darkness

THE BARN WAS like an intimate church. Lol could sense it around him, a rich and velvety warmth. He could see the long beeswax candles, creamy stems aglow, and imagine tendrils of soft scented smoke curling to the rafters.

He stood for a moment, giving in to the deceptive luxury of heat – experiencing the enchantment of the barn as, he felt sure, Moon would have known it. Then catching his breath when the total silence gave way to an ashy sigh – the collapse of crumbling logs in the hearth with a spasm of golden splinters, the small implosion bringing a glint from a single nail protruding from the wall over the fireplace. A nail where once hung a picture of a smiling man with his Land Rover.

Which brought Lol out of it, tensing him – because another black-framed photo hung there now: of a long-haired woman in a long dress.

The candle-holders were like dead saplings, two of them framing a high-backed black chair, thronelike. And, standing beside the chair – Lol nearly screamed – was a priest in full holy vestments.

Merrily was gesturing wildly for a verger, a cleaner, anybody with a mop and bucket – people staring at her from both sides of the aisle, as though she was some shrill, house-proud harpy.

What she was seeing was the defiled altar at St Cosmas, blistered with half-dried sacrificial blood – while *this* blood was close to the centre of the Cathedral, and it was still warm and it was human blood, bright and pure, and there was so damned much of it.

The choir sang on. The Boy Bishop and his entourage were now out of sight, out of earshot, paying homage to Cantilupe in all his fragments.

She should be there, too. She should be with them in the ruins of the tomb, where the barrier was down, where Thomas Dobbs had fallen. Yet – yes, all right, *irrationally* maybe – she also had to dispose of the blood... the most magical medium for the manifestation of... what? *What?* Anyway, she couldn't be in both places, and there was no one else... absolutely nobody else.

Sophie was tending to the woman, the contents of her large handbag emptied out on the pew, the woman's head tilted back – Sophie dabbing her nose and lips with a wet pad, the woman struggling to say how sorry she was, what a time for a nosebleed to happen.

'She has them now and then,' a bulky grey-haired man was explaining in a low, embarrassed voice to nobody in particular. 'Not on this scale, I have to say. It's nerves, I suppose. It'll stop in a minute.'

Merrily said sharply, 'Nerves?'

'Oh,' he mumbled, 'mother of the Boy Bishop, all that. Stressful time all round.'

'You're Dick Lyden?'

'Yes, I am. Look, can't you leave the cleaning-up until after the service. Nobody's going to step in it.'

'That's not what I'm worried about, Mr Lyden. This is his *mother's* blood?' She was talking to herself, searching for the significance of this.

'I don't want the boy to see the fuss.' Dick Lyden pulled out a white handkerchief and began to mop his wife's splashes from his shoes. 'He's temperamental, you see.'

* * *

Someone had given James Lyden one of the votive candles from near where the shrine had stood, and he waited there while they pushed back the partition screen.

'Not how we'd like it to be,' Jane heard this big minister with the bushy beard say. 'Still, I'm sure St Thomas would understand.'

'Absolutely,' James Lyden said, like he couldn't give a toss one way or the other.

There was no sign of Rowenna.

Pressed into the side of one of the pointed arches screening off the transept, no more than six yards away from them, Jane saw it all as the bearded minister held open the partition door to the sundered tomb.

Only the minister and the Boy Bishop went up to the stones – as though it was not just stone slabs in there, but Cantilupe's mummified body. The two candle-bearing boys in white tunics waited either side of the door, like sentries. One of them, a stocky shock-haired guy, saw Jane and raised a friendly eyebrow. She'd never seen him before and pretended she hadn't noticed.

The bearded minister stood before one of the side-panels with those mutilated figures of knights on it – their faces obliterated like someone had attacked them centuries ago with a hammer and a stone-chisel, and a lot of hatred.

The minister crossed his hands over his stomach, gazed down with closed eyes. He saw nothing.

'Almighty God,' he said, 'let us this night remember Your servant, Thomas, guardian of this cathedral church, defender of the weak, healer of the sick, friend to the poor, who well understood the action of Our Lord when His disciples asked of Him: which is the greatest in the Kingdom of God and He shewed to them a child and set him in the midst of them.'

Jane saw James Lyden's full lips twist into a sour and superior sneer.

The minister said, 'Father, we ask that the humility demon-strated by Thomas Cantilupe throughout his time as bishop here might be shared this night and always by your servant James.'

'No chance,' Jane breathed grimly, and the shock-haired boy must have seen the expression on her face, because he grinned.

'It is to our shame,' the minister went on, 'that Thomas's shrine, this cathedral's most sacred jewel, should be in pieces, but we know that James will return here when it is once again whole.'

Wouldn't put money on it. This time Jane looked down at her shoes, and kept her mouth shut.

Which was more than James did when he put down his candle on a mason's bench, and bent reverently to kiss the stone. Jane reckoned he must have spent some while dredging up this disgusting, venomous wedge of thick saliva.

When his face came up smiling, she felt sick. She also felt something strange and piercingly frightening: an unmistakable awareness, in her stomach, of the nearness of evil. She gasped, because it weakened her, her legs felt numb, and she wanted to be away from here, but was not sure she could move. She felt herself sinking into the stone of the arch. She felt soiled and corrupted, not so much by what she'd seen but by what she realized it meant, and she groped for the words she'd intoned with all the sincerity of a budgie – while Mum held her hands – before the altar at Ledwardine.

Christ be with us, Christ within us.

And then the electric lights went out.

'Look, darling,' he said, 'it's Mr Robinson. You remember Mr Robinson.'

Tim Purefoy held a large glass of red wine close to the table-cloth white of his surplice.

Anna wore a simple black shift, quite low-cut. She was a beautiful woman; she threw off a sensual charge like a miasma. Like an aura, Lol supposed.

'You know,' she said, 'I thought, one day, there would be somebody. I really didn't think it would be you.'

'The brother, perhaps.' Tim lowered himself, with a grateful sigh, into the chair. 'All rage and bombast, amounting, in the end, to very little – like most of them.'

'Or the exorcist,' Anna said, 'Jane's mother. I did so want to meet her before we moved on.'

'But not this little chap here. No, indeed. Hidden depths, do you think?' A bar of pewtery moonlight cut through the high window, reaching almost to the top of Tim Purefoy's pale curls. He held up a dark bottle without a label. 'Glass of wine, old son?'

'No thanks,' Lol said tightly. 'I... seem to be interrupting something.' Everything he said seemed to emerge slowly, the way words sometimes did in dreams, as though the breath which carried them had to tunnel its way through the atmosphere.

'Not at all.' Tim Purefoy took a long, unhurried sip of wine. 'It's finished now. It's done. We're glad to have the company, aren't we, darling?'

'Done?'

'Ah, now, Mr Robinson...' Tim put down his glass then used both hands to pull the white surplice over his head, letting it fall in a heap to the flags. 'You must have some idea of what we're about, or you wouldn't be here.'

Anna Purefoy brought Lol a chair and stood in front of him until he sat down – like he was going to be executed, sacrificed. Anna looked young and fit and energized, as if she'd just had sex. She must, he thought, be about sixty, however. 'Sure you won't have a glass of wine?'

Before you die?

'Communion wine?' Lol said.

Tim Purefoy laughed. 'With a tincture of bat's blood.'

'It's our own plum wine, silly.' Anna took the bottle from her husband and held it out to Lol. 'See? You really shouldn't believe everything you read about people like us.'

Lol remembered her patting floury hands on her apron. *One can buy a marvellous loaf at any one of a half-dozen places in town, but one somehow feels obliged, living in a house this old.*

He was almost disarmed by the ordinariness of it, the civility, the domesticity: candles like these, in holders like these, available in all good branches of Habitat. He blinked and forced himself to remember Katherine Moon congealing in her bath of blood – glancing across towards the bathroom door, holding the image of the dead, grinning Moon pickled like red cabbage. In *that* room over there, beyond *those stairs*. Behind *that door*.

Visualization, Athena White had said. *Willpower*.

'Thank you.' Lol accepted the stoppered wine bottle from Anna. He held it up for a moment before grasping it by the neck and smashing it into the stone fireplace. He felt the sting of glass-shards as the fire hissed in rage. Rivers of wine and blood ran down his wrist. And down over the hanging photograph of Moon.

'Now, tell me what you did to her,' Lol whispered.

The choir faded into trails of unconducted melody.

'Please remain in your seats.' The Bishop's voice, crisply from the speakers. 'We appear to have a power failure, but we're doing all we—' And then the PA system cut out.

Merrily spotted Mick in his mitre, by candlelight amid jumping shadows, before the candles began to go out, one by one, the air laden with the odour of cooling wax, until there was only the oval of light on the corona, like a Catherine wheel over the central altar – the last holy outpost.

She pulled the cross from under her cloak, standing close to the pool of blood on the tiles, though she couldn't see it now. A baby began to cry.

She looked across the aisle and the pews, towards the main door, to where the big black stove should have been jetting red, and saw nothing. The stove was out, too. The Cathedral gone dark – gone cold.

'*Jesus,*' – Merrily feeling the fear like a ball of lead in her solar plexus – '*may all that is You flow into me.*'

'James?' the bearded minister called out. 'Are you there?'

Jane stepped out from the archway and heard the swish of heavy robes as the Boy Bishop brushed past her in the dark. The candles held by the two attendants, the sentries, were also out. Only one small flame glowed – the two-inch votive candle given to James Lyden, now lying on the mason's bench. Jane ran and snatched it up, hid the flame behind her hand, and moved out into the transept, listening for the swish of the robes.

Lyden was going somewhere, being taken somewhere, escorted.

She heard him again – his voice this time. '*Yeah, OK.*' She followed quietly, though maybe not quietly enough, wishing she had her trainers on instead of her stupid best shoes.

She could see him now – a black, mitred silhouette against the wan light from the huge diamond-paned gothic windows in the nave.

Moonlight. Shadows of people, unmoving. Jane heard anxious whispers and a baby's cry mingling into a vast soup of echoes. Where was Mum? Where was Mum with the cross? Why wasn't she rushing for the pulpit, because, Christ, if there was a time for an exorcism, a time for the soul police to make like an armed response unit, this was it.

She could no longer see the mitred silhouette. Where had he gone, the sneering bastard who'd spat on the saint's tomb, and brought darkness? Although, of course, she knew it hadn't really happened like that. Somebody had hit a big fusebox somewhere. It was all coincidence, theatrics.

Jane stumbled, stepped into space, groping for stone, nearly dropping her stub of a candle. Hearing quick footsteps receding ahead of her.

Steps. Stone steps going down.

The crypt? The Boy Bishop was going into the crypt.

Jane had never been down there, although it was open to visitors. Mum had seen it. Mum said it was no big deal. No, there weren't stacks of old coffins, nothing like that. Tombs at one end, effigies, but not as many as you might expect. It was just a bare stone cellar really, and not as big as you'd imagine.

Jane stayed where she was at the top of the steps.

Afraid, actually.

Admit it: afraid of being down there with Rowenna's creepy boyfriend in his medieval robes, afraid of what slimeball stuff she might see him doing. The guy was a shit. Just like Danny Gittoes had broken into Ledwardine Church for Rowenna, James Lyden had spat on the tomb of the saint for her. Another sex-slave to Rowenna, who in turn was a friend of Angela. How long had Rowenna known Angela?

Aware of this long slime-trail of evil unravelling before her, Jane edged down two steps, listening hard.

Nothing.

She raised the stub of votive candle in its little metal holder. Perhaps she held the light of St Thomas, the guardian.

Could she believe that?

What did it matter? Jane shrugged helplessly to herself and went down into the crypt.

51

Sacrilege

'BLOOD,' LOL SAID. 'I've been learning all about blood.'

Feeling – God help him – the energy of it.

It had been the right thing to do. Another couple of minutes and the Purefoys would have had him apologizing for disturbing their religious observance.

Tim scowled. 'Mr Robinson, there are several ways we could react to your outburst of juvenile violence. The simplest would be to call the police.'

'Do it,' Lol said.

'If you think we would have any explaining to do,' Anna said, 'you're quite wrong. We have an interest in ritual magic. It's entirely legal.'

'I am an ordained priest of God,' Tim said. 'My God is the God of Abraham and Moses and Solomon, the God who rewards knowledge and learning; the God who shows us strength, who accepts that plague and pestilence have their roles…'

'Stop dressing it up.'

'… the God to whom Satan was a – an albeit occasionally troublesome – serving angel. Calling me a Satanist, as I suspect you were about to do, is therefore, something of an insult. For which' – Tim Purefoy waved a hand – 'I excuse you, because it was said in ignorance.'

'We were both brought up in the Christian tradition,' Anna interrupted. 'It took us a while to realize that Christianity was

493

introduced primarily as a constraint on human potential, which has to be removed if we are to survive and progress.'

'Let's say it's simply run its course,' Tim added, with the fervour of the converted. 'The Church has no energy left; it's riddled with greed and corruption. In this country alone, it's sitting on billions of pounds which could be put to more sensible use.'

'Even if we didn't lift a finger, it would destroy itself within the next fifty years. But the signs are there in the sky – too many to be ignored. We cannot ignore *signs*.'

'The signs are what brought us here to Hereford,' Tim said. 'But I don't think you want to know about that. I think you want to know about the death of Katherine Moon. I think you're here for reassurance that there was nothing you could have done to save her, am I right?'

'And we're happy to give you that.' Anna smiled and reached across the firelight for his bloodied hand. Her fingers were slim and cool.

George Curtiss had taken charge, talking to vergers, organizing people by sporadic candlelight, shouting from the pulpit, explaining.

As though he could.

Merrily noticed that candles had to be repeatedly relit; it was like last night, when she and Huw were at the saint's tomb. She stumbled past the central altar – only three candles left alight on the corona – looking around for Jane and the Bishop.

She found Mick Hunter eventually in the deep seclusion of his throne beyond the choir-stalls. The throne was of dark oak, many pinnacled, itself a miniature cathedral. He came out to join her, having removed the mitre. His sigh was like an audible scowl.

'Merrily, of all the people I could do without in this situation...'

'You really… really have to let me do it, Mick.' Keeping her voice low and steady. 'You can look away, you can grit your teeth – but you have to let me do it.'

'Do it?'

'You know exactly what I mean. You've got darkness and cold and spilt blood in your Cathedral. What you must do now is wind up the service, get the congregation out of here, lock the doors, and just… just let me do it.'

He stared down at her and, although it was too dark to see his face, she sensed his dismay and disbelief.

'All right,' she said, 'why don't you ask God? Why don't you go and kneel down quietly in front of your high altar and ask Him? Ask Him if He's happy about this?'

The Bishop didn't move. There were just the two of them here in the holiest place. She dropped the wooden cross and bent to pick it up.

'I made a mistake, didn't I?' Mick Hunter said. 'I made a big mistake with you.'

She straightened up. 'Looks like you did.'

'Do you remember what I said to you last night when you asked me if I wanted your resignation from the post of Deliverance Consultant?'

'You told me to get a good night's sleep and forget about it.'

'And?'

'I couldn't sleep.'

'Very well,' he said. 'Put it in writing for me tomorrow.'

'Mick—'

'Bishop,' he said, 'I think.'

Jane heard him breathing, so she knew roughly where he was – like, somewhere in the crypt, because the breathing filled the whole, intimidating blackness of it. She had her coat open and the candle cupped in her hand inside. She caught a finger in the flame and nearly yelped.

Christ be with me, she heard inside her head. In Mum's voice. *Mum be with me* – that might be more use!

Just words, like a mantra – words to repeat and hold on to, to try and shout down your fear, like those poor, doomed soldiers in the First World War singing in the trenches. *Christ within me.*

She walked towards the sound of breathing, which came quicker now, with a snorting and a snuffling. Gross. What *was* this? Maybe she should get back up the steps and shout for help. But there was a power cut; and by the time she could get someone with a lamp down here, it would be over, whatever it was. Like she couldn't guess.

She shouted, 'Freeze!'

Bringing the candle out from under her coat, she held it as high as she could reach.

A hundred quaking shadows broke out over the crypt, and James Lyden's eyes opened wide in shock, his mouth agape.

'Oh!' Jane recoiled in disgust.

There he was, the Boy Bishop, with one gaitered leg on a long-dead woman's stone face. His chasuble was tented over Rowenna, now emerging – who for just a moment looked so gratifyingly ridiculous on her knees that Jane laughed out loud.

'You total slimeballs!'

But she was nervous, realizing this wasn't just some irreverent stunt – the Boy Bishop in full regalia, except presumably for his underpants. This was an act of deliberate sacrilege. It was meant to have an unholy resonance.

Get out of here!

Jane turned and made a dash for the steps.

But crashed into a wall. In the dark you quickly lost any sense of direction.

When she turned back, Rowenna was already between her and the steps leading out. Suddenly James's arms encircled her from behind, his breath pumping against her neck.

Jane screamed.

Rowenna was easing the candle from between her fingers.

'Oh, kitten,' she said thickly. 'Oh, kitten, what *are* we going to do with you now?'

Jane glared at her with open hostility. 'Does our friend here know you do the same with Danny Gittoes?'

Holding the candle steady, between their two faces, Rowenna looked untroubled.

Jane said, 'Does he know about those clergymen in Salisbury?'

Rowenna shook her head sadly.

'I now know everything about you,' Jane continued. 'I know exactly what you are.'

Rowenna smiled sympathetically. 'You're not really getting any of this, are you? What *I* am is a woman, while *you* are still very much a child.'

Jane glared at her in silent fury, as Rowenna just shook her head. Looking at her now, you detected the kind of lazy arrogance in her eyes that you hadn't picked up on before – and the coldness.

'You must realize we were only friends because someone wanted your mother monitored, yeah?'

'Who?'

'And that sort of thing is how I make a bit of money sometimes.'

'Someone at the Pod? Angela? You set me up for Angela, didn't you?'

Annoyance contorted Rowenna's small mouth. 'Oh, please. I was ahead of where the Pod are *years* ago. Though it was quite touching to think of you standing at the window in your little nightie, solemnly saluting the sun and moon, and thinking you were plugged into the Ancient Wisdom.'

'You bitch—'

'Pity it all went wrong, though. I could have really shown you things that would've blown you away.'

'Oh, you're just so full of shit, Rowenna. I—'

Rowenna suddenly slapped Jane's face, knocking her head back into James's chest. 'Don't push your luck with me any more. Given time, I could really do things to you. I could make you totally fucking *crazy*.'

Jane felt James Lyden's breath hot on her neck, and struggled vainly. 'You're even fooling yourself.'

'You don't know anything.' Rowenna held the candle very close to Jane's face, so that she could feel its heat. 'Remember that suit? The greasy old suit I had Danny hide in the vestry?'

'Yeah, who told you to do that?'

'*Nobody* told me. I don't take anyone's orders... unless I want to.' Rowenna wore a really sickly, incense-smelling scent that seemed to fill up the entire crypt. 'I just couldn't resist it after you'd told me how Denzil Joy had so badly scared your mother. I thought that would be really interesting – to see if I could make him *stick* to her.'

'What?'

Rowenna put her face very close to Jane's and *breathed* the words into her. For the first time, Jane knew what it meant to have one's skin crawl.

'I found his widow's name in the phone book, so I sent James round to collect any old clothes for charity. And next I got into *her*: the Reverend Merrily Watkins. I nicked some of her cigarettes when I was at the vicarage, and I smoked them slowly and visualized, and I did a few other things and... OK, maybe I asked for a little assistance. It's amazing what help you can get when you're working on the clergy – on the enemy. And it worked, didn't it? It really made her sweat; it made her ill. You told me she was ill. And I bet she didn't tell you the half of it.'

Jane felt sick. She must be lying. She *couldn't* have done all that.

'You're... just *evil*.'

'I'm special, kitten. I'm *very* special.' Rowenna moved away.

'No, you're not. You're just... maybe you *are* a lot older than me. You're, like, old before your time – old and corrupted.'

'Right.' Rowenna stepped away from her. 'That's it. James?'

James answered, 'Yes?' in this really subservient way.

'Hit her for me, would you? Hit her hard.'

James said, 'What?'

'*Hit* the little cunt!'

'No!' Jane turned and hurled herself against him. Turned in his arms and pushed out at his face.

Which made him angry, and he let go for an instant, and then he punched her hard in the mouth. And then Rowenna's hand came at her like a claw, grabbed a handful of her hair and pulled her forward. Jane felt a crippling pain in the stomach and doubled up in agony. Another wrench at her hair pulled her upright, so James could hit her again in the face – enjoying it now, excited.

'Yes,' Rowenna hissed. '*Yes!*'

As Jane's legs gave way, and the stone floor rushed up towards her.

Perhaps she passed out then. For a moment, at least, she forgot where she was.

'We can't!' she heard from somewhere in the distance.

'Go on, do it!'

Rowenna? Jane heard Rowenna's voice again from yesterday. *Death can also just mean the end of something before a new beginning.* She saw Rowenna pointing her knife across the table... *Lord Satan, take me!...* the Tower struck by lightning, people falling out of the crack... a long way down, on to the hard, cold stone floor.

Jane felt very afraid. *Must get up.* She opened her eyes once and saw, in a lick of light, another face right under her own, with dead stone eyelids.

They'd laid her out on one of the effigies.

She tried to lift her head from that stone face. But she couldn't, felt too heavy, as if all the stones of St Thomas's tomb were piled on top of her. Then the candlelight went away, as they pushed her further down against the stone surface. She felt stone lips directly under hers.

'Never go off on your own with an exposed flame,' Rowenna said. 'It's bad news, kitten. Night-night then.'

A stunning pain on the back of her head and neck.

Time passed. No more voices.

Only smoke.

Smoke in her throat. Her head was full of smoke – and words. And Mum whispering…

Let me not run from the love that You offer
But hold me safe from the forces of evil.

But Mum was not here. It was just a mantra in her head.

'Thank God for that,' George Curtiss grunted from the pulpit, as the lights came back on.

There was laughter now in the nave – half nervous, half relieved – as George's words were picked up by the suddenly resensitized microphone.

'Well, ah… we don't know what caused this, but it was most unfortunate, very ill timed. However, at least, ah… at least it demonstrates to our Boy Bishop that the life of a clergyman is not without incident.'

The Boy Bishop stood, head bowed, beneath the edge of the corona, in front of the central altar itself. Mick Hunter stood behind him, one hand on the boy's shoulder.

'We'd like to thank you all for being so patient. I realize some of you do need to get home…'

Merrily stood in the aisle, near the back of the nave, looking around for Jane, and very worried now. *This is all that matters, isn't it? This is all there is.*

Something was wrong. Something else was wrong. The power seemed to be restored, but there was something missing. A dullness lingered – a number of bulbs failing to re-function, perhaps. The round spotlights in the lofty, vaulted ceiling appeared isolated, like soulless security lamps around an industrial compound.

'It's been suggested,' George said, 'that we now carry on with the ceremony, with the prayers and the Boy Bishop's sermon, but omit the final hymn. So, ah... thank you.'

And no warmth either. The warm lustre had gone from the stones; they had a grey tinge like mould, their myriad colours no longer separated.

George Curtiss stepped down.

An air of dereliction, abandonment, deadness – as though something had entered under the cover of darkness, and something else had been taken away.

Dear God, don't say that.

Under her cloak, the cross drooped from Merrily's fingers, as the choir began – a little uncertainly, it sounded – with a reprise of the plainsong which had opened the proceedings.

Sophie had appeared at her side. 'What happened?'

'Sophie, have you seen Jane?'

'I'm sorry, no. Merrily, what did Michael say to you?'

'Basically he sacked me.'

'But he can't just—'

'He can.'

She looked for the puddle of blood left by Mrs Lyden's nose-bleed. It was hardly visible, carried off on many shoes into the darkness outside.

'Don't give in, Merrily.' Sophie said. 'You mustn't give in.'

'What can I do?'

Mick had melted away into the shadows. James Lyden, Bishop of Hereford, was alone, sitting on his backless chair, notes in hand, waiting for the choir to finish.

'I don't like that boy,' Sophie said.

The choristers ended their plainsong with a raggedness and a disharmony so slight that it was all the more unsettling. The sound of scared choirboys? By contrast, James Lyden's voice was almost shockingly clear and precise and confident: a natural orator.

'A short while ago, when I took my vows, the Lord Bishop asked me if I would be faithful and keep the promises made for me at my baptism.'

'You must stop him,' Sophie murmured.

'I can't. Suppose it... Suppose there's nothing.'

'Of course,' James said, 'I don't *remember* my baptism. It was a long time ago and it was in London, where I was born. I had no choice then, and the promises were made *for* me because I could not speak for myself.'

Sophie gripped her arm. '*Please.*'

'But now I *can.*' James looked up. Even from here, you could see how bright his eyes were. Drug-bright? 'Now I can speak for myself.'

'Don't let him. Stop him, Merrily – or I'll do it myself.'

'All right.' Merrily brought out the cross. It didn't matter now what anyone thought of her. Or how the Bishop might react, because he already had. The worst that could happen...

No, the best – the best that could happen!

... was that she'd make a complete fool of herself and never be able to show her face in Hereford again. Or in Ledwardine either.

Untying the cloak at her neck, she began to walk up the aisle towards James Lyden.

As James noticed her, his lips twisted in a kind of excitement. She kept on walking. The backs of her legs felt weak. *Just keep going. Stay in motion or freeze for ever.*

Members of the remaining congregation were now turning to look at her. There were whispers and mutterings. She kept staring only at James Lyden.

Who stood up, in all his majesty.

Whose voice was raised and hardened.

Who said, 'But, as we have all seen tonight, there is one who speaks more... eloquently... than I. And his name... his name is...'

'*No!*'

Merrily let the cloak fall from her shoulders, brought up the wooden cross, and walked straight towards the Boy Bishop, her gaze focused on those fixed, shining, infested eyes below the mitre.

52

A Small Brilliance

LOL WAS SEEING himself with Moon down below the ramparts of Dinedor Camp. They were burying the crow, one of his hands still sticky with blood and slime… for him, the first stain on the idyll. He saw Moon turning away, her shoulders trembling – something reawoken in her.

'Did you ever watch her charm a crow?' Anna Purefoy asked. 'It might be in a tree as much as fifty, a hundred yards away, and she would cup her hands and make a cawing noise in the back of her throat. And the crow would leave its tree, like a speck of black dust, and come to her. I don't think she quite knew what she was doing – or was even aware that she was going to do it until it began to happen.'

It fell dead at my feet. Out of the sky. Isn't that incredible?

'It was simply something she could always do,' Tim added. 'Further proof that she was very special.'

Lol glanced at the red-stained photograph of Moon over the fireplace. Not one he'd seen before; they must have taken it themselves. Athena White had told him how they would use photographs, memorabilia of a dead person as an aid to visualization.

He turned back to the Purefoys. 'Why don't you both sit down.' He didn't trust them. He imagined Anna Purefoy suddenly striking like a cobra.

'As you wish.' She slipped into one of the cane chairs. Tim hesitated and then lowered himself into the high-backed wooden throne.

'After she was dead,' Lol said, 'you left out that cutting from the *Hereford Times*, like a suicide note. She'd probably never even seen it, had she?'

'It doesn't matter.' Tim yawned. 'That's a trivial detail.'

Lol made himself sit in the other cane chair, keeping about ten feet between himself and them.

'How did you kill her?'

'Oh, really!' Anna leaned forward in the firelight, a dark shadow suddenly spearing between her breasts.

'Darling—'

'No, I won't have this, Tim. Murder is a crime. We did not kill Katherine. We showed her the path she was destined to find, and she took it – according to the values of the Celtic ethos. We talked for hours and hours with Katherine. She could never relate to this era – this commercial, secular world, this erratic world, this panicking period in history. She knew she didn't want to *be* here, and she was looking for a way *back*.'

'Bollocks,' Lol said, although he realized it wasn't.

'And anyway,' Anna said, 'to the Iron Age Celt, death is merely a short, shadowy passage, to be entered boldly in the utter and total certainty of an afterlife. A Celtic human sacrifice was often a *willing* sacrifice. Katherine always knew she wouldn't enjoy a long life – I showed her that in the cards, though she didn't need me to – and therefore she was able to give what remained of it a purpose.'

'We helped her return to the bosom of her tradition,' Tim said comfortably.

'It was very beautiful,' Anna said softly. 'There was snow all around, but the bathroom was warm. We helped her put candles around the bath. She was naked and warm and smiling.'

'No!' Lol said.

But he saw again Moon's thin arms gleaming pale gold, lit by the four tall church candles, one at each corner of the white bathtub. Her teeth were bared. Her hands – something black and knobbled across Moon's open hands.

'But you didn't give her an afterlife, did you?'

He saw those sharp little teeth bared in excitement, Moon panting in the sprinkling light: energized, euphoric, slashing, gouging. And then lying back at peace, relieved to feel her life-blood jetting from opened veins.

The tragedy and the horror of it made him pant with emotion. The Purefoys had done this, as surely as if they'd waylaid her like a ripper in a country lane. But it was actually worse than that…

Hands sweating on the edge of the chair seat, he flung at them what Athena White had explained to him.

'If a sacrifice is swift, the spirit is believed to progress immediately to a… better place. But if the death is protracted, the magician has time to bind the spirit to his will, so that it remains earthbound and subject to the commands of—'

'Oh, really' – Tim half rose – 'what nonsense…'

'It might well be,' Lol said, 'but *you* don't think it is. You think you still have her… and through her an access to her ancestors and to the whole pre-Christian, pagan Celtic tradition.'

He sprang up. He was sure Moon's image there on the wall was shining not with the candlelight, nor the moonlight, but with a sad grey light of its own.

'You just prey on inadequates and sick people like Moon, and attract little psychos like Rowenna and other people desperate for an identity and—'

'People like you,' Anna said gently.

'No.' He backed away, as she arose.

'Katherine told us about you, Laurence. She said you would often make her feel better because you were so insecure yourself, and had a history of mental instability.'

507

'That was a long time ago.'

Tim laughed. Anna held out her hands to Lol. Her face, in the mellow light, was beautiful and looked so exquisitely kind.

'It wasn't *such* a long time ago. And it doesn't go away, does it, Laurence? It's part of you. You have no certainty of anything, and you're drawn to people who do have.'

He stared into the explicit kindness of her, searching for the acid he knew had to be there, because this was the black siren, the woman who had moulded Moon into her own fatal fantasy and would have taken Jane too – to use as well.

Anna smiled with compassion, and he knew that if he let her touch him his resistance would be burned away.

She said softly, 'Laurence, think about this. What sent you to Katherine? Why did you come here tonight?'

Lol closed his eyes for just a moment. At once he saw a small, slim dark woman in black, with eyes that had to laugh at the nonsense of it all. He blinked furiously to send her away; this was no place for—

'Ah.' Anna was shaking her head, half amused – an infants' school headmistress with a silly child who would never learn. 'Why are you… why *are* you so obsessed with the little woman priest?'

'You can only…' His mind rebelled. Up against the far wall, facing this smiling Anna and the candles in the barn bay, he refused to be shocked, refused to believe she'd pulled the image of Merrily from his head. 'You can only think in terms of obsession, can't you? Love doesn't mean a thing.'

There were suddenly two bright orbs in the air.

'Love,' Tim Purefoy said, 'is the pretty lie we use to justify and glorify our lust. And the feeble term used in Christian theology to dignify weakness and sentiment.'

Both Purefoys were gazing with placid candour at Lol, as the bright orbs exploded, and Lol's ears were filled with roaring and the night went white.

* * *

A shadow fell across Merrily as she walked towards the altar with the cross in her hands.

The old priest stood next to her in the aisle. He wore a black cassock, stained, plucked and holed. He looked very ill, pale beyond pale. She had no idea how he came to be here – only why. His eyes looked directly into hers. His eyes were like crystals in an eroded cliff–face. They carried no apology. There was a bubble of spit in a corner of his mouth.

He held out a hand ridged and gnarled as a shrivelled parsnip.

Jesus Christ was the first exorcist – letters on a white page.

And Huw Owen on a mountainside in Wales. *I don't want stuff letting in. A lot of bad energy's crowding the portals. I want to keep all the doors locked and the chains up.*

Merrily nodded.

She put the cross into Thomas Dobbs's hand and stepped aside, with her back to a pew-end.

Jesus Christ was the first exorcist.

The Boy Bishop stood up, letting his notes flutter to the tiles. He held his crozier at arm's length, like a spear. His two candle-bearers had melted away, but Mick Hunter still stood a few paces behind him. Merrily saw a series of expressions blurring James's face. She thought of Francis Bacon's popes.

She thought that James's face was not now his own.

The Cathedral had filled with a huge and hungry hush.

Thomas Dobbs stopped about ten feet short of the boy – under the jagged halo of the corona. When he spoke, his voice was slurred and growly, dense with phlegm and bile, and the words tumbled out of him, unstoppable, like a rockslide.

'IN THE NAME OF... OF THE LIVING GOD, I CALL... I CALL YOU *OUT*!

'IN... NAME OF... GOD OF ALL CREATION...

'... NAME OF HIS SON JES... JESUS CHRIST... I CALL YOU *OUT*...

'I CALL YOU OUT AND...

'*BANISH YOU.*'

509

Merrily watched his pocked monument of a face, only one side of it working. She could almost feel the strength leaving his body, the despair at the heart of his struggle against his own weakness.

The Boy Bishop let his crozier fall, and ran down the aisle. Merrily saw Dick Lyden squeezing out of his pew, striding after his son. Where the boy had stood, she saw the slightly unclear figure of a slim woman in a long dress, with hair down to her waist, like dark folded wings, and then – as though Merrily had blinked – the woman was no longer there. She saw Dobbs clench his teeth so hard she felt they were going to split and fragment, and she saw his arm winching stiffly upward like a girder, pointing.

'DEVIL... UNCLEAN SPIR... IT!'

No more than a harsh rasp this time, and then he turned away, stumbling, and he and Merrily came face to face.

He put up a hand to her.

She didn't move. She didn't speak. There was nothing to say. She had no tradition.

Slowly, she bowed her head.

Felt the heat of his hand a second before his fingers touched her cheek.

Merrily looked up then, and saw in his old, knowing eyes, a small brilliance, before he died.

53

Silly Woman

LOL GAZED INTO Anna Purefoy's pale eyes. There was no obvious expression in them: no fear, no alarm. Only perhaps the beginning of surprise, or was he imagining that?

There was dust in her fine, fair hair.

No blood at all – Anna's neck was simply broken. It wasn't obvious exactly what had done that, but it wasn't important, was it? Not important now.

He didn't touch her. He just stood up. Strangely, although part of the loft had come down, six of the ten candles were still alight. No shadows, other than his own, appeared to be moving.

He couldn't look for very long at Tim Purefoy, who was, mostly, still in his chair, the chair itself crushed into the stairs. The black bull-bars had torn Tim almost in half. One of his legs was...

God! Lol turned away, towards the car. The smell from Tim's body was hot and foul, and there was still running blood and what might be intestine over the windscreen of the Mitsubishi Intercooler Super-Turbo-whatever the hell it was called.

And something else, half across the roof, which he thought was Moon's futon fallen from the toppled loft. Making it impossible to see inside the vehicle. The steaming silence, though, was ominous.

Also, the old oak pillar. Nothing but old oak or steel would have stopped the bull-barred Mitsubishi. It had torn down the glazed bay like cellophane, exploded the urbane Tim Purefoy like a rotten melon. But the pillar had held.

He couldn't make himself go past Tim; he didn't want to know the details. Instead he squeezed around the back, stepping over the smashed pieces of the chair he'd been sitting in a few minutes ago. If he hadn't finally lost it… if Anna Purefoy hadn't pursued him, gleefully taunting him with her knowledge of his obsession for 'the little woman priest'… he would have been the first to be hit.

When he reached the other side of the car, he found the driver's window wound down. Right down – as if that was how it had been when the Mitsubishi rammed the glass-covered bay. As though the driver had needed to hear the impact – and the screams.

But there had been no screams audible above the engine's roar and the sounds of destruction. All too fast, too explosively unexpected.

Denny smiled out at him. 'Bodged job, eh? I always said it was a… bodged job. They never meant to… turn it into holiday 'commodation. Never planned to renovate it, till… till Kathy showed up. Dead, are they?'

'Mm,' Lol said.

'But *you're* all right. I never… I never thought you'd be here. I thought you were a…' Denny laughed out some blood. '… a bit of a nancy, if I'm honest. No… no… you stay there. Don't fucking look down here, man. Not having you throwing up on my motor.'

'Shut up now,' Lol said. 'I'll have an ambulance here as soon as I can find the bloody phone.'

'I think on the table – bottom of the stairs. Be part of my fucking sump now.'

Lol tried the driver's door. 'Don't be stupid, mate,' Denny said. 'You open that, I'll just fall out in several pieces. An Iron Age Celt dies in his chariot. I tell you about my dream? A mystic now, man – finally a fucking mystic.'

Lol saw that Denny's earring was gone. Or maybe the ear itself.

'You're so… indiscreet, Lol. That's your problem. You don't trust yourself – always got to tell somebody.'

Lol sighed. 'The extension. You heard me leaving that message for Merrily.'

'Been eavesdropping on your calls for weeks, Laurence. Needed to hear what you were saying to Lyden – about Kathy. Could never figure why you weren't all over Kathy. She attractive, this vicar?'

'Listen,' Lol said. 'I'm going over to the farm. I'll have to break in and use their phone.'

'If that makes you feel better. But if I've gone to the ancestors, time you get back…'

'I'll be less than five minutes. I'll smash a window in the kitchen.'

'Got a lot to say to those primitive fuckers,' Denny muttered. 'To the ancestors.'

'Don't go away,' Lol said.

'No. Cold in here, en't it? Must be the extra ventilation.'

Denny laughed his ruined laugh.

Headlights and warblers. *Déjà vu*. The ambulance cutting across the green again, directly to the north porch. A police car behind the ambulance. Behind that, a plain Rover: Howe.

'Later, Annie,' Merrily said, 'please? Is that all right? I need to see that Jane's…'

'Just don't go off anywhere,' Howe said.

'No further than the hospital.'

'No,' Jane protested, sitting up in the back of the ambulance, a paramedic hanging on to her arm. 'You're not coming. *I'm* not going. This is ridiculous. It's just like… mild concussion.'

'Could be a hairline fracture, Jane,' the paramedic warned.

'No way. This guy's just blowing it up on account of having his hands all over me.'

'I had my hands all over you,' the boy in white said patiently, 'because you were on fire.'

'Sure,' Jane said. Some of her hair was singed, and she had quite a deep cut on her forehead and bruising on the left side of her jaw and under her left eye. 'And, like, if you're wearing a dress and your name's Irene, you think nobody's going to suspect anything.'

'Eirion,' the boy said. There were black smuts all over his hands and his white alb.

'Whatever.'

'I'll be here for quite a while,' Annie Howe told Merrily. 'We have to talk in depth, Ms Watkins.' She pulled Eirion away from the ambulance. 'I think you need to tell me how she got on fire.'

'She was down in the crypt – with a candle. She said she must have tripped, but...' He hesitated. 'There was nobody else there when I got to her, OK? But she was face-down and her coat was on fire and... I really think you need to talk to James Lyden.'

'Who's he?'

'The Boy Bishop. His parents were looking for him. They've probably taken him home. They live in one of those Edwardian houses in Barton Street. And you need to talk to his girlfriend.'

'Oh, yes,' Merrily said, 'I think you definitely want to talk to James's girlfriend.'

'Name?'

'Melissa,' Eirion said. 'But she seems to have gone.'

Merrily said, 'Melissa?'

'I don't know her other name. James told me she lives with her foster-parents on a farm up on Dinedor Hill. He knows where it is – he's been up there a couple of times.'

'Jesus Christ,' Merrily said.

She went into the Cathedral and stayed away from everyone, even Sophie. Especially from Sophie – she mustn't be involved.

Merrily saw that there was a blanket over the body of Thomas Dobbs, and two uniformed policeman guarding it. The nave had a secular feel, like some huge market hall. Spiritual work to be done, here – but by whom?

Jane had absolutely refused to let Merrily go with her to the hospital, but in the end she had accepted Eirion's company. Merrily smiled faintly. The boy must have masochistic tendencies.

Across the nave, over by Bishop Stanbury's ornate chantry, she saw Huw Owen pacing about, hands deep in the pockets of his RAF greatcoat. She hadn't spoken to him yet, although George Curtiss had told her it had been Huw who'd brought Dobbs along, after helping him sign himself out of the General Hospital.

Dobbs's last stand. Where was the *squatter* now? Should James Lyden be exorcized, or merely counselled by his father? Where would they go from here? Who would work from the office with ☧ on the door? Not a woman, that was for sure.

A hand on her shoulder, but she didn't turn round. She knew his smell: light sweat, sex.

'A busy day, Merrily.'

'Indeed, Bishop.'

'Were you looking for me?'

'I don't know. Perhaps.'

He came round to face her. He'd changed into his jogging gear. His thick brown hair looked damp with sweat.

'I have to run sometimes, to clear it all away. It's very calming. I run through the streets and nobody knows who I am.'

'Oh, I think they do, Bishop. They've all seen your picture, running. But you can only run so far, can't you?'

Mick didn't smile. 'Let's go for a walk, shall we?'

'All right.'

She followed him out of the south door, towards the cloisters, along a narrow, flagged floor, dim and intimate. She'd left her cloak in the Cathedral and felt cold in her jumper and skirt, but was determined not to show it.

'This farce will be in the papers,' he said.

'*Something* will be in the papers.'

'What does that mean?'

'I imagine you're excellent at news management.'

'Said in a somewhat derogatory way.'

'Oh no,' she said. 'I'm impressed.'

'No, you aren't. You think I'm just an ambitious adminis-trator, with few spiritual qualities.'

'If any,' Merrily agreed. *What the hell.* Jane was going to be all right, Huw was there in the Cathedral. *What the hell!*

The Bishop leaned against a door to his left, and the cold bit hard. They were almost outside.

This was the tourist part of the Cathedral – in summer, anyway. A stone-walled courtyard, a snackbar, steps and benches and tables. The Bishop held open the door for her and followed her out, pulling the door shut behind them. They were on a raised stone path bordered by flowerbeds and evergreen shrubs. There was a circular lawn with a dead fountain in the middle, a picturesquely ruined wall behind it, overhung by decorative trees and vines. Idyllic in summer: you could be miles from the city.

Deserted now under the icy moon.

'You,' Mick Hunter said mildly, 'are an unbelievable little bitch – an incredible cock-teaser.'

'Uh-huh.' Merrily shook her head, moving back to the door. 'This is not what I wanted to talk about.'

The Bishop placed himself in front of the door, shaking his head slowly. 'All right, what *do* you want to talk about?'

'Dobbs?'

'You want me to express regret? Very well, I regret it.'

Merrily folded her arms against the cold. There was no deli-cate way to put this. 'When Canon Dobbs was dying, he put out his arm and he pointed, and he managed to say, "Devil...

unclean spirit." And everyone thought he was pointing at James Lyden. But I saw he was pointing at someone standing just to the left of James – in the shadows for once.'

Hunter didn't deny it. 'Does it surprise you that he hated me?'

'Under the circumstances, hardly. When you arrived, he was an old man in bad health. He was due to retire at any time, but *you* pushed him out. When he wouldn't resign voluntarily, you chose to humiliate him. Thus antagonizing the Dean and the Chapter and countless other people – people who really counted.'

'One can't be sentimental about these things.'

'This wasn't pragmatism, Bishop. This was lunacy. When you told me last night that you'd been advised against appointing a female Deliverance consultant, it didn't strike me at the time, but later I thought, that's not the kind of thing he does. He's a politician. He might appoint me later, when he's proved himself, but not… I mean, I bet the people who advised you against it were those people whose support you really needed.'

He said nothing.

'It had never really made obvious sense, but I thought – and Sophie often said – that you were young and radical and a bit reckless. But you're also clever and cautious. You never put a foot wrong. How would some hot-headed revolutionary *ever* make bishop under the age of forty-five? How could he ever make bishop at all?'

'Merrily,' he said. 'Did it ever occur to you that I simply fancied the hell out of you?'

'God forgive me, it did. It occurred to me you were looking for a nice, safe legover, and what safer option than a female cleric with ambition and no husband? Sure, I thought that for quite a while. I even came to the conclusion I could handle it if we weren't alone too often.'

'How plucky of you.' He moved out of the doorway. His face was two-dimensionally gaunt – light and shadow – in the moonlight.

'But I still wondered why it was so important for Dobbs – the hardest, possibly the most uncompromising exorcist in the business – to be out of the way *now*? And *quickly*. Who could it possibly help to have a barely qualified novice floundering about? Someone who really didn't know the score on certain aspects of the situation. Someone whose appointment was politically sensitive. Someone who could be pushed around, blamed, bullied...'

'You're talking nonsense, Merrily. It's been an emotional few days for you, and you're—'

'Acting like a silly woman.'

He said, 'You know, frankly, I couldn't believe it when you wouldn't let me take you home and fuck you that night. It was such an *amazing* night... with the new snow and the ambulance and that wonderful charge in the air. We were all so *high*.'

'High?' She stared at him. 'High on an old man having a stroke? Wow! Even better tonight, then, Mick. This time he really died. I bet you nearly came in your episcopal briefs.'

The Bishop slapped her face.

She said, '*What?*'

He'd hardly moved his body, simply reached out and done it. Almost lazily, as if to show that if she really annoyed him he could knock her head from her shoulders without breaking more sweat than it took to circuit High Town.

'There are policemen in the Cathedral,' Merrily said.

'It's a cathedral, Merrily. It has very thick walls and windows which don't open. You aren't supposed to hear what goes on outside.'

'I can't believe you did that.'

'You can believe anything you want to believe. You can believe or disbelieve at will.'

'I think we should go, Bishop, before you do or say something else that won't help your glittering career.'

She was now realizing how stupid she'd been. She could have told Annie Howe. She could have called Huw over. Earlier,

Sophie had offered to come with her. But, as usual, she hadn't been able to quite believe she wouldn't be making a complete fool of herself in front of others. And she had thought she'd be quite safe virtually anywhere in the shadow of the Cathedral.

He seemed quite relaxed, but he wasn't going to let her through the door. She found she was backing away on to the circular lawn.

'Do you know young James Lyden?' The Bishop put a foot on to the grass, already brittle with frost.

'Not really.'

'Not a popular boy. Even I don't like him awfully. He behaved rather badly today. What do you think's going to happen to him?'

'I don't know. His father's a psychotherapist. Perhaps *he'll* be able to handle it.'

'I don't think so – neither does James. Where do you think he is now?'

'I believe his parents took him home,' she said cautiously. What was *this* about?

'Wrong,' the Bishop said. 'James gave his old man the slip. The last thing James wanted was to go back home in disgrace – Hereford-cred is Dick Lyden's *raison d'être*. The boy's now undone all the good work for him. I told James he could hang out at the Palace for a while. Nobody knows he's there. Nobody there but me today, as Val left for the Cotswolds this morning. Rather an unpleasant, maladjusted boy, our James.'

'Yes.'

'He nearly killed your daughter.'

'Yes.'

'And who knows what he'll do now?' Mick said.

He came towards her, moving as an athlete, his arms loose. She knew that if she tried to run past him, towards the closed-down snackbar and the steps, he'd catch her easily. She stopped in the middle of the circular lawn, near the fountain with its stone pot on top. She put her hands up. He waited, a couple of yards away, moonlight on his hair.

'Look—' She tried to produce a laugh. 'How about we treat this like last night's conversation and pretend it never happened?'

Somewhere, over God knew how many intervening walls, she heard a car start up. That was the only sound.

'I don't think so,' he said quietly. 'I think you'd better carry on talking.'

'I think I've said all I want to say.'

'But not all I want to know.'

She found she'd now backed up against the ruined wall, far too high to get over. Probably the Bishop's Palace garden behind.

'There are people,' she said, 'who wish us ill. And I think – whether unwillingly, or because of blackmail, or something – you've been playing on *their* side.'

Her right shoulder rammed against a projecting stone, and she winced.

'All the signs for them… Cantilupe's shrine in pieces, I suppose, was the main one… I mean, if Dobbs had still been official, the spiritual defences would have been so much stronger, wouldn't they? Instead of him having to struggle alone and furtively at night, exposed to whatever psychic influences were at work.'

She began to edge, inch by inch, along the wall. There was a lower section further along, no more than three feet high. OK, she might wind up on the Palace lawn, but she could make it down to the river bank and…

Oh Jesus, that was wrong, wasn't it?

But what alternative was there? She kept moving – imperceptibly, she hoped.

'Try pinching yourself,' the Bishop said. 'It might all be a dream, a silly fantasy.'

'I don't think so. And I still don't know what you believe, if anything. I don't even know if you believe that what they're doing is likely to have any effect whatsoever.'

He smiled and stepped back from her. 'You know, I never wanted to be a bishop. There've been far too many in my family. From an early age I knew what unholy shits most of them were, so I never wanted to be one of them. No, I wanted to be a rock star – or a cabinet minister. I actually quite envied poor Tony, for a while, but politicians... everyone *suspects* them, don't they?'

'Do they?'

'Politicians are capable of anything, whereas bishops... bishops somehow are still seen as quite remarkably saintly. They might occasionally make some ill-advised remark about the fantasy of a virgin birth, but they don't embezzle large sums, fuck other people's wives or... what? What else don't they do, Merrily? What else don't bishops do?'

'Oh God,' she said. 'Don't make me say it.'

He straightened up, a foot taller than her.

'Let's go in now,' she said. 'You've already sacked me. I'm pretty stupid, really. A lousy exorcist, too.' She shook her head. 'I'll go away immediately. I'll apply for vicar of Penzance.'

'Merrily, what else don't bishops do?'

'I don't *know* that you did it. And if you did, I don't understand why – or even if it was an accident.'

'Go on.'

'Paul Sayer – the Satanist dragged from the river.'

'Ah,' he said.

'I think you know how he died,' she said.

And she dived for the low wall.

He caught her easily and threw her down, well away from the wall, into the frozen flowerbed under the central fountain. He slapped her hard, backwards, forwards, across both cheeks, shocking away her scream as he straddled her, pushing her skirt up and thrusting a hand between her legs.

He gave a long, ragged, rueful sigh.

Then took his hand away.

She froze up.

'The really unfortunate part, for me, Merrily,' he said, 'is that I cannot give you what you so richly deserve and would probably end up rather enjoying.'

She couldn't move. She heard herself panting in terror, panting so loud that it might have been coming from someone else lying next to her.

'DNA,' he said. 'D-N-bloody-A.'

Her spine was chilled, literally: the frost melting through her jumper as he pressed her into the soil. She tried to pray, while at the same time looking to each side of her for a possible weapon.

'Because this isn't me, of course,' he told her. 'Bishops don't do this. It's never considered feasible for a bishop to even contemplate doing this to a woman. A bishop's whereabouts on the night in question are rarely – even in these suspicious times – ever questioned. Especially… if there's an unpleasant, arrogant, sociopathic teenager like young James Lyden on the loose. Having been found hiding in the Bishop's Palace and unceremoniously ejected therefrom by the understandably irate Bishop, he wanders the grounds…'

'You can't *possibly*—'

'My dear child, you have no *idea* of the things I've got away with… I really do believe I am… protected.'

'You're mad. I can't believe—' She panicked then, pushing against him, tossing her head from side to side, summoning a scream.

He jammed an arm into her mouth. 'No,' he said coldly, his other hand flattening a breast. 'Not that. *Never* that.'

Over his shoulder, she could see the Cathedral wall and one of the high, diamond-paned windows – with lights behind. With police, and perhaps a doctor summoned to examine Thomas Dobbs's body, or an electrician to find out what went wrong earlier? Vergers, canons, all within twenty feet – as the Bishop of Hereford placed his long, sensitive fingers round her throat.

'You rejected me, Mrs Watkins. On a personal level, that was the most insulting thing of all.'

'I want to pray,' she said.

He laughed.

'Does that really mean nothing to you?'

He took his hands from her throat.

'I don't believe in God,' he said, 'except as something created by man in what he liked to believe was his image. I don't believe in Satan. I don't believe in saints – or demons. I accept the psychological power of symbolism, of costume drama.'

She said, 'You really don't see it, do you?' She squirmed to a sitting position, her back to the fountain. 'You don't see what you are!'

He recoiled slightly, puzzled.

'You don't realize… that a non-believer who manipulates—' she struggled to her feet as she spoke, '… who manipulates the belief system to promote his own power and influence…' she snatched the stone pot from the top of the fountain; it was heavier than she expected; she almost let it fall; '… is the most *satanic*… person of all.'

She was sobbing.

'Put it down,' the Bishop said.

She managed to raise the pot, with both hands, over her head. She backed on to the path.

Mick relaxed, spread his hands. 'You going to throw that at me?'

He was about four feet away from her. If she threw it at him with all her strength, he would catch it easily. If she came close enough to try to hit him with it, he would simply take it away from her.

His eyes caught the full moon. His eyes were at their wildest; she sensed enjoyment, a need to be at all times very close to the edge.

He shrugged.

'I was going to let you pray. I was going to let you kneel and pray. I accept the level of your faith. Very well, I'll use that pot, if you like. You can kneel and pray and, while you're talking to God, I can bring it down very hard, very cleanly, on the back of your head. Bargain?'

Her arms were aching, but she kept the pot raised, like an offering to the moon.

'It distresses me that you have to die,' Mick Hunter said. 'The way it's turned out with you, that leaves me sad. I do want you to know that I'm capable of feeling real distress.'

He walked towards her with his arms outstretched.

'Merrily?'

There was nothing more to say. She arched her back, feeling a momentary acute pain in her spine, and hurled the stone pot into the great gothic diamond-paned window.

54

Friends in Dark Places

YOU COULD SEE him sliding it into her. It was quite dark, but the camera came in close, and there was the beam of a torch or lamp on their fuzzy, shadowed loins. Candles wavered out of focus, balls of light in the background. You could make out the glimmer of a gothic window. Beneath the woman's buttocks was what might have been an altar-cloth.

'Is that him?' Annie Howe asked. 'Is it as simple as this?'

They knew from his parents that, for a period during his time at Oxford, he'd had long hair – though it was not fashionable at the time – and also a beard. But there seemed to be no actual pictures of him from those days.

'It could be him,' Merrily said. 'Then, again…'

'You going to invite his wife to look at this?' Huw wondered.

'If necessary,' Howe said. 'I'm advised it may not be entirely politic at this stage to expose a bishop's wife to pornography, and ask her if she recognizes her husband. She's coming back this afternoon from her parents' house in Gloucestershire. I've already spoken to her on the phone, and she didn't seem as shocked as she might be. Any reason for that?'

'It's a marriage,' Merrily said, 'and maybe a political marriage, at that. Put it this way, their kids go to boarding school, and Val seems to spend a lot of time away from home.'

'Interesting,' Howe said.

Her office at headquarters was no surprise. Minimalist was the word; the TV and video looked like serious clutter. Merrily found this calming for once; there were no layers here. She wondered if she dared light a cigarette. Perhaps not. Beyond the big window, the sky was grey and calm: one of those un-Christmassy mild days which so often precede Christmas.

'All right.' Howe stopped Paul Sayer's tape and rewound it. 'Let's look at it one more time.'

'Actually,' Lol said, 'that woman... Could I look at the woman?'

Howe glanced at him with tilted head, and set the tape rolling again.

The woman on the possible-altar wore a blindfold and a gag, but the more times you watched the scene, the less it seemed like rape. Too smooth. *She was ready*, Merrily thought.

'It's Anna Purefoy.' Lol leaned forward from the plastic chair next to Merrily's.

'Are you sure?' Howe asked him. 'This woman looks quite young. I'm told the film could be twenty years old. I thought we might be looking at the very early days of home-video, but my sergeant suggests it was transferred from something called Super Eight cine-film. Even so, Anna would have been in her late thirties, early forties.'

'It's her,' Lol insisted.

'Aye, they like to take care of themselves.' Huw Owen was occupying a corner of Howe's desk. He was the untidiest object in the immaculate room.

'I'm sorry, Mr Owen?'

'Secret of eternal youth, lass – sometimes you'd think they'd found it. Then they'll go suddenly to seed, or become gross like Crowley. Drugs were no help, mind, in his case.'

Howe stood with her back to the window. She appeared, for some reason, uncharmed at being addressed as 'lass'.

'Well, it's clear that this tape is never going to be usable in evidence, even if we could put our hands on the original. But it does prompt speculation. Would you like to speculate for us, Mr Owen?'

'I get the feeling *you* were at university,' Huw said. 'Did they have any kind of occult society at your place?'

'There were a hundred different societies, but I was never a joiner.'

'I can imagine,' Huw said. 'Well, you look at most universities, you'll find some kind of experimental mystical group – harmless enough in most cases, but one association leads to another.'

Merrily said, 'I have a problem with that. I can't see Mick having any interest at all in mysticism.'

'Happen a reaction against his solid clergy family?'

'His reaction, then, would be to avoid *any* kind of religious experience.'

'My knowledge of theology is limited,' Howe said, 'but what we've just been watching is not what I would immediately think of as religious.'

'No,' Merrily said, 'it's plain sex. If you're looking for serious motivating forces in Mick's life, you'd have to put sex close to the top. He'd be nineteen or twenty then, newly liberated from the bosom of what was probably a less-than-liberal family. Suppose he thought he was getting involved with people who could, I don't know, extend his experience in all kinds of inter-esting ways.'

'Very astute, lass.' Huw patted her shoulder. 'As you've been finding out, clergy and the children of clergy are always fair game.'

'Yes.'

'So we've got a lad from a high-placed clergy family, up at Oxford. What was he reading?'

'History,' Howe said, 'and politics.'

'He could have become anything,' Merrily said, 'yet winds up following his father into the Church. You just can't see him as a curate, somehow.' She looked up at Howe. 'It's like imagining Annie here directing traffic.'

Howe scowled.

'That's interesting,' Huw said. 'Why *did* he do it? You really want me to develop a theory, Inspector?'

'Go ahead.'

'All right. You've got this smart, handsome lad from a dog-collar dynasty, putting it around Oxford like a sailor on shore-leave. And he's drawn into summat – drawn in, to put it crudely, by his dick. He's having the time of his life – the best time ever. He doesn't see the little rat eyes in the dark.'

'Meaning what, Mr Owen?'

'There *is* a network. It might not put out a monthly news-letter, but it does exist. The general aim is anti-Christian. They might be several different groups, but that's their one rallying point – the destruction of the Christian Church.'

'I'd have thought,' Howe said drily, 'that they could simply sit back and watch the Church take *itself* apart.'

'She's got a point,' Merrily said, the need for a cigarette starting to tell.

'Merrily, lass, you'd be very naive if you thought the Church's problems were *entirely* self-generated.'

'Sorry, go on.'

"They've got a good intelligence network, the rat-eyes. The Internet now, more primitive then but, just like Moscow was head-hunting at Oxford and Cambridge in the sixties, the rat-eyes had their antennae out.'

Lol said, 'Anna Purefoy was in Oxfordshire then. She worked for the county council. She'd been fired from the MOD after some fundamentalist junior minister found out she was involved in magic, along with a few other people – a purge.'

'Part of the honey-trap then,' Huw said. 'Beautiful, experienced older woman. Aye, I think we can rule out rape in them pictures. Happen she said she enjoyed being tied up. If that *is* Hunter, it's an interesting connection, but I'd be looking for something harder. Suppose they stitched our lad up good? Suppose they had him full of drugs, and suppose he really did

528

rape somebody – a young girl, say. Suppose they even arranged for him to kill somebody.'

Annie Howe began to look uneasy. 'That stuff's surely apocryphal.'

'That *stuff* happens all the time,' Huw told her. 'You coppers hate to think there's ever a murder you don't know about, but there's thousands of folk still missing. All right, say they've stitched him up – tight enough to have him looking at public disgrace and a long prison sentence.'

Howe sighed. 'Go on, then.'

'What do they want of him? I think they want him in the Church.'

'Oh, wow,' Merrily murmured.

'Make your father a happy man, they'd say. Repent of your evil ways. Make restitution. Join the family business. Either that or go down, all the way to the gutter. Well, he's in a panic, is our lad: self-disgust and a hangover on a grand scale. In need of redemption. So he goes home to his loving family, and the result, after the nightmares and the cold sweats, is the Reverend Michael Henry Hunter, a reformed character.'

'It's a brilliant theory, Huw. Is there a precedent?'

'Happen.'

'Meaning one you never proved.'

Huw looked down at his trainers. 'I once exorcised a young curate from Halifax who admitted celebrating a black mass. It was to get them off his back, he said. Blackmail again. I never met anybody more full of remorse.'

'You think Mick—?'

'It's sometimes what *they* do. They get in touch after he's ordained, with "Do us this one thing and we'll leave you alone for ever." Ha! You likely don't know this, Inspector, but having a reverse-eucharist performed by an ordained cleric is a *very* powerfully dark thing. And a fully *turned* cleric is… lord of all.'

'Like Tim Purefoy,' Lol said.

'There's one as is better dead, God forgive me.'

'Hold on,' Howe said. 'Are you saying these – whoever they are… possibly the Purefoys – might have been in touch with Hunter throughout his whole career?'

'Very likely smoothing his path for him. A satanic bishop? Some prize, eh?'

'Except he wasn't really,' Merrily said. 'He was a man with no committed religious beliefs at all. Perhaps that's how he could live with it. "I don't believe in the Devil" – he said that to me. Perhaps he really believed he was using *them*.'

'Very likely, lass.' Huw opened out his hands. '*Very* likely. But it doesn't change a thing.'

'But what a career, Huw! What an incredibly *lucky* career. He never put a foot wrong, said all the right things to all the right people, charmed everyone he met with his energy and his sincerity. He actually told me he believed he was protected.'

'Obstacles would be moved out of his path. Look at how he got this job – his one rival has a convenient heart attack. Oh, aye, he could very well come to believe he was protected. But not by God, not by the Devil – by his own dynamism, his willpower, his bloody destiny. But what's the truth of it, Merrily? The truth is he's a demonic force, whether he believes in it or not.'

'He believed he was invulnerable, obviously.' Annie Howe switched off the TV and went to sit down behind her desk, behind a legal notepad. 'Certainly, if he seemed to think he could murder Ms Watkins in the actual Cathedral precincts, and we'd simply arrest James Lyden for it…'

'Do you think you would have, lass?'

'I hate to think so, but… well, we might have. As Lyden had already, that same evening, attacked Jane Watkins and left her unconscious in the crypt with her coat on fire. We're trying to persuade the CPS to go for attempted murder on that, by the way, but I don't suppose they will. Tell me your feelings on Sayer, Mr Owen.'

'Headbanger.'

530

'Meaning an amateur, a hanger-on.'

'If he possessed this tape, he might have been more than that – or not. Did he have a computer? Was he on the Internet?'

'He was, come to think of it.'

'You can dredge all kinds of dirt off the Net. If we assume he did know it was Mick Hunter on that tape, he might've tried a bit of blackmail. And Hunter sees the tape… or happen he's seen it before. He knows it looks bugger-all like him now, so he's not worried about the tape, but he doesn't like the idea of this lad Sayer walking round spreading bad rumours. Aye, he might well've bopped him over the head and dragged him down to the Wye. Cool as you like, popped him in a boat – I bet he had a boat, didn't he, athletic bugger like him wi' a river at the bottom of the garden. Then rowed him downstream. Who in a million years would ever look towards the Bishop's Palace…?'

'I don't think Hunter was even supposed to be here that night,' Merrily said. 'Out of town, as I recall.'

Huw snorted.

There was a long silence. Merrily looked at Lol, remembering she hadn't been all that convinced when he'd first told her about Katherine Moon. And yet Lol himself had actually underestimated the full extent of it. They both needed a long walk – somewhere you could feel you weren't looking through a dirty spiderweb.

'There isn't a shred of evidence for any of this, Mr Owen, is there?' said Annie Howe.

'We're none of us coppers, lass. Just poor clergy and a lad wi' a guitar.'

'As for the other stuff: the ley-lines, the sacrifice of crows, the alleged *presence* in the Cathedral…' Howe pushed her notepad away. 'I don't want to know about *any* of it. I don't know how you people can pretend to… to do your job at all. To me, it's a complete fantasy world.'

Lol said, 'Have you talked to James Lyden?'

'I have *tried* to talk to James Lyden. He blames the girl – Rowenna Napier. We found her car, by the way – at the car park at the Severn Bridge motorway services. We've circulated a description. Her family seems to have given up on her. Lyden still thinks she's called Melissa, and that she lived with her now late foster-parents, with whom he'd spent many an interesting hour at their farmhouse on Dinedor Hill.'

'She seems to have used a number of identities,' Merrily said.

'But, in the end, just one,' said Huw.

Howe looked at him.

'The archetypal Scarlet Woman, lass. The temptress.'

Merrily thought, *What's he saying?* It was true that everything about Rowenna disturbed her: preying like a succubus on the Salisbury clergy, obviously dominating her own family – why *had* Mrs Straker suddenly clammed up? – and pulling off that insidiously effective psychic attack with the dregs of Denzil Joy. Rowenna was terribly dangerous – and still out there.

'She certainly seems to have acquired a considerable amount of money,' Howe said.

'For services rendered,' Huw told her.

'Certainly the basis for a few questions when we do find her. And I *do* want to find that girl – and Michael Hunter – before someone at Division decides to take this case out of my hands. Which is why I'm talking to… to people like you. Ms Watkins, when you suggested to Hunter that he knew something about the death of Paul Sayer…?'

'I'm sorry. I chose that moment to try and get away. Paul Sayer was never mentioned again.'

'But you raised it with him purely because your secretary told you she recognized Sayer from one of my photographs, yes?'

'It was the day you came into the Deliverance office. She recognized Sayer as a man who had actually come into the office asking for the Bishop – making Mick angry in a way Sophie says she'd never seen before – in a way that seemed to her… unepiscopal. Sophie's very discreet and very loyal, but also very observant.'

'This was not on the night he died, however.'

'No. A couple of days earlier.'

'Hold on.' Howe picked up a phone. 'Douglas, could somebody bring in Mrs Sophie Hill from the Bishop's office?… No, *now*… Thank you.'

'What you have to understand about Sophie,' said Merrily, 'is that the Cathedral is her life. She worried about this thing for days. She kept half-approaching me and then backing off.'

'Sure,' Howe said. 'Damn it, I think I'm going to have some divers in the Wye again.'

Huw slid from her desk. 'For Hunter?'

'What do you think?'

'Unlikely. He moves fast, that lad, in his jogging gear.'

Merrily closed her eyes for a moment, trying to remember which way Hunter had gone after the stone pot had made such a gloriously jagged, noisy hole in ancient glass. He'd stared at her for a moment, then she'd turned and run away – as lights were coming on everywhere, a verger and a policeman thrusting out of the door.

'And Hunter has friends,' Huw said. 'More friends than even he knows. Friends in dark places.'

55

Location Classified

THEY SAT AMONGST the stones and they lit a candle for Tommy Canty.

Huw held the candle over each disfigured knight in turn, making a blessing for each. Merrily wondered if it had been the Bishop himself who had taken away the single knight and then brought it back, making sure that the tomb was still lying in pieces for the time of the Boy Bishop ceremony.

They would probably never know. Huw was convinced Mick Hunter would now be abroad. Italy, he thought; there were a number of dark sanctuaries in Italy. *How did he know that?*

So many questions.

DS Franny Bliss had been summoned back to St Cosmas and St Damien after reports from the two ornithologist ladies that a couple of people had been seen acting suspiciously close to the church, which the ladies apparently had been virtually staking out ever since. As a result, Craig the crow-catcher was in the cells, now suspected of greater involvement in the desecration than previously thought.

So, once again last night, simultaneous action along the Dinedor Line – with the Cathedral in the middle. Jane had seen Rowenna making a call on her mobile phone – perhaps to the Purefoys – as the Boy Bishop was about to be installed. And then, coincidentally or not, a power failure. Its cause had still not been established.

Lol was convinced that, this time, the Purefoys – always assuming they were controlling the assault, which was by no means certain – believed they were using the very spirit, the element, the essence of Katherine Moon to try to awaken something aggressively pre-Christian. They *believed* it, so at some level it was happening? And what form had their ritual – over by the time Lol arrived – actually taken? This all needed thinking about. Perhaps Merrily would be compelled to consult (Oh God!) Miss Athena White.

'But they were right, weren't they, lass?' Huw was stroking a stone.

'Mm?'

'The demon manifested in clerical clothing?'

'Yes, I suppose it did.'

And where was it now? Where was the *squatter*? Did it die with Dobbs? Did it flee with Mick? Was it over?

'Over?' Huw laughed a lot. 'The oldest war in the world, over? I'll tell you what, though...' He grew sober. 'We're up against it now. The Church is on its knees now, and the more we get weakened by public apathy, the more they'll put the boot in.'

'Jane thinks there's a new spirituality on the rise, replacing organized worship.'

'With all respect to the lass,' Huw said, 'it's people like Jane who'll turn religion into a minority sport.'

'She sees it more in terms of a period of cataclysmic psychic upheaval.'

'Could be,' Huw said. 'But if that happens, they'll still need somebody to police it. And, all the time, we're going to have folk like your Inspector Howe dismissing us as loonies. We're going to have battles with psychologists and social workers. We're going to be attacked by fellers like that Dick Lyden, who thinks Dobbs was persecuting his poor maladjusted son. And, naturally, we're always going to be regarded with suspicion within the Church itself.'

536

Merrily stood up and dusted her knees. 'Hunter wanted me to draft a paper on New Deliverance. He suggested this would be an approach acceptable to psychologists and social workers.'

'For New Deliverance, read Soft Deliverance,' Huw said.

'I suppose that's right.'

'Happen that was going to be one of Mick's principal contributions: pioneer of Soft Deliverance. On the surface, decently liberal – exorcism by committee – but, underneath, the gradual dismantling of the final human barrier against satanic evil.'

Merrily shook her head, dubious, bewildered.

'Stick with it, lass,' Huw said. 'You've come too far now.'

'I don't know. The new bishop may not want me.'

'There's that,' Huw said.

'Anyway, there's a lot to think about. Lol and I are going to drive up into the Malverns, or somewhere – to do some walking and talking. He's very confused and spooked, after his showdown with the Purefoys. It's all going round in his head; he's realizing how close he came to winding up as dead as they are, and he's thinking: *What is this about?*'

'I gather that lad Denny Moon died this morning.'

'Yes.' She didn't want to talk about what Lol had heard from a porter in the Accident and Emergency unit at the General.

'Poor bugger. Always some casualties, Merrily, luv. Always.'

The porter said that, a few seconds after Denny was pronounced dead, a woman patient who'd been brought in after falling down some steps had begun to scream, and the nurses had had to open a window to let out a large black bird.

Huw was saying, 'Incidentally, I don't know who the Purefoys have left their place to, and I don't like to think. But I reckon it could do with some attention smartish if we don't want yet more hassle.'

She shook her head. 'I don't think I could.'

Huw said, 'Oh, aye, I think you could.'

'You were the one who tried to talk me out of this whole thing!'

'That were because there was no tradition *then*,' Huw said. 'I think you've started one. Too late to back out now. You know what I'd do?'

'What?'

'Bugger the Malverns, they'll not go away. Take the lad up to Dinedor and do a little service of restitution for the spirit of this Katherine Moon. And for her brother. And their parents. See what happens.'

'I dread to think.'

'Don't dread,' said Huw. 'Second Law of Deliverance: *never* dread. Don't do it in the barn; it might be dangerous in there – I mean falling masonry and that. Go to the tip of the owd ramparts, and look out down the line, through All Saints and *this* place, to St Cosmas and St Damien.'

'Will you come?'

'I will not. It's not my patch.'

'What about the major exorcism? Who do we consult?'

'I think...' Huw looked up at the enormous stained-glass window, suddenly aglow with unexpected winter sunshine. 'I think we can leave it alone. Stand back, lass.'

He began to lug one of the stone panels of the Cantilupe tomb to one side, revealing a bundle of white and gold cloth about the size of a tobacco pouch. He bent down and gathered it up.

Merrily leaned over his shoulder. 'What on earth have you got there, Huw?'

'Picked it up before I fetched Dobbs from the hospital. Planted it here before the service – with all due ceremony, naturally – so it was there throughout.'

He unrolled the cloth. There was a fragment of what looked at first like brick: dark red-brown, and brittle.

'Holy relics, lass.' Huw said. 'The undying power of holy relics.'

Dark red.

'Oh, my God,' Merrily said. 'His bones were supposed to have bled, weren't they?'

538

'Bit of the skull, apparently. Borrowed it from some monks. Location classified.'

'God.' She put out a finger.

'Aye, go on, lass. It's all right. You wouldn't have got within ten yards of the bugger when he were alive, mind, but there you go. Times change.'

He let her touch the piece of bone, and then rolled it up in its cloth again and slipped it into an inside pocket of his blue canvas jacket, next to his heart.

'Come on, then, Tommy,' he said.

Closing Credits

IT'S ALWAYS DIFFICULT setting a novel in real locations without appearing to implicate real people... which is why I've always avoided meeting the Bishop of Hereford.

However, the book would have been impossible without invaluable background information from a Hereford Deliverance minister, who prefers, like Merrily, to keep a low profile; from the Director of the Hereford Cathedral Perpetual Trust, Sue Embrey, who provided crucial information on the Cathedral and the tomb of Thomas Cantilupe and was always really helpful and encouraging; from Ron Shoesmith, the archaeologist overseeing renovation of the Canty tomb; from Richard Powell, of Capps and Capps, the mason who performed the actual renovation (without losing any bits) and from Brian Chave, who showed me Merrily's office and Mick's lair.

For information on Dinedor Hill and Cathedral-related hauntings, thanks to Hereford journalists Nicola Goodwin and George Children (whose excellent book, *Prehistoric Sites of Herefordshire*, co-written with George Nash, is published by Logaston Press).

Also thanks to Nick Whitehead, Andrew Hewson, Jill Dibbling, Penny Arnold and, of course, Pam Baker for the awful story of The Real Denzil Joy (oh, yes, there are some nurses who still have nightmares...). And Mark Owen thought it was time he got a mention, so here it is.

Finally, at the production end... thanks to my wife, Carol, who combined a massive, wide-ranging and detailed four-week professional (if unpaid) edit with some absolutely vital plot-surgery.

Lol Robinson's songs can be found on two full-length CDs, *Songs from Lucy's Cottage* and *A Message from the Morning* (which includes *Moon's Tune*) by Lol Robinson and Hazey Jane II, produced by Prof Levin and Allan Watson.

The *Midwinter* locations are included in *Merrily's Border* by Phil Rickman, with photographs by John Mason. (Logaston Press)

Full details on the website www.philrickman.co.uk

PHIL RICKMAN

THE MERRILY WATKINS SERIES

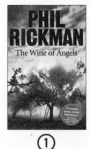
(1) The Wine of Angels

(2) Midwinter of the Spirit

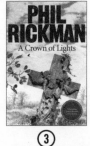
(3) A Crown of Lights

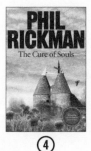
(4) The Cure of Souls

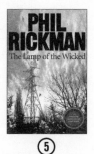
(5) The Lamp of the Wicked

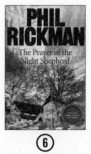
(6) The Prayer of the Night Shepherd

(7) The Smile of a Ghost

SINGLE MUM. PARISH PRIEST.
COSY?
I DON'T THINK SO...